HOSTAGE MOON

Visit us at www.boldstrokesbooks.com

HOSTAGE MOON

by

AJ Quinn

2011

HOSTAGE MOON

ISBN 10: 1-60282-568-8
ISBN 13: 978-1-60282-568-0

This Trade Paperback Original Is Published By
Bold Strokes Books, Inc.
P.O. Box 249
Valley Falls, NY 12185

First Edition: October 2011

Credits
Editor: Ruth Sternglantz
Production Design: Susan Ramundo
Cover Design By Sheri (graphicartist2020@hotmail.com)

Acknowledgments

My heartfelt thanks to Radclyffe for drawing together an amazing group of people and creating a place where storytellers can gather and dreams really can come true.

Dedication

For BJ, who listened, encouraged, and supported me throughout this adventure. Thanks for believing in me.

PROLOGUE

March 22, 6:35 a.m.

Her first sensation was pain—blinding pain lancing through her body. A wave of dizziness followed. Coming fast and hard, it hit with such force that all she could do was keep her eyes pressed tightly closed and try to ride it out. She repressed the urge to moan as reality faded away.

"You are mine."

The words seemed to reverberate around her as awareness returned. She started to open her eyes, but the act triggered another flash of pain. She immediately shut them, preferring the darkness and the illusion of protection it offered. Confused and fighting an unnamed fear, she tried to concentrate on the jumble of nearby sounds—the muted rumble of traffic, a car horn, the wail of a siren. But she didn't know where she was and had no idea where she'd been.

With awareness came the realization that the air was brutally cold. But in spite of the temperature, beads of sweat formed on her brow. Involuntary shivers coursed through her body, and her jaw clenched spasmodically. More than anything, she wanted to go back to sleep, to escape the cold and pain, but some primal instinct knew not to take that course of action.

Instead, she forced her eyes open and tried to bring into focus a world that swirled around her like a mist. She tried to remember what had happened to her, but she couldn't push past the pain that enveloped her mind and racked her body. With a low moan, she slipped back into the comforting darkness.

"You are mine."

She awoke with a start, unable to tell whether someone nearby had spoken or the words were simply in her head. Uncertain, she began to assess her situation. Her throat felt as if she had swallowed shards of glass. It hurt to breathe, and she was having difficulty seeing out of one eye. She recognized the metallic taste of blood in her mouth and felt the first hint of panic.

She lifted her head, conscious of her heart pounding erratically in her chest. Her last clear memory was…Damn. What was wrong with her? Why couldn't she remember?

With concerted effort, she raised herself onto her elbows and, after a brief struggle, managed to push her back up against a cold wall, her legs stretched out in front of her. Taking shallow, labored breaths, she waited for the dizziness to pass, braced herself against the wall, and made it first to her knees, then onto her feet. She shivered, swaying unsteadily, her legs threatening to buckle and her vision swimming as she walked toward the light. A lifetime later, she managed to get beyond the mouth of the alley and stood by the water's edge. Looking up, her gaze swept over a full moon suspended above a familiar skyline.

Without conscious thought, her hand reached automatically and found her phone hooked to her belt. She hastily unclipped it, silently praying it still had a charge. An instant later, she turned it on and hit a speed-dial number.

"Hey," she said hoarsely when a sleepy voice finally answered.

"Hunter?" The sleepiness vanished instantly. "Where the hell are you? Do you realize everyone's been looking for you?"

"I'm sorry," she whispered softly. She hated that her voice sounded so strained.

There was a moment of dead silence, followed by the sound of a deep breath being released. "Shit—no, I'm sorry. Are you all right? Where are you?"

"New York. Brooklyn, I think."

"New York? What the…you were scheduled to leave New York yesterday. But when the limo arrived to pick you up, you were nowhere to be found. Where the hell have you been? Talk to me. What's going on with you?"

Her heart hammered in her chest as the lights in the sky danced in a crazy pattern and adrenaline pumped through her in a fight-or-flight rush. She gulped a deep breath, then another.

"I don't know," she said, unsuccessfully fighting the rising panic evident in her voice. "Matt, I don't know what's going on. I don't know where I've been. And I especially don't know why I just woke up in an alley near the East River or how I got here."

"Okay—okay. Take it easy. Are you hurt?"

She raised a hand and touched the side of her head where it continued to throb. Drew it back and stared at the dark blood staining her fingers and palm and tried to comprehend.

"Damn it, Hunter, answer me. Are you hurt?"

"I'm not sure…there's some blood…I'm pretty sure most of it's mine."

❖

He watched her from the shadows of the rooftop.

He had seen the confusion on her face from the moment her eyes opened. Watched her struggle as she tried to think, tried to move beyond the pain. But the drugs he had given her were still flowing fast and hard through her system. It would be some time before she would be able to think clearly.

Of course, she wouldn't know that—at least not yet.

He continued to watch as she made her phone call. He was disappointed that he couldn't hear her conversation, but now wasn't the time to take any unnecessary chances, and he couldn't risk moving closer. So he waited. Once she completed her call, she began making her way slowly toward the lights, stumbling as the drugs played havoc with her body and mind.

Still he watched and waited. Just a little longer. Just a matter of time.

It happened as she reached the intersection. She had thrust her shaking hands into the pockets of her jeans, felt something, and pulled out the note he had purposefully left there. He watched her read it.

You are mine.

He smiled and walked away.

CHAPTER ONE

Six months later

All actions have consequences.

Sara Wilder knew that to be one of the basic tenets of life, and it was certainly one she should have remembered when her cell phone began to vibrate. For an instant, she stopped her restless pacing in the departures lounge and considered not answering it. Even the little voice of reason inside her head told her to ignore the incoming call, reminding her that calls so late in the day seldom brought good news.

But it seemed the fates had conspired, and a sequence of events had been set in motion. She should have been on a plane bound for Bali and her first real vacation in years. Two weeks of glorious beaches and dense jungles that beckoned and called out for exploration. But her flight had been inexplicably delayed, leaving her stuck on the ground at San Francisco International with her phone on.

In the end, she answered the phone even as she noted the name on the call display. FBI Special Agent David Granger—former mentor, friend, and, perhaps most importantly, her partner until her resignation from the bureau eight months earlier.

She had met David when she had been a raw recruit out of Stanford, armed with a brand new doctorate in psychology and an indefatigable belief that she could make a difference. He'd been a field counselor assigned to her training group, and initially, he'd been tough on her. Demanding. Pushing her to excel, both during and after completion of her training at Quantico. But over time, he'd proven equally generous with his support, and she'd been able to carve a niche for herself within the Behavioral Analysis Unit.

It wasn't until much later, over shots of tequila in a bar somewhere in Texas, that he admitted he'd seen something special in her. And when all was said and done, they had made a formidable team. Still—

"Whatever you want, the answer is no," she said.

"It's been a while," David chided. "You could try saying hello first."

Sara sighed. "Hello, David. Whatever you want, the answer is no."

"Hear me out, Sara. I only want you to take a quick look at a crime scene…and maybe give me your impression."

"Not interested." She swallowed hard. "I quit…eight months ago. Remember?"

"I'm not likely to forget," he replied softly. "But I'm not calling to try to get you reinstated in your old job. And you know I wouldn't be calling if I didn't really need your help. Please, Sara."

In the end, it was the simple plea that worked. It was a tactic Sara always found impossible to ignore—a fact David knew all too well. Smiling tiredly at the customer service agent, she explained her situation and made arrangements to have her luggage returned to her. Thirty minutes later, with doubt and uncertainty shadowing her footsteps, she walked out of the airport.

Just before midnight, the cab she had hailed pulled up to the curb in an upscale residential neighborhood. The driver turned and gave an apologetic shrug. "Sorry, but this is as far as I can take you," he said, although they were still almost a block from her destination.

A glance through the passenger-side window revealed several black-and-whites blocking the road, their flashing red and blue lights marking the perimeter of the site. Beyond them were the glowing spotlights from several news vans that lined the street, backlighting the growing crowd of curious onlookers drawn by the drama that was being played out.

"Looks like somebody sent out invitations," she said. She paid her fare and exited the vehicle. Showing her driver's license in lieu of FBI credentials she no longer had, she gave her name to the uniformed officer in charge of perimeter security. Intent on keeping both the media and spectators behind the yellow tape, he barely glanced at her and nodded.

David had obviously cleared her, Sara realized. She allowed herself a ghost of a smile and gave a moment's consideration to his probable reaction when he saw how she was dressed. Khakis and a red polo shirt instead of the conservative, tailored suits she had always favored on the job in the past. She looked startlingly out of place, a stark contrast to the uniforms and suits that now surrounded her, and she hoped David, a stickler for protocol, remembered she had been at the airport on her way to a tropical destination when he called.

Giving a mental shrug, she pushed past the yellow tape and along the narrow walkway. She carefully avoided the crime scene markers that indicated evidence—in this case, what looked to be bloody footprints—and made her way to the front of the house. At the door, she paused briefly, inhaled deeply several times, and cleared her mind before entering the house.

"Dr. Sara Wilder." She flashed her ID to the uniform at the door and watched him write down her name and driver's license number before stepping aside.

"They're upstairs," he said.

From the doorway, she could see various crime scene techs engaged in the meticulous process of collecting physical evidence. Just inside, to the left of the door, she paused long enough to grab a pair of latex gloves and some booties from boxes on a table and slipped them on. Moving farther down the hallway, a staircase opened up on her right. At the top of the stairs, she spotted David speaking to a couple of SFPD homicide inspectors.

A fifteen-year veteran of the FBI, David Granger was a solidly built man of forty. Just under six feet in height, he had the muscular build of a weight lifter and a long-standing affection for Italian suits. He saw her as she approached and smiled.

"Sara. Thanks for getting here so quickly."

"Well, it turns out the airport wasn't that far away," Sara responded dryly, even as her lips curved slightly upward. There was no denying they had a lot of history between them, and regardless of the circumstances, it felt good to see him again. Even so, there was no need to give everything away.

As David offered an apologetic shrug, Sara became aware of his scrutiny. Beyond her attire, he was undoubtedly noting the physical changes that were evident since he had last seen her. She knew she looked different. Her pale blond hair was longer, falling just past her collar, and she had managed to regain most of the weight she had lost while working on the last investigation they had worked together—the Pelham case. But more noteworthy, she knew she had finally shed the haunted look that had seemed permanently etched on her face during those last few months. Instead, her eyes were now clear, and she looked and felt relaxed and healthy.

Just thinking about the Pelham case, even all these months later, still made her shudder. But not because of the particularly heinous nature of Pelham's string of rapes and murders.

Instead, it was the reminder of how much she detested politics. She'd underestimated the politics attached to the Pelham investigation. Specifically, the political pressure that had been brought to bear when one of the victims turned out to be the sixteen-year-old daughter of a well-connected judge.

Politics had never been Sara's forte. But politics and circumstantial evidence had resulted in a rush to judgment at the local level and led to the arrest of an innocent man. And in the time it took Sara to convince anyone they had the wrong man, Hugh Marshall had been brutally attacked by a gang of inmates at Rikers, while Richard Pelham had remained free to commit two more murders before ultimately being caught.

The overwhelming sense of failure had left a bitter aftertaste and ended her career.

Clearly aware the two SFPD inspectors were standing back watching them with apparent interest, David's mouth quirked into a wry grin. He quickly introduced Carlos Sanchez and Rick Wilson and then added, "C'mon, let's get started. Why don't you take a look around first? See what your Spidey senses pick up."

Sara nodded wordlessly. For the next few minutes, David, Sanchez, and Wilson stood back and waited, observing while Sara seemed to communicate with the victim's home, wondering what it would tell her.

She remained motionless in the middle of the room for a minute, her arms wrapped around her midriff. She felt nothing and could see no visible signs that the space had been disturbed in any way. It did not seem likely that the killer had come up here. But the victim had lived here, had spent the last few hours of her life here, and she needed to get to know her.

Sara believed it was important to study the victim. If she understood the victim, she felt she had a much better chance of figuring out how she'd crossed paths with her killer. Did she pick up strangers at bars? Had she inadvertently invited a killer back to her house? At first glance, it didn't feel that way.

The master bedroom was decorated simply. Wooden blinds, colorful throw rugs scattered over hardwood floors. The bed had been neatly turned down, but the sheets remained crisp and taut and had not been slept in. The dresser was covered with an assortment of creams and lotions, their scents competing with the faint but unmistakable odor of blood and death that hung in the still night air.

The entire room was pristine. Only a dark blue sweatshirt looked vaguely out of place, and even that had been carefully folded and placed on a chair near the bed. But there were no scented candles, no condoms, no toys, nor any other sign the bedroom had been set up for seduction. What else could it have been? Maybe she simply had recognized him from someplace and let him in.

David indicated vaguely with a nod of his head. "There are two other bedrooms on this floor. One was set up as a home office. The other looks like a guest room and doesn't appear to have been used in quite some time."

She thrust her hands into her pockets and moved past David out of the master bedroom. After briefly looking into the other two bedrooms, she turned and headed back down the stairs. David and the two inspectors followed.

"The victim's name is Shelly Barrett. Neighbors describe her as quiet." Sara knew it was David's habit to catalogue—people, places, events—believing life was kept simpler if everything could be neatly labeled. He pulled out a well-used notebook and glanced at it. "Single. Twenty-six. She was a graphic designer."

The body had already been removed and was in the hands of the medical examiner's office. But as Sara listened to the murmured conversations swirling around her, it became quickly apparent the members of the joint FBI and SFPD task force assigned to the case already knew what they were facing. Shelly Barrett was the latest victim—the fifth victim—of a serial killer.

The tension evident among the investigators spoke volumes. Collectively, they would be fervently hoping this victim would give them something the first four had been unable to provide. Sara had been there often enough in the past. She knew they were praying for a break. Something, no matter how small or seemingly insignificant, that would help them identify a killer before he could strike again. Just as she knew David was counting on his former partner to help him in that regard.

Reaching the bottom of the stairs, they turned right toward the rear of the house. By comparison with the nearly obsessive neatness of the upstairs bedrooms, this part of the house was in total disarray. Overturned furniture, a broken lamp, spatters of dark blood marring the gleaming hardwood floors and whitewashed walls.

Here was the terror, the evil. It felt imprinted in the air.

"She put up one hell of a struggle."

Sara wasn't sure who made the comment but she silently disagreed. Walking through the lower level of the house, she could feel Shelly Barrett's terror as she tried to elude her assailant. Terror evident in the chaos and destruction she could see. But the chaos wasn't about struggle. Shelly Barrett had simply tried to throw obstacles in her wake—a chair, a lamp, a small side table. A valiant but ultimately fruitless attempt to slow down her killer's relentless pursuit.

"The ME's initial estimate put the time of death sometime between eight and midnight last night," David said. "Barrett frequently worked from home, but a co-worker got concerned when she failed to show for a meeting this afternoon and wasn't answering her phone. When she came by the house to check, she saw the blood on the front steps and called it in."

David paused and consulted his notes. "There appear to be defensive wounds to her forearms, but he didn't use the knife to kill her. Just to frighten her. Subdue her. That's the one clear difference between this and the other four crime scenes we're attributing to the same UNSUB."

Sara frowned. Without knowing the details of the four previous murders, she was left to speculate what the unknown subject of the investigation had done differently this time. "What do you mean? What's different?"

"This one's more...I don't know...frenzied. As if either it didn't quite go according to plan or he started losing it. In all other aspects, though, they're all the same. No sign of forced entry. The victim was killed by a single gunshot to the right temple. A contact wound. If it's the same as the others, it'll be a thirty-eight. There was blood splatter evident on the victim's right hand. First officer on the scene called it in as a suicide."

Sanchez snorted. "Dumb rookie."

Sara raised a questioning brow as she waited for the punch line. When it came, it was Wilson who gave it.

"No gun," he explained. "The UNSUB somehow gets the victim to shoot herself. Same as all the others. But he's not doing it to make it look like a suicide. Otherwise, he wouldn't take the gun with him when he leaves."

"Victim was fully dressed when she was found." Sanchez picked up the narrative from his partner. "No sign of sexual assault. No sign of a robbery either. Just this."

They turned another corner, and Sara got her first full view into the mind of a madman.

The blood spatter on the wall and floor indicated where the killer had finished what he started. Sara stared at the dark stained floor and the outline where the body had been found. She tuned out all distractions, concentrated on committing the scene to memory. Looked for anything that would offer insight into the unknown subject. She then let her eyes drift slowly upward.

He had spent a lot of time here. Had left numerous messages scrawled across the walls, written in red. Simulating blood, no doubt.

At first glance, Sara could see most of the writing consisted of rambling fantasies. But there, in the middle of the wall, an island surrounded by the sea of disjointed thoughts, stood one clear message, printed larger than the rest.

> *Hunter,*
> *You are mine.*
> *It's time for daddy's girl to come home.*

CHAPTER TWO

Three hours later, Sara slipped on the rimless reading glasses that had been nesting in her hair, as eyestrain competed with the pounding in her head. She knew David was watching her study the five photographs he had just removed from the case file and spread across his desk.

"These are all the victims. One per month for the last five months, starting with Sandra Holman." David's index finger restlessly tapped the photograph corresponding with the first victim. "Five foot nine, twenty-seven years old. An architect. She was found in her apartment near Golden Gate Park back in April. Killed by a single shot to the temple from a thirty-eight."

As Sara watched and listened, she acknowledged if only to herself that David was deliberately and indelibly planting the victims' images in her mind. He was making them real. Their names, their faces, their lives. Knowing that would make it all but impossible for her to walk away from them, and therefore from him. But even recognizing she was being manipulated, she couldn't blame him. After all, given a reversal in their roles, it was what she would have done.

David glanced at her as if he could hear the thoughts going on in her head. He continued his narrative as he moved on to the second victim.

"The same signature was repeated." He tapped the next photograph on his desk. "Deanna Gordon was a lawyer. Five foot eight, and at twenty-nine, the oldest of the five victims. She was found in her home in North Beach a month after the first killing."

The litany of murder continued. June's victim had been a five-foot-ten, twenty-eight year-old associate professor named Nina Tyler. July followed with another twenty-eight year old. A five-foot-nine programmer named Rita Stavros. And then, of course, there was Shelly Barrett, the victim corresponding to the crime scene they had attended earlier that evening.

Sara felt drained as she studied the photographs. Five victims dead as a result of self-inflicted wounds. Five young women whose lives had been ruthlessly cut short. Five women who would never have the opportunity to live out their dreams. The burning question was why.

"The similarities between the victims are obvious," she said finally. "All were in their mid-to-late twenties, attractive, taller than average. They all had dark hair, blue eyes. And all would appear to have been successful professionals."

"Mm-hmm. In addition, they all lived alone. But we're not talking victims of opportunity. Too many similarities to be just a coincidence—"

"And you don't believe in coincidences," Sara finished for him.

"Right." David smiled tiredly. "No question. They were specific targets. Still, as far as we've been able to determine, there's no connection between the victims. They didn't live in the same neighborhood. Didn't shop in the same stores. Didn't frequent the same clubs. And there were no personal or professional connections. Which means we don't know where or when they crossed paths with their killer."

"Then what's the common denominator?"

David responded by reaching into the case file. He extracted another photograph and handed it to Sara.

For a long moment, she stared at a close-up of a drop dead gorgeous brunette whose face was instantly seared into memory. Her dark hair hung loosely past her shoulders and framed an exquisite face with high cheekbones and intense blue eyes. Her lips were full and had formed a sensuous smile as she stared directly into the camera. It was, when all was said and done, an unforgettable face. Heart-stoppingly beautiful and perfect but for a small scar that cut the corner of her right eyebrow.

Sara looked back at David. "She's stunning. And there is an obvious superficial similarity to your victims. Who is she?"

"She's the original," David said. "Her name is Hunter Roswell."

Sara's eyes narrowed briefly. "As in 'Hunter, you are mine'?"

"Yeah. We've managed to keep this out of the media so far, but there were actually messages left at each of the crime scenes. Our problem was until now, we weren't clear who the UNSUB was trying to communicate with, but this last one—the message you saw tonight—tied it all together. We were finally able to identify who the messages were meant for." David tapped the photograph Sara was holding. "Roswell."

"How did you make the connection?"

"The reference to 'daddy's girl.' It's an old…nickname of Roswell's," David explained. "But while it makes it easier to know who he's targeting, in some ways this thing's gotten more complicated and has political nightmare written all over it."

"Why? Who is Hunter Roswell?"

"That's the million-dollar question, isn't it?" David said and absently rubbed his chin. "The short answer is she's the head of a high-tech security firm called the Roswell Group. Cutting edge when it comes to biometrics. Retinal scans. Face and voice recognition. Hand and palm geometry. Behavior pattern recognition. The full monty."

As David explained, the Roswell Group was as good as it got, handling both corporate and government contracts, but not limiting themselves exclusively to the US government. His understanding was Roswell was working with a number of governments in various European countries and in the Middle East as well. They also worked closely with law enforcement, both at home and abroad.

"The general consensus is Hunter Roswell can take a computer system and a piece of software and make it howl at the moon. Her company designs unbelievable security systems," he said, "and they also develop a lot of the offender and geographic profiling software being used by law enforcement agencies."

Something in David's voice caught Sara's attention. "I take it she's connected."

"No question. She's got powerful relatives that extend beyond the Roswell Group," David replied carefully. "We're talking old money and big business, primarily shipping and hotels, and Junior provides the security for all of it."

"Nepotism at its finest," Sara said.

"You'd think so," David grinned. "But the truth is she's that good. And at the end of the day, we're still talking high profile. What it means is we have to tread lightly and very carefully. We can't afford to make any mistakes. Otherwise, the family will put a phalanx of lawyers around Roswell that no one will get through, and we're going to need her cooperation if we want to identify our boy."

Sara's expression grew thoughtful. "You mentioned messages left at the other crime scenes. Were they similar to the one tonight?"

"Yeah. Although the earlier messages weren't specifically addressed to Hunter, like tonight's, they shared one common theme— 'You are mine.'" David fell silent, his eyes drawn to Roswell's picture. When he spoke again, both tiredness and frustration were evident in his voice. "But there was no mention of 'daddy's girl' or any message about coming home before tonight."

"And home for Roswell is San Francisco?"

"Um, yeah…or at least it was," David said. "The Roswell Group has offices in San Francisco, New York, and London. Until a few months ago, Roswell traveled between the three offices, but she worked out of their San Francisco office."

"And that changed?"

"About six months ago. Since then, she's been working exclusively out of their London office. No idea why, and no one's provided any explanations. But we know there's a connection somewhere between our UNSUB and Roswell, and I don't believe it's a coincidence the killing spree began just after she went to London." David paused and cleared his throat. "Our biggest challenge is we don't have the luxury of time."

"Because the killer is decompensating?" Sara asked. "Or because he seems to be following a lunar cycle?"

"Caught that, did you?" David gave her a weary grin.

"Come on, David," Sara chided. "We both know the full moon has always been linked to incidents that occur during its phase. But in this case, it would appear to be warranted. Near as I can tell, each of the murders you're looking at has taken place around a full moon."

"Yeah," David acknowledged. "Just one of the little details we're trying to keep out of the media. It certainly helped that in a couple of the cases, the victims weren't immediately discovered, and the actual times of death haven't been made public. Otherwise, the headlines in the papers would be screaming about a full-moon killer and scaring tall, dark-haired women half to death."

Sara leaned forward, placing her elbows on the desk. "And the public would probably fail to make the distinction between correlation and causation. Just because there is a relationship between the full moon and certain behavior, it doesn't mean the moon caused the behavior."

"Agreed, but while the full moon isn't causing the UNSUB's behavior, he is definitely using it to establish his timetable," David said. "And with the last crime scene indicating a loss of control, it may be he's no longer satisfied with killing surrogates. He may be getting ready to move on to Roswell herself, which means the pressure to solve this—to find him before he goes anywhere near Roswell—will increase exponentially."

Politics.

Sara raised her eyebrows and stared at David for a long, silent moment. Finally, she probed. "And what is it you want from me?"

"What I would really like is for you to come with me to London. I got clearance to use you as a consultant on the task force, and I'd like you with me when I meet with Roswell. I'd like your help in further developing the profile." He paused and rubbed the bridge of his nose. "I know I told you I wasn't looking to get you directly involved in the investigation. But the truth is I could really use your help on this one."

Sara didn't miss the uncertainty in David's voice. "Why?"

There was a moment of hesitation before he answered. "I don't know how Roswell's going to respond to any of this or how much push back we can expect. But I think having you there will help."

"Why?" she asked again.

David sighed and sank back in his seat. "Because I know her."

"You know Roswell personally?" Warning bells sounded in her head, and Sara began to wonder just how concerned she should be by David's revelation. "How well?"

"I certainly wouldn't say we're friends, and obviously we don't run in the same social circles, but we've crossed paths a few times over the years."

David's answer was so vague Sara could all but visualize him tap dancing in her head. She steepled her fingers and stared at them contemplatively. It was one thing to feel she was missing something vital. It was something entirely different to believe she was being deliberately misled.

"Talk to me," she said quietly. "Because I have to tell you, it really looks like you're holding something critical back for some reason, and I don't like it."

"Sara—"

"No, I'm sorry, but if you truly want my help, then I would suggest you come clean and make sure I understand everything that's going on." She paused for an instant and deliberately kept her voice devoid of sympathy. "As in right now, David, or I'm out of here and on the first flight I can get to Bali."

There was a long, tense pause while they stared at each other, and Sara almost believed David would refuse, would let her walk away. But then his shoulders slumped, and he closed his eyes.

"You're right, of course." His voice sounded infinitely weary. "I first met Hunter Roswell just about ten years ago. At the time, I had been assigned to a team charged with protecting the US Attorney General's daughter after several specific and credible threats were made against her. 'Daddy's girl' was the code name the security detail had for Hunter."

Sara grew still. But then a sigh escaped as the pieces began to fall into place. "Oh God, I never made the connection with the name," she said. "Hunter Roswell. Her father was Michael Roswell?"

David nodded and looked down at the expanse of desk that lay between them. "It was a clusterfuck of epic proportion. I…the security detail…we failed to protect Hunter. The militia group that had made the threats succeeded in kidnapping her, and Michael Roswell was killed during a botched attempt to rescue his only child."

Sara watched David carefully as she quickly tried to process the information. "Is that what this is about?" she asked softly. "Do you believe there's a connection? Do you think there's a chance what happened to Hunter Roswell ten years ago is somehow connected with the serial killer you're currently trying to identify?"

David finally looked up. "I don't know. It's a distinct possibility, and I think we need to find out."

But that was his fear, Sara realized.

❖

David crossed to a pot of stale coffee resting on a hot plate. After pouring himself another cup, he raised the pot in Sara's direction. "Want some?"

Sara stared at the muddy looking contents in the pot and shuddered. "I think I've had enough," she responded, glancing at the untouched cup of coffee in her hand. Her head continued to pound in a steady rhythm while she tried to gather her thoughts.

"Help me make sure I understand this," she said. "You believe Hunter Roswell is the key to whoever is killing these women. In fact, you believe she's his real target. But you're challenged by the fact that she's extremely well connected, which makes the situation politically dangerous and potentially career limiting. It also doesn't help that she's currently out of the country."

David nodded somberly.

Sara slid off her glasses and began absently gnawing on the tip of one earpiece. "Then there's the UNSUB. Based on his messages, he's probably an erotomanic stalker. Erotomanics typically react badly to any perceived rejection by their victims and will turn to violence when the relationship with the object of their affection looks hopeless. It's likely he interpreted Roswell leaving the country six months ago as rejection, which triggered his killing spree."

"Mm-hmm." David drew the sound out.

"Obviously, part of what's missing here is what motivated Roswell to shift her base of operations to London. Have you considered the possibility her move was precipitated by some kind of contact with her stalker?"

David nodded again. "It's certainly a possibility."

Sara sighed. "Fine. Since she's the key to all of this, what can you tell me about Hunter Roswell? How involved is she in the day-to-day operations of her business? What does she do for fun and relaxation? Where might she have come into contact with her stalker? In other words, what's she like?"

David responded without any apparent conscious thought. "She's painfully beautiful and intimidatingly intelligent." An instant later, David looked up and met Sara's eyes with some difficulty. "Shit. Can you please pretend you didn't hear that?"

"Not a chance." Sara laughed and then relented. "But for old times, I'm willing to save that conversation for later. Maybe over drinks. In the meantime, you're going to tell me all about Hunter Roswell. She seems kind of young to head up a company. Is she a trust-fund baby?"

Her shift in direction allowed David to move past his discomfort. "Yes," he said, then stopped and corrected himself. "I mean, no."

Sara tilted her head. "Well? Which is it?"

"Both, I guess. She got control of her first trust fund at twenty-five, and another is set to kick in on her thirtieth birthday. In the meantime, she's made a fortune of her own. She's got a couple of partners in the Roswell Group, but make no mistake: she's the brains behind the operation. She's got more intelligence than should be considered safe for one human being."

"Just how smart are we talking about?"

David opened the case file once again and quickly scanned a document. "Let's see…an IQ estimated at somewhere around one eighty. Private school education, graduated high school at thirteen. A couple of PhDs from Oxford, and then she started the Roswell Group. All before her twenty-first birthday."

"Sweet Jesus," Sara breathed. "That's not even remotely human."

"I did warn you, but I know what you mean. You'll find Hunter is like no one you've ever dealt with. She mixes easily with Fortune 500 types, has a high-octane temper and a reputation for not taking no for an answer. Put it this way—in this business, you learn to take stories with a grain of salt. But in Hunter's case, I always wonder how much has been left out."

Sara raised an eyebrow at the picture being painted. "And there's no question? No doubt in your mind Hunter Roswell is the intended target?" She waited patiently—for about ten seconds. "David?"

"No," David replied. "No question. No doubt."

Suddenly Sara's eyes narrowed, and the smile left her face. "That's really what this is all about…why you want me to go to London with you, isn't it?" As she spoke, her frown deepened. "This isn't about cooperation or helping you to identify a killer. You want to give the UNSUB what he's asking for. You want to talk Hunter Roswell into coming back to San Francisco. She's your bait. Tell me I'm wrong, David."

There was a long pause before David responded. "You're not wrong. Yes, I want her to come back, but it's not what you're thinking."

"You're willing to put her at risk?"

"No." David shook his head adamantly. "In fact, it's the opposite. I need to prove we can cover her."

"Why—" Sara froze for a moment, holding up a hand as understanding dawned. "You do know you can't undo the past, don't you?"

"I know that—damn, at least I think I know that. That's not important right now. What's important is we'll have her covered by both FBI and local law enforcement, and she's got an operations team working with her that's capable of providing her with personal protection around the clock. They're all former law enforcement or former military and are considered second to none. She won't be at risk."

"And have you considered your objectivity might be in question here? What if you're wrong, David?" Sara asked softly.

"That's the point, isn't it? I'm not wrong, and with you and me working together, we'll make sure of it. It'll be like old times. Better. If I learned anything from the Pelham case, it's that I should have listened to you sooner. Please. I know this case is riddled with politics, and I know how much you hate that. But I really need you on this."

Sara knew all the reasons she should simply walk away. Walk away now, and maybe she could still salvage part of her vacation. Instead, she heard her own voice saying, "I'll go to London with you. But I'm making no promises beyond that."

CHAPTER THREE

Hunter Roswell stepped outside to the sound of thunder rolling in the distance. She paused long enough to pull up the collar of her long black coat and tipped her head back, watching as lightning cut jagged streaks against the dark storm clouds that hovered overhead. An instant later, another flash split the sky, tearing it open and allowing a soft rain to begin falling.

Despite the storm that had been threatening all morning, the streets were alive. Filled with people and a frenetic energy Hunter always thought of as distinctly London—a city that never failed to exhilarate, stimulate, and invigorate her in equal measures. She stood still, closed her eyes, and simply let the life force of the city surround her and fill her senses.

It was noisy and vibrant, the air filled with fragmentary sounds. Tourists crowding the sidewalk ducked under overhangs to wait out the rain, their voices blending with the never-ending rumble of the cars and buses going past. Somewhere nearby a police siren began to wail, its mournful sound gradually diminishing as it moved toward its destination. And clearly audible above the din was the sound of the rain.

Hunter loved the rain.

Their lips brushed gently, light feather touches. She could taste the rain on the soft lips touching her own, feel it on her skin. "Have you ever made love in the rain?" she asked.

The memory washed over her, and for a fleeting moment, Hunter became lost in the visceral recall. Hot, hungry mouths, sweat-soaked bodies, and tangled limbs moving in synchronous rhythm while thunder rumbled overhead and rain lashed against the windows.

There was just something about rainstorms that always seemed to awaken her id. Just the sound or scent of rain alone inevitably fueled her libido and left her in a perpetual state of wanting. But now was not the time, she acknowledged with a sigh.

Opening her eyes, she took a deep breath and moved toward the limousine waiting patiently at the curb. The sounds of the city receded as she got in and the uniformed driver closed the door. Moments after she was seated, the car began to maneuver slowly through the congested, rain-soaked streets, edging its way into the outside lane of traffic.

❖

Five minutes passed silently. Then, as if suddenly aware she wasn't alone, Hunter looked up. Seated across from her was Sir Nigel Wainwright, the man who represented the closest thing to a father figure in her life. A good friend of both her parents, he had played an integral role in her life, starting from the time she had enrolled at Oxford at the age of thirteen.

Her intellect hadn't seemed to frighten Nigel, the way it did most adults in her life at that time. Instead, it was as if he had felt challenged by her insatiable appetite for knowledge and had discovered in himself the joy of teaching her. They discovered a shared passion for history, literature, art, and music, although he failed to understand her love of progressive and psychedelic rock.

And while he didn't share her fascination with computers and technology, she knew he had come to rely on her insights and suggestions when it came to securing his many business interests. Just as she knew he appreciated her at times uncanny understanding of the vagaries of the market, which continued to make him a wealthy man.

Drawn back into the present, she felt the intensity of Nigel's gaze as he watched her and forced herself to remain cool, calm, completely composed. Meeting his eyes, she raised an elegant eyebrow.

"See something you like, old man?"

"Maybe." He gave the expected reply, bringing a faint smile to Hunter's lips.

"Let me know when you decide," she said. But then her smile faded as she saw the expression on his face. She moistened her lips, took in a deep breath of rain-filled air, and braced herself, turning blindly to the window for a moment. "What is it you want to know, Nigel?"

"On a serious note, my dear," he said, "I'd like to know why these American police officers have come to see you."

Hunter shrugged and leaned forward, elbows resting on her knees, as she grew pensive. All she knew was Quito, her personal assistant, had sent her a heads up in a text message earlier. He had warned her two FBI agents had shown up without prior notice and were insisting on meeting with her. Coincident with the arrival of the two agents, Matt Logan, one of her business partners, had flown in unannounced, and wanted to see her.

Neither fact pleased her.

Straightening, Hunter frowned slightly and made a noncommittal sound. "I guess we'll find out soon enough."

Seated to Hunter's right, Peter McNeil stiffened perceptibly, the first indication that he had been listening to the conversation. He remained silent. But as head of security for the Roswell Group in general and Hunter Roswell specifically, Hunter knew his preference would be to get any questions answered up front, which in this case meant before letting the two FBI agents anywhere near her.

But that wasn't about to happen. Experience should have taught him by now that Hunter maintained tight control over any decisions that directly affected her. And on this particular occasion, she was not only not asking for advice, she was not interested in what he would consider to be due diligence.

Hunter felt Peter's reaction and instinctively reached out with one hand to reassure him. "It's all right, Peter," she said. "I wouldn't have agreed to meet with them if I thought it would cause a problem. Besides, I know one of agents, David Granger, and at least for now, I'm willing to trust him."

"How can you say that? How can you even think it?" Peter retorted. "He's the bloody FBI, for God's sake. You, of all people, should know what they're like."

Peter's off-hand comment penetrated her guard and had the blood draining out of her face. She could feel it and knew her sudden pallor would leave no room for doubt about where her thoughts had taken her.

But Peter was still frustrated, angry. That she would deal with, Hunter decided. She shuddered slightly then straightened her shoulders and brought her eyes back into sharp focus. But before there could be any kind of escalation of their disagreement, Nigel intervened.

"Hunter," he said, "are you certain you're not in some kind of trouble?"

"Me?" Hunter responded, grateful for his intervention, gracing Nigel with a smile that didn't quite reach her eyes. "To my knowledge, I've done nothing that would warrant any level of interest from the FBI."

Nigel leaned back and sighed. "Then what is it? And don't tell me nothing is wrong, because I can see it in your eyes. You've not been sleeping."

Hunter looked up with a start. She had expected the question to come from Matt, once he got a good look at her. But not Nigel, who had played the role of surrogate father for so long she sometimes forgot how perceptive he could be and how well he knew her. She felt a pang of guilt. "I don't know. Maybe you're just seeing that I stayed out much too late last night and didn't get any sleep."

"And I suppose the papers will be full of speculation about you and that politician once again. Or was it the musician this time?"

"Tennis player…" Hunter said and flashed a weak grin.

Nigel's eyes narrowed. Hunter winced at that. Of all people, Nigel would know there was something else at play and had been for quite some time. She could feel his penetrating gaze as he studied her face, and worried about how far he would push her.

As he continued to watch her, she began counting the seconds as they ticked by. Just eight more minutes and they would arrive at the Roswell building. She could meet with Matt, deal with the FBI, and not have to contend with this conversation with Nigel. Just a few more minutes and—

"Will you at least tell me if the arrival of these agents has anything to do with whatever brought you to London and has kept you here all this time?"

Hunter's grin disappeared.

It had been six months since she had shown up at her London office, no doubt looking as if she could feel the hot breath of the hounds of hell on the back of her neck. She had dodged all of Nigel's gentle attempts at inquiry. Instead, she had simply stated her intent to expand the Roswell Group's European operations.

A force to be reckoned with when she set her mind on something, she had spent the past six months accomplishing just that. Driven like never before, she had worked nonstop, pushed relentlessly, traveled constantly. But success notwithstanding, she was aware Nigel—and possibly others—had been left with the impression that she was running *from* rather than *to* something.

Rightfully so.

Thunder rumbled as Hunter considered Nigel's question. She wondered how best to answer. How much to prevaricate. Images flashed in her mind of their own volition. The resulting emotions briefly flickered across her unguarded face before she was able to slip a practiced mask back into place. Taking a deep breath, she made an effort to bring her heart rate back to normal. But the turmoil in her soul remained.

"Hunter?"

Aware Nigel was waiting for an answer to his question, Hunter swallowed and took another calming breath before smiling slightly. "Sorry, mind's wandering."

As he waited for her response, Hunter wondered if she could simply deny the existence of any problem. Deny anything other than a business reason for her extended stay in the UK. But after an interminable silence, she looked up and gave the only truthful answer she had.

"I'm sorry, Nigel. It's not that I don't want to answer you. It's that I honestly don't know if anything's connected."

"But the arrival of these agents does signal your imminent return to California, doesn't it." He made it a statement, not a question, because Hunter knew he could see his answer in her eyes.

"Probably...yes. It's been good to be here. Really good. I've missed London. I've missed you. But it's probably time to go home."

She'd been away for longer stretches of time in the past, but this absence was weighing more heavily on her. *Perhaps because this time you've stayed away out of cowardice*, her pragmatic conscience pricked her.

Was that really the reason? Had what happened in New York left her so unnerved she had opted to hide in England and bury herself in work? Of course, that led to the real question. *Why?*

And she knew the answer to that question.

The incident in New York had left her battered physically. But the toll had been greater emotionally, representing the second time in her life a stranger had wrested control from her. And while there was still much she couldn't remember about what had happened in New York, it had triggered such an onslaught of memories and nightmares it had left her reeling.

But she ought to go home, she knew that now. She needed to make her peace with the past. She needed to make her peace with herself. And hiding out in London wasn't going to get her what she needed.

And perhaps, the pragmatist said, *that was what going home really meant.* Perhaps it was simply a metaphor.

"Tell me what I can do to help," Nigel said.

Hunter blinked, tried to bring things into focus. She had expected pushback, not quiet acceptance and support. She closed her eyes briefly, letting the emotions wash over her. Then, leaning forward, she placed a gentle kiss on Nigel's cheek, surprising them both.

"Thank you," she said softly. "You have been my mentor and my greatest ally for as far back as I can remember. Right now, I'm not sure what the problem might be. But I promise if I find myself in trouble and need any help, I will come to you."

"Whatever you need. Whenever you need it, Hunter," Nigel stated unequivocally.

CHAPTER FOUR

The uniformed security guard at the Roswell Group's London office stared impassively at the two FBI agents as they displayed their IDs and made their request. A quick phone call later, he informed Sara and David that Hunter Roswell was not in the building. Nor had she advised anyone that she was expecting visitors…*which she certainly would have done had she known they were coming*. This was said with such obvious disdain Sara had to bite her cheek to keep from laughing.

After several more phone calls, security personnel escorted them to a small waiting room on the ground floor "until Ms. Roswell could be notified." As the door closed, David cursed under his breath and slumped into one of the rich leather chairs. Sara took off her jacket and did her best to relax while trying to ignore him.

She was quite thankful when it turned out they had to wait less than an hour before the door opened again. Her first impression was of a tall, slightly built Hispanic male in his early twenties, with dark, nearly black eyes set in a beautiful face. He was dressed in an impeccable gray suit, and a black shirt and tie. All of which contrasted rather nicely, in Sara's opinion, with his peroxide-tipped, spiky hairstyle and the tiny diamond stud in one ear.

"Special Agent Granger? Special Agent Wilder? I'm Quito Ramirez, Ms. Roswell's personal assistant," he said as he extended his hand. "She apologizes, but she's been held up in traffic and has asked me to ensure you're comfortable until she arrives. If you'll follow me, I'll get you through security."

Quito guided them to a discreet office on the ground floor, where security staff obtained palm prints, fingerprints, and photographs while running retinal scans and voice- and facial-recognition programs. They were asked to relinquish their government-issued Glocks, which Sara did gladly, David with some reluctance. In response, a dark-haired man with a French accent flexed his muscles and politely assured David he would not need his weapon while on Roswell property. He then added, almost as an afterthought, that the weapon would be promptly returned upon his departure.

Sara was impressed. The entire procedure from start to finish was handled with absolute courtesy and efficiency. In what seemed like no time at all, they were provided with temporary access cards, which Quito informed them had to be worn visibly at all times during their visit.

"I'm curious," David commented casually as he clipped the card to his lapel. "I've visited both your New York and San Francisco offices in the past and didn't have to go through this level of clearance. Is there a reason for the heightened security?"

"I'm not sure when you visited previously," Quito replied politely, "but this is SOP for access to the executive-level floors, and Ms. Roswell requested you be brought to her office."

Sara noted that he hadn't really answered the question. At the same time, he left no room for doubt that what Ms. Roswell asked for, Ms. Roswell got.

"Your access cards will be valid until midnight," Quito added.

"What happens then?" Sara said. "Do we turn into pumpkins?"

"Nah." Quito flashed a quick grin, providing a first glimpse of youth under his carefully maintained professional persona. "It...just stops opening things. You'll be locked down until morning. Or until someone comes along and finds you."

As he spoke, he steered them through a series of metal detectors and X-ray scanners, before continuing toward a bank of elevators. Sara wondered what he would have said had he not censored himself. She felt there was a great deal more to the access card than the simple explanation provided but decided this was not the time to challenge Quito on the subject.

"I notice you don't wear an access card," she said instead.

"I don't need one," he replied. "There are scanners located throughout the building that are programmed to recognize authorized personnel. A combination of handprints, fingerprints, retinal scans, or the works depending on what area you want to access."

He paused and indicated a small silver-and-black pin on his lapel bearing the Roswell Group insignia. "I'm also wearing this. From the time I enter the building until well after I leave, security can pinpoint exactly where I am. They can also tell if someone other than me is wearing it."

"Good God," Sara whispered. "Big Brother really *is* watching."

"More like big sister," Quito countered with another quick grin. "Hunter…um, Ms. Roswell…she designed all the security systems we use in each of our offices. Says it gives her somewhere to play and razzle-dazzle…you know, try new things out that might impress potential clients."

An elevator door opened, and Quito inclined his head, indicating that Sara and David should precede him. Once inside, he pressed the only button on the wall panel. "This elevator only goes to the executive offices," he explained in response to Sara's quizzical look. Further conversation was pre-empted as the elevator swiftly reached its destination and the door opened soundlessly. "Welcome to the inner ring."

Did he just quote C.S. Lewis? Sara stared at the young man with growing fascination. As she followed him down a softly lit hallway, she began to wonder at what point she would most likely encounter a large white rabbit.

Near the end of the hallway, Quito opened the door to a corner office suite. Leading them through the reception area, he opened a second door that led into a large office. Tastefully decorated in soothing shades of burgundy and gray, it was large enough to comfortably accommodate a sleek curved desk and leather chair, and two soft leather couches.

Classy and understated, Sara thought, but she noted the remarkable lack of personal items. No framed diplomas. No photographs. No fingerprints or clues to the personality that normally resided within the office walls.

"Can I get you anything to drink while you're waiting?" Quito asked. "Coffee, tea, water?"

Sara and David responded simultaneously with requests for coffee. Quito laughed softly and promised to return quickly before excusing himself.

David immediately dropped onto one of the couches. Sara walked past him and over to the large windows, from which she could see the rain-drenched streets below. She wasn't sure what she was searching for as she watched the rain pour from the sky and streak across the windows. But there was something comforting about the thunderstorm, something familiar and special she couldn't put her finger on. Right now, she would take whatever comfort she could get.

Why do I let myself get talked into these situations?

It was, of course, a little late to be asking that particular question. She knew it was her need to find closure—not only for herself, but possibly for David as well—that was, in part, driving her present actions.

Over the past eight months, she had asked herself hundreds of times if there was anything she could have done differently, anything that would have changed what happened during the Pelham investigation. The question had haunted her, and after months of endless debates with Kate, her old college roommate and closest friend, with her parents, and indeed with herself, she finally accepted there wasn't. It had come as an incredible relief to know that.

Perhaps that's what made it easier for her to recognize David still carried much self-blame and a tremendous amount of guilt over what had happened ten years earlier when Hunter Roswell had been kidnapped and Michael Roswell had been killed. It also made it all but impossible for her to deny David's appeal for help.

She was also sufficiently self-aware to recognize there were enough similarities between the Pelham case and this one—two high-profile serial killer cases—to cause her discomfort. But there was also an undeniable pull to work on and solve a complex and psychologically intriguing case.

But that didn't stop her head from aching and her body from desperately craving caffeine. It also didn't help that she had just spent far too many hours in an overheated airplane packed full of bodies—her personal idea of hell. She rubbed her temples and tried to ignore the fatigue she was feeling.

Behind her, David continued to mutter about being made to wait. Sara wanted to point out they had arrived without warning, and unless she was psychic, Hunter Roswell would have had no prior knowledge her presence would be required at the office today. But she decided it wasn't worth the argument with a tired and obviously irritable David. Instead, she concentrated on watching the storm as it slashed across the city. She had almost succeeded in tuning him out when a low, husky voice interrupted her musings.

"I hear you've been looking for me, Special Agent Granger."

Sara heard David respond as she turned away from the window. She didn't need his greeting to identify the tall, slim woman standing at the door. But the photograph David had shown her notwithstanding, the woman wasn't entirely what Sara had expected.

Perhaps it had something to do with the white linen shirt left carelessly untucked or the threadbare blue jeans with holes in interesting places. Hardly the expected attire for a CEO doing business with numerous governments and Fortune 500 companies.

Still, even casually dressed, wearing little makeup, and with her hair windblown and damp from the rain, Hunter Roswell had something that David's photograph had failed to capture. It went beyond the stunningly beautiful face and the intense blue eyes. Beyond the long and lean body and a heady, tantalizing scent.

Unexpectedly, Sara felt something inside her stir, and her professional façade slipped slightly as she caught herself staring longer than she should have. The realization caused a hot blush to spread across her face while she tried to figure out what the hell had just happened. But try as she might, she couldn't pull her eyes away long enough to discern what it was about Hunter Roswell that drew her in and held her. And perhaps it didn't really matter because Hunter seemed equally content to stare back, her killer blue eyes pinning Sara where she stood.

Hunter recovered first and pushed off the doorframe. Entering the room with a fluid grace and an aura of confidence, her face gave nothing away. But as she extended her right hand, her cool gaze seemed to warm, and her lips curved ever so slightly.

"Hi. Hunter Roswell. I don't believe I've had the pleasure—?"

The voice was deep and whiskey-warm, the accent unmistakably American laced with a hint of England. It rolled over Sara, and she smiled wryly as she found herself looking up. Although she stood just over five-eight, Hunter Roswell topped her by at least a couple of inches. She took the long and slender hand, adorned with a single wide platinum ring, and returned the handshake. And as their hands connected, she could feel both warmth and strength.

"Sara Wilder," she responded. Her voice sounded unusually husky to her own ears, and she blushed again as she cleared her throat.

Hunter's eyes narrowed slightly, and Sara knew those cool, quick eyes were assessing everything. An instant later, the moment was broken when Quito returned with a tray from which wafted the rich aroma of freshly brewed coffee.

Just the scent of the strong coffee alone provided Sara with an immediate and welcome kick, and she anticipated the warm rush of instant energy coursing through her tired body. Nodding her thanks, she gratefully accepted a cup and took a sip.

"God, this is really good," she said with pleasure and let the caffeine do its job.

After ensuring both visitors had been looked after, Quito handed a tall silver-and-black mug to Hunter. She responded by unleashing a grin like a thunderbolt and mouthed *my life saver* in the young man's direction. Quito returned her grin with obvious adulation before asking whether anything else was needed. Taking his cue from Hunter, he quietly left the room.

Hunter's grin had Sara staring at her mouth. It was full and sensual, evoking an almost visceral response. Her pulse stuttered and it became difficult to think. No, David's photograph had not done Hunter Roswell justice at all. But there was something else. She groped to identify it but a definition eluded her.

Hunter watched Quito leave before turning and motioning toward the two couches. "Please make yourselves comfortable."

Sara glanced at David. They automatically chose to sit on the same couch and waited expectantly for Hunter to follow suit. Instead, she roamed the office with a restless energy before stopping in front of the window to stare out at the endless mist, much as Sara had done earlier.

Unwillingly fascinated, Sara took the opportunity to observe Hunter. She watched her rake her fingers through her damp hair, a nervous habit she was probably unaware of, and it wasn't difficult to see the subtle signs of strain that were evident. Hunter's body was tense, her shoulders were stiff, and there were faint lines of fatigue and shadows darkening her eyes. Was it merely unhappiness with the FBI's unexpected intrusion into her life? Or was there something else?

As if sensing her thoughts, Hunter turned away from the window and stared at Sara. Openly. Deliberately. Blatantly. Then slowly, very slowly, she smiled, and Sara felt the power of that smile ram into her.

Sex, Sara realized abruptly as her mouth went dry. Hunter Roswell exuded raw, unapologetic sex.

Seemingly unaware of the undercurrents, David cleared his throat. "I really appreciate your agreeing to see us, Hunter. I know we arrived without any notice, but if you give us the chance to explain, you'll quickly understand the urgency of our situation."

Hunter lowered her coffee mug and tilted her head. "It's not a problem. I hope you don't mind, but since one of my business partners, Matt Logan, happens to be in town, I've asked him to join us." Hunter glanced absently at her watch. "He was wrapping up a conference call, so we shouldn't have long to wait."

David stiffened slightly before murmuring his acquiescence. Sara maintained a neutral expression and remained silent, continuing to watch Hunter as she closed her eyes and sipped her coffee.

"If you don't mind my asking, where did you find Quito?" Sara asked, hoping the conversation would enable her to gain some insight into Hunter Roswell. But if she was honest, she was also responding to an intrinsic need to connect with her and chose what she thought was a safe starting point. She was ill-prepared for Hunter's response.

"The Latin Kings," Hunter said nonchalantly, naming a youth gang with a history of guns and violence.

Sara's eyes widened. "You're kidding?"

"I think it was about five years ago. I was in L.A. on business when Quito and some friends decided they wanted the car I was driving."

"And?"

"I decided I wasn't ready to give it up." Hunter shrugged, sipped her coffee, and closed her eyes again, momentarily caught up in the past. "It turned out there wasn't a lot of room for negotiating. When the dust settled, all that remained standing was me and this skinny sixteen-year-old holding a three fifty-seven that was bigger than he was. He was shaking so badly I was afraid he was going to shoot me by accident."

"What did you do?"

Hunter's eyes opened and she flashed Sara a grin. "I took him home with me."

"You *what*?"

"Well, I fed him first." She said it as if that explained everything. "It's amazing what two people can work out over burgers and fries. In fact, more people ought to try it."

"And he's been with you ever since?"

"We hammered out a deal we could both live with," Hunter replied enigmatically.

"What kind of deal?" Sara asked.

Although the soft voice was serious, Hunter thought she detected a flicker of amusement in her eyes. "He told me about his family, and one of the first things we agreed on was if his mother concurred, I would move the family to San Francisco."

"And she agreed just like that?"

Actually, when I showed up at her door with her errant son in tow, Cecilia Ramirez thought heaven had sent her an angel—a tall, dark-haired angel. "We talked, and Cecilia agreed because it got both her children away from the gang influences in their neighborhood. It didn't hurt that Quito also agreed to go back to school, and I agreed to tutor him whenever my schedule permitted. If I was unavailable, we both agreed a member of my OPS team could fill in and help him with his studies."

"That's quite the deal. You must be one hell of a negotiator."

"So they say." Hunter grinned. "It also didn't hurt that I threw in some additional incentives."

Sara's eyes narrowed slightly. "What kind of incentives?"

"For one thing, shortly after they moved, Cecilia began training at one of the de León family hotels under my mother so she no longer had to work three jobs. And when he finished high school, I arranged for an internship for Quito as my personal assistant and agreed to cover his tuition while he completes his degree in business. And when she's not in school at Stanford, his sister Annie's interning in the legal department at Roswell. She thinks she wants to be a lawyer."

Sara shook her head and looked as though she was trying very hard to stifle a laugh. "That's crazy, you know that?"

"Certifiable," Hunter said affably. "More coffee?"

The conversation was interrupted as the office door opened, and they were joined by Matt Logan. Rangy and just a little over six feet tall, he had dark eyes that missed nothing and closely cropped dark hair.

"Sorry to have kept everyone waiting," he said.

He passed Hunter, touching her lightly on the shoulder. He then shook hands with Sara and David before dropping onto the vacant couch opposite them.

Hunter remained standing. When she turned back to David and Sara, the warmth and humor that had been present a moment earlier were gone.

"Before we start, I would be remiss if I didn't ask. Do I need to have legal representation? My chief legal counsel is in California, but I'm sure one of our local lawyers will be more than happy to fill in."

"Christ no," David replied quickly and seemed surprised.

"But I take it you're here in an official capacity?"

"Well, yeah. I mean, yes, we're here as part of an official investigation. But it's not like you're a suspect."

"That's a relief." Hunter smiled humorlessly and thrust her hands into the front pockets of her jeans. "Then why don't you tell me what has brought two federal agents to my doorstep?"

As she watched, David and Sara glanced at each other. Sara shrugged in a barely perceptible move and remained silent, while David took the lead. "We're dealing with a situation back home—in San Francisco—and we're actually hoping you can help us. Maybe shed some light," he began tentatively. He inclined his head and appeared to consider his next words carefully. "Perhaps it would help if I started at the beginning."

"Why not?" Hunter said.

"Over the past five months, we've had five women murdered by what is clearly the same perpetrator. Same weapon was used in all five instances, a thirty-eight caliber. But the physical evidence is nonexistent. All the kills are clean, no DNA, no tangible leads."

"And you want me to try running the data from your murders on the new program we're beta testing?" Hunter's lips curved in a faintly perplexed smile.

David frowned and shook his head. "I wasn't aware you were testing any new software."

"We're always testing new programs, David. It's what we do," Hunter admonished gently. "If that's not the help you want, then why are you here?"

"Actually, we're here because of the victimology. When we looked at the victims, while there were no obvious links connecting them to each other, they had a number of things in common."

Hunter felt the faint stirrings of impatience as David paused once again. "I'm sure there's a good reason you're delivering this piecemeal. Are you going to make me ask?"

David straightened his shoulders. "Point taken," he acknowledged. "All the victims were single, professional women in their mid-to-late twenties, and they all fit a specific physical type. Taller than average, between five eight and five eleven, with dark hair and blue eyes."

Hunter turned and stared in silent contemplation at her reflection in the window before looking back at David. "Tell me you've got more to go on to bring you all the way to London. For God's sake, David, there've got to be literally hundreds of women other than me who live in and around the Bay Area and match that physical description." But before David could respond, she already knew she wasn't going to like the answer. She could see it in his eyes. "What is it? Why are you connecting this to me? What haven't you told me?"

"You're right, there's more. In each instance, the killer left a message at the crime scene. His earlier messages contained one brief sentence: 'You are mine.'"

Unable to prevent it, Hunter's mind flashed to New York and the carefully printed message she had found in her pocket. She closed her eyes and fought something akin to panic that welled up inside her, spreading through her chest and threatening to overwhelm her.

Sara noted the almost immediate state change David's words elicited in Hunter. There was a sharp, indrawn breath and a tightening of her shoulders as a fleeting shadow crossed her face.

"However, in the most recent crime scene, he left a considerably longer message, and for the first time, his message was addressed," David continued. "That's what brings us here today. We're here because the message was addressed to you."

"What the hell does that mean?" Temper flashed visibly in her eyes before she reined it in. "Damn it, David. What's going on?"

Sara watched Hunter turn and look at Matt, holding his eyes briefly as she searched for some kind of answer. Nothing.

Hunter's frustration came out in her tone as she turned back expectantly to face David. "I really need someone to explain."

"Hunter, the message was addressed to you by name," David said quickly and raised his hand to discourage any disagreement.

"And before you start arguing with me, there's something else you need to know. The message also said it was time for daddy's girl to come home."

David pressed on, even as Sara saw his words hit home. "I'm sorry, but unless you're prepared to show me another Hunter who was once called daddy's girl, there can be no question you are the intended recipient."

In the silence that followed David's revelation, Hunter wrapped her arms tightly around herself. The reference to daddy's girl was obviously not what she had expected, and watching the exchange, Sara knew David's words had wounded Hunter severely. She stood hollow eyed, holding her body deathly still, and for an instant, she glanced down at her chest as if possibly wondering why the damage David had inflicted wasn't bleeding visibly. At the same time, her face became frighteningly pale.

But it wasn't the lack of color that worried Sara. It was the slow deadening in the previously clear blue eyes and the first signs of mild shock as evidenced in the slight loss of focus.

Though obviously shaken, Hunter appeared to try to regain control. "Jesus, David, I can't do this. I can't go back there again. You, of all people, should know that. You were there." She paused, momentarily unable to speak, then struggled to continue. "I'm sorry. Will you excuse me for a moment." Hunter bolted for the door.

"Hunter—"

Hunter flinched and looked back at Sara, pain starkly evident in her eyes. She swallowed hard and moistened her lips. But whatever she might have said, the words simply died in her throat. She turned away, grabbed the doorknob, yanked the door open, and was gone. The door automatically closed behind her, leaving the room far emptier without her vibrant presence.

Matt jumped up, reached for the telephone on the desk, and quickly punched in a number. "Peter? Hunter just left her office. She's...Don't let her leave the building...Yeah, that's right...Just find her, damn it. Make sure she's okay. And as soon as you find her, let me know where the hell she is."

Chapter Five

Leaving her office, Hunter moved quickly down the hallway and ducked into a small bathroom. It wasn't until she was behind the closed door that she allowed herself to feel anything. Fighting waves of nausea, she splashed some cold water on her face and then dried off with a towel, before facing her reflection in the mirror. It was a reflection she barely recognized these days. Her eyes were bloodshot and burning with fatigue, her face unnaturally pale and drawn.

Trying to keep herself from groaning, she sank to the floor, dropping her head between her knees as she took a number of long, deep breaths and let them out slowly. After a few breaths, the tightness in her chest began to ease, leaving her physically and emotionally drained. But she couldn't shake the sense her carefully structured world was imploding and tumbling into chaos.

She knew she didn't have a lot of time before someone—most likely Peter—found her. On cue, she heard a soft knock on the door, followed by the muffled sound of someone calling her name as the doorknob turned.

As the door opened, she glanced up and was surprised to see Sara leaning against the frame, a bottle of water and something that promised pain relief in her hands. She noted the concerned expression on her face and, after a brief hesitation, managed to give her a weak smile.

Sara silently regarded Hunter's tense form before entering and dropping to the floor beside her. She opened the ibuprofen container, then handed her the water bottle and two tablets. With a short nod of thanks, Hunter downed the tablets and followed them with a few swallows of water.

"I hope you don't mind. Someone named Peter let Matt know where you were, and I figured you'd be about ready to deal with that headache I could see brewing a little earlier," Sara said. "I also wanted the chance to talk to you. Are you okay?"

"I'll survive," Hunter replied. She deliberately kept her voice light but knew her face would tell a different story. "Of course, I'd probably do even better if I thought there was a chance I could sneak out of here without anyone seeing me."

"Sorry." Sara shook her head ruefully. "Matt and David are still waiting for you in your office. And then, of course, there's me."

"Right." Her voice was both weary and resigned.

For a few minutes, neither one spoke. Finally, Hunter turned her head toward Sara and looked at her. "Maybe you can help me with something."

The temperature had dropped, but Sara didn't flinch. At least not visibly. "I'll certainly give it a try."

"Given the fact that he and I share some history, I can come up with a pretty good explanation as to why Special Agent Granger is here. But I can't seem to make you fit into the equation. So, if you wouldn't mind telling me, why exactly are you here?"

"Ah. Well—" Sara paused uncertainly, as she contemplated how best to deliver an appropriate response to Hunter's question.

"I'm sorry. I'm tired and I'm being rude." Hunter lifted a hand to rub at her temple.

"No, it's all right. It's just that David and I also share some history. I suppose I should start by telling you I'm a psychologist currently consulting with the FBI on the serial murders David mentioned to you." Sara felt an almost imperceptible change in Hunter's body language. Uncertain of its cause, she took a careful breath before continuing. "Before that, until about eight months ago, I worked with the FBI in the Behavioral Analysis Unit. David was my partner."

"What happened eight months ago?"

"I resigned."

"Why?"

Sara shrugged. "I don't know how much news you follow—"

"Try me."

"Okay. For a period of almost a year, up until eight months ago, I was part of a joint NYPD and FBI task force working on a case involving a serial rapist-murderer."

"You were part of the Pelham investigation?"

Sara's eyes narrowed as she nodded. "Right the first time."

Hunter tilted her head and assessed Sara. "I ran the data on Marshall after he was arrested. According to the offender-profiling software we were testing, in spite of the circumstantial evidence piling up against him, there was less than a forty percent probability he committed those murders. He didn't have the intellectual capacity—"

"I know. I tried to convince them they'd arrested the wrong man," Sara said softly. "But no one up the chain of command was interested in hearing it. By the time I got someone to listen to me, Marshall was already in the hospital, and Pelham had increased the victim count."

"I'm sorry. That had to be hard." Hunter grimaced. "Do you blame yourself for what happened to Marshall?"

Sara shook her head. "No. It's not that I blame myself for what happened. But the bottom line is I do share in the responsibility."

"Is that why you quit?"

She released a breath, then shrugged. "I resigned two days after Pelham was arrested."

"And started consulting?"

"Initially, I did some consulting work with Seattle PD. More recently, I've been staying in San Francisco with my old college roommate and doing some guest lectures at Berkeley. I just completed a twelve-week series in criminal and abnormal psych."

Hunter moved her shoulders restlessly. "How was that?"

"Different." Sara gave a slight grin. "But I liked it enough that I'm weighing an offer from Stanford and considering relocating permanently to the West Coast. I went to school there and still have family in the area. And in the meantime, I'm helping David out with this case."

"Interesting." The word was said in a carelessly polite tone that seemed to indicate the end of their conversation.

"Listen," Sara said. "It's all right to ask for help, and for what it's worth, I'd really like to help you. Just let me do my job."

"Right. You're a psychologist." Hunter dragged a hand through her hair and sighed. "The only problem could be I have this thing about shrinks. Psychiatrists, psychologists. It really makes no difference. Nothing personal, you understand. Just a case of some bad history, which makes it impossible—"

"I can appreciate that, but it only makes it difficult, not impossible." Sara could feel the increase in Hunter's tension. Deciding she had gotten as far as she was going to for the time being, Sara pushed herself to her feet. "Will you at least think about it?"

Hunter sighed again, let her head fall back, and closed her eyes. "I'll think about it," she agreed softly and kept her eyes closed as Sara left.

❖

Almost twenty minutes after Sara had left her, Hunter re-entered her office, straightening her shoulders as she stepped back into the room. She remained by the door with her arms crossed loosely across her chest, glancing from Matt to David and finally to Sara. She could discern nothing but concern from the benign expressions on their faces.

"My apologies," she said quietly. She was still feeling off balance, and in spite of her best intentions, her voice still held an edge, and a frown creased her forehead. She narrowed her eyes and tried to ignore both the throbbing at her temples and the emotions that were vibrating through her. But she could see no escape and braced herself for a fight.

"You okay?" Matt asked. He should have known better, and the look she gave him was cold as winter.

"I'm fine," she said. "Let's put everything on the table. David, if I understand correctly, you have five murder victims you believe were killed for no reason other than they happened to bear some resemblance to me. You also have a killer leaving notes at the crime scenes that would seem to connect him to a time in my life I would just as soon forget. You've come a long way to talk to me, so you must have something in mind. Where do you see us going from here?"

David cleared his throat. "I believe we need to take a fresh look at what happened ten years ago. The fact that the killer knows enough to call you daddy's girl tells us his connection with you most likely originates there. We just need to find it."

"How do you propose to do that?"

"Well, the first thing we should do is review the original case files with you. See if that triggers anything—"

"You mean other than nightmares?" Hunter let out an explosive breath of frustration. "Thanks, but I already have those."

David took a reflexive step back.

"We believe the killer started as a stalker. Specifically an erotomanic," Sara interjected softly, drawing Hunter's attention away from David. "That's a stalker with a delusional belief that the object of his or her attention reciprocates the affection. Or will, given time and opportunity, come to share a desire for intimacy. Erotomanic stalkers may know they are not actually having a relationship with their victims, but firmly believe they will someday."

"And that means—"

"It means he believes he is destined to be with you, and if he only pursues you hard enough and long enough, you will come to love him as he loves you."

Hunter's eyes narrowed warily. "Go on."

"But there are associated behaviors and psychopathologies in the evolution of these types of stalkers, and the fact that he's trying to contact you through the message he left at the last crime scene is not good."

"Why?"

"It's indicative of a stalker who feels as if he's been, in some way, betrayed by the object of his affections. Betrayed by you, in other words," Sara explained.

"Considering his message says he wants you to come home," David added, "it's likely the trigger to his killing spree was your extended stay in the UK."

Sara noted another brief state change in Hunter before her expression resumed its carefully guarded state. *Definitely something there*, she thought, but this was not the time to pursue it. Instead, she picked up where David left off.

"When that happens, when an erotomanic stalker feels betrayed, it often leads to violence against the target," Sara said. "But the stalker in this case, at least for the time being, has been either venting his anger or practicing on surrogates—women who bear a close resemblance to you, at least physically. And possibly more deeply, if you consider the women he chose lived alone and all were successful professionals."

Hunter closed her eyes and raked her fingers through her hair. "You're really saying those women died because they reminded someone of me, aren't you?" she said, her voice filled with fatigue and resignation.

"Hunter," Matt interjected. "This is not your fault."

"I'm not trying to take blame here. I'm merely clarifying the facts," Hunter responded quietly. "You said earlier there were no obvious links between the victims, but that's not quite correct, is it? I'm the link. They all died because they looked like me. At the very least in the eyes of someone connected to me. And from what you're telling me, it's likely more women will die unless whoever is doing this is stopped."

"Yes," David said. "That's why we're here, which I believe was your original question."

"And the answer would be?"

"We'd like you to work with Sara. She's a psychologist. Works with our Behavioral Analysis Unit."

"Used to work with the BAU," Hunter corrected. She crossed her arms, temper smoldering visibly in her eyes. "Not being straight with me is not going to earn you any points, David."

"Look, it's clear whoever is doing this—stalking you and killing these women—is connected to what happened to you ten years ago. The reference to daddy's girl makes that abundantly clear. That connection belongs to a specific time period, and the number of people who would know to use it in reference to you has got to be pretty select."

"And?"

"Do you think it's just a coincidence we're coming up on the tenth anniversary of everything that happened?" David asked. "Our challenge is that beyond the official storyline, we actually have very little concrete knowledge regarding what happened back then. Your father's family—Patrick Roswell specifically—managed to keep a lot of the details under wraps. Especially where you were concerned."

Hunter's brow furrowed. "What does that have to do with anything?"

"If we're going to identify and stop this guy, we need to consider everything. The FBI and SFPD already have a task force working on this case. They're currently interviewing and re-interviewing family, friends, coworkers, and neighbors of the victims. The UNSUB spent time following them. Watching them. Someone has to have seen something. In the meantime, we need to look at anyone who was around you or connected to you in any way ten years ago. Because that's where we're going to find our killer."

"What are you suggesting?" Hunter asked in a cool, even tone.

"I'm suggesting as both a psychologist and someone with extensive experience with the BAU, Sara can help you revisit what happened and help you...help *us* identify whoever's doing this before he kills again," he said. "At the same time, we'll be able to provide you with round-the-clock protection."

"Meaning what?"

"Meaning Sara stays with you at all times, and we'll assign a team to provide you with twenty-four seven surveillance and protection."

Hunter stared at David for an interminable moment. Her eyes never wavered from his, her expression intent. "For how long?"

"For as long as we need to."

In the ensuing silence, Sara wondered if in that moment, Hunter had seen David not as he now appeared, but as he had been ten years earlier. Part of some nameless, faceless security detail assigned to protect daddy's girl. Eager to prove himself, but ultimately failing. And she couldn't help but wonder if both David and Hunter were looking for the same thing.

The possibility of absolution. Redemption.

"Sorry, but I've no real interest in opening up and spilling the details of my life story to anyone. No offense intended, Dr. Wilder. I'm sure you're very good at what you do. But if that's what you're all waiting for, you know where the door is," she said flatly, closing down the lines of communication. "I've even less interest in having the FBI assign a security detail to protect me. As I recall, the last time the bureau tried to blanket me with protection, it didn't turn out too well for anyone. So thanks, but I think I'll pass."

"Hunter, you can't—" David took a step forward and reached for Hunter's arm.

Without warning, Hunter stopped David mid-reach, holding his arm with what appeared to be a surprisingly strong grip. "I'm sorry. Did you think that was a suggestion on my part?" The words were said softly with anger just behind them. "Be careful, David. You're on my territory right now, and 'you can't' are words I don't tolerate very well."

She continued to stare at David, trapping him with her eyes. "I know I've always had a reputation for having a temper. But it's only fair that I warn you…I'm not the kid I was ten years ago. I tolerate a lot less bullshit now than I did when you first met me."

Sara could feel the heat of Hunter's temper and decided she preferred it to her icy control. She watched her for a moment longer and waited to see if Matt would say something. But when he failed to react, she decided to take pity on David and intervened. "Hunter, since you obviously have no desire to follow David's suggestion, why don't you tell us what you think might work for you?"

Hunter drew a deep breath, then another, as she obviously tried to pull some of her self-control back around her. Her hands twisted together before she clenched her fists and held them still. She took one more breath, and in the ensuing silence, it was clear she had come to some decisions.

"All right," she said, sounding calm, almost bored. "It would seem to me the logical next step will be to convince me to go home to draw out this stalker."

As David nodded, Sara narrowed her eyes and tried to anticipate where Hunter was leading them. In spite of her spiking anger, her voice was remarkably cool. Hunter fascinated her, and Sara studied her face more closely, watched the emotions play over it. And because she could also see the fatigue and the ghosts and the grief, she realized Hunter was walking a fine line.

"Let me save you the time and trouble. There's a fundraiser this evening for the children's hospital I've committed to attending. Once the dinner's over, I plan on taking one of the corporate jets back to San Francisco."

Hunter paused and turned to look directly at Sara. "You and David are both welcome to fly back with me. Unless, of course, you have a particular affection for sitting elbow-to-elbow while someone kicks the back of your seat." She flashed a hint of a grin. "If that's the case, you're more than welcome to fly commercial."

"I'm going to need some time to set up protection—" David began.

Hunter froze him with a look. "I'm going back on my terms, David. That means no FBI security detail. No surveillance. Nothing." She paused and shifted her gaze until it met Sara's once again. "When I get home, I will give serious consideration to how the doctor and I might work together. In the meantime, if I detect a hint of FBI surveillance anywhere near me, any cooperation on my part will vanish. Am I making myself understood?"

David glanced at Sara and then gave a slight nod.

Sara looked on with rising concern and disbelief. Hunter, in her present frame of mind, without adequate protection and in close proximity to her stalker, was a disaster waiting to happen. She found herself wishing she'd had the time before coming to London to learn more about what had happened ten years earlier and resolved to correct that oversight at the earliest possible moment. Preferably directly from Hunter. In the meantime, she took comfort in knowing she would be working with Hunter and could provide some level of protection.

Clearly satisfied she had made the right decision, Hunter turned to leave when David called out to her. "Hunter, wait."

She stopped with her hand on the door, glanced back at him, and waited.

"About that new program you said you're beta testing," he said. "I know you've no reason to want to do me any favors right now, but is there any chance you could run some of our current data and maybe some stuff from ten years ago and see if anything interesting pops up?"

"Already started the process of downloading what I'll need to run it." Hunter sounded no more than casually interested. "I haven't looked at it in great detail, but I can tell you the data from your San Francisco murders comes up a little light. But if you can add anything of value—like the missing ME reports—e-mail them to me. In the meantime, I'll run what's available and let you know if I come up with anything."

Allowing no opportunity for further discussion, Hunter turned and walked out of the office, leaving Sara with an aching head as she tried to make sense of what had just transpired. "What did she mean? How can she already be preparing to run the data?"

Matt grinned broadly. "I would say she accessed the FBI files."

"Accessed?" Sara's eyes widened slightly and her eyebrows rose in disbelief. "Are you telling me she hacked the FBI?"

"No one would ever suggest such a thing," Matt said mildly. "That would be illegal. To say nothing of the fact that the FBI files would at best get her the current data. To access the old stuff from ten years ago, she'd probably have to tap into the Justice Department archives as well."

As Sara shook her head, Matt paused and flashed another grin. "Yeah, that sounds about right," he said. "That's my girl."

CHAPTER SIX

The converted Boeing 767 belonging to the Roswell Group departed London shortly before ten p.m. local time and began making its way back to the US. Once the jet achieved cruising altitude, Sara finally began to relax and found herself taking an interest in her surroundings.

The aircraft's luxurious interior had clearly been designed to maximize comfort, and she glanced appreciatively at the natural and tranquil tones that had been incorporated in the decor. The leather seats were butter soft, the lighting recessed, and there were crystal vases with fresh-cut flowers. It was, she acknowledged, a far cry from the overcrowded flight that had brought her to London. *Was that only yesterday?*

Her thoughts were temporarily disrupted as the pilot's voice— soft, feminine, and distinctly British—came over the speakers and advised the passengers they were now free to move about. Seated to her left, Matt and Quito immediately unbuckled their seatbelts and excused themselves from the main lounge. Matt disappeared into what looked like a well-appointed office, while Quito laid claim to a leather sofa and plugged his headphones into the onboard sound system.

A moment later, a leanly muscled man approached and crouched down beside her seat. Peter McNeil quickly introduced himself to Sara as Hunter's chief of security. In his late thirties with short blond hair and blue eyes, he had a slow, sharp smile.

"I thought I should introduce myself, since I believe we'll be crossing paths frequently once we get home," he said. "In the meantime, the princess doesn't stand much on ceremony, so make yourself comfortable, and help yourself if there's anything you want."

Sara nodded, her smile never faltering. "Okay."

After sending a curt nod in David's direction, Peter stood and followed four people Sara understood to be the members of Hunter's operations team as they raided a well-stocked galley. In a matter of minutes, they returned with platters heaped with sandwiches and a bucket of beer, before setting up a poker game at a nearby table.

"Well, I don't know about you," David said, "but I understand there's actually a small theater on board with a good collection of first-run movies. Interested?"

Sara shook her head. "I'll pass," she said and watched David amble away.

Trying to ease the low-grade headache that seemed to have lain siege permanently in her head, she rubbed her temples, then picked up a magazine. But she was unable to concentrate as her mind replayed the latter part of the day.

She and David had run into Hunter outside the Roswell building while trying to decide where to grab a quick bite to eat. The rain had stopped, and as they discussed possible options, Hunter materialized on the steps beside them. She looked positively stunning in a black silk dress with a tantalizingly deep neckline and a slit up the side that showed off a long smooth thigh. She had left her hair falling loosely over her shoulders, and diamonds glinted brilliantly in her ears.

Feeling vaguely nonplussed, Sara took in the elegant hollows and angles of her face, the finely delineated arms and shoulders, the long and slender body. She sucked in an involuntary breath as she caught herself staring and tried to focus on what Hunter was saying.

"There's a small pub a couple of blocks up," Hunter offered. "It has an excellent kitchen and a good atmosphere. Tell Shelby I sent you, and she'll take care of you."

As she spoke, a limousine pulled up to the curb. Sara watched the driver open the door, allowing a distinguished silver-haired man in a tuxedo to exit the vehicle. He smiled and climbed the steps toward them.

"Hunter," he said, gently taking Hunter's hand and bringing it briefly to his lips. "You look positively exquisite, my dear. You'll do wonders for both my reputation and my ego this evening."

"I see you're on your best behavior, old man," Hunter teased. She softly brushed her lips against his cheek before turning to facilitate introductions. "Sir Nigel Wainwright...Special Agent David Granger and Dr. Sara Wilder."

"Of course, the two American FBI agents," he said.

Sara felt his eyes shrewdly assessing both her and David as they shook hands. He appeared to dismiss David almost immediately before turning his attention to Sara. "May I ask who I'm holding responsible for keeping this wild child out of trouble once she's stateside? Would that be you, Dr. Wilder?"

Sara looked into Nigel's eyes and noted both humor and affection evident there. She was also keenly aware Hunter was watching their exchange with great interest.

"To be honest, I'm not sure how to answer you," she said. "As a consultant on this case, I imagine I will be working quite closely with Hunter, but I'd wager no one keeps her out of trouble unless it's what she chooses."

Nigel laughed with delight as he turned to Hunter. "You're in trouble, my dear, if after such a short time Dr. Wilder has figured you out."

Hunter arched an eyebrow.

"I certainly wouldn't say I've figured her out," Sara interjected quickly before Hunter could speak. "But I'm certainly up for a challenge," she added with a grin.

"Of that I have no doubt," Nigel responded. He watched Hunter trying not to laugh at their conversation before she turned and walked away to speak with David. Sara watched his expression soften and gentle. He remained silent until Hunter was far enough away to ensure she was unable to hear their conversation.

"I look at her like this and wonder why there's someone out there who wants nothing more than to hurt her. But I know he exists, and unless you can stop him, I'm afraid he may succeed in killing her."

"All I can tell you is I'm going to do everything in my power to see that doesn't happen," Sara responded.

Nigel nodded. He watched Hunter a moment longer before turning to look at Sara, his expression resolute. "Hunter won't make things easy for you."

"Why is that?"

"Her intellect is both her greatest strength and weakness. It allows her to make great leaps in logic the majority of people cannot follow. But she also uses it to substantiate her disregard for most authority, which leads her to take risks others might consider unacceptable."

Sara considered the implications of his words. "I take it she's spoken to you about what she's facing in San Francisco?"

"Michael Roswell was a good friend, as is Marlena, Hunter's mother." It might have been ten years since Michael Roswell's death, but Sara could still hear the sorrow in Nigel's voice. "I would never presume to fill Michael's role in Hunter's life. But she's been like a daughter to me for many years and often comes to me when something's troubling her."

"As she did six months ago?" Sara probed.

Nigel looked at her as if reassessing his opinion and smiled. "As she did six months ago."

"Do you know—?"

"No." Nigel shook his head. "I only know something happened in New York, but I don't know the specifics of what drove her here. I merely provided the shelter she needed. A place where she could heal physically and emotionally."

"Why did she need to heal?" The question came out more sharply than Sara intended, but Nigel seemed not to notice.

"When she first arrived, her face was bruised, and there were bandages around her hands and wrists. She also moved stiffly as if she was in pain. But she never mentioned what had happened, and I didn't press her."

Nigel lifted a brow and continued to watch Hunter. "All I can tell you is I saw something in her eyes I'd never seen before. It looked like fear. But I have no idea what put it there, and she has never talked about it. Consequently I don't know how to help her."

Sara thought about what Nigel was saying and tried to put his words into context with who Hunter Roswell appeared to be—a woman who wanted no one's protection and clearly intended to look after herself.

As if reading her thoughts, Nigel turned to her. "Don't let her fool you. Hunter is more vulnerable than most people realize and certainly more than she will ever admit, even to herself. That said, her happiness and well-being are of the utmost importance to me. I cannot stress that enough."

He paused, lowered his voice, and handed her a card with all of his contact information on it. "We almost lost Hunter ten years ago, and no one is prepared to face that risk again, especially not like this. If you need anything—anything whatsoever to ensure she is kept physically and emotionally protected—I expect you to contact me. I will put whatever resources I have at your disposal. Whatever it takes to keep her safe. Do you understand?"

Sara nodded, and a silent understanding passed between them. A moment later, they both smiled as Hunter approached and wrapped long, slender fingers lightly around Nigel's arm.

"I'm sorry to interrupt, Nigel, but if we're going to make the fundraiser and still leave enough time for me to fly out this evening, we really should be going."

"Of course, my dear," Nigel said before turning back briefly to look at Sara. "A pleasure, Dr. Wilder. I'm quite certain we will see each other again before too long."

Sara watched them make their way to the waiting limousine and drive away before rejoining David.

When she next saw them, Hunter and Nigel were standing beside the limo, parked on the tarmac in the shadow of the Roswell jet. They were engaged in what looked to be a very intense conversation. A conversation which continued long after the jet was loaded and everyone else was on board.

From her vantage point near the door, Sara observed the discussion continue until finally, in what could only be interpreted as capitulation, Hunter threw her arms up and nodded. Obviously pleased with the outcome, Nigel enveloped her in his arms. A moment later, he watched her turn and board the jet. She proceeded directly into the cockpit, where she remained until the jet achieved cruising altitude. Shortly thereafter, she walked through the cabin and headed to an enclosed area near the rear of the jet.

❖

As the jet drew inexorably closer to San Francisco, Hunter began to pound on a heavy punching bag set up in a small gym near the rear of the aircraft. She attacked it relentlessly as if her life depended on it. Left, right, left, right. Again and again in time with the driving beat of the music she had selected, expelling her breath each time she connected with the heavy bag.

Even as a child, she had always been filled with a kind of restless energy, physically and mentally. No matter how hard she tried, she could never slow her mind down enough to relax, and her body slowed down only when there was no other choice.

Tonight she desperately wanted sleep…sleep without dreams, without guilt, without fear. But she knew just as a killer waited for her at home, nightmares were lurking in the shadows waiting to begin. Recurring dreams populated with ghosts conjured from the past. If she couldn't sleep, at the very least annihilating the heavy bag would stop her from thinking. And not thinking ranked very high on her priority list.

Still, she couldn't help but imagine Sara, as an FBI psychologist, would probably have a field day interpreting her dreams.

Dropping her hands, Hunter rotated her shoulders and tried to loosen up. Then with lightening speed, she resumed her assault on the bag, her hands moving in a series of explosive jabs as she circled left to right and worked the bag up and down.

Damn Matt. Damn David. Damn the FBI. Damn them all.

As the flurry of punches continued, her movements picked up speed, and she pushed herself harder until all that powered her was adrenaline. Her breathing became ragged, and pain and strain reminded her of physical limitations. But she continued to push herself beyond them, pushing as her mind emptied, pushing until she could no longer lift her arms. Until all she could do was drop to her knees in exhaustion, stretching a hand out to catch herself as she hit the floor. Surprised to feel a sob constrict her throat, she closed her eyes.

She wasn't certain how long she remained like that, but when she opened her eyes again, she knew immediately she was no longer alone. Looking up, she saw Sara Wilder standing in the doorway.

Hunter closed her eyes and then slowly blinked to make sure she hadn't conjured her out of her overtired imagination. But when she opened her eyes, Sara was still standing there, holding the towel Hunter had dropped on the floor in one hand, a bottle of water in the other.

She looked serious and supremely self-assured in her impeccably tailored blue suit. But then she smiled, for just an instant, and Hunter's eyes were drawn to her mouth. Sara's lips were soft and full. And as Hunter stared a moment longer, she found herself lost for several heartbeats in an arresting face framed by pale blond hair and a pair of misty green eyes that seemed filled with quiet understanding.

Realizing she was staring, Hunter eased back and met Sara's gaze. "Hey, doc. Wanna spar?" she asked, while trying to catch her breath.

Sara glanced down, pale eyebrows rising slightly, her lips curved into an amused, self-deprecating smile. "So you can kick my ass? Go figure, but I don't think I'm ready for that right now. But thanks for the offer."

Sara looked at Hunter a little longer, watching as emotions she couldn't name danced across shadowed blue eyes. Hunter let out a shuddering breath and flashed an apologetic smile, but she didn't say anything else. Her face was flushed, her chest heaving, her breathing fast and audible. All bearing testament to the display of lethal grace and power Sara had just witnessed. But also making her look wild and untamable.

Sweet Jesus. She could be the poster child for transgression.

The thought worried Sara. Under the present circumstances, it was totally inappropriate, even if it was also undeniably true. Pushing it aside, she tossed Hunter the towel she had been holding and dropped to the floor beside her. After helping her remove the hand wraps, she offered the water bottle.

"You okay?"

Hunter nodded as she brought the bottle to her lips and drank deeply. It was obvious the adrenaline rush had dissipated, but she didn't appear any more relaxed. She gave a rueful laugh and tried to flex her left hand, her knuckles already swollen and bruised. She immediately hissed and cradled her throbbing hand.

"You're going to want to put some ice on that," Sara said mildly before asking, "Do you want to talk about it?"

Hunter took a moment before responding and then lowered her voice to a conspiratorial whisper. "You should probably know I've been giving serious thought to turning the plane around and heading back to London." She bit her lower lip as her eyes met Sara's, and Sara thought she detected a flicker of humor once again. "Of course, I can always be persuaded to head for Paris, if you would prefer a different destination."

"Since I've never been to Paris, I can't really offer an opinion. I guess that means I'll leave the decision up to you," Sara conceded, smiling. "Are you having second thoughts?"

Her question elicited a shake of Hunter's head and a weak smile. "Having second thoughts about going home would imply I had first thoughts, wouldn't it?"

Sara laughed. "That's true."

They sat without speaking for a couple of minutes as Hunter's labored breathing returned to normal. After another minute passed, she tilted her head back, and when at last she spoke, her voice sounded tired and uncertain. "The problem is I don't want to do this."

"What don't you want to do?"

"I don't want to sift through the rubble and ashes of the past." Hunter stopped as if trying to collect her rambling thoughts. "Don't get me wrong, I know I don't have a lot of choice. I know my past is where we're going to find this killer you're looking for. It's just that there are other things buried back there, and I'm pretty sure I'm not ready to deal with any of it."

"It might help if you remember a couple of things," Sara said gently. "The first is you won't be alone. The second is I can help you not only to identify a killer but to deal with those other things as well…if you'll let me."

She sensed the moment Hunter began to withdraw and gave her arm an urgent squeeze. "Hunter, I really want to help you. Please don't look at me as the enemy…"

She let her words trail into silence, uncertain how to continue. Hunter met her eyes for an instant, and Sara felt a stab of disappointment when Hunter closed her eyes and turned her head away. But not before she saw the grief and pain swimming in their depths.

So she sat back and waited.

Almost a full minute passed before Hunter opened her eyes again. Raking a hand through her hair, she drew in a deep breath and then released it on a sigh. "Can you teach me to live with the past? With what happened to me?"

Sara's pulse jumped. She knew only the bare bones of what had happened to Hunter ten years earlier. But there was no questioning the profound effects that still lingered.

"I can try." Her gaze trailed across Hunter's face, and her voice dropped to a whisper. "You'd be surprised how much it can help just to talk about things, and most people will tell you I'm a really good listener."

Hunter stared into Sara's face. Her eyes were soft and clear, and her voice was full of compassion waiting to be shared. But the question remained. Ten years spent burying her feelings had left her ill-prepared for the level of introspection required of her. It wasn't like she could change the past, she mused. The question was whether she could open herself up. Did she even know how?

"Right now, all I really want to do is stop thinking," she said. Making the admission was as difficult as trying to stop thinking, and she forced herself to release a cleansing breath.

Sara's expression softened. "It doesn't really work. But you already know that, don't you?"

Hunter stared at Sara intently, trying to read the expression on her face.

Was Sara trying to let her know she too was familiar with those dark and desolate moments? Had she experienced moments when she wanted nothing more than to close off her mind? When she didn't want to think about the past or the future? When the moment was complicated enough and more than she could handle?

For some reason, she didn't want to think of Sara hurting to that extent and kept her voice mild to counteract the sudden surge of confusing and conflicting emotions. "It's a bad habit of mine… wishing for the impossible."

"Which is why the better option would be for you to talk to me," Sara continued, "and let me help you."

Hunter acknowledged the wisdom in Sara's words. But as she pushed her damp hair back behind one ear, she felt a flash of wary uncertainty. "The problem is…Look, it's not you. It's just that I don't have a great track record doing this."

"Doing what?"

"Talking about what I'm thinking or feeling."

"Try," Sara encouraged gently. *Talk to me. Please let me help.*

The music suddenly stopped, and as a pervasive silence enveloped them, Sara let her head roll back and come to rest against the wall. When the silence lengthened, she tilted her head to one side and regarded Hunter. What was it she had said? Something about having a *thing* about shrinks. *Nothing personal, you understand. Just a case of bad history.*

"Maybe that's where we need to start," she said out loud.

"Where's that?"

"When we were back at your London office. You said you have a problem with my profession."

Hunter arched one dark brow. "That's true, but…just so you understand, I have nothing against you personally—"

"Does it matter?" Sara asked bluntly. She could see Hunter starting to close herself off. "What's important here is you need to move beyond those issues, whatever they may be, if I'm going to help you." She stopped short as she heard the edge creep into her voice. *Not the recommended approach.*

She leaned closer and consciously softened her voice. "What I'm trying to say is I want to help you—and I believe I can help you—but we don't have the luxury of time. We need to identify whoever is stalking you, and we need to do it quickly before he strikes again."

Hunter nodded.

"So I guess I need to know what I can do to make this easier for you. To make you feel more comfortable talking to me, working with me. I can't change my profession. Tell me what I can do. Is there something I can tell you about myself that you don't already know?"

Hunter took another long swallow from the water bottle and then leaned forward, dangling the bottle from her fingertips between her knees. "What do you mean?"

"I mean what could you possibly need or want to know? From what I've been told about the Roswell Group, I can only surmise your chief of security will already have developed an in-depth file on me. I can't begin to imagine what he won't have covered. So what can I possibly add?"

"To Peter's file?" In response to Sara's nod, Hunter frowned. "I wouldn't know. I haven't read it."

"Why not?"

"Saw no reason to," Hunter replied mildly. "The truth is unless I'm negotiating a business deal, I've always preferred getting to know people on my own terms, over time. Face-to-face rather than by reading one of Peter's files."

Sara considered Hunter's response. "I guess that's something we have in common."

"Does that mean you haven't read the file David has on me?" A second passed, then another, while Hunter waited for an answer. When Sara shook her head, Hunter expelled what was possibly a sigh of relief.

It seemed some levels of trust were more easily achieved than others, Sara realized, and as she looked at the fatigue etched on Hunter's face, she came to a decision. One that would not make David very happy.

"I know there's a lot of pressure to resolve what's going on," she began. "But we don't need to do everything right now. Why don't you try to get some rest. Once we get back home, as soon as you're ready to talk, I'll be there to listen, and we'll figure this all out. It's all going to be all right."

Hunter didn't respond immediately. When she did, her voice was filled with emotion, her angular face pale and intense. "Thanks."

For the longest time after her simple reply, Hunter remained silent. After several minutes of silence elapsed, Sara was on the verge of accepting Hunter wasn't going to talk further when she heard her sigh.

"My father died when I was seventeen." Hunter paused, needing to push past the tightness in her throat but obviously wanting to choose her words carefully. "When he died, my mother was devastated. She fell apart, unable to handle her own grief, let alone mine. My father's family, my grandfather Patrick specifically, stepped in and took over. I know he was only trying to help…"

Sara watched Hunter struggle to give voice to her pain. Unable to help without running the risk of shutting her down completely, she sat back and waited for Hunter to continue. A minute later, her patience was rewarded.

"My grandfather Patrick…the senior senator from California… is nothing if not determined. During that first week I was hospitalized, he arranged for virtually every specialist in the country to come see me and assess what was going on inside my head." The words were softly spoken but revealed a multitude of emotions, not the least of which was residual anger. "It seemed like an endless parade of psychiatrists and psychologists, all dropping by my room. Each of them wanted to be the hero. Each of them wanted to be the one to fix me. I can't remember how many actually came to see me."

Sara's eyes reflected empathetic understanding, her voice gentle. "But you did eventually find someone to talk to, didn't you?"

"That's true. Ironically, she was actually on staff at the hospital but hadn't been asked for a consult. Too young, too inexperienced to satisfy Grandfather Patrick, I guess. But she quickly became my safe haven and over time we became, and are still, good friends."

Hunter smiled as she focused on the one good memory, remembering her first encounter with Lindsay. "We met by accident. All I really wanted was to breathe fresh air and be alone for a little while. That's when I discovered the roof garden." She gave a rueful laugh. "I began by pretending to swallow the pills intended to help me sleep, and then I'd pretend to be asleep when the night nurse came to check on me. One night in particular—"

She paused at the memory of falling asleep on the roof staring up at an endless sky. "I woke up mid-nightmare, screaming, while this woman I'd never met held on to me," Hunter said starkly. "She eventually told me her name was Lindsay Carson, and she promised to stay with me for as long as I needed her. I didn't want to let go. Eventually, I calmed down enough that she was able to get me back to my room, and she kept her promise. She stayed with me until daybreak, and then she came back when I asked her to, regardless of Grandfather Patrick's objections."

As the memory receded, Hunter turned toward Sara. "You must be really good to get me to say any of that out loud." She offered Sara a smile that died before it reached her eyes. "In fact, you've gotten me to tell you more than I told most of my other psychiatrists combined. You should be quite pleased with yourself, Dr. Wilder."

In spite of the attempt at humor, Sara heard the stormy emotion in Hunter's voice, saw the muscles along her jaw tighten. *All without the benefit of actually addressing her demons. Just circling around them.* She weighed the need to push Hunter for more against an inexplicable urge to provide succor. A minute passed, then two, while she found herself waiting once again.

"I adored my father," Hunter said at last, when Sara remained silent. "I'm not sure if you're aware of the circumstances—that I was there with him when he died." She stopped for an instant and shook her head. "No, that's not quite accurate. He was carrying me to safety when the shooting started. Which is ironic, don't you think, because the bullet that killed him went through him and ended up lodged in me."

Her hand moved unconsciously, and her fingers searched out the spot. She appeared almost surprised not to find it bleeding. "Sometimes I can still hear the killshot."

Unable to stop herself, Sara reached out and curled her fingers around Hunter's wrist. "Hunter—" she said, only to have Hunter shake her off.

"No, please let me finish this," she persisted, her voice flat and remote, struggling even as the words sat perched on her tongue begging to be released. Her eyes grew unfocused and her face paled as the memories rushed to the surface, and the edges between the past and present blurred. Unconsciously, she hugged herself as she attempted to control the grief that threatened to overwhelm her. She looked at Sara, looked through her, seeing only the past.

"Everything happened so damn quickly. One minute he was there, carrying me. Telling me to hold on. Promising everything would be all right. The next minute, he was hit, and we were both falling to the ground. I watched him die, and there wasn't a damn thing I could do except tell him I loved him and try to hold him while we both bled."

Hunter stopped, caught in the nexus between the past and the present. She stared down at her own hands not really seeing anything, then refocused on Sara and pushed on.

"In case you're wondering…the reason I'm telling you this is if you need to know who I am…if you need to understand who I am in order to catch the bastard that killed those women in San Francisco just because they looked like me, then you need to know that was my single most defining moment."

Hunter's words hung suspended in the air between them for seconds that felt like forever. Sara felt the silence lengthen as she tried to formulate a response.

"I won't trivialize it by telling you I know how you feel, because I don't," she finally said. "I've never lost someone I love, and I can't imagine losing anyone I care about like that. I do, however, understand this is difficult for you, and the last thing I want to do is to cause you any more pain."

Hunter's brow rose. "I can sense a *but* coming."

"You'd be right," Sara said. "That's because no matter how difficult—how painful—I know this process is going to be for you, we don't have a choice. We know the five murder victims were chosen because they reminded the killer of you, and the killer's reference to daddy's girl tells us his connection to you dates back to the time when your father died. We'll have to examine that period in your life, look at everyone who was with you, around you, even peripherally—even knowing it will be painful for you—because that was when he chose you."

"That makes sense." Hunter's voice was remarkably calm. She leaned her head back against the wall, closed her eyes, as if resigning herself to the inevitability. She confirmed it a moment later when she asked, "Will you give me some time and let me work through this?"

"Of course." Sara shifted slightly and glanced at Hunter, then found she was unable to look away. Hunter's world had been rocked off its axis, and sitting emotionally and physically exhausted and disheveled on the floor, the protective shell of arrogance she usually wore had slipped off. It left her clearly exposed for Sara to see that beneath the strength and intelligence, beneath the passion and temper, resided an unexpected vulnerability. Unbidden, Sara's own feelings made her furrow her brow. Protectiveness. Tenderness.

"You're nothing like I expected," she found herself saying.

"I'm well aware of the tabloid image I have," Hunter said. "I can imagine what you expected. To think you still agreed to come to London with David to meet with me."

As she turned to face Sara, a slow, sexy smile touched her lips and made Sara's mouth go dry. "But here you are, so let me see if I can help you separate fact from fiction. I'm almost twenty-eight years old and have an education in electrical and computer systems engineering. I've known both my business partners since I was fifteen, one of whom happens to be my best friend. I'm highly competitive, can't resist a challenge, and enjoy almost any kind of physical activity."

Unbidden, Sara's pulse began to race, and she couldn't help but smile. "Is there anything else you think I should know?"

Hunter's eyes glinted dangerously, and her voice seemed to drop an octave. "Yes. I have a weakness for fast cars, classic rock, and intelligent women." She paused ever so briefly. "Now you'll have to decide if coming to London to meet with me is going to be a good thing or a bad thing. Which will it be, do you suppose?"

Oh God, that voice needs to be declared a lethal weapon. And then a second thought occurred to Sara. *Is she flirting with me?* She swallowed hard and found herself struggling to respond as a shiver ran along her spine.

"I'll have to let you know," she said.

In that instant, she became acutely aware of Hunter's body pressed against hers. She could feel the heat, the subtle shift of muscles, and the soft and steady heartbeat as well as her own almost immediate physical response to the currents suddenly running between them. Her thoughts drifted momentarily, and she shivered again.

Reluctantly, she exhaled and shifted away just a little. She cleared her throat and tried to think. Tried to remember a time when a woman she had just met managed to intrigue and captivate her so thoroughly. Somehow, she couldn't think of a single instance.

In fact, she couldn't remember the last time she had felt like this. She felt disoriented, her heart was hammering, and in the back of her mind, Sara thought she heard a warning sound about the dangers of getting too close to this particular woman. But the sound was almost instantly lost in the heated rush of blood she felt coursing through her veins.

Struggling to refocus on the job at hand, Sara sensed Hunter was at her emotional limit. She knew if she pushed too hard, the small opening she'd just been given would quickly disappear.

Instead, she let the silence settle comfortably between them before changing the subject.

"Could I ask one more personal question?"

"One more? I guess it would depend on the nature of the question and whether I can tell you it's none of your business." Hunter studied her bruised knuckles before looking up. "Listen, don't believe everything you've heard or read about me in the papers. If there is something you need to know, just ask me, and I'll do my damnedest to give you a straight answer."

"Okay." Sara smiled. "I know you were at a fundraiser earlier this evening. Or was that yesterday?" She shook her head and gave a soft laugh. "No matter. At a guess, your mind was probably occupied with other things, and I was wondering when the last time was that you actually had anything to eat." She laid her hand on her own abdomen, and as if on cue, her stomach grumbled. "Because I don't know about you, but I'm starving."

"Personal question, hmm?" Hunter's grin was audible. "The truth is I can't remember having anything other than coffee in the last twenty-four hours."

"That is so not good, Roswell," Sara chided and was rewarded with a genuine laugh. "But the question is whether there happens to be any food on board this fancy jet of yours."

"I'll let you in on a secret." Hunter's grin widened as she leaned forward. "My team is aware I'm hopeless in a kitchen. I mean, hitting the switch on the coffeemaker is about the extent of my cooking skills. So under normal circumstances, you can expect to find the galley stocked with everything imaginable."

Sara gave Hunter an appraising glance, gliding over the lean, sculpted body before moving slowly down her long jean-clad thighs. "You're a little skinny. I guess they want to make sure you eat every now and then, right?"

"I guess, but I'm afraid we're not going to find anything fancy on board tonight. I really didn't give much advance warning to prepare for the flight." She laughed as Sara affected a pout. "Still, if it's just something to eat you're interested in, I'm sure I know where we can find something to tide you over. Just give me a minute to clean up."

She got to her feet with effortless grace, pausing for an instant. "Maybe when this is over, I'll take you to see Paris. You said you've never been, and it's one of my favorite cities. A little bit of notice and you'd be amazed what we can cook up," she added with a cheeky grin before disappearing into an adjoining lavatory.

Sara felt an inexplicable sense of loss from almost the moment Hunter closed the door between them. She pondered the unexpected turn in the conversation and found she missed the contact with Hunter's warm skin. It would seem when Hunter left a room, she left a vacuum. One that retained faint traces of her deliciously sexy scent.

CHAPTER SEVEN

Hunter freshened up and exchanged her damp T-shirt for a clean shirt that, at a glance, probably belonged to Matt. Rolling the sleeves halfway up her forearms, she splashed cold water on her face and ran her still-wet hands through her hair. After a cursory glance in the mirror, she shrugged at her reflection before rejoining Sara.

Sara's warm hand gripped hers, and their fingers entwined as she tugged Sara to her feet. Their touch brought a flash of pleasure that was both unexpected and a little surprising. And when Sara didn't immediately release her hand, Hunter was startled to realize she wasn't quite ready to let go. Instead, something irrepressible deep inside made her hold on until after she had led the way through the main cabin toward the front of the jet, where a card game was in progress. Only then did she regretfully pull her hand away.

They found four of the players frowning over their cards, while Peter leaned back in his seat, a large stack of poker chips in front of him and a self-satisfied grin on his face. The chatter and teasing at the table melted momentarily as they approached. Hunter readily accepted a lollipop Peter handed her and stuck it in her mouth while she watched the hand get played. When it was over, she grinned in delight.

"Well done," she told Peter before turning back to Sara. "Sara Wilder, meet my wolf pack."

At Sara's inquisitive look, the player closest to her spoke up. "We're the operations team for the Roswell Group, better known as Hunter's wolves." He stuck out a large, callused hand. "I'm Scott Prentiss and this is the rest of the pack—Rachel Jones, Conner Reese, and Adrienne Beaumont. I believe you've already met Peter."

As they went around the table, Sara acknowledged the flurry of introductions with brief handshakes. When they finished, Peter looked at Hunter expectantly. "Are we dealing you in, or should we just get out our wallets now and hand them over to you?"

His comment elicited laughter from the other team members as they began to make room for Hunter and Sara at the table. But Hunter shook her head and smiled wryly, shifting the lollipop from one side of her mouth to the other.

"Thanks, but I don't think it looks good for me to keep winning all your money. Next thing I know, you'll all be asking for a raise." She paused and raised an eyebrow at what little remained of the original sandwich platter on the table. "Besides, we were just passing through on our way to get something to eat. I trust you left something worth eating."

"What can I say?" Peter shrugged and his boyish face split with a sheepish grin. "Some of us didn't go to a fancy fundraiser, and we were hungry."

Hunter rolled her eyes and gave Sara's hand a little tug, pulling her along as she led the way to the galley.

Sara leaned against a counter while Hunter reached into an overhead cabinet, pulled down a tray, and placed it on the counter. An instant later, she bent over, head in the fridge. "Not a lot of choice, but I think we might have the makings of a picnic," she said as she pulled out an assortment of containers and placed them on the tray. "We've got roast beef, some hard rolls, lettuce, tomato, and mayonnaise. There's also something that looks like potato salad."

She opened another cabinet and added china plates to the tray, along with some cutlery, before ducking her head back into the fridge. "Do you want beer or water? Or there's a bottle of Chardonnay here, if that interests you."

Sara inhaled sharply as she watched Hunter's denim-clad hips do a quick, enthusiastic bump and grind as she found some dijon. Distracted by the view, it took her a moment to realize Hunter was waiting for an answer.

"Beer's good," Sara said. As she watched, a bottle of Corona made its way onto the tray along with a bottle of water. "If you'd rather have the beer, I'm good with the Chardonnay."

Hunter's quick, amused grin flashed over her shoulder, lingering in her eyes as they connected with Sara's. "There's plenty of beer. But I'm planning on flying later, and I generally find it works better for everyone if I haven't been drinking. Bottle or glass?"

"Bottle's fine." It took a moment for Sara to process what Hunter had said and her eyes narrowed. "You're planning on flying—as in this plane?"

That elicited a genuine laugh. "Don't look so horrified, Sara. I've been a licensed pilot longer than I've had my driver's license. Trust me. You're in good hands."

Sara found herself staring at Hunter's hands and lost track of the conversation.

Having fit as many items as possible into a haphazard pile, Hunter grabbed the tray and indicated with her head Sara should follow as they made their way into what appeared to be a small stateroom, complete with a double bed and a comfortable seating area.

Hunter placed the overloaded tray on a table and then walked over to a cabinet housing electronic equipment that would make even the most technologically savvy envious. Soft jazz, bluesy and mellow, immediately filled the room, and for the next few minutes, they concentrated on pulling their meal together. Finally satisfied with what she had created, Sara took a large bite of her sandwich and groaned in ecstasy. A couple of bites later, she washed it down with the ice-cold beer. And then, she decided, it was time to ease back into work.

"Your team seems quite impressive. Have they been with you long?"

"That depends on who you're talking about," Hunter replied easily. "Peter and Scott were in the military with Matt, and they were both there when it all got started so I guess you could say they've been part of Roswell the longest."

"And when was that? How did it come about?" Picking up her sandwich, she took another bite before meeting Hunter's gaze.

"That would have been almost eight years ago, in a little godforsaken corner of South America." Hunter poured some water into a crystal glass filled with ice and watched Sara over the rim. "Matt and the guys were attempting to start up a private security business and had gone down there to meet with one of the British oil companies. As I recall, the company was pumping the oil to the Caribbean through a pipeline, and it had become a regular target for the Marxist guerrilla forces and drug cartels operating in the area. Matt convinced them he should have a look to assess their situation and see what could be done to better secure the pipeline."

"So, what happened?"

"While they were there, a group of guerrilla fighters overran the security at the drill site and took Matt and a pair of oil company execs hostage. They demanded several million in exchange for their release and threatened to kill them if their demands weren't met."

Sara's eyes widened as she set her beer on the table. "Jesus. Obviously the oil company paid the ransom—" Something in Hunter's expression stopped her and her mind flashed back to an image of Nigel Wainwright. Warning her Hunter was inclined to take risks others might consider unacceptable. "What did you do?"

Hunter reached for the bottle of water, refilled her glass, and took a drink, her gaze never leaving Sara's. "We're not that different, you and I."

"That's an interesting statement, but I'm not certain I understand what you mean."

Amusement darkened Hunter's eyes. "You came to London— and, in fact, you're sitting here with me right now—because of your relationship with David. I was motivated to help Matt in much the same way, and as a good friend, I did what I felt I had to do. I just happen to be an obsessive overachiever."

"What did you do?"

"When I first learned Matt was being held hostage, I flew into Bogota, then met up with Peter and Scott somewhere near the foothills of the Andes. They wanted to mount a rescue operation and had put together a plan, including hiring some local talent."

"You mean mercenaries, don't you?"

Hunter hesitated and then shrugged. Slowly, she lowered her glass, set it aside. "I suppose…yes. The challenge was the only way to access the drill site was by helicopter, and Matt had taken the oil company chopper with him. Peter knew where there were some Mi-24s that belonged to the local military unit, but they weren't being exactly cooperative, and we didn't have a lot of time if we were going to act before the deadline the guerrillas had given…So I borrowed one."

"You borrowed…wait a minute…what's an Mi-24?"

"It's a Russian attack helicopter. After the fall of the Soviet Union, a lot of Latin American countries bought old Soviet aircraft for their armed forces."

"And you borrowed—" Sara braced her hands on the table and aimed a narrowed look. "No, sweet Jesus, you *stole* a military attack helicopter to conduct a rescue operation against a group of armed guerrillas? And you knew how to fly the thing?"

"Sara…" Hunter drew in a deep breath and settled back into the soft leather of her chair. "I borrowed the helicopter. The reason I say that is because I brought it back after we'd rescued Matt and the oil company execs. And yes, I knew how to fly the damn thing. I've always had this thing with flying machines. I can't explain it, but you can put me into anything that flies, and I can figure out how to fly it."

Sara couldn't help herself. She started to laugh, allowing the vague tension between them to dissipate. "You're crazy, you know that, don't you?"

"I believe you've told me that before."

Still shaking her head, Sara drained her beer and placed the empty bottle on the table. "Okay, so you returned the helicopter you borrowed. Were there any repercussions from the local military?"

Hunter grinned. "Well, they weren't too pleased their helicopter had some holes that hadn't been there previously, and they arrested Peter and Scott."

"What about you and Matt?"

"Well," Hunter shifted uncomfortably, "it turned out I picked up a bit of shrapnel—"

Sara searched Hunter's face. "Oh God, how bad?"

"It was nothing. Just a scratch really," she said, "but it was enough to put me in the local hospital for about a week. The military kept me under armed guard and were waiting to arrest me, but the doctor looking after me wasn't a fan of the military and wouldn't release me. And by the time I was medically cleared, Matt had gotten hold of the chairman of the oil company. Did I mention that happened to be Sir Nigel Wainwright?"

Sara shook her head and laughed once again. "I guess it helps to have friends in high places." Of course, she also understood wealth—the kind Hunter Roswell could claim in her own right— could have smoothed any bumps she'd encountered if Nigel hadn't been available.

"Yeah, well." Hunter's lips curved. "Nigel quickly flew in and took charge of the situation. By the time I was ready to be released from the hospital, he had cleared up any outstanding issues with the military. And in the meantime, Matt and I had spent a lot of time talking and agreed on the foundation for what became the Roswell Group. The rest evolved over time, and we began recruiting key personnel from law enforcement and the military, staring with Peter and Scott."

"That's one hell of a beginning," Sara said softly.

"It was." Hunter's amused eyes remained steady on Sara's. "But I've always believed anything worth starting should start out with a bang."

CHAPTER EIGHT

After clearing the remnants of their meal, Hunter grabbed a fresh pot of coffee from the galley and brought it back to where Sara was seated in the comfort of the small stateroom. Watching Sara as she poured them each a cup, she decided it felt nice having her here on board the jet. Almost as if they were friends. As if she wasn't sitting there on behalf of the FBI, waiting to get into her head.

The thought made her frown and she began weighing the seemingly infinite courses of action that would be possible once she got home. She needed to talk to Tessa. She needed to—she bit her lip and began making mental notes. Several more minutes passed in silence before she glanced up and realized Sara had been watching her. Studying her intensely, as if trying to read something in her face, and yet patient with her reflective silence.

Hunter smiled hesitantly. "What?"

"I'd love to know what's been going through your mind for the last few minutes," Sara responded with a slow smile.

"Trust me, it's not that fascinating. Let's see if I can help you." She tilted her head to the side. "Mostly, I've been putting together a list of all the things I need to do once I get home. I've been away for about six months, which means there'll be some catch-up to do at the office. There are also a couple of contracts that still need to be finalized."

"Is that it?"

"Hardly." Hunter smothered a grin. "On the personal side, I was thinking I need to let my mother know I'm home again and find a way to tell her what's going on before she hears it from someone else or through the media. I'll also need to get my house in order, call the cleaning service, maybe get some groceries. Not that I'm planning on doing any cooking or anything crazy."

"Of course not."

"No, but with how Matt and Peter are reacting over this whole stalker situation, I've got a feeling I'm going to find myself having a lot of company."

"Anything else?"

"Yes, I've been thinking about how little I actually know about stalkers, but I'm sure there's a wiki I can start with and then take it from there."

"You think too much." Sara looked amused. "Do you always create mental lists of things to do?"

Hunter thought about it and gave a wry grin as she made another mental note. "Sometimes. Sure. Why not?"

Sara rolled her eyes. "I can't do much to help out with some of what's on your list, but maybe I can help you with answers to whatever you'd like to know about stalkers. In fact, maybe we can do something quid pro quo."

"Quid pro quo?" Hunter looked at Sara cautiously as she considered what her offer meant. She was former FBI. Smart, competent, confident. She had eyes that missed very little and it would be perilous to take her lightly. "And what do you want in exchange?"

"For you to answer some personal questions," Sara said softly. "You know the sooner we understand the connection between you and the stalker, the faster we'll be able to identify and stop him. But to do that, we…*I* need to understand you. It's how I work—how I've always worked."

Hunter's shoulders tensed. "What does that mean exactly?"

"That means I need to ask a lot of questions, especially about who you were ten years ago and who might have been around you at that time. Small details you might not even think will help."

A myriad of feelings flashed through Hunter's mind. Fear, indecision, grief, and deep weariness. She had known this was coming. It had only been a matter of time. But for some reason, she hadn't expected it so soon. She squeezed her eyes shut, desperate for calm. For control. For a wisdom that suddenly seemed beyond her. Confused and uncertain, caught in a wave of emotions that almost brought her to her knees, she got up and poured herself another cup of coffee.

As she stared at the coffee she had just poured, she felt a hand on her arm. For just a moment, a fraction of a breath, she remained frozen. And then, finally, she turned to find Sara's gaze upon her. Offering compassion. Support. Solace.

"It'll be okay, Hunter. Trust me. You can do this." Her voice was pitched low. Soothing. The kind of tone psychologists and psychiatrists probably used the world over.

Without saying a word, Hunter sat back down. She swallowed nervously and stared at her shaking hands. She didn't know what to do, and she couldn't seem to engage her brain enough to figure it out. That was a first. But she could also hear the soft-spoken, nearly hypnotic words of assurance, and she wanted to believe her. *Almost* believed her. And maybe that was enough for now.

Her eyes remained steady on Sara's. "Can I ask you something?" she asked.

"Of course."

"Why are you so certain the stalker is male?"

Sara stared at her and then, slowly, understanding dawned in her eyes and a faint smile appeared. "Realistically," she said softly, "stalkers can be either male or female, but the majority of documented stalking cases—approximately eighty percent—involve men stalking women. The initial FBI profile concurred and has him pegged as a white male in his late twenties to early forties."

"What else is the profile going to tell me?"

"The typical profile of a delusional stalker is an unmarried loner, unable to establish or sustain close relationships. Since delusional stalkers are both threatened by and yearn for closeness, they often pick victims who are unattainable in some way."

Hunter noted that Sara slipped easily into the role of teacher, and she found herself enjoying the soft cadence of her voice.

"Like a celebrity stalker?"

Sara nodded. "That's right. His—for the sake of argument, let's say it's a man—obsession is based in fantasy. What he can't get in reality, he achieves through fantasy, and when he tries to act out his fantasy in real life, he expects the victim to play their role and return his affection. But when the affection isn't returned, when the victim doesn't fall in line and play along, he's likely to become violent. What makes delusionals even more dangerous is they tend to objectify their victims—an object they alone must possess and control."

"And what do you think?" When Sara's eyes narrowed, Hunter laughed softly. "Come on, Sara, David wanted you to be part of this for a reason. You just gave me an overview. Now tell me what you think."

Sara hesitated and appeared to consider her request. "All right," she said after a moment had passed. "I think he's highly intelligent but has an inflated sense of his own intelligence, and he's driven by ego to improve with each killing. He sees himself as dominant, controlling, and he needs to get it right. He's educated, financially independent, and has had ample time to follow you and study your habits. And his MO—his modus operandi or method of committing the crime—shows he's organized, meticulous. He's planned each of his crimes carefully and has left no forensic evidence or clues."

Hunter remained silent for a minute as thoughts chased each other in her head, before finally raising her gaze so she could stare levelly at Sara. "What about the fact that he knew to call me daddy's girl? I mean Jesus, that goes back almost ten years. How is that even possible? I can't wrap my brain around it."

"Actually, some studies show delusional stalkers are the most tenacious of all," Sara said. "In fact, erotomanic delusions themselves typically last an average of ten years."

Hunter folded her arms across her chest and took a deep breath. "Do you think it's possible you're looking for someone who was part of the original security detail assigned to protect me? Or maybe involved in the aftermath of the kidnapping as part of the negotiation and recovery team?"

"You mean law enforcement? It's certainly something we have to consider, insomuch as the man we're looking for not only knows the code name that was used but also knows enough to leave no trace evidence behind," Sara admitted. "David filled me in on the basics of what happened ten years ago, and while I don't know precisely who was involved, I do know the case involved law enforcement personnel from local, state, and federal levels. That's why I need your help. But there are other possibilities we need to consider."

"Like what?"

"Like the studies that show only twenty percent of female victims are stalked by strangers."

Hunter frowned. "Someone close to me?"

"It's possible, Hunter. Almost sixty percent are stalked by either intimate partners or ex-intimate partners. That scenario would put the UNSUB close enough to you to be familiar with your security code name. I know you were only seventeen, but I'm going to need to know if you were involved with anyone immediately before or after the kidnapping. Anyone with whom you might have shared the code name or who was close enough to overhear it being used."

Hunter's instincts screamed for her to stop this conversation. The smart thing—the prudent thing—would be to have someone else provide Sara with the details she was seeking about parts of her less-than-illustrious youth. Matt came to mind.

Sara felt Hunter stiffen and saw something that looked like regret and unease flash across her face. In the deafening silence that followed, she became aware she had inadvertently stumbled onto a sensitive subject. With rising concern that Hunter could end the conversation, Sara changed tactics. "Can we talk a bit about what happened? About the kidnapping?"

Hunter stared at her in silence before finally nodding stiffly. She seemed calm enough, but Sara could sense the turmoil beneath the deceptively calm expression. "How much do you already know?" she asked.

Sara closed her eyes and tried to recall what David had told her. "I know your father was the US Attorney General at the time, and you were kidnapped by a survivalist group led by a man named… damn, I'm sorry, I can't remember his name."

"Kyle Brenner."

"Brenner, right. If I remember correctly, the kidnapping was tagged as retribution for the death of Brenner's son, who was killed during a joint ATF-FBI raid on a militia compound somewhere in Oregon. And I know the hostage recovery went horribly wrong, and people on both sides got killed, including your father."

"You've got the gist of what happened," Hunter said. She took a deep breath and then glanced up at Sara, her face pale and strained. "What was never made public was after the Oregon raid, Brenner threatened my father."

"Threatened him how?"

"Sent him a message telling him he should hold his little girl and tell her he loved her while he still had a chance. Because she wouldn't be around much longer."

Sara nodded her head mutely. Her throat was dry, and she sipped her coffee as she waited for Hunter to continue. She wanted to ask how Hunter knew this level of detail, then realized she was better off not knowing the answer. *She probably hacked the files.*

"You need to understand my father never wanted the dark part of his world to touch his family, so he did what he thought was best under the circumstances. He brought me home from England where I was going to school and surrounded me with round-the-clock security, code-named daddy's girl. But he never told me about the threats. Never explained why he had brought me home."

When Hunter paused, Sara found herself waiting with growing concern, her dread increasing with each passing second. She watched as Hunter's chin dropped, and when her eyes finally lifted once again, they revealed a world of sorrow.

"The day Brenner grabbed me, my father and I had one hell of an argument. I confronted him that morning, demanded to know what was going on."

"What did your father do?"

"He blew me off." Hunter shrugged tiredly. "Except he forgot we were really very much alike. He forgot there was simply too much of his DNA in me for me to do what I was told without question. He forgot I'd inherited his damned temper. His headstrong will. His single-minded intensity."

Sara closed her eyes. Her chest tightened; she knew what was coming next. "You slipped away from your security detail, didn't you?"

Hunter exhaled deeply and nodded her head. "And Brenner and four of his boys were able to grab me." She swallowed hard, and Sara could see the pain so readily apparent on her face. "They held me for just over three weeks."

Hunter's earlier question came back to her with a vengeance. *Can you teach me to live with the past? With what happened to me?* Swallowing hard, Sara squared her shoulders. What had they done to her during those three weeks? She wasn't certain she wanted to know as she waited for Hunter to continue.

"I won't get into what happened during those three weeks," she said softly, staring at Sara unflinchingly as if reading her mind. "That's for another place and time. Or maybe never. What's important here—what no one counted on—was Brenner had a change of heart at the last minute."

"What do you mean?"

"For whatever reason, Brenner couldn't bring himself to kill me, and instead, he contacted my father and began negotiating for my release. But then it all went to hell and what was meant to be a hostage recovery turned into a bloodbath. In the end, my father, an FBI agent named Robert Simms, and four of the kidnappers were killed."

"And what about you?" Sara asked. "What happened to you?"

"I was admitted to the trauma center at San Francisco General just after three in the morning," Hunter replied quietly, "covered in my father's blood."

"Jesus Christ, Hunter. How the hell did you survive?"

"Sometimes, I'm not certain I did," Hunter replied starkly. "But it brings us back to your earlier question."

"What question was that?"

"Earlier, you started to ask me about any personal involvements I might have had ten years ago."

"That's right. I know you were only seventeen—"

"Sara," Hunter interrupted her gently. Her tone was dry and a wry smile curved her lips. "I was never seventeen. At least, not in the way you mean it."

Sara nodded, not certain how to respond.

"After the kidnapping and after my father was killed…it was like I became a different person. When I was finally released from the hospital, I didn't know where to go. My mother was still struggling to cope, and I felt like I was a constant reminder of everything she'd lost."

"You blamed yourself."

"Yes. I couldn't handle it, ended up handling it all rather badly, and ran away to Europe. And…well, you might say I went a little crazy. Got a little out of control."

Sara looked at Hunter and was shocked to see her blush unexpectedly. "How out of control?"

"At seventeen, I was…damn, how can I put this? At seventeen, finding any number of willing partners was never a problem for me. And that might become a problem for *you*."

"Why?"

Hunter turned away. "Because they were mostly one-night stands, Sara, and I didn't always know their names," she said flatly. "And the ones that weren't…let's just say one or two might not take it lightly if the FBI were to suddenly start directing any level of scrutiny into their private affairs, particularly if it means revealing the existence of an intimate relationship with me ten years ago."

Sara blinked slowly. "I'm not sure I understand what you're saying. We're trying to find and stop someone who has killed five women so far and poses a very real threat to you. Surely, if they were once intimate with you, that has to count for something?"

"Of course it counts, but—look, does the name Dimitri Kozlov mean anything to you?"

"The Russian billionaire? Runs a global empire and has his fingers in shipping, mining, electronics, and armaments?" Sara's eyes narrowed. Kozlov was a handsome, ruthless businessman in his late sixties—making him forty years Hunter's senior. "You were involved with Dimitri Kozlov?"

"I was involved…I had a relationship with Dominique—his wife."

"The model? Sweet Jesus, Hunter. What were you thinking?"

"That she was beautiful," Hunter replied softly. "That she was gentle and kind. She found me on a beach one night and was worried I meant to harm myself."

"And did you? Did you mean yourself harm?"

Hunter shrugged. "I don't know. All I know for sure is she helped me to see alcohol and parties and an endless string of one-night stands wouldn't make it hurt any less."

Sara's eyes met Hunter's, fierce with determination, achingly sad, and she touched her cheek in a tender gesture. "I'm glad she was there for you. That she was able to help."

"Then maybe you'll understand why I wouldn't want to put our relationship under a spotlight. Dimitri knew, but it would still hurt them both if Dominique was forced to openly admit that ten years ago, she had an affair with the seventeen-year-old daughter of an assassinated American politician."

"I do understand," Sara said.

"Thank you." Hunter flashed a smile filled with gratitude. "You didn't think this was going to be easy, did you?"

Sara's grin fought its way to the surface, and she laughed softly in response.

CHAPTER NINE

S ara awoke to the gentle pressure of a hand shaking her shoulder. When she opened her eyes, she found Peter McNeil standing over her.

"We'll be landing in less than an hour," he said, "and I thought you'd appreciate the opportunity to freshen up. You'll find all the comforts of home in the bathroom on your right. In the meantime, can I get you some coffee?"

"That'd be great. Just cream, thanks."

Sara spent several minutes freshening up and chasing away the edges of sleep. When she returned to the main cabin, she glanced at her watch, only to realize she no longer had any idea what time it was.

"It's just before midnight, San Francisco time," Peter provided.

"Thanks. I've changed time zones so many times in the past few days I'm no longer sure if I should be considering breakfast or dinner when I get home," Sara said. She sipped the strong coffee Peter gave her and sighed. "This is really good."

Peter laughed. "Hunter considers coffee a basic food group, so she has the stuff delivered by some guy who I swear only handpicks the beans under a waning moon."

At the mention of Hunter's name, Sara automatically looked around, but failed to catch sight of her and hoped she was finally sleeping. "Where is Hunter?" she asked.

Peter indicated the cockpit. "She chased J.J. out of the left seat about four hours ago."

"She's flying the plane?" Silence pressed in and Sara frowned. "Do you know if she got any sleep?"

"No idea," Peter replied and shrugged. "But it's no great surprise. When she gets focused on something or is working out a problem in her head, she tends to forget to eat and sleep and doesn't stop until she's exhausted. Even then, she keeps going until she drops. I think it has something to do with the fact that her brain doesn't function like a normal person's."

"You're saying she's always been like this?"

"At least for as long as I've known her, and I've known her since Matt introduced us about ten years ago," Peter replied carefully. "If you want to know more, you need to speak to Matt. He's known her the longest."

"And how long is that?"

"Since she was fifteen. I met Hunter when my father was working for Michael Roswell in the Department of Justice," Matt Logan answered as he approached. "You should have seen Hunter back then. All legs and sass." He broke off and gave Sara a slightly self-deprecating smile. "Let's just say after I met her, it came as a shock to discover she was only fifteen. Any coffee left?"

"There's a fresh pot," Peter answered. "I was about to get myself a cup. I can get some for you if you'd like." He walked away without waiting for a response.

Sara turned and faced Matt. "I hope you don't mind all these questions," she said.

Matt shook his head. "Anything that's going to help," he said. "Look, I know the FBI wants Hunter back in San Francisco in response to the killer's message found at the last crime scene. But maybe, instead of bringing her closer to this guy that's stalking her, we should be thinking about taking Hunter off the streets completely."

David, tired and rumpled, looked up from the coffee he was mindlessly stirring. "Why would you want to do that? You know we're prepared to protect her going forward. Hunter just needs to say the word."

Sara noted an almost imperceptible state change in Peter, and wondered once again if there was more at play than she knew. "You head up security for her, Peter," she said. "What do you think?"

"I'm all for removing Hunter from any possible danger," Peter replied without having to give the matter a moment's thought. "But if we do move her, we really should take her to a safe house. It's a pretty good bet this stalker knows where she lives, where she works, where she hangs out."

"I disagree," David fired back. "Hiding Hunter will accomplish nothing other than to possibly feed this guy's rage. We just need to be smart about this and make sure we've got her covered at all times. Then, when he makes his move, we can nail him."

"Do I get a say in this?" Hunter's voice was mild, but there was a discernable edge as she approached from the cockpit.

Peter and David started to speak at the same time. Hunter stared impassively at them until she had heard enough. Finally she raised both hands in an unmistakable cue for silence.

"Let's be clear about this. I decided it was right for me to go home, not anyone else, and that's what I'm doing," she glanced at her watch, "in less than an hour. And while I'm not sure what I'm going to do after we land, I can tell you this much. I won't have my life ruled by fear of what this stalker may or may not do. And I don't give a damn whether anyone agrees with me. In case you haven't noticed, I am not asking for opinions."

She paused, suddenly aware of how very tired she was. Worse, she could only imagine how difficult things would get in the coming days. But there was nothing she could do about that. Not now.

"Don't try to make my decisions for me," she continued more calmly, straightening her shoulders. "And just so we're clear, neither am I going to accept being wrapped in cotton and surrounded with FBI agents."

Before anyone could say a word, Hunter turned and walked toward the galley, her long strides quickly eating up the distance.

After a moment's hesitation, Sara followed her with no clear plan of what she would say. She couldn't blame Hunter for being angry, but as much as she might wish she could change things, the reality of what awaited them in San Francisco was dictating the course of action. As she approached, she watched Hunter pour herself some coffee and noted the slight trembling of her hand, the shadows under her eyes.

"I'm sorry. We were being insensitive," Sara said. "Believe me. If I was in your position, I'd be just as upset. But you don't want to do anything to put yourself at greater risk just because you're angry."

Hunter glanced up, bristling visibly, and Sara could see both fury and fatigue. "Have you ever been? In my position? Having people expecting you to relinquish control of your life while they make decisions for you as if you're—"

"As if you were incapable of making decisions for yourself?" Sara finished for her. Reacting without thinking, she curled her hand around Hunter's wrist. "No, but that's not the point. What you need to understand is that top of mind for everyone right now is keeping you healthy and whole. Alive."

"And you were hired to do that, I know." There was no more anger in Hunter's voice. It had dissipated as quickly as it had appeared, leaving only a bone-deep weariness.

I'm trying very hard to remember this is a job, Sara thought, her gaze dropping to where her hand lingered on Hunter's wrist. She squeezed it once before letting go, but swore she could still feel the warmth of Hunter's skin, smell the faint and intoxicating scent. "Still, I'm sorry."

"There's no need to apologize." Hunter paused and looked as if she had more to say. As they stood silently staring at each other, she gnawed on her bottom lip then reached into the pocket of her jeans and pulled out a card. She held it in her hand a moment longer before she handed it wordlessly to Sara.

Sara stared at the card and tried to make sense of what she was looking at.

"That's every conceivable means of contacting me," Hunter explained softly. "Home and work addresses, cell, home and office numbers."

Glancing at the card one more time, Sara looked up at Hunter, the question evident in her eyes.

Hunter smiled wistfully. "I guess I thought if you and I are going to try to work together, you should know how to reach me at any time."

Sara found she liked the sound of that. As she absorbed the words, she watched Hunter pick up her coffee, take a sip and grimace.

"God, I've maxed out on coffee," she said. "I didn't think that was possible."

❖

Just before one in the morning, the jet touched down in San Francisco and taxied to a stop in front of a hangar owned by the Roswell Group. On board, everyone waited to be processed by US Customs and Border Protection. The CBP official barely glanced at Hunter's documents before allowing her to slip out of the plane and into the misty night.

Sara could only observe and smile wryly. *Roswell jet, Roswell passport, in the home state of Senator Patrick Roswell.*

Through the open hatch, she watched as Hunter stopped on the apron just beyond the jet's wing. In less than a minute, a black Maserati pulled alongside. When the driver's door opened, a long-legged brunette exited the vehicle. She tossed the keys to Hunter, who caught them easily before being enveloped in a full-bodied embrace.

"Aw, shit."

"Problem?" Sara asked Peter as she watched the unknown woman kiss Hunter soundly. She couldn't see her clearly, but there was something vaguely familiar about her, and Sara looked around for a better observation point. An instant later, it was no longer relevant as Hunter slipped into the driver's seat. Barely waiting for the brunette to get in beside her, she gunned the engine and, like a chimera, disappeared from view.

"Damn. Hunter must have arranged this so she could make her escape," Peter said. "I should have anticipated this."

A few minutes later, Peter's suspicion was confirmed with the arrival of three limousines to take everyone to their respective destinations, courtesy of Hunter Roswell. Too tired to argue, Sara relinquished her bag to a dark-suited driver and got into the closest limousine. Matt followed Sara and David into the vehicle and stretched his long frame into the leather seat.

Sara asked, "Is Hunter going to be okay? She really shouldn't be alone before we know what we're dealing with."

Matt smiled reassuringly. "She'll be fine. She's tougher than she looks."

Sara wasn't entirely convinced.

"We need to consider her stalker has been watching and following her for a long time," David said. "He'll know all her habits. That means some changes will have to be made in Hunter's routine, at least in the short term, and that includes not leaving her alone."

"Then we can be grateful that, at the moment, we know she's not alone," Matt responded.

"Speaking of not being alone, do you know the woman that picked Hunter up?"

Matt turned back to Sara and nodded. "Tessa Kinser."

A warning bell sounded in Sara's head, and then the fog cleared and it came to her. "Tessa Kinser…the lawyer?" *Kate's current lover? Sweet Jesus, talk about six degrees of separation.*

"Mm-hmm. The one and only. Do you know her?"

"We've had occasion to meet."

"Tessa heads up legal for both the Roswell Group and Hunter personally. They've been best of friends for years."

Her instant relief that the gorgeous brunette with Hunter was just a friend concerned Sara. It shouldn't matter. *And maybe if you tell yourself that long enough, you'll start to believe it,* she thought before grinning uncertainly.

"Hunter's best friend is her lawyer?" she asked wryly, then relaxed into the seat and let her eyes close.

"Yeah, strange as it might sound." Matt laughed. "As I recall, they originally met while at Oxford, and then hooked up again stateside. But Tessa showing up does make me wonder whether she came as Hunter's lawyer or her friend. It also makes me wonder what the hell is going on in Hunter's oversized brain."

An interesting question that needs to be answered quickly, Sara thought. *Because somewhere out there, a killer is planning his next move.*

Chapter Ten

The air was whisper soft and carried the scent of the sea. Drawn to the window by the first light of day, Hunter faced the panoramic views that stretched out before her and felt something shift inside her.

She had missed this, she realized, more than she had known. Missed the moodiness of the ocean and the breathtaking vistas across the Pacific, the Marin Headlands and the Golden Gate Bridge. She had even missed the soothing presence of the fog which shrouded the bridge in the distance.

Inside the house, the shadows were close and the silence pressed in all around her. The stereo was silent, the TV was dark, and the thick panes of window glass shut out the noises of the night other than the persistent sound of the waves that stirred the pebbles along the shoreline.

She was finally alone. With that realization, some of the tension she had been feeling dissipated. Her head still ached and her eyes burned, but the agonizing pressure in her chest had eased.

Swirling the coffee in her mug as she paced, she stopped in front of the baby grand piano which sat glistening and hauntingly silent in the barely furnished living room. With one hand, she ran her fingers along the keyboard, letting the notes echo through the empty room. Unable to resist, she played the first few chords of a Chopin étude before turning away.

The house was exactly as she had left it six months earlier. Sparsely furnished with unopened boxes still leaning haphazardly against the whitewashed walls. She knew the cleaning service Matt had arranged to come in once a week could have unpacked the boxes. But it hadn't been her intention to have strangers decide where things should go. Of course, neither had it been her intention to leave the house vacant for so long when she had purchased it.

The purchase had been a rare spur-of-the-moment decision. She had fallen in love at first sight with the house—its romantic architecture, the serenity of the grounds, and the unbelievable views. Buying it had also given her a vague sense of establishing roots. Of belonging. But she had barely taken possession and begun the process of moving in when she had flown to New York for a meeting and had not been back since.

Until now.

Hunter suddenly felt overwhelmingly weary, her legs seemingly incapable of holding her up. Putting her coffee mug in the kitchen sink, she walked back into the living room and sank down on the leather couch. Drawing her knees up to her chest, she wrapped both arms around her legs and pressed her face to them.

The stress of the last twenty-four hours hit her all at once, including the inescapable reality that her life would only get worse, not better, over the next few days. She was equally aware she alone was responsible for setting events in motion, and if things got out of hand, she had only herself to blame.

After leaving the airport, her team, and the FBI behind, she had called in a few favors and arranged an encounter with Ellis McKay, a syndicated columnist she knew fairly well. Ellis gladly accommodated her and suggested they meet at a popular underground club where people went for no reason other than to be seen. That more than suited Hunter's purpose. The resulting photograph of Tessa and Hunter set to run in the paper would hopefully be enough to make the stalker notice daddy's girl had come home.

Foolish? Perhaps. But Hunter desperately wanted to do something to stop another woman from being killed. She needed to figure out who he was. Where he fit in her past. More importantly, how to stop him.

Tessa hadn't agreed with the tactic and had strongly voiced her opinion against Hunter's plan. But in the end, she had come through for her, supporting Hunter partly in the name of friendship, but mostly because at two in the morning, she was incapable of coming up with a reasonable alternative.

A quick glance at her watch confirmed it was coming up on six a.m., and after almost thirty-eight hours with little sleep, Hunter knew she had nothing left in reserve. She needed to sleep. She needed to empty her mind. Not spend two hours tossing and turning on the couch, hoping for sleep while at the same time dreading the nightmares she knew were waiting just beyond her field of vision.

But the shadows from her past were always there, haunting her. And therein lay her dilemma. For all her wealth and intellect, for all her connections, she had no weapons in her arsenal to deal with ghosts. Maybe coming back to San Francisco hadn't been such a good idea after all.

She sighed as the tendrils of the ever-present dream continued to swirl around her. It was always the same. Kyle Brenner. Her father. Rivers of blood. Images of a time that had forever altered her life and left her too often with a scream trapped in her throat. The problem was now, much like then, there was nothing she could do to alter the inevitable outcome.

Releasing an oath, she got up and made her way up the winding staircase, heading for the master suite bath and the enormous steam shower. She quickly undressed, fiddled with the temperature controls, and turned on the water, then stepped into the cross streams.

A moan of pure relief escaped her as the jets of steaming water washed over her body from three directions. Bracing her hands against one wall, she dipped her head and let the near-scalding water flow over her. Felt it soothe her tired body while she slowly turned. Allowed it to wash away the fatigue while the heat massaged and loosened her muscles.

As the water began to ease some of the tension, she reached for the shampoo and found her thoughts drifting to Sara Wilder. In short order, the former FBI agent had somehow managed to penetrate her defenses, and Hunter found herself intrigued. Because there was no question. One look at her and she'd been interested. One word and she'd been captivated.

And it wasn't just that she found her beautiful, although her body hummed with awareness, and she felt a nearly irresistible urge to explore the physical attraction. Sara was the kind of woman who could make Hunter look, and then look again. To pretend to be anything other than attracted to her was simply a lie, and Hunter could easily foresee a time when it would become difficult to maintain an appropriate distance.

But could she really consider acting on the attraction with everything that was happening? Something inside her wanted to take a chance.

So what are you going to do about it?

The thought that she would probably see Sara again today made her smile.

Twenty minutes later, she shut off the water and grabbed a towel as she wandered into the bedroom. Glass doors and windows extended from floor to ceiling and led to a terrace with a spectacular view of the ocean and Marin Headland. Gazing quietly into the early morning light, she quickly dressed.

A few minutes later, having pulled on well-worn jeans, a white polo shirt, and her leather jacket, she headed back down the stairs and out the front door. And immediately came face-to-face with Peter, leaning casually against the wall.

"Good morning," he grinned. "Going somewhere?"

"Try not to sound so chipper, and I might not have to kill you," Hunter responded in a low, tired voice as she slipped her sunglasses on. "Why are you here?"

"We thought it might be a good idea to keep you covered." He cocked his head and indicated the dark SUV where she could see the silhouettes of two other team members. "At least until we can get the lay of the land. Maybe then we can actually have a plan instead of having to improvise."

Hunter heard the unmistakable reprimand, rolled her eyes and sighed. "Did you at least manage to get some sleep?"

"Scott and Rachel had the house covered from the time we landed until I got here just a few minutes ago." He paused and gave Hunter a look that said he was about to get serious. "It was the best we could do under the circumstances, especially since we had no idea where you went when you took off with Tessa. I don't need to tell you no one was very happy about that. Not me. Not Matt. And certainly not the FBI."

"I'm sure," Hunter said dismissively then stopped short. Her lack of sleep was making her hold on her temper tenuous at best, and Peter had done nothing to deserve her anger. Sighing softly, she allowed well-ingrained manners to take over. "Look, I'm sorry, I don't mean to take it out on you. And I didn't mean to make things difficult. I just had some things I needed to do that wouldn't have worked out quite as well with an entourage."

"Don't you mean you needed to do some things you knew I'd never approve or agree to from a security perspective?"

Hunter lowered her sunglasses until her eyes cleared the bridge, and she flashed an unrepentant grin. "Yes."

Peter grinned back. "Damn it, Hunter, you're still a brat."

"I can't help it," she laughed, hooking his arm with hers as they walked down the long cobblestone drive. "And I wouldn't mind the company, so why don't you come with me in my car. Just let Conner and Adrienne know we need to stop and pick up some food before we get to the office."

Peter grabbed the small two-way clipped to his belt, speaking softly as he relayed the information while matching Hunter's long strides toward her car. A minute later, the front gates opened and the Maserati joined the early morning traffic, with the black BMW SUV following close behind.

They stopped at a local café along the way and picked up a bag of beignets and several large coffees. The French-style doughnuts, lavishly covered with powdered sugar, were a favorite indulgence of Hunter's. *The breakfast of champions*, she sighed with a grin, as they reached their destination.

The Roswell Group's corporate headquarters occupied most of a two-building complex in the city's financial district. The guard raised the gate as the Maserati and BMW approached and waved the two vehicles through. Minutes later, Hunter led the way as they entered the first building and took the elevator up to the top floor, which housed both the executive offices and the primary operations center.

"What's the plan?" Peter asked, looking eager to get started.

"Before we left London, I asked Quito to get me copies of the old case files and anything related to the current murders," Hunter explained. "Hopefully everything will have been delivered here by now."

She entered her office and opened the door that led to the adjoining conference room. In spite of the early hour, Quito was already opening boxes and sorting the documents. He quickly moved to Hunter's side, grinning happily as he reached for the bags of take-out and placed their contents on a nearby credenza.

Once food and coffee were distributed, Hunter gave a sigh of appreciation as she bit into a beignet and selected a file from the pile closest to her. "I want to review and break everything down, case by case. Maybe you can set up the whiteboard over there." She indicated the far wall with her hand.

She stared at the volume of information in front of her. At best, it would take several hours to sift through all the material Quito had pulled together. Muttering to herself, she settled back into a chair and began to read.

The original FBI profile, developed before Hunter had been identified as the primary target, had been included in the first file she opened. It expanded on the summary Sara had provided, indicating a stalker driven by his all-consuming loneliness and all-pervasive fantasies. It surmised he would have a well-established delusional fantasy in which he had a special relationship with his chosen victim, based on the belief she was the perfect match for him.

It also indicated while efforts to contact victims were common, erotomanic stalkers were known to keep their delusion a secret. They studied their victims, often from afar, and reacted badly to any perceived rejection by their victims. The profile concluded with a rather prophetic warning that when the relationship looked hopeless, many erotomanic stalkers embarked on a violent spree of self-destruction.

She read the document several times, each time wondering when and how she had first encountered him. She knew it was inevitable they would eventually meet face-to-face. Would she know him? Had they ever really met? Connected? Or was it all part of a twisted fantasy in a deluded mind? The questions looped endlessly in her mind.

As seconds stretched into minutes, then morphed into hours, Hunter switched her focus from the killer to his victims until it felt like she knew each of the women—where they lived, where they worked, where they played. But she was no closer to finding anything that might identify where or when they came into contact with their killer.

After four hours, having used up an all too brief second wind, her mind began to stutter. Stacks of paper and folders were now scattered on the table around her, in a pattern recognizable only to her. The walls, however, were covered with meticulously arranged photographs and documents corresponding with the deaths of the five victims, including crime-scene photos and investigator's notes, organized in painstaking chronological order by Quito under Peter's watchful eye.

One box remained unopened. It held the case files pertaining to the incident ten years earlier. But Hunter wasn't ready to confront the part of her life she desperately wanted to keep buried deep in her mind. She wasn't ready to view the photographs she knew the box contained. She wasn't ready to read the formal, emotionless reports that detailed her kidnapping and her father's death.

Not yet.

Instead, she rested her chin on her fist and stared balefully at the computer in front of her. She silently scanned the data that scrolled by and contemplated doing another search. Reaching for the keyboard, she quickly tapped a query then waited for a response. The frown creasing her forehead deepened as she continued to read the endless loop of information that appeared on the laptop screen.

Frustrated, she swiveled her chair away from the table and stared out the window. It was there, laid out in front of her, like a picture just out of focus. What was she missing?

"I guess it would be kind of stupid to ask how you are. You look like hell."

Startled, Hunter stiffened and looked up. She felt the heat of temper dance along her skin as she cast a glance up at Matt and bit back an automatic retort. He was probably right. "Then I look as good as I feel," she said finally, directing a scowl in his direction before leaning back into her chair. Closing her eyes, she wondered if she could get away with killing a business partner. *Probably not.*

Matt gave a shrug and walked around the table, looking at the documents displayed on the walls. Photographs, computer printouts, newspaper articles.

"You've been busy," he said, clearly astounded at the amount of information which had been gathered in such a short period of time.

"Quito did an amazing job."

Matt nodded. "But why are you all alone? I thought you had help."

"Hmm…I did…I do. I believe the last time I saw them, they were going to make a fresh pot of coffee."

"Not wired enough?" he asked with a grin. He then indicated the files on the table. "How's this coming?"

"I don't know," Hunter responded, frustration evident in her voice. "There's something here I'm not seeing." She paused and looked around the conference room. "Mostly, I'm not seeing how all of this connects with anything that happened ten years ago. I know it has to, because there's no other rational explanation for him to have known to call me daddy's girl. But—"

"You're not going to be able to figure it out until you get some rest." Matt regarded Hunter silently. "Tell me truthfully. Have you slept at all?"

"A couple of hours. Sort of." She shrugged and worked to keep her expression nonchalant. "I tried for more, but I couldn't find a way to shut down."

"Hunter—"

"I'm all right." She sat up a little straighter and tightened her fingers on the edge of the table. "Don't pick a fight with me, Matt. Not today."

It should have worked. Matt should have known, from the set of her jaw and the edge in her voice, not to push. And for an instant, she almost believed he would leave her alone as he walked toward the wall and stared at the documents neatly pinned there. But then—

"Is it everything in general or is there something in particular that's not letting you shut down?"

Isn't having a serial killer targeting me enough? Hunter pinched the bridge of her nose, trying to ward off a headache. "I can't stop thinking he killed those women because of me…because he couldn't get to me. And he couldn't get to me because I ran away to London."

"C'mon, Hunter, lighten up and give yourself a break," Matt said gently. "If you weren't so tired, you would know responsibility for the deaths of those five women lies squarely with the man who pulled the trigger. No one else is to blame. But you're not ready to accept that. Not until you get your ass home and get some sleep."

But Hunter was no longer paying attention to him. Instead, she sat in front of the laptop, her gaze glued to the monitor. Her fingers flew over the keyboard as she opened and scrolled through a series of new e-mails.

"Hunter?"

"Oh, shit," she whispered.

She heard Matt walk up behind her as she continued to softly swear. Felt him peer over her shoulder at the documents she had called up on the split screen, and knew that, at a bare minimum, he would recognize them as the medical examiner's reports David had sent her. But he wouldn't understand what had caused her reaction.

And there was no question it had shaken her. Her mouth was slightly open and she could hear her own shaky breaths as she struggled to inhale under the weight of emotion that had her in its grasp.

"Hunter? What is it?"

She couldn't answer. She had stopped listening, stopped scrolling, and as she stared at the documents on the screen, she began to shake, but could do nothing to control it. No more than she could stop the voice, whispering incessantly in her ear.

Tell me, Hunter, what's it worth to you?

Matt reached around her and closed the laptop, then grasped Hunter's wrists. He held them tightly as he turned her chair, forcing her to face him. Feeling his gaze on her face, she squeezed her eyes shut, trying to stop the tears that pooled in their depths and threatened to fall. She knew that in itself would stun him. Especially since he was one of the few people who would know she hadn't cried since the day her father died.

"Hunter? Damn it, talk to me. What's in the ME's reports?"

"It's been here all along. How could I have missed this?" She hated that her voice was shaky and fought to regain control.

"What the hell do you think you missed?"

"The connection...the connection to daddy's girl. He didn't pull the trigger, Matt. They did. That's what was missing—what was in the ME's reports. All of his victims shot themselves. That's the damned connection between then and what's happening now." Hunter reached for the phone on the conference table and hit an extension. "Tessa? How quickly do you think we can pull some strings?"

Chapter Eleven

Late morning sunlight dappled the room, but as far as Sara was concerned, getting out of bed was proving to be a challenge.

Still groggy from too many time zones and too little solid sleep, she groaned as she pushed back the covers to get up. Stumbling into the bathroom, she grabbed a toothbrush and squeezed out some toothpaste and then turned on the water and stepped into the shower. But the cool spray did nothing to dispel her desire to go back to bed. Nor did the scent of coffee a short while later, which preceded a soft knock on the bathroom door.

"Good morning, sunshine. I didn't hear you come in last night, so I'll assume you got in late. I checked in on you when I got up, but you were really out of it."

Kate Montgomery stood in the doorway, warm dark brown eyes smiling as she held a heavenly scented mug. The trauma surgeon looked lean and athletic, dressed in khaki cargo shorts and a white T-shirt. Her auburn hair fell in a carelessly casual style and framed an attractive face that reflected her keen intellect.

"I've brought you some coffee."

"You're a goddess among women, Kate. Thanks," Sara said as she shut off the water, wrapped herself in an oversized towel, and knotted it just above her breasts. "Shouldn't you be at the hospital saving lives?"

"I'm not scheduled to work until this afternoon." Kate's welcoming smile froze as she got a closer look at Sara. "Jesus, Sara, what's going on? For someone who just got out of bed, you look all done in." As she pulled her closer and pushed blond hair back from Sara's forehead, Kate's brow creased. "When was the last time you had a physical?"

"Good Lord, Kate, I'm fine. I certainly don't need a physical, so stop playing doctor. I'm just overtired," Sara said. She moved out of Kate's reach, picked up the coffee mug, and sipped the strong brew. "Damn, you make good coffee. Rest assured I'm not coming down with anything. I just didn't get in until almost two this morning and I was so wired I had a hard time falling asleep. So instead, I spent some time reviewing case files and making notes."

Kate continued to study Sara's face, gazing silently a little longer. It was quickly apparent she sensed something was amiss but wasn't certain what she was reading. "What else? Tell me what's happened."

"Nothing's happened," Sara answered, her response coming out more sharply than she intended. *Not unless you count being knocked on your ass by the most gorgeous woman you've ever met,* she thought wryly and then wondered why she was prevaricating. She and Kate had been friends since their student days at Stanford, and Kate's ability to see right through her no longer came as a surprise.

"Uh-huh." Watching Sara dry her hair, Kate leaned back against the doorframe. "Try again. Tell me what's going on."

"It's nothing, really." Sara sighed before continuing in a quiet tone. "If you must know, I've been thinking about someone I just met. I can't seem to stop, and I have absolutely no idea what, if anything, I'm going to do about it."

"Well, I'd say only a woman could put that look on your face, and you've got to know if that's the case, I think it's great." Kate grinned broadly. "You need a life. And if she's local and will keep you in San Francisco instead of going back east, so much the better."

Kate continued to probe. "Tell me about her. Where did you meet and when are you seeing her again? Better still, when do I get to meet her? You know, to make sure she's good enough for my best friend. I assume she's hot."

"Hot?" Sara closed her eyes and flashed to an image of Hunter. *No, not hot. More like sizzling.* She sighed softly as she considered the implications of her attraction to Hunter. Lectured herself on the futility of her interest, not the least of which was Hunter Roswell was absolutely off-limits. "Yeah, she's hot, but it's not like that."

Opening her eyes, she tilted her head and glanced at Kate. For as long as they'd known each other, Kate had been her confidante. Even when they had been on opposite coasts—Sara in New York and Kate in San Francisco—it had always been Kate she had called. And day or night, whether she needed a sounding board about a case that was frustrating her or to commiserate about a relationship that had run its course, Kate had always been there for her, listening and providing sage advice.

But sometimes talking, even with an old friend, wasn't easy. What could she say? The physical attraction was easy to explain. But Hunter had also gotten under her skin. *You're a fool, Wilder. There's not a chance in hell.*

"What's going on?" Kate asked gently.

"It's complicated."

"Isn't it always?" Kate laughed. "Want to talk about it?"

"Isn't that supposed to be my line?" Sara quipped. "If you must know, she's someone I met through this case David Granger asked me to consult on."

Kate had always been easy to read. In that instant, her expression became one of guarded concern. "The serial killer case? Is that going to be a problem?"

Sara thought carefully before replying. "No. At least I don't think so." She hesitated as she met Kate's steady gaze. "It's not about professional boundaries or ethics. I mean, we don't have a doctor-patient relationship, and it's not like she's a suspect."

"Then what do you have?"

Sara shrugged. "I'm not sure. She's directly involved in the case. Actually, all the evidence would seem to indicate the serial killer is stalking her, and the FBI has determined it's someone from her past. David wants me to help her identify him so he can be stopped."

"Does helping her put you in any kind of danger?" Kate regarded her steadily.

Sara knew the risks inherent in her job when she had been with the FBI had always been of concern to Kate and quickly shook her head. "Danger?" she said. "Only of being foolish."

Still she hesitated.

How did she explain that she found herself inexorably drawn to Hunter? That the combination of intelligence, strength, and vulnerability added layers to the attraction? And if she was being honest, that Hunter was drop-dead gorgeous and stirred in her a surge of pure, unadulterated lust?

How did she explain that, in so many ways, Hunter Roswell seemed to represent everything she ever wanted in a woman, and everything she feared? That she knew, on an intuitive level, Hunter could leave her aching with just one look but also had the power to leave her heart shattered and bleeding if she wasn't careful?

She wondered when the last time was she'd been this attracted to someone and realized she couldn't remember the last time she had even been on a date.

"Sara? What is it, hon?"

Sara caught Kate's reflection in the mirror, saw the concern in her eyes and shrugged. "This is going to sound cliché, but she's not like anyone I've ever met. I barely know her, but somehow she's managed to stir all these feelings in me. And I know it's probably just a silly infatuation, but I swear I felt something the moment I saw her…as if we had some kind of connection."

"No one you've previously met was able to hold your interest for very long," Kate reminded her. "While there may be things about this woman that complicate your life, I'm going to go out on a limb and suggest that's not necessarily a bad thing. In fact, I think you should stop overanalyzing and just go for it. Just remember I'm always here for you, okay?"

"Thank you," Sara responded, closing her eyes. A brief smile crossed her face. "How about I get dressed and then join you downstairs for more coffee?"

It didn't take long for Sara to get dressed, and a few minutes later, she followed the scent of freshly brewing coffee into the kitchen. There she discovered a rumpled and tired-looking FBI agent sitting at the table with Kate.

"Special Agent Granger, is this going to become a habit?" Sara teased.

David rubbed his face with both hands. "Sorry," he said. Examining her with tired brown eyes, he shook his head and grinned. "I know you didn't manage to get much more sleep than I did. How the hell do you manage to look so good?"

"Good genes." Sara laughed. "But compliments from David Granger? You must really want something."

"Actually, I'm here because I can answer the question everyone was asking only a few hours ago. But yes, it also means I need your help again. That's why I come bearing gifts." As evidence, he held out a bag of bagels.

"Smart man." Sara flashed him a smile and grabbed a still-warm bagel from the bag, nibbling on it while Kate brought the coffeepot to the table and refilled Sara's mug. "So, what's this question you can answer?"

"Where our runaway genius went after she disappeared from the airport in the wee hours of the morning," David responded triumphantly. "It would seem our girl has been very busy."

"What makes you say that?"

In response, David produced a copy of the *Chronicle* and placed it on the table. As he indicated a photograph above the fold with a tap of his finger, a quick glance confirmed what Sara already suspected.

The photograph was a candid shot of three remarkably beautiful women at a trendy club. The dark-haired woman on the left was identified in the caption as Tessa Kinser while the exotic Versace model on the right was further identified only as Rafaela. Both stood with their arms draped around the beautiful woman who had haunted what little sleep Sara had managed to get. Hunter Roswell stared up at her, a sexy half-smile on her face.

"Shit," Sara exclaimed. At the same time, she heard Kate's sharply drawn breath and glanced in her direction.

Kate's face was impassive, and Sara briefly wondered if she had simply reacted to a newspaper photograph of her lover, obviously enjoying herself with two beautiful women. The other possibility, which she was now forced to consider, was Kate had reacted to *who* was with Tessa.

She stared at Hunter's image, at the smile that could melt the hearts of women from eighteen to eighty, and considered that Kate had been dating Tessa for several months, ostensibly while Hunter was in England. Wasn't it still possible she knew Hunter as well?

And what does that mean?

Pushing that thought aside for the moment, Sara tried to concentrate on what the photograph meant for their case. That was where her focus needed to be. On the case. "Someone worked awfully hard to get that photo into today's edition, don't you think? It's a dangerous move."

"Exactly," David responded. "It's as if she's trying to wave a red flag in front of the UNSUB to let him know she's back. But we don't know how or when he'll respond. In part, that's why I need you to come with me."

"Oh? Do tell. Where are we going this time? And please, tell me we don't need to fly anywhere," Sara whined good-naturedly.

"I can assure you we won't need a plane for where we're going, because we're going to San Quentin."

Sara's eyes widened. "Whatever for?"

"As I said, our girl's been busy. I'm not sure how many strings they had to pull, but Tessa Kinser arranged for Hunter to meet with Kyle Brenner this afternoon. And between the two of them, they've somehow managed to bypass the time it typically takes to get a visit approved. In fact, I'm told they got everything arranged in less than an hour."

Sara looked up in undisguised surprise. "It's called connections. But Kyle Brenner? Isn't he—"

"The man who kidnapped Hunter ten years ago. He was charged, tried, and convicted in the deaths of Michael Roswell and Special Agent Robert Simms," David finished for her. "He's been sitting on death row since his sentencing while his case goes through the appeals process. I understand that until today he's had no visitors, with the exception of his lawyers."

"And Brenner agreed to meet with Hunter?"

David scowled. "I'm told he couldn't agree to the meeting quickly enough."

"How did you find out?"

"I've had someone keeping an eye on Brenner ever since Hunter's name first came up in our investigation," David admitted. "With the reference to daddy's girl and the probability the current murders are somehow connected to what happened ten years ago, I thought there was a very real chance this might happen. That someone would want or need to see Brenner."

"I don't know, David," Sara rubbed her temple as it began to throb. "I'm concerned about how Hunter will deal with actually seeing Brenner. I don't think people realize just how emotionally fragile she is. I also don't believe she's ever reconciled herself with what happened back then."

David shrugged. "That may be the case, but there's not much you or I can do to stop this. All we can really do is be there to pick up the pieces if things go south." He glanced at his watch. "And that means you've got to get ready if we want to actually get there before Hunter."

Sara glanced down at her casual attire and smiled. "I guess that means you want me to change into something a little more appropriate." Without waiting for David to respond, she turned and headed upstairs, aware that Kate was trailing her.

"Hunter Roswell?" Kate asked incredulously as soon as they stepped into the guest bedroom Sara was using. "Hunter Roswell is the woman you were talking about earlier, isn't she?"

"Yes," Sara admitted reluctantly.

"Honey, that's not a minor complication we're talking about. Hunter Roswell's in a league of her own where complications are concerned. And for the record, she's as hot as you can get."

"I know." Sara exhaled softly. "It occurred to me you might know her, considering you've been dating Tessa and she just happens to be Hunter's closest friend."

"I can see how you might think that, but I actually met Hunter first." There was a slight hesitation before Kate continued. "It was Hunter who introduced me to Tessa rather than the other way around."

Sara quietly processed that piece of information while pulling clothes out of the closet. "How long have you known her?" she asked, managing to keep her tone even and curious. But she knew exactly what kind of woman Kate found attractive, and Hunter Roswell more than filled all of Kate's requirements.

"About five years." Kate watched while Sara dropped the shorts and T-shirt she had been wearing onto the bed and changed into a conservative dark suit and a pale-blue silk blouse. "I met her just after I finished my fellowship and started on staff in the trauma center. We were both involved in a fundraiser for the children's health center at the hospital."

Kate reluctantly admitted she had felt both challenged and more than a little embarrassed that Hunter turned her down late one evening when she suggested they go somewhere a little more private for a drink.

Sara raised an eyebrow and sent Kate a long, contemplative look.

"What do you want me to say?" As Kate reacted to the look, her voice took on a slightly defensive tone. "Everyone was trying to get close to her. And why not? She was rich, successful, more intelligent than any one person had a right to be, and she had a reputation for being adventurous—in and out of bed. It also didn't hurt that she was goddamned gorgeous." Kate continued, the defensiveness gone, a wry note in its place. "I had just completed six grueling years of surgical residency and suddenly found myself face-to-face with a woman who encompassed all the complexity and intensity I thrived on. I was cocky and full of myself, and when I met her, I honestly believed Hunter was meant to be my reward for all the years of hard work. I wanted her like I had never wanted anyone else before."

Sara wasn't certain she wanted to hear the rest and tried to smother the unexpected bolt of jealously that lanced through her. It didn't make her feel particularly happy, and she wasn't prepared to question the reasons, but one thing was abundantly clear. She didn't want to even think of the possibility Hunter and Kate had been lovers.

Still, she forced herself to ask. "What happened?"

Kate laughed and looked a little self-conscious as she shook her head. "I was relentless in my pursuit, and Hunter was exquisitely gentle in suggesting we would make better friends than lovers. Who knew she would be right?"

Sara closed her eyes as a tremulous wave of relief coursed through her. She was aware Kate was still watching her and felt her concern when she reached out tentatively and put a hand on her shoulder.

"Sara?"

Opening her eyes, Sara glanced at Kate. "Hmm?"

"Just be careful, okay? Hunter's been running from something for a long time, and until she stops, she's not going to be able to let anyone get too close. That makes her heartbreak territory."

Sara's smile faded slightly. "I'll try to keep that in mind."

Kate nodded. "Are we going to be okay with all of this?"

"Of course," Sara said softly.

Chapter Twelve

For an early weekday afternoon, traffic proved surprisingly heavy. Sara watched as David tried not to lose his patience when they were forced to remain behind a truck intent on driving well below the speed limit. But in spite of his best efforts to make up time, they arrived half an hour later than intended.

Their destination, San Quentin, was the oldest prison in the state. Overlooking the bay just north of San Francisco, it was home to California's only death row chamber, housing all of the state's male death row inmates among the over five thousand inmates residing within its historic walls. It was also the only home Kyle Brenner had known since his conviction nine years earlier.

Clearly visible from the San Rafael Bridge, from the outside the prison looked like any aging building. The bricks were faded and worn, the metal trimmings old and rusty. But as Sara and David drew closer, there was no mistaking this was no ordinary building. The sight of the looming, fortresslike walls and the grim series of sally ports and security gates sent an involuntary shiver down Sara's back, as if an icy hand had touched her.

The guard at the first gate verified their identification, pointed the way, and directed them to the main visiting area. The gates closing behind them gave an echoing clang as they moved to the next security gate. There, another guard sitting in a booth rechecked their paperwork, then buzzed the door open. Glass and metal slid heavily and they went through.

At the next clearance checkpoint, the man that met them greeted David by name. David quickly introduced Sara to John Rayburn, who provided an update as he escorted them through a labyrinth of dim cement passageways to a small room.

"The show's about to begin so you're just in time. The guards are on their way down, escorting Brenner to the visiting room," Rayburn stated. "You know, I don't know how the hell Roswell managed it, but she actually arranged a private contact visit."

Sara spun around in disbelief. A contact visit wouldn't offer Hunter even the illusion of protection. There would be no Plexiglas partition separating her from Brenner. They would not be communicating over a telephone. Instead, she would be sitting at a table across from Brenner, meeting with him face-to-face.

"For God's sake, David. Tell me this is some kind of joke," she snapped in frustration. "You're not going to let her meet Brenner like that, are you?"

"She's Patrick Roswell's only grandchild. That carries a lot of political clout, so it's not like we have any choice in this," he responded.

"If it makes you feel any better, Brenner will be fully shackled," Rayburn added, "and there will be guards posted outside the room who can intervene at a moment's notice in case the situation starts to tank. Best we can do under the circumstances, because the set-up wasn't our choice. It's what we were asked to provide."

Sara opened her mouth to protest but could form no words. It wasn't the risk of Brenner inflicting physical injury that concerned Sara. She worried about the psychological impact on Hunter of meeting her old nemesis face-to-face. But it wasn't something she was prepared to discuss with David or Rayburn, so she nodded, slipping into her own façade of control.

Rayburn pointed to the video monitors lined up along one wall in the room and handed Sara a headset that had been lying on the table. "The room where Roswell is meeting Brenner is wired for sound and there are video cameras set up. We should be able to see and hear everything."

The monitors displayed a bleak gray room where every other hue seemed to have bled away. As Sara adjusted the headphones, the screen in front of her suddenly came to life, and a muscular man wearing prison blues shuffled into view. His wrists were handcuffed and attached to a belly chain, and his ankles were shackled. Flanked by four guards, he was pushed unceremoniously into a chair.

"Just remember we're watching you," one of the guards said before they left and assumed their positions outside the room.

Kyle Brenner sat at the table with a bored expression on his craggy, once-handsome face as he looked around. His complexion was prison pale, and he was sporting a series of tattoos spreading from under his shirt collar up his neck. When his eyes settled on the camera, his body stiffened before a cruel smile flashed briefly on his face and he sat back to wait.

A few minutes later, Hunter appeared, escorted by a guard. Instead of her customary casual style, she was dressed monochromatically in a charcoal-gray silk suit, the blue of her eyes providing the only points of color. She looked, in a word, dangerous.

Sara saw the guard whisper something to her before leaving. But Hunter didn't react to whatever he said. Nor did she move farther into the room. Instead, she remained standing by the door, casually assessing the room before finally turning and staring at Brenner. He stared back and a long silence ensued.

To no one's surprise, it was Brenner who broke the silence first.

"Well, well, Hunter. You were a knockout at seventeen, but mm-hmm, I had no idea. You look so fine, babe." As he spoke, he stared insolently at her, but Hunter gave no indication that she noticed, even as his eyes seemed to take in every visible inch of her. "Since you're so good at pulling strings and calling in favors, perhaps next time you could arrange for us to have a conjugal visit."

"What?" Hunter's low voice drawled. "Are you telling me the prison doctors have been able to fix your little problem?"

On the video monitor, Brenner's shoulders stiffened perceptibly and his face grew dark and taut. Behind Sara, David said, "Ouch," and Rayburn snickered.

Hunter paused and let out a humorless laugh. "What's the matter? Did I hit a nerve?"

"Don't make me laugh, Hunter. I don't have nerves." He smiled at her and seemed so calm that Sara was instantly on alert.

"I thought it was a conscience you didn't have," Hunter countered. "Or was that a heart?"

Brenner's eyes narrowed, and in Sara's estimation, appeared to reappraise the woman in front of him. "You asked for this meeting, babe. You obviously want something from me, so it's best you remember how this works and play nice."

Brenner's tone sounded threatening. But Hunter's reaction gave Sara no indication she felt any fear. Instead, she simply sighed and sank into the chair across the table from him, her expression neutral.

"You're right," she said. She leaned heavily on her arms, her eyes shadowed. "I do want to talk to you. About what happened ten years ago."

"Our time together? That sure was a fun time, wasn't it?" Brenner's face broke into a leering smile. "I knew we made a connection back then. Just like I knew you couldn't stay away from me forever. It was just a matter of time before you came to see me." Brenner laughed softly. "Do you still dream about me? Do you miss my special touch?"

Sara grew increasingly uncomfortable with the direction the conversation was taking. "David," she said hesitantly. "Brenner held her for what…three weeks? At that time, was there any indication he—?"

David stared at Brenner's image on the monitor. "Physically abused her? Yes, because it was obvious from her injuries. Psychologically abused her? Again, there was no doubt. We might not have known what that bastard did to her, but the kid was so damned messed up it was virtually impossible to get a coherent statement from her. Sexually abused her? That what you're asking?" David shook his head. "She claimed not to remember anything."

"You didn't believe her?"

"There's more to it than that. One of the residents at the hospital implied there were signs of what he would only describe as torture. And the shrink who ended up treating her suggested she might be suffering from some kind of dissociative amnesia." David shrugged. "But she didn't rule out the possibility that Hunter's lack of recall might have been caused by physical trauma."

"Was there evidence of a head injury?" Sara asked.

"No one was volunteering to share the details of her medical records with us. We could only go by how things looked," David answered bluntly. "And in that regard, her own mother must have had a hard time recognizing her for all the bruises and bandages."

He paused as if trying to recollect long-ago details. "We picked up bits and pieces, mostly gossip from the EMTs and nurses. In terms of a head injury, she had a pretty severe concussion, and there was some kind of facial fracture. Anything else would be pure conjecture."

"How come?"

"By the time she came out of surgery, her father's family had closed ranks around her," David responded. "They weren't sharing information with us, and Patrick Roswell carried too much political clout for anyone to go up against him. Afterward, not a lot was made public during the trial."

Sara jotted some notes while maintaining a vigilant eye on the monitor where Kyle Brenner could be seen leaning back in his chair. It seemed as if he was trying to reconcile the adult version of Hunter sitting across from him with the teenager he had kidnapped. She wondered if Hunter was scared. She wondered if Hunter suspected Sara was watching.

"You want to talk about old times, go right ahead," Brenner said. "I ain't got nowhere to go, and you're better looking than anything I've seen in a long time."

They stared at each other like two gunslingers waiting to see who would draw first. The silence went on interminably, before Hunter lifted a dark eyebrow. "Just like that?"

Brenner nodded. "Sure, babe. Why not? What have I got to lose? And if I help you, maybe you get Granddaddy to put in a good word with the governor."

Taking a deep breath, Hunter crossed her arms to hide the fact that her hands were shaking. She wondered who was watching them. She wondered if Sara was there, if she could see her hands tremble. That Brenner could still elicit a fear response in her was enough to ignite her temper, and when she spoke, her voice held a discernible edge of anger.

"All right. Ten years ago, there were five of you in the house with me. Geddrick, Watters, Johnson, and McSwain never made it out," she stated. "Only you got out alive."

"You too, babe," Brenner corrected. "Let's not forget you got out alive."

"And me," Hunter acknowledged, her voice soft. "Who else would know what happened in that house?"

Whatever motive Brenner had attributed to Hunter's sudden desire to see him, this obviously wasn't according to his game plan. Her question had caught him by surprise. His eyes narrowed and he sat up straighter. "What do you mean?"

"I mean"—Hunter leaned forward, paused to push back the hair falling in her eyes—"six people knew what went on inside that house. Four never made it out alive, leaving just you and me." She stared at Brenner intently and her voice became softer still. "I need to know if there is anyone else who would know what happened in that house during those three weeks. I need to know who you told."

Brenner stared at Hunter, his expression unchanging. And then he began to laugh, leaving little doubt he was enjoying the moment. "Aw, is someone messing with your head, babe? C'mon, tell Kyle all about it. It'll be just like old times."

Hunter leaned across the table toward Brenner and didn't bother to mute the anger in her voice. "Just answer the damned question."

Brenner stopped laughing abruptly and stared back at Hunter. "They've really gotten to you, haven't they. How much do they know?"

"Enough," she answered starkly. "Maybe too much."

Brenner leaned closer, obviously aware if he moved too far, got too close, the guards would come in and end the visit. An outcome he was obviously not prepared to accept just yet. "What's my answer worth to you, Hunter?" he whispered.

Hunter froze.

She made a small, choked sound deep in her throat that spoke of anger and fear and grief.

Why have you brought me home...Damn it, why won't you tell me what's going on...Well, look what we've found...I do believe it's daddy's little girl and she's all alone...What's it worth to you, Hunter...Hold your fire...Hold your fire...He's down...They're both down...We're losing him...

And through sheer strength of will, Hunter pulled herself together.

What's it worth to you, Hunter...

She took a deep shuddering breath to steady herself and used it to help stay in the moment.

What's it worth to you, Hunter...

Fear abated and anger took its place. This was the man who had killed her father. This was the man who had left her mother devastated and barely able to cope for far too long. This was the man who had left her with her psyche shattered and driven her to the edge of self-destruction. She felt her temper flare, and as she used it to gather strength, she mimicked Brenner's pose. Leaning in toward him. Bringing their heads so close she could feel his breath, hot and fetid against her skin.

"Fuck you, Brenner," she hissed.

Kyle Brenner sat back, a startled expression on his face combined with something else. And then he threw his head back and gave a sharp laugh. "Got your fight back, haven't you, babe."

"You have no idea." Her voice dropped to a low growl.

Brenner's eyes glinted, and then surprisingly, he nodded his head. "Okay. I'll give you this one. You might even say maybe I owe you something—for old times," he said. "The answer is no. No one else would know what went on. Not even my goddamned lawyers knew. If someone's playing games with you, I sure as hell didn't give them the ammunition, 'cause I told no one."

❖

As she watched the interchange play out, Sara frowned. "Damn it," she said. "She knows more than she's told us." She turned to look at David, her eyebrows raised in question. "Do you have any idea what they're talking about?"

But David shook his head.

Had Hunter figured out the connection between what had happened to her ten years earlier and the man who was presently stalking her? Everything Sara had just witnessed would seem to indicate she had, but if that was the case, how quickly could they use the connection to identify the UNSUB? She felt like a voyeur as she continued to watch Brenner inch close to Hunter once again.

"Listen, babe. I got something you need to know."

Intense blue eyes glinted preternaturally as Hunter looked at Brenner. "Other than the answer to my question, what could you know that would possibly be of interest to me?"

When Brenner glanced briefly at the video camera, Sara felt a red flag go up. *What the hell is he up to?* Fascinated, she watched Brenner lean closer still.

"Don't you want to know why, Hunter? Why I never killed you like I said I was going to?" he asked as his voice dropped to a whisper.

Sara could not hear everything he was saying. But Hunter's reaction told her all she needed to know. Her face became impossibly pale, and there were waves of white-hot pain emanating from her. She stood up abruptly, sending her chair crashing to the floor.

"Get her out of there, David," Sara cried out.

She continued to watch, horrified, as Hunter leaned across the table toward Brenner, her mouth pressed close to the inmate's ear, and she whispered something.

Brenner's face immediately hardened. Clearly enraged, he tried to raise his hands in an attempt to grab Hunter's arm. The chain linking his handcuffs to the belly chain he wore prevented the move and stopped him abruptly. *"Goddamnsonofabitch—"*

Sara could hear Rayburn on the phone issuing instructions, and in a matter of seconds, the guards who had been stationed outside the visiting room quickly entered and roughly pulled Brenner away. Holding him between them, they began to drag him out of the room.

Too late, Brenner realized his time had run out, and he looked over his shoulder at Hunter.

"You'll come back to visit me, babe. You know you'll need to come back to see me, and I'll be right here waiting for you," he shouted, before he disappeared from view as the door closed.

❖

Hunter moved quickly. Endeavoring to outrun the memories that held her ensnared, she exited the oppressive building by the shortest route, making her way back to the parking lot while trying to avoid looking like she was running away. She reached her car and blindly keyed the remote, intent on escaping.

And just what are you trying to escape, the pragmatist asked. *This oppressive and depressing place? The past is done and can't be changed. The future has yet to be determined. So what are you running from?*

"Hunter, wait—"

The soft voice calling out her name compelled her to stop the incessant debate before she could formulate an answer. Almost grateful, she turned and saw Sara approaching her. She paused, her eyes narrowing as the realization hit that she was happy to see her. With a shrug, she moved away from her car and walked toward Sara, aware she was being openly and rather intently scrutinized.

"Why am I not surprised to see you here?" Hunter's voice trailed into silence and she stuck her hands in her pockets. She drew closer as she spoke, slowing down until they stood only a few feet apart. It was then she noted David was there as well, approaching from the left. The smile that had been playing on her lips faded and revealed her disappointment.

"Since I'm pretty sure we agreed to work together, I thought I'd check and see how you're doing."

Hunter stiffened and every muscle in her body tensed. It was taking everything she had just to keep her emotions in check, and she felt a sudden flash of concern that the walls she had spent years erecting were in danger of breaking apart. Her heart was hammering, and she found herself vacillating between digging in for yet another battle and total surrender.

Sara stared at her in silence, a focused look in her eyes as if reading her mind. "Have you ever thought of sleeping? You look like hell, Roswell."

Unexpectedly, Hunter laughed and discovered laughter released some of the tightly wound tension. "I get the feeling having you around will not be very good for my ego," she said.

Sara looked at her for an instant, a faint smile on her lips. "Somehow, I don't think your ego needs any help from me," she responded dryly, but her eyes softened as they met Hunter's gaze. Moving closer, Sara touched Hunter's cheek, tracing the slashing cheekbone and the shadows under her eyes with her thumb. "How about we get out of here and you tell me what that conversation with Kyle Brenner was all about?"

Hunter swallowed and tried to formulate an appropriate response. But before she could put voice to her clouded thoughts, the ground beneath their feet shook with a powerful tremor.

She saw a brilliant flash of light and felt an intense blast of heat as the force of the explosion hit them. Dimly, she realized she was airborne. The blast knocked her off her feet and then slammed her to the ground. Head pounding and ears ringing, she felt her breath driven from her lungs, and for the longest time, drawing in any air to breathe was a physical impossibility.

Something sharp glanced off her temple, something hot struck her shoulder, and she could feel bits of glass and metal showering down all around them. As more debris landed, in a move driven more by instinct than thought, Hunter threw herself protectively over Sara and then covered her own head with her arms.

She remained motionless until she was reasonably certain the debris had stopped falling. Only then did she raise her head. Ignoring the stinging pain in her shoulder, she glanced around and slowly became aware that beneath her, Sara was deathly still. Her eyes were closed, her face pale.

"Sara?" she whispered. "Please answer me."

There was no response, and Hunter felt an irrational flash of fear. With unsteady fingers, she shifted to check for a pulse. Relief coursed through her as she found one, the heart beneath her fingers beating clear and strong, and she dropped her head until her forehead was pressed against Sara's.

As she took several deep breaths and considered her options, she heard someone talking but couldn't make out what they were saying. The voice seemed to be coming from a distance, but she wasn't sure if that was a result of the impact of her head against the asphalt or because the echo of the explosion was still resonating in her ears.

Something wet and warm trickled down her face. Irritated, she brushed it aside only to find blood painting her fingers when she brought them away from her face. Pain was also seeping through. With her lungs still struggling to pull in some much-needed oxygen, she attempted to lift her body off Sara, whose eyelids were beginning to flutter. She saw Peter approaching, weapon drawn as he tried to assess for any additional threat. And by this time, David was also upon them.

Peter quickly knelt down beside her and put a hand on her shoulder.

"Take it easy, Hunter. You're bleeding," he said. "You probably don't want to move until—"

"I'm okay." She managed to focus and winced as she made it to her knees, breathing haltingly. "Shit," she gasped, holding her head with both hands. She closed her eyes against a wave of pain as she tried to ride it out.

Sara lay on the ground a minute longer, peering up at Hunter in confusion. Pushing up onto her elbows, she looked beyond Hunter and Peter to the flames that consumed what had once been a black Maserati. "Your car," she said.

Hunter nodded and then winced as the motion caused the throbbing in her head to intensify. She could see emergency personnel doing what they could to contain the fire and could hear the sound of several vehicles pulling up and stopping, brakes squealing and voices shouting as fire and rescue took over the scene and paramedics began to assess the damage.

Sara's eyes followed the activity before she turned back and looked at Hunter. "Are you all right?"

"I've been better. You do this often?"

"What, get blown up?" Sara grinned weakly and opened her mouth to say something else. But another explosion, this one feeling almost as strong as the first, sent a shockwave that drove her head into the pavement. She gave a small sigh as her eyes closed.

Chapter Thirteen

S ara fought her way up through several layers of disjointed images and finally opened her eyes. She felt groggy and disoriented, but she knew instantly where she was. The scent of antiseptic and the IV dripping slowly into her arm made that much readily apparent. She also remembered why she was there—the sound of the explosion and the smell of smoke had stayed with her.

What she couldn't automatically determine was the nature and extent of her injuries. All she knew for certain was her entire body ached, and her head throbbed.

Gradually she became aware someone else was in the room. She turned her head toward the sound, but when she tried to speak, her mouth was too dry and the words became trapped in her throat. Gritting her teeth, she tried to move but was stopped by the pain and found herself unable to hold back the groan that worked its way up from deep inside her.

Almost immediately, a familiar face came into view as Kate leaned forward and placed a featherlight kiss on Sara's brow. When Kate straightened, she smiled and lightly brushed Sara's hair off her face.

"Welcome back, sweetie."

"Thanks, I think," Sara said hoarsely. She tried to push herself up and groaned before sinking back onto the bed. "How long was I out?"

"Keep still," Kate instructed as she pressed the button on the control panel which raised the top of the bed. "You haven't been unconscious the whole time. You actually came around a couple of times. Once in the ER when they brought you in, then again when they took you down to X-ray. Don't you remember?"

Her brows furrowed in concentration, and Sara realized she had lost all sense of time. "I don't remember," she said. "Is it still Wednesday?"

"Yes, and Luke Skywalker is still the president," Kate said with a grin.

"Smart-ass."

Kate fussed and adjusted the pillow for her. "You got off lucky. I thought you told me you weren't in any danger?"

"I wasn't...I'm not," Sara quickly replied. "I think I was unintended collateral damage. Just happened to be standing too close to the car when it blew up, I guess."

Kate looked down at Sara and brushed her fingers across her cheek. "I couldn't believe my eyes when I saw you being wheeled into the ER on a gurney," she said, looking visibly shaken. "You scared several years of life out of me."

"Sorry about that. Really I am, but it couldn't be helped," Sara said so dryly Kate's lips twitched. She shifted slightly, reaching out and squeezing Kate's hand. "So what's the prognosis, Dr. Montgomery? Will I live?"

Kate smiled weakly in response. "The worst of it is a mild concussion. But you do have an interesting assortment of colorful bruises. You're going to be sore as hell for a few days, but that's as bad as it gets."

"Good to know." Sara started to laugh. An instant later, she froze and her heart began hammering painfully in her chest, causing one of the monitors to beep.

"What is it?" Kate asked. "What's wrong?"

"Shit. Kate, what about Hunter? We were talking in the parking lot when her car exploded, and I'm pretty sure she was hurt. She was bleeding—I remember seeing blood on her face and neck. Where is she? Do you know if she's okay?"

"Is Hunter okay?" Kate smiled, moved slightly to her right, and indicated with a sweep of her hand. "You tell me."

As Sara slowly turned her head to the side, she could see a body sprawled in a chair next to the bed. Hunter looked slightly singed, her face still smudged with soot and ash. There was some bruising evident on her right arm, along with a nasty scrape that looked to be seeping blood, and there was a neat white bandage on her forehead. Somewhere along the way, she had also exchanged her torn and burned silk suit for dark blue surgical scrubs.

But she was still the most beautiful sight Sara had seen in a long time. And the almost fierce sense of protection Hunter inspired no longer surprised her.

"Is she actually sleeping?" she whispered.

"Closer to unconscious, but yes, she's asleep." Kate lowered her eyes and looked vaguely uncomfortable. "Who would have guessed she could manage to do it without hanging upside down in a cave somewhere."

Sara laughed and immediately grabbed her abdomen and groaned as various aches and pains made their presence known. "Well, if you're trying to tell me she's Batgirl, then that means I flew back from London in the Batplane and I guess that was the Batmobile that blew up." She peered closer at the long body awkwardly folded and deathly still in the high-backed chair. *How the hell can she sleep like that? She can't possibly be comfortable.*

"I don't know about that. All I can tell you is she's been quite a handful to deal with."

"Why is that?"

"When they brought her into the ER with you, she was barely coherent and could hardly stay upright. To top it off, she initially didn't want to let me stitch up the cut on her head or treat the burns on her shoulder, and she flatly refused to let me admit her. Wouldn't listen to a word Tessa had to say either, even though she had to know being admitted would be the best thing for her. Said she would sign whatever papers were necessary and she would leave AMA if that's what she had to do."

It all made perfect sense to Sara, but Kate wouldn't know finding herself in the emergency department at San Francisco General would be enough to send Hunter into a panic. Especially right now, at a time when she was being forced to confront all her memories of the darkest time in her life.

"She hates hospitals, which makes it understandable she would be willing to leave against medical advice." Sara's eyes narrowed. "Tessa was here?"

Kate nodded. "Hunter's bodyguard called her. But she wasn't able to influence Hunter either. Since there was nothing we could do, we simply kept an eye on her until she finally crashed. Which seemed to take forever, I might add." Kate paused and raised a brow, giving Sara a speculative look that made her shift uncomfortably. "She happened to be in here because she wanted to check on you. She made it clear she was going to stay by your side until you woke up. Don't you find that the least bit curious?"

Sara shook her head. "Natural concern," she said, watching as Kate gently lifted Hunter's wrist and checked her pulse. Kate then found an extra blanket and draped it over Hunter's inert body. A short time later, she was paged to trauma admitting. Uttering a quick "Catch you later," she hurried out of the room.

Sara watched her leave and released a long, slow breath. She ran a trembling hand back through her hair and sighed again. Unable to go back to sleep, she lay back, content to watch the steady rise and fall of Hunter's chest as she slept.

Hunter stirred restlessly in the darkness, her body vibrating with tension as the dream began. She whimpered softly and tried to curl up into a protective ball, but the dream still managed to slip past her defenses and left her helplessly caught in its grasp.

She was back where it had all started, locked in a small, dark room.

She had lost all sense of time.

When they first brought her to the room, they had kept a hood over her head, tied tightly around her neck, which prevented her from seeing anything. During that time, her arms had been tightly bound at the wrists, and although she had twisted her hands until her wrists were raw and bleeding, she had been unable to loosen the hood.

No food. No water. They also prevented her from getting any sleep, so she spent the endless hours pacing the room out. Fifteen steps by fourteen steps. Near as she could tell, the room was windowless, cold, and dirty. From the smell, it was probably in a basement, and had only a battered mattress on the floor for furnishing. There was a single wooden door representing the only point of exit, but that was always locked.

By the end of the first day, she knew every nook and cranny, every crack in the walls. She thought endlessly about escape. Of finding a way to get past the locked door. But she was too much of a realist and knew with doomed certainty there was no way out.

With the passage of time, she became tired and cold and hungry. So very hungry. And she hurt everywhere. A whimper tore from her throat, but she would not give in to the scream that desperately sought to escape.

You want food? You want to sleep? Then tell me, what's it worth to you, Hunter?

The disembodied voice coming from the darkness made her stomach clench in fear and anticipation. She hadn't heard him unlock the door. Hadn't heard him come in. How had she missed that?

The first blow, when it came, stunned her. She fell hard to the floor and curled into a fetal position.

I asked you a question.

Rough hands reached for her, held her, hurt her, striking her again and again.

What's it worth to you, Hunter?

Again and again, she tried to crawl away. Again and again, the hands stopped her. Again and again, the voice demanded she answer the question.

What's it worth to you, Hunter?

"Hunter—"

"I don't know." The words were torn from her throat and echoed in the room.

"Hunter, it's just a dream," the soft voice said. "You're safe now."

Hunter awoke with a start, gasping for breath. She felt herself surface as if from a dive, fighting to break through the barrier between dreams and reality, aware her heart was beating fiercely, threatening to explode in her chest.

She blinked several times and ran her tongue slowly over dry lips while she tried to focus burning and gritty eyes. It was still dark, and it took a moment longer before she knew for certain she wasn't in the old house with Brenner. Instead, she was in the private hospital room she had arranged for Sara to be moved into when she had been admitted.

"It was a nightmare, Hunter. It's all right now. Everything is all right."

Dazed, Hunter's eyes tracked to the figure kneeling beside her. Gradually, the face came into focus, until Hunter could clearly see her, her concerned expression readily apparent.

"Sara?"

"Yes. Are you okay?"

"I'm all right." She squeezed the bridge of her nose between her thumb and forefinger and tried to clear her head. As usual, the nightmare had left her with a throbbing headache. "How long was I asleep?"

"Does it really matter?" Sara asked pragmatically. "You obviously needed the sleep, and if you know what's good for you, you'll try to get a few more hours. If it'll help, you might consider asking for something. We are in a hospital, after all."

Reaching out slowly with one hand, she gently encircled Hunter's wrist. Almost immediately, Hunter's body went rigid with tension but Sara didn't release her hold. After a couple of minutes during which neither of them spoke, Hunter gradually began to relax as the nightmare loosened its grip on her and receded into the shadows. But her breathing remained rapid and shallow, and her heartbeat danced skittishly.

"Do you want to tell me about the dreams?"

The instant she said it, Sara knew she'd made a mistake. She'd pushed too fast, too soon. In the span of a few seconds at most, she watched Hunter's expression change from distressed to the cool façade she was quickly beginning to recognize.

"I'm sorry," she said before Hunter could respond. "I only asked because I thought it might help you to talk about them. Sometimes it helps just to say things out loud, and as I've said before, I'm a good listener."

Hunter nodded noncommittally and closed her eyes. When she spoke, her voice seemed calmer, almost resigned. "What's there to tell? I can't control the dreams. They've been coming more frequently, and I can't seem to stop them no matter what techniques I try."

"Have you tried—"

"Nothing works. And while sedatives may help me sleep, they don't stop the dreams. They only make it more difficult to wake up from the nightmares."

Sara heard the tension in her voice and stayed where she was, kneeling on the floor beside Hunter. Without thinking, she pushed aside an errant wisp of dark hair that had worked its way across Hunter's cheek. She continued to watch her, gently stroking her arm and calming her just by her very presence. When Hunter didn't move, didn't say anything, Sara began to wonder if she had fallen back asleep. But then she heard her sigh.

"Sara, I'm so sorry you were hurt because of me. You… those other women…you have to believe I'd undo it all if I could." She caught her bottom lip between her teeth. "You might want to reconsider working with me on this. Getting too close will only get you hurt."

On so many different levels, Sara thought as she looked at Hunter's face, pale and bruised and filled with sorrow. When Hunter opened her mouth to speak again, Sara silenced her with gentle fingers pressed against her lips. "Hush for a minute and listen to me, okay?"

Hunter nodded mutely.

Seeing that she wasn't going to be interrupted, Sara removed her fingers from Hunter's mouth, almost immediately missing the soft, warm contact.

"Please don't apologize for something you can't control. None of this is your doing, Hunter. And as for my getting hurt, I'm the big bad FBI agent, remember? That means I'm supposed to be faster than a speeding bullet and able to leap tall buildings."

Looking remote and introspective, Hunter remained silent. Finally, she nodded, a smile hinting at the corners of her mouth. "Ex-FBI agent…which probably means they changed the secret handshake and took away your secret decoder ring."

"Okay, ex-FBI agent." Sara rolled her eyes and grinned. "But sort of back on the job, even if it's only temporary, which means I'm both willing and able to do what it takes to find whoever is responsible for all of this madness and help bring him to justice. To do that, I'm going to need your help. So no more apologies and no more regrets, okay? We just need to be careful."

"Okay." Hunter turned her head as if to study Sara more closely. "You know, for a big bad *former* FBI agent, you look like a feather could knock you down right now. Shouldn't you still be in that bed over there instead of trying to look after my sorry ass?"

"Probably," Sara responded, a faint smile on her lips. "I feel like I'm wading in quicksand and things are getting a little fuzzy around the edges." She paused for an instant. "Can I ask you a personal question?"

Hunter's smile faded. "I believe I told you before. You can always ask."

"It's not that complicated." Sara squinted and looked more closely at Hunter's face. "How many eyes do you have? How many should I be seeing?"

"Two. Just two."

"Damn. Wrong answer."

"It's probably the concussion." Hunter raised her eyes to Sara's face. "How about I help you get back into bed?"

"Kate said it's just a mild concussion," Sara grumbled. She tried to ignore the pounding in her head but found it was difficult to ignore the heat in Hunter's gaze. Relenting, she gave a slight nod. "But going back to bed sounds like a plan."

She watched Hunter rise to her feet and allowed her to slip an arm around her waist for support as she slowly stood up. Fighting the vertigo that was brought on by the movement, she let out a low groan and felt her knees turn to water.

Hunter immediately stopped and tightened her grip. She managed through sheer force of will to keep both of them upright and was grateful they didn't end up on the floor. Keenly focused on Sara's face, she waited a few seconds before saying, "Let me know when you're okay to move."

Sara blinked and nodded. Turning her head toward Hunter, she managed a weak smile and indicated the hospital bed that suddenly seemed very far away. "Shall we try that again?"

Moving slowly, Hunter held Sara tightly and helped her back into bed. As Sara's head hit the pillow, the two women regarded each other. "You know, I usually require a date of some sort before letting a woman take me to bed," Sara murmured as she sank deeper into the bed. "Even a gorgeous one."

Sara was asleep before Hunter finished pulling a blanket up over her. She watched her a moment longer as an unguarded smile curved her lips.

The psychiatry floor was relatively quiet as Hunter stepped off the elevator and made her way down the hall. It was still too early for morning rounds, but she knew from experience the chief of psychiatry would already be in her office. She knocked softly then opened the door as a warm and vibrant voice called out enter.

Dr. Lindsay Carson's office was a reflection of the woman herself—classy and soothing. She was a petite woman with short dark hair threaded with silver framing delicate features. She also had remarkable dark-chocolate eyes that reflected an equal mix of compassion, humor, and a love of life.

Looking in, Hunter could see Lindsay's face register first surprise and then genuine pleasure as she opened the door and stepped into view. Lindsay quickly pushed her large leather chair away from her desk and stood up, her smile widening as she moved quickly toward her visitor.

"I don't see you for more than—what's it been now? Six... seven months? And now look at you," she admonished gently as she brushed Hunter's hair back and touched the bandage on her forehead. "What have you done to yourself this time?"

When Lindsay looked at her and winced with sympathy, Hunter decided she probably looked worse than she felt. That was saying something, since the lightweight cotton scrubs she was wearing felt heavy on her bruised body.

"I forgot to duck and cover," she said wryly.

Lindsay's eyes narrowed briefly on the surgical scrubs. "Did they give you something for the pain?"

"Yes. Why?"

"I can tell by the way you're moving that you're hurting. When did you last take something?"

"A while ago," Hunter responded vaguely, glancing away from Lindsay's patient gaze for an instant before looking back and smothering a sigh. "Yesterday afternoon in the ER. You know I don't like taking meds. They muddle my brain so I can't think."

Lindsay nodded. "All right. But at least take some aspirin. It'll give you some relief and help with the inflammation."

Her smile widened as she pulled Hunter into a fierce embrace. "It's so good to have you home, Hunter. If it's at all possible, you've gotten more beautiful in the last few months. But you look tired. Now come and sit down. Tell me what you've been up to and why you're showing up at my office door at six thirty in the morning looking like one of my residents after a rough night in the emergency department."

With an arm tucked around Hunter's waist, Lindsay guided her to a pair of comfortable wing chairs that sat by the window, choosing one while motioning for Hunter to take the other. "You've not been sleeping," Lindsay noted with some concern.

"I'm fine, don't fuss."

Lindsay laughed. "Sorry. Can't help it—it comes with the territory, and with you in particular, it seems to be a constant refrain. But for now, I'll leave it alone. I get the distinct impression this isn't a social visit, so talk to me. Tell me, how can I help?"

Hunter let herself sink into the deep, comfortable cushion and leaned her head against the back of the chair. She gathered a breath and made a conscious effort to keep her voice slow and easy.

"I need to ask you a question," she began. "But I don't want to hurt or insult you, and I'm afraid I will end up doing both."

Lindsay reached out, took Hunter's right hand in both of hers, and squeezed reassuringly. "Hunter, we've known each other for almost ten years, and you should know by now, without my telling you, that you are one of my favorite people. I should think you would also know I can handle one of your direct questions without taking offense. Go ahead. Ask your question."

"I need to know—" Hunter hesitated and, in an uncharacteristic move that was likely to raise Lindsay's level of concern, averted her gaze briefly before starting again. "I need to know if you shared what we talked about during our sessions with anyone."

Obviously baffled, Lindsay released Hunter's hand and sat back. "Hunter?"

"You once told me anything I said to you would stay here." Hunter indicated the elegant office with a hand gesture. "That our conversations would stay just between us."

"Of course. What's going on, Hunter? I thought we moved past trust issues a long time ago. What's happened to make you question it now?"

Hunter didn't respond immediately. When she finally spoke, it was tentative as she searched for the words. "There's someone out there who knows far too much…I don't know, maybe everything. About things I've talked about only with you."

Lindsay leaned forward. "Hunter—" she started to say, but Hunter stopped her.

"Please, just listen for a moment," she managed. "All I know is he's replicating what happened ten years ago in order to kill women. Five so far. Women whose only mistake is they looked enough like me to catch his attention. I know he's not finished yet. And I know—I know when he's finished practicing with them, he's coming after me. I have to stop him before he does that. I have to stop him before he kills someone else."

"Why aren't the authorities dealing with this? The police, the FBI?" Lindsay asked.

"They are." Hunter looked up and met Lindsay's eyes, feeling vulnerable and unsure of herself. "The FBI came to see me in London. After the last murder. The killer…the killer left a note addressed to me at the crime scene. The note said he wanted me to come home."

She felt Lindsay's eyes on her face, searching for answers. And then she heard her sigh and felt her gentle touch on her hand. And the soft question. "What you're telling me is bad enough. And that's starting to frighten me, so I need to know. What are you not telling me?"

Hunter stood and began pacing the length of the office, arms folded across her chest. And then slowly she stopped and turned to face Lindsay.

"He knows too much—" A muscle in Hunter's jaw twitched as memories flashed and shattered in her mind. Her hands shook as she forced herself to slow down and continue. "And he's using what he knows. He's using his knowledge of what happened to me…what Brenner did to me…to murder his victims."

"What do you mean?"

"All of his victims shot themselves." Hunter drew a deep, shuddering breath. "Damn it, Linds, he's playing Brenner's damned game with them, except so far, they've all lost. So far, I'm the only one who's managed to walk away. But this person—whoever he is—he wants to change that."

Lindsay stood and gathered Hunter into her arms. "Shh, it's okay, Hunter. I've got you," she said gently. "We're not going to let him hurt you. I promise."

CHAPTER FOURTEEN

S ara finished toweling her hair as she stepped back into her hospital room. She felt much better after the shower, which had removed the lingering traces of smoke and eased some of the stiffness in her body. Dropping the towel on the chair, she immediately noticed the stack of neatly folded clothes at the foot of the bed.

Yes. Clean jeans and a polo shirt. At least she wouldn't be going home wearing the faded blue hospital gown she currently had on, she thought with a grin. *Thank you, Kate.*

"A tall redhead dropped them off. She said to tell you she'd be waiting downstairs with a limo to take you wherever you want to go, whenever they decide to release you."

Sara turned at the sound of the unfamiliar voice. Standing in the doorway was a petite, forty-something brunette wearing a white lab coat over a cream-colored silk blouse and black slacks. Clipped to her left breast pocket was a plastic hospital ID card identifying her as Dr. L. Carson.

"Sorry, I was expecting Dr. Montgomery." Sara smiled uncertainly. "Can I help you?"

"If you mean Kate Montgomery, I saw her heading into the OR with an MVA emergency case about an hour ago. I wouldn't count on seeing her for at least two or three more hours. I'm here because a mutual acquaintance asked if I would stop by and talk to you. I'm Lindsay Carson."

"Sara Wilder." Sara shook the doctor's hand and frowned in confusion. "We have a mutual acquaintance?"

"Hunter Roswell," Lindsay responded with a warm smile.

Intrigued, Sara quickly realized who this had to be. "You're Hunter's safe haven."

Lindsay laughed with delight. "I haven't heard that term in a long, long time. You must know Hunter quite well if she told you about that."

"Not really. I mean I've not known her for very long." Along with being her safe haven, Hunter had also described Lindsay Carson as a good friend, and Sara did not want the doctor to be under any misconception.

"Well, I'd have to say 'very long' is a relative term," Lindsay said. "You've obviously known Hunter long enough if she told you I was her safe haven. And you must have breached some of her walls since she's asked me to come talk to you."

"You've seen Hunter?" Sara stood stiffly and could feel a blush rising on her face. She couldn't remember falling asleep, but she must have done so almost immediately after Hunter had helped her get back into bed. Nor could she shake the sense of unease she'd been feeling since awakening to find Hunter gone. "When did you see her? Was she okay?"

Lindsay nodded reassuringly. "She came to see me early this morning. As to how she was, I'd say that's a matter for some debate. By that I mean she was sporting an assortment of relatively fresh bruises, stitches, and burns. She also seems to have lost some weight she could ill afford to lose over the past few months."

She paused and smiled as she tilted her head to one side. "This, of course, made me wonder what she'd gotten herself into this time. Then she told me a tale about an exploding car and a stalker-serial killer. And then she told me about you, how you are trying to help her figure out the identity of the person stalking her so he can be stopped."

"That's certainly my intention. But I believe Hunter is finding it to be a rather painful process."

"That would explain why she asked me to come talk to you," Lindsay said gently. "If you're feeling up to it, why don't you get dressed, and we'll go to the cafeteria and have some coffee while we talk. In the meantime, I'll let the nurses' station know where you're going to be in case anyone comes looking for you."

Sara agreed and fifteen minutes later, they went through the cafeteria line and took their coffees to a small unoccupied table in a relatively quiet corner.

"Hunter tells me you're a psychologist as well as former FBI. How much do you know about what happened to her ten years ago?" Lindsay began without preamble.

"Right to the point," Sara commented dryly. "I would have to say my knowledge is limited."

"How limited?"

"I know the basics. I know Hunter was kidnapped by Kyle Brenner and held for three weeks, and her father was killed while trying to rescue her. But I've no knowledge of what Brenner did to her during the three weeks he held her captive. I've been told Hunter's family made sure no details were ever leaked. Not even during Brenner's trial." Sara paused and then added, "That's pretty much what I know."

Lindsay looked quizzically across the table at Sara. "Considering who Michael Roswell was and the circumstances surrounding his death, I would have thought the FBI would have a rather extensive file on the subject."

"They probably do." Sara shifted uncomfortably. "I haven't read it."

"Why not?"

There was an awkward silence. Sara stared at the table and reminded herself that Lindsay Carson was not only Hunter's friend, she was also a highly regarded psychiatrist. She cleared her throat and lifted her chin. "For some reason, my not reading her file seems important to Hunter."

Lindsay's warm chocolate eyes gentled. "Good enough reason," she said. "And what has Hunter told you?"

"Not a lot." Sara leaned back in her seat as she recalled her conversation with Hunter during the flight from London. "She described what happened to her as being the defining moment in terms of who she is but admits she has difficulty talking about it. She also mentioned she has issues talking to psychiatrists and psychologists, other than you."

"And now you," Lindsay added, sounding pleased.

"And now me," Sara agreed.

Lindsay nodded slowly. "You should know there have been many times when I have cursed Patrick Roswell. Regardless of intentions, his arrogance and highhanded tactics in dealing with Hunter after her father was killed caused a lot of damage and left a lot of residual scars. But that's for another time."

Dark brows creased in thought. "Hunter explained her connection with her stalker is somehow tied to what happened to her ten years ago. And she recognizes that no matter how painful it might be, opening up about what happened will be critical to your being able to identify him before he kills someone else. But she's not yet able to talk to you about what happened, and right now, there are some things you need to know. Let me tell you a story."

Now that she had Sara's undivided attention, Lindsay seemed uncertain where to start. After a protracted silence, she looked up and cleared her throat. "On the night Michael Roswell was killed, Hunter was brought into the emergency department conscious and nonresponsive. And in less time than it took to complete morning rounds several hours later, she was the talk of the hospital."

"Why is that?"

Lindsay leaned forward. "It helps if you understand that hospitals are filled with every kind of human drama—birth, death, and everything in between. They are also notorious for gossip. And Hunter's situation might well have been scripted in Hollywood. Stop and think about it. The beautiful, wealthy, young kidnap victim. The gun battle between the authorities and the kidnappers. And the kidnap victim's father tragically killed while saving his only child."

Sara nodded thoughtfully. "I never thought of it like that."

"It didn't help that within minutes of her being brought here, there was a media scrum on the front lawn which lasted for days, and at times, it seemed as if there were more Secret Service and FBI agents in the hospital than there were medical personnel."

Lindsay grew quiet. After what seemed to Sara like a long stretch of silence, she sighed, and with her coffee cup cradled in her hands, she sat back in her chair.

"A lot of what I'm about to tell you isn't public knowledge," she began again. "After her father was killed, Hunter's mother fell apart completely. It was totally understandable. Marlena had just spent three weeks under enormous pressure trying to cope with Hunter's kidnapping when she suddenly lost the love of her life and her only child was hospitalized in critical condition. It all proved too much and left her in no shape to deal with things when Patrick Roswell, with all his political clout, took control, determined to fix Hunter."

"Funny, that's exactly the term Hunter used," Sara mused.

"Not really surprising. Patrick Roswell can be quite overbearing at the best of times, and in this particular situation, he pulled out all the stops. He used his considerable resources and influence and brought in every renowned specialist in the country to treat Hunter." Lindsay sat up straighter. "By the time I actually met her, Hunter had been in the hospital for just over two weeks. During that time, she had been examined and treated by an endless array of medical practitioners—neurologists, orthopedic surgeons, ophthalmologists, and psychiatrists, as well as a number of physiotherapists."

Sara winced as she tried to imagine what it must have been like. "How did Hunter react to all of that? Somehow, I can't imagine her not objecting."

"Initially she was all but catatonic, and I'm not sure how much she was aware of the circus surrounding her. Things didn't get really bad until she actually started to improve. That was when it hit her that her father was really dead and she had missed his funeral."

"Oh hell. I didn't know that." Sara felt empathetic pain flare deep within her. "What did she do?"

"She shut down. She stopped communicating with everyone, and it became a kind of power struggle. The more the experts pressured her to talk to them, the more she refused and the more out of control things became. Two weeks into her hospitalization, she was barely eating or sleeping, was suffering from night terrors, and began exhibiting signs of claustrophobia. But no one picked up on it."

"Why not?"

Lindsay shrugged. "I suppose, in part, because Hunter wasn't telling anyone anything. The nursing staff was too busy trying to deal with the FBI, the Secret Service, the media, and all the medical specialists that had been brought in, and unfortunately, no one noticed when Hunter stopped taking her meds and started sneaking up to the roof at night."

Lindsay's pager went off at that moment, and their conversation was put on hold while she left the table to respond.

While she waited, Sara stretched out her bruised and aching body and nursed her coffee. She let her thoughts drift back to Hunter. Tried to sort out and define her feelings. She recognized that she needed only to think her name and emotions tumbled forth, leaving her struggling to contain an undeniable and growing attraction.

Images of hot, uninhibited sex came immediately to mind. But just as quickly came the realization that there was more drawing her to Hunter than a suddenly reawakened libido. But what did that mean?

She knew Hunter was bright, sensitive, funny, caring. She knew she liked her—a lot—and wanted to get to know her even better. She could see them developing a real friendship. The problem—the temptation—was if she allowed herself to think about it, she could see them developing so much more.

With a sigh, she acknowledged she was quickly drifting into dangerous waters, and sooner rather than later, she would have to deal with that. But for now, there was only one thing she knew with absolute certainty. She was going to do whatever it took to help Hunter get through this.

She was still lost in thought a few minutes later when Lindsay returned.

"Sorry about that. Sometimes residents just need to be reassured." She frowned and tilted her head as she looked at Sara. "Where was I?"

"The roof?"

"Right…the roof. On one particular night, as luck would have it, Hunter wasn't the only one seeking fresh air and open spaces on the roof. I saw her almost immediately when I went up and knew who she was, of course. But I quickly ascertained she had no intent to harm herself and figured she could use a break, so I let her be."

"Did she know you saw her?"

"Oh yes, she knew. We actually made eye contact. And when I didn't immediately report her presence to her watchers, she gave me a little nod and seemed to relax. A short while later, I was about to head back down when I noticed she had fallen asleep." Lindsay closed her eyes briefly. "I don't know why I decided to stay close. I think I just wanted to make sure she would be okay."

"What happened?" Sara prodded gently.

"She scared me half to death when she suddenly started to scream. By the time I got to her, she was deep in the throes of some hellish nightmare and was oblivious to her surroundings. I was terrified she would hurt herself. I grabbed her and held on until she was calm enough that I could get her back down to her room. From there, it was like a dam had burst, and I spent the better part of that night listening to a battered and broken teenager try to talk about things no one should ever have to experience.

"In the morning, the chief pulled me aside just as we were about to begin rounds and told me Patrick Roswell wanted to talk to me." Lindsay's lips quirked into a small grin at the memory. "I figured he had heard I had talked to Hunter without his permission, and I was about to lose my job."

"But obviously, that turned out not to be the case."

"Indeed." Lindsay's smile broadened. "Instead, it turned out Patrick Roswell's granddaughter had started communicating again. With her first words, she demanded to see her grandfather and told him, in no uncertain terms, not to bother arranging for any more specialists because she would refuse to see them. And then she told him Lindsay Carson—a doctor he had never heard of—was the only doctor she was willing to see."

"That must have gone over well," Sara said. Lindsay laughed and some of the tension dissipated. But the respite lasted only for the time it took Lindsay to resume her story.

"To say Patrick Roswell was not a happy man would be a gross understatement. He threatened Hunter with a competency hearing. Thankfully, that seemed to energize Marlena, and she responded with a threat of her own. She told Patrick if he didn't leave Hunter alone, she would guarantee he would never see his only grandchild again."

Sara raised both eyebrows. "From what I've read and heard about him, I can't imagine Senator Roswell backing down."

"Marlena left him with very little choice." Lindsay paused and took a deep breath. "Over the next several days, Hunter started talking to me about what had happened to her. And considering how she looked when she was admitted—the extent of her physical injuries—I expected it to be bad. But somehow, it was worse."

Sara found herself bracing as if in anticipation of a physical blow. "What did Brenner do to her?" she asked in a hollow tone.

"Hunter said the first few days following her kidnapping were all about breaking her psychologically. This was apparently something Brenner had been studying for some time. They kept her awake, cold, hungry, and blindfolded, and subjected her to random physical attacks."

Lindsay explained most of the physical trauma Hunter had suffered happened during those first few days. "She said they would always ask her the same question—'What's it worth to you, Hunter? You want to eat? Sleep? What's it worth to you?' The only problem was she didn't know how to respond. She didn't know what they wanted to hear."

Closing her eyes, Lindsay paused once again. "I'm sorry," she said softly. "You need to understand that, at seventeen, Hunter was this unbelievably gifted, beautiful young woman with no frame of reference for the evil she had encountered."

Sara considered Lindsay's choice of words. "Do you believe in evil, Doctor?"

"Not previously," Lindsay answered without hesitation. "But after listening to Hunter describe what was done to her? Yes. Without question."

Watching her, Sara realized the intervening years had blurred and ultimately erased the lines that denoted the doctor-patient relationship. Lindsay and Hunter had become close. Good friends. Recognizing just how difficult this was for the psychiatrist, Sara laid a comforting hand over Lindsay's, squeezed it briefly, and waited for her to continue.

"I'm not going to go into great detail about what was done to Hunter. It's not relevant to the point at hand. But when we're done here, Hunter authorized me to give you copies of the notes from my sessions with her. What's important for you to know is after they figured they'd softened her up enough, Brenner introduced Hunter to what she called his game."

Something in Lindsay's voice had Sara's heart feeling like it was going to pound right out of her chest. "Brenner's game?"

Lindsay nodded. "According to Hunter, Brenner handed her a revolver loaded with only one bullet and gave her the opportunity to gamble for favors. Brenner's game was his own version of Russian roulette. One pull of the trigger—one favor earned. And if she didn't feel like playing, his boys simply beat her until she agreed to play. She ended up with two facial fractures, a concussion, a separated shoulder, and most of her ribs broken before it was all over."

Oh God. A strangled sound escaped Sara's throat, and she was afraid she was going to be sick. She looked across the table at Lindsay, the horror she felt undoubtedly reflected in her face, in her eyes. And then it hit her—the reason Lindsay was telling her this particular story. More importantly, the reason Hunter wanted her to know.

"The stalker. He knows this is what Brenner did to her," she said flatly. "That's why all the victims have shot themselves. He's replicating Brenner's game."

"Yes."

"And Hunter knows this." It was all making a horrible kind of sense. "That's why she went to see Brenner yesterday. She wanted to know if he had told anyone about what happened in that house ten years ago. He told her he hadn't."

"Did you believe him?"

Sara didn't have to give the question any thought. "Actually, yes. I did."

"It would seem Hunter believed him as well," Lindsay said. "That's why she came to see me earlier this morning. She wanted to know if I had shared any part of what she told me with anyone."

"And had you?"

"No. Not before today. At least not directly." Her voice trailed off. "But this is a hospital, Sara, and at the time, everyone knew I was working with Hunter. Initially I saw her daily on an in-patient basis. But I continued to work with her for some time after she was released. Even when she took off for Europe. She would phone me from wherever she happened to be at the moment, and we would talk until she could get to sleep. If anyone really wanted to know what we talked about, it would have been relatively easy to find out."

"How?"

Lindsay tugged on the sleeves of her lab coat. "Sadly, medical files can be accessed. Computer records can be hacked. And before you ask, you need to know there are over five thousand attending physicians, residents, interns, nurses, healthcare workers, and other professionals working here. And they serve an endless stream of people on a daily basis—both in-patients and out-patients. That leaves a lot of potential suspects."

"Maybe," Sara responded thoughtfully. "But it narrows the initial point of contact between Hunter and her stalker to a specific place and time. That gives us somewhere to start, which is more than we had an hour ago."

"Even if you had the ability to narrow it down to anyone who was at the hospital during the nearly four weeks Hunter was a patient, do you have any idea how many people that might be?"

"No," Sara said solemnly before flashing a smile. "But with your help, we can start by eliminating anyone who doesn't match the profile we've developed. And maybe you can think back and see if anyone stands out in your mind. Someone who maybe showed a little too much interest in Hunter. Maybe asked too many questions or watched her a little too closely."

"I'll see what I can do. But you need to understand I won't do anything that will put Hunter in greater jeopardy than she is already."

"Then we don't have a problem."

"Actually," Lindsay said with a sigh, "the problem is knowing Hunter as I do, I can tell you she's going to be doing her own search and may try to draw the stalker out on her own. Get in his line of sight and make him turn to her before he's ready. That way, another woman won't be forced to play the game in her place."

Sara felt her chest tighten painfully, and her heart skipped a beat. "What do you mean before he's ready?"

"Hunter believes the killer won't come after her until the full moon in October. That means there's still another woman out there who doesn't know she's about to become a killer's target for September."

"I don't understand. Why would he wait until October when Hunter's home now, just like he wanted?"

"To understand, you have to know lunar folklore," Lindsay said. "You're dealing with a killer who is following a lunar cycle, and in myth and folklore, each full moon is given a name."

"Shit...that's right...and October's moon is known as the blood moon."

"Indeed. The name is said to have been used by Native Americans as they tracked and killed their prey by autumn moonlight," Lindsay said. "But the full moon in October is also known as Hunter's Moon. And I happen to agree with Hunter. Even if it wasn't part of his original plan, symbolically, October's full moon is too perfect for him to pass up."

Unhappily, Sara concurred. "But I will tell you this. Whether he comes after her now or in October, Hunter is not about to become his sixth—or seventh—victim. Because whoever is stalking her will not only have to get through Hunter's own security team, he will also have to get through me."

Lindsay stared at Sara. "Why? I understand from Hunter you are no longer with the FBI. Why are you willing to go to the mat for Hunter?"

Sara waited just a heartbeat before shrugging. "Why doesn't matter. The only thing that's important right now is figuring out *how*."

CHAPTER FIFTEEN

The late afternoon sun was sinking fast on the horizon, its
fading light brushing the pale walls of Hunter's office with
muted shades of gold. As the light slashed across the room, Hunter
looked at the chaos that surrounded her and groaned. Reaching for
the bottle of water on the desk, she took a sip as she sent the final
report to print. She then swiveled her chair toward the window,
leaned back, and stared at the dying sun.

Somehow the day had gotten away from her, and now her eyes
burned and her head ached from studying the endless streams of
data. She closed her eyes for just a moment, let exhaustion creep
in, and allowed her mind to wander. There was so much she didn't
know. So many how and why questions without answers and so
many possible places to look for them. She let her mind drift back
over the long-ago events, wondered what details lay in the rubble
that might provide direction to her search.

The parameters, as she saw them, were simple enough. She
had been brought to the trauma center at San Francisco General on
October third almost ten years earlier and had been released on the
morning of the twenty-ninth. Sometime during that twenty-seven
day window, the first encounter with her stalker had occurred.

The challenge was he could have been anyone. An attending
physician, a resident, or an intern. Or he could just as easily have
been an EMT, a nurse, an orderly, or a janitor. In fact, she realized
dejectedly, he could simply have been one of the countless people

who had been a patient or a visitor to the hospital during that time period. But it made the most sense that he was an employee, if for no other reason than the heightened security provided by the FBI, SFPD, and Secret Service, which had ensured she had no interactions with other patients or visitors.

She would focus on hospital employees. She would trust the profile the FBI had developed was accurate and begin to eliminate anyone who didn't fit. She would look for a single male, currently in his late twenties to early forties and living in the Bay Area. Should be simple enough. *It's like a puzzle. You find the pieces, you fit them together, and you get the answer.*

Feeling the solitude of the office pressing in on her, Hunter got up, stretched, and crossed the room to the window. Turning her back on the humming computer, the mess of files scattered on the desk, and the continuous stream of documents collating on the printer, she rested her forehead against the cool glass and rubbed the back of her neck, as the toll of the past week washed over her in waves.

She was feeling both listless and unnaturally calm. She knew she'd not been eating or sleeping much, and if her reflection in the window was any indication, it showed. Particularly in the shadows beneath her eyes which stood out starkly against the paleness of her face. The only consolation was she was making progress. Wrapping her arms securely around herself, she stood motionless and stared out the window, her gaze following a sailboat tacking against the wind as it made its way across the bay.

She wasn't certain how long she remained staring out at the bay before she recognized she was no longer alone. Tessa stood in the doorway to her office, her reflection staring back at her in the glass. Hunter didn't want to see the look of compassion that darkened her eyes. And yet, as she looked at her reflection—at once so familiar and so dear to her—she couldn't help but recall the girl she had met at Oxford.

The Brits had probably found it amusing to pair the two disparate Americans as roommates. The gifted young prodigy from California working on her second PhD, and the brash and cocky

New Yorker who wanted to see and experience everything the world had to offer. It certainly shouldn't have worked.

But instead of a disaster, it had been the start of an amazing and enduring friendship. It was Tessa who had willingly followed her lead as they backpacked through Europe. Tessa who had walked away from the partnership track at the law firm she had joined to come aboard the fledgling Roswell Group. Tessa who had taught her the infinite wonders of loving a woman.

"Hey," Tessa said as she stepped into the room. "Are you okay?"

Hunter sighed. "Yes. Why does everyone keep asking me that?" Her voice was soft with exhaustion and strain.

There was a pause the length of a heartbeat before Tessa responded. "Maybe because it's late and everyone else wants to call it a day, but you're oblivious to what's going on around you," she said, clearly watching Hunter's face reflected in the glass.

"I didn't ask anyone to stay here with me."

"I know you didn't, but Jesus, look at you." Tessa's face softened for the briefest moment and she expelled a long sigh. "Your team is here because they're concerned about you, just as I am."

"I don't need anyone worrying about me. I'm fine."

"Of course you are," Tessa snapped back. "That's why you're losing weight and there are shadows under your eyes. It doesn't look like you've eaten or slept in days. Why would anyone be concerned?"

Hunter's anger rose and evaporated in the span of the same heartbeat. Tipping her head back, she closed her eyes. "I'm sorry, Tessa. It's just been a long day. Can we start over?" She lowered her voice to an almost-whisper then arched both brows. "Why are you still here? I thought you had a hot date tonight with a lovely doctor?"

Tessa tilted her head in silent acknowledgment and waved the file in her hands before dropping it on Hunter's desk. "I wanted to finish reviewing the new casino contract before I left. It took longer than I expected, and I lost all track of time. But that shouldn't come as a surprise considering Channing drafted it. My God, but that man can go on." She sighed melodramatically, and then looked at Hunter. "What about you? What have you been working on?"

"Accessing the hospital database." Hunter grinned at the pained look Tessa gave her. "The first cut's not quite finished, but the last time I checked it had well over a thousand possibilities."

"Jesus." Tessa looked suitably overwhelmed. "Do you have a way of narrowing the search any further?"

"Sort of. I mean, this is just a preliminary list of people who were employed at the hospital ten years ago who would match the profile today. Once the initial cut is complete, I plan on looking closer at anyone associated with the ER, psychiatry, and neurology that fits the profile. Those would be the departments I had the most interactions with at the time, so they present the most likely possibilities. I know it's not much, but at least it gives us a place to start."

Tessa flashed a wicked-looking grin. "For good measure, you should also run the list of specialists your grandfather Patrick brought in for consults."

"I doubt any of them would fit the profile in terms of age," Hunter responded dryly. "In fact, knowing my grandfather, I'm surprised any of them were still practicing medicine ten years ago. After all, he couldn't have his only granddaughter treated by someone who was...oh, I don't know...*young*."

"God forbid." Tessa laughed and then glanced at her watch. "Oh shit. Look at the time. Are you hungry? I bet you haven't eaten anything all day."

Hunter shrugged and shook her head. She hadn't had dinner and couldn't remember lunch. In fact, she couldn't remember having anything all day other than coffee, something that was becoming habitual.

Tessa slipped her arm around Hunter's shoulders. "Come on then, you need something to eat. I was supposed to meet Kate at Vertigo and I'm late." Tessa began to gently coax Hunter in the direction of the door. "If you come with me, you'll be able to catch up with what we've done at the club over the last six months and, more importantly, distract Kate from the fact that I'm late again."

Hunter sighed and stopped their forward motion. "Tessa, you know normally I would love to go with you, and I do want to see how the club looks with all the work that's been done. But today has been a pretty long day—"

"That feels like it's already lasted a week," Tessa deadpanned, finishing for her.

"Yeah, something like that." Hunter grinned tiredly. "I was really looking forward to some downtime. Can I take a rain check?"

"You can always have a rain check." Tessa's eyes softened as she framed Hunter's face between her hands. "But I know this face. I know when you've pushed yourself past the point of exhaustion. I know when you're sad or unhappy. I know when something's got you teetering on the edge. And right now your face is telling me you really need to go out and have a little fun."

Hunter raised one eyebrow. "Really? My face told you all that?"

"Yes, really. Just answer one question for me. When was the last time you went out just for fun and cut loose?"

"Um…my second-to-last night in London. I believe the story and photos appeared in the *Tattler*."

"The tennis player. Right. Okay, I concede." Tessa laughed. "But I still think you need to come out with me."

Something in her tone had Hunter's eyes narrowing with suspicion. "Why is that?"

Tessa shrugged nonchalantly. "Maybe because Kate's bringing a friend—"

"Damn it, Tessa. I'm really not interested," Hunter said through gritted teeth. "Jesus, isn't my life already complicated enough without you and Kate trying to fix me up with someone?"

"Not even if it's with Sara?" Tessa asked before adding softly, "Tell me you're not interested, and I'll call Kate and put her off. But be honest with me, and more importantly be honest with yourself. Because I saw the way you were looking at Sara in the hospital. And just for the record, I think it's about time, my friend."

Feeling inexplicably panicked, Hunter turned toward Tessa but remained silent. *When did I lose control over my life?* Unsure what to do with her hands, she thrust them into her pockets.

There was no disguising Tessa's look of triumph. Picking up Hunter's jacket from the back of the chair, she held it out for her. "C'mon, gorgeous," she said. "Let's go eat and have a little fun."

❖

Club Vertigo was an old converted warehouse. A once-dilapidated brick building, it had been restored from the ground up and now housed one of the area's hottest nightspots. "Good luck getting in," the cab driver said with cheerful pessimism as Kate and Sara exited the vehicle.

But in spite of a queue wrapped partway around the building, Kate and Sara were quickly ushered in by the black-clad doorman. Once inside, a similarly attired hostess took over. Flashing a welcoming smile, she led them past the dinner crowd waiting at the bar for a second-floor table to clear. With friendly efficiency, they were ushered up the stairs to a booth.

Sara looked at Kate in surprise.

"Trust me, it's not whatever you may be thinking," Kate said with a laugh. "Tessa's one of the owners, and we've been here a number of times—both while they were doing renovations and since the club opened. A lot of the staff know me."

"I thought Tessa was the chief legal counsel at Roswell."

"She is," Kate replied. "She and Hunter bought this place about a year ago and totally gutted it. They had a soft opening about a month ago, in part because Hunter was away. The grand opening is planned for a couple of weeks from now to coincide with Tessa's birthday. It's by invitation only, and they've got Darcy Cole headlining the evening's entertainment. Wanna come?"

"Absolutely. I caught her as part of a benefit concert series in Central Park last summer. I thought she was amazing," Sara replied, then frowned as she thought about what Kate had just said. "Wait a minute. Are you suggesting Hunter was already scheduled to return for the grand opening?"

"Without a doubt. Tessa told me there was no way Hunter would miss her birthday. But if you're wondering whether whoever is stalking Hunter knew she was coming back, I would have to say no. My understanding is it's a personal thing, not something that would be widely known. Apparently, it's got something to do with keeping an old promise."

Kate's eyes suddenly widened. "Oh Christ. You don't suppose they made some stupid schoolgirl promise about marrying each other if they were both still single by the time Tessa turned thirty, do you?"

Sara laughed and shook her head. "Somehow, I can't picture it."

"That's because you haven't seen them together." Kate's voice held a slight edge. "There's this…this chemistry between them. It sizzles. In fact, I'm pretty sure they used to be lovers."

Sara heard the uncertainty in Kate's voice and kept her tone light. "If that's true, I would focus on the used-to-be part. I mean, it's not as if you were celibate before you met Tessa," she chided gently and then paused as a waiter approached.

"Buenas noches, Katarina…señorita," the waiter said as chilled champagne in a bucket appeared at their side and four glasses were placed on the table, reflecting the candlelight. "Compliments of the house."

Sara's gaze narrowed as she looked from the glasses to Kate. "*Katarina?* Do you want to tell me why you were insistent on having a third wheel tagging along this evening?" She stared meaningfully at the four glasses. "Or is there something else you were meaning to tell me, and it just slipped your mind?"

Whatever Kate said as she responded was lost.

In the midst of the noise, chatter, people, and music that made up the ambient sounds of the restaurant, the room suddenly seemed to fall silent as Sara caught sight of the two women approaching their table. Tessa nonchalantly sauntering through the room, Hunter slightly behind her, strolling casually, one hand tucked in her pocket.

Both women looked relaxed and absolutely comfortable in their surroundings, in their own skin. They were obviously working the room, stopping briefly here and there, talking to both restaurant patrons and staff as they slowly moved through the crowd. And in a club where people came to see and be seen, they were turning more than their fair share of heads as the restaurant filled up.

It should be a sin to look that good, Sara thought wryly. But it was an honest assessment. For the first time, she realized both women were remarkably similar. Although Tessa was slightly taller and Hunter slightly leaner, both were tall, dark, and model gorgeous. In addition, the two women exuded an air of confidence, intelligence—and yes, arrogance. The difference that defined who they were was in their eyes. Tessa's were a cool slate gray. Hunter's were a hot laser blue.

In that instant, Hunter's gaze suddenly lifted above the crowd. Her head tilted slightly, and she met Sara's eyes with a look that was piercing and intense. Even as they connected, Hunter's eyes darkened, smoldered, and emitted one hundred thousand volts of pure sexual energy.

Everything else faded dimly into the background, until all that remained were two women, drawn inexorably together. Sara felt her pulse racing and sensed the unmistakable stirring of desire, the heat settling deep within her.

"If you don't stop staring at her like that, she's going to spontaneously combust." Kate's amused voice sounded in her ear, causing Sara to jump.

Sara felt a deep blush heat her face and neck, and she shot Kate a look that was a mixture of amusement and embarrassment tinged with insecurity. "I have no idea what you're talking about."

"Right. Of course you don't," Kate said with a laugh. She wrapped her arm around Sara's shoulder and gave her a friendly squeeze. "But you have to admit—they're really something, aren't they? Lesbian poster girls."

"I suppose," Sara nodded appreciatively. "I mean, if you happen to like your women drop-dead gorgeous."

They were both laughing when Tessa and Hunter reached their booth. Tessa slid in easily beside Kate, while Hunter sat on the opposite side beside Sara.

"Hey there," Hunter said softly, the beginnings of a beguiling smile touching her mouth.

Sara's stomach fluttered, and she licked her lips before offering a smile of her own in response. "Hey there yourself."

She caught a trace of Hunter's enticing scent, and a tiny shiver of anticipation ran along her spine as heat sparked between them. Already forgotten was the tension she'd felt when she'd thought Kate was trying to set her up with someone. Instead, she realized she was relaxed and happy.

For a moment, Sara considered hiding her unexpected pleasure with the direction the evening was taking and with life in general. But then, just as quickly, she dismissed the thought, choosing instead to revel in the unexpected and leaving herself open to whatever the night might bring.

CHAPTER SIXTEEN

I hope you don't mind," Tessa said as Hunter's leg brushed against Sara's under the table, "but in honor of Hunter's first visit to the club since we opened, I've taken the liberty of arranging a meal that you won't find anywhere on the menu."

Sara nodded absently, not caring if they dined on hot dogs and fries as long as Hunter's leg didn't move away.

"Hunter?" Tessa asked. "Is that okay with you?"

Hunter raised her head and gazed blankly at Tessa. "Hmm?"

"To think, she used to be so articulate," Tessa said with a laugh.

For the next two hours, they were kept wined and gastronomically entertained, while Tessa and Hunter shared amusing stories about their days at Oxford. The teasing banter between the two women was fast paced and at times acerbic, but was obviously borne of a deep and enduring friendship. The jibes and jokes flew constantly, and Hunter and Tessa seemed equally adept at holding her own.

Sara leaned back in her seat and sipped her wine. She marveled at the easy conversation they shared during dinner and could not remember when she had laughed as much over the course of an evening. Hunter appeared relaxed, and Sara was glad to see that, at least for the moment, most of the tension had faded from her eyes.

As the evening progressed, much to her delight, Sara discovered Hunter not only possessed a razor-sharp wit but knew when to use it. She also learned, unexpectedly, that Hunter expressed herself through touch. On several occasions during dinner, she had reached out quite naturally and squeezed Sara's hand or touched her arm. Fleeting connections that had nevertheless felt like caresses.

She saw Hunter laugh in response to something Tessa was saying and enjoyed the opportunity to simply watch her. Be with her. It was the first time she had seen her so unguarded, although she had to know every diner's gaze had been drawn to her at some point during the evening. Sara could hardly blame them. Sitting there with a sexy smile on her face and the candlelight reflecting in her eyes, Hunter was easily the most compelling woman in the room.

She was also beginning to feel very much like Hunter's date, which meant her social life had just taken a very intriguing turn. Especially if she considered this would make it her first date since before the start of the Pelham case.

Christ. That's almost two years ago. What am I doing?

Sara felt the onset of a sudden attack of nerves and wondered how one slim woman could knock her feet out from under her in a way no one had before. She repressed a shudder and felt totally self-conscious. She no longer knew how to act on a date, and despite their obvious chemistry, she really didn't know Hunter. The only thing they had in common was the stalker. What exactly did that mean?

Abruptly, she realized she had drifted away from the conversation at the table. She brought her attention back only to find Hunter staring at her with hot eyes and a lazy half-smile on her face. She closed her eyes, shivered, and felt the breath leave her body—the flash of arousal in response to that brief look was instantaneous and nearly overwhelming. She sighed and acknowledged that before the evening was through, she would need to find some semblance of self-control.

After dinner, by unspoken consensus, the four women moved to a table being held for them on the patio and ordered a round of drinks. The seductive beat of the music was drifting out, and after a few minutes, Tessa grabbed Hunter's hand and pulled her to her feet.

"It's been a while, but I seem to recall you were pretty good on the dance floor," she said. "Come and dance with me, Roswell."

Hunter smiled nonchalantly and let Tessa take her by the hand and lead her onto the dance floor. The two women danced with a sexy grace and rhythm, and Sara was not surprised to see they fit together perfectly. As she watched, Hunter led Tessa through a complex set of moves. Tessa followed flawlessly, and they looked as if they had been dancing together for years.

Of course, why wouldn't they.

Kate seemed to be enjoying the show as well, smiling as Hunter spun Tessa and then came up slowly behind her and started to gyrate sensuously against her. When Hunter placed her hands on Tessa's hips, Tessa's eyes drifted closed. She moved her hips against Hunter's pelvis and then pressed closer. An instant later, her face became suffused with what could only be described as pleasure as Hunter ran her hands intimately along her sides and brushed her lips against Tessa's neck.

That elicited a jealous growl from Kate who got swiftly to her feet and moved in the direction of the dance floor.

"Time to separate those two before they burst into flames or get arrested," she said before turning back to Sara. "Don't just sit there, girlfriend. If they get arrested, we'll have a hell of a mess on our hands. Between the two of them, they represent both the lawyer we'll need and the source of bail money. Come and dance with Hunter while I remind Tessa she's supposed to be with me."

Dance with Hunter? Now there's a hardship.

Sara got to her feet, aware she was a little lightheaded, and remembered too late she had consumed a fair amount of champagne and wine with dinner. Moving a little more slowly, she followed Kate onto the dance floor. She couldn't help but laugh as Kate stood in front of Tessa and pantomimed that she was cutting in.

In response, Hunter released Tessa and swept an unsuspecting Kate into her arms. She then dipped, spun, and held Kate close before spinning her again directly into Tessa's waiting arms in a well-choreographed move.

Laughing, Hunter turned to Sara and held out her hand. Almost instantly, the look in her eyes changed. Amusement faded and was quickly replaced by heat.

"Dance with me, *querida*?" she said, her voice dropping to a lazy, liquid purr.

The low, sexy voice wrapped itself around Sara's senses and a delicious shiver ran down her spine. Just the thought of being on the dance floor moving to the sensual beat with Hunter's body pressed close was enough to make her mouth go dry. Her heart began to beat faster and breathing became a conscious act.

"I thought you'd never ask," she answered, allowing Hunter to pull her toward the dance floor, willingly losing herself in the blue of her eyes.

As she moved closer to Hunter, Sara became conscious of the heavy bass beat vibrating through the floorboards. She was cognizant of every place their bodies touched. She could feel the heat radiating from Hunter's body against her skin as their bodies fit together, thigh between thighs, and felt instantly intoxicated by the increasingly familiar scent of Hunter's perfume.

Pressing closer still, she could feel Hunter's abdominal muscles twitch as a tremor ran through her. She could feel Hunter's heart start to race. Closing her eyes, Sara allowed herself to enjoy this unexpected pleasure—the knowledge that she was not alone in how she was feeling.

When the music ended, she stood an instant longer, swaying to a rhythm that lingered in her head before fading like whispers in the night air. For that moment she just breathed, willing her racing heart to slow down. She felt a strange sense of loss as Hunter released her, but shook it off. Then she turned her head a little, opened her eyes, and was startled to realize just how close they still were.

Hunter didn't move, didn't say a word. She just kept her eyes on Sara, making her feel as if she'd been touched. Intimately.

"Let's get out of here," Hunter murmured and reached for her hand.

Danger signals flared, warning Sara of an impending train wreck, both personally and professionally. Then without hesitation, she accepted Hunter's outstretched hand.

"Where are we going?" she asked, curious.

"Does it really matter?"

Wordlessly, Sara shook her head.

❖

The night breeze toyed with Hunter's hair as she and Sara stepped outside the club. The streetlights cast a soft glow around them, and they continued to hold hands as they walked. Sauntering slowly past the clubs, bars, and restaurants that lined the street, enveloped by the competing strains of blues, jazz, and classic rock that spilled out into the night through numerous open windows and doors.

As they passed others who were likewise enjoying the sultry summer evening, Hunter tried to imagine how it would feel to be just like everyone else. Anonymous. Living an ordinary life. Simply out for an evening with good friends and then walking a beautiful woman home.

But that would mean imagining she didn't have a serial killer stalking her. And pretending there was no security team trailing her somewhere in the shadows. And acting as if the beautiful woman holding her hand wasn't really a former FBI agent, who was, even now, probably carrying some kind of weapon.

Still, if only for a little while, Hunter wanted nothing more than to pretend.

Walking beside her, Sara began to slow her pace until she forced them to come to a standstill. "You know we really shouldn't be doing this, don't you?" she said softly when Hunter looked at her.

Hunter froze. She glanced at their still-joined hands and quickly released her hold on Sara's hand as if it was a live electrical wire. *What are you doing?*

She took a step back while murmuring, "Oh Jesus. I wasn't thinking. My personal life has never been much of a secret. What people think about who I'm with…man or woman…it's not something I've ever worried about…I'm sorry if—"

Just as quickly, Sara moved forward until their bodies were as close as they could get without actually touching and their breath mingled in the stillness of the evening air. She then reached out, grasped Hunter's hand once again, and threaded their fingers together, watching Hunter's face as their fingers became entwined.

"You misunderstood me," she said as she squeezed Hunter's hand. "I simply meant we shouldn't be out unprotected in the dark when we still don't have the slightest idea who is stalking you."

"Oh." Hunter smiled again, a little laugh on her lips, and she did not pull her hand away. Instead, she raised their joined hands and touched her lips to Sara's fingers. "We may not know everyone who's stalking me, darlin'," she drawled wryly, "but I can assure you we're hardly what you could call alone and unprotected."

Hunter chewed her lower lip and considered her options. Truthfully, she wasn't that worried for herself. But the last thing she wanted was to place Sara in the midst of a situation that was eventually going to become dangerous. Even if Sara was a former FBI agent.

"But you're right," she concluded, her voice soft and tinged with regret. "There's no sense in taking unnecessary chances."

Having made the decision, she raised her free hand and signaled with her fingers. Within seconds, a dark limousine pulled up to the curb, and simultaneously, Peter materialized from the shadows. Hunter had a quiet word with him while the limo driver held the door open for Sara to get into the vehicle.

A couple of minutes later, Hunter got into the limousine beside Sara and sank back into the soft leather seat with a sigh. Sara slid along the seat until their thighs touched and laid her hand on Hunter's leg. Smiling, Hunter responded by raising her arm and wrapping it around Sara's shoulders, pulling her even closer until Sara's head was resting against her shoulder.

Hunter felt the proximity acutely, and for a little while, she closed her eyes and relished the sensation, allowing herself to enjoy their closeness as well as the energy that seemed to be sparking between them. *And yes, the sexual tension*, she acknowledged with a smile. Feeling strangely content, she relaxed her head against the back of the seat. Then opening her eyes once again, she watched the lights of the city stream by through the darkened window.

"You know, I've always hated riding in these things," she said after a few more minutes had passed. "It reminds me I need to pick up my new car in the morning."

In the brief silence that followed, Hunter could feel Sara studying her, could see her biting her lip against whatever question she obviously wanted to ask. "Go ahead. Ask your question."

Sara watched her for another few seconds then gave an odd smile. "It's just I'm not sure what kind of car you're picking up in the morning," she said casually. "But you do know everyone would prefer that you replace the Maserati with something a little less conspicuous, don't you? Or maybe even consider only using the limo until this is all resolved?"

Hunter dismissed the notion with a laugh. "If that's the case, I'd say *everyone* will have to learn to live with disappointment."

Sara nodded, as if she had expected Hunter's response. She tapped her fingers on the seat and they continued in silence a minute longer. "So what is it with you and limos?"

"I grew up being driven to places in them. They're just big and boring...not exactly what a girl needs to make a good first impression." Hunter rolled her eyes, her sigh long-suffering and exaggeratedly dramatic.

Sara chuckled. "I wouldn't think you need that much help to make a good first impression. After all, you're employed, don't have a criminal record, you're reasonably bright, and you're not that hard on the eyes. Hell, when you stop and think about it, you're actually a pretty good catch."

"Thanks, I think. Good to know your criteria. But my grandfather Patrick would have to disagree with you. He thinks that's part of why I've made it to the advanced age of twenty-seven—almost twenty-eight—without having found and married Mr. Right."

"And have you been looking?" Sara asked. "For *Mr.* Right?"

"Not exactly, no. And Grandfather Patrick would tell you that's the other part of the problem. Or at least as far as he's concerned."

"What do you mean?"

Hunter grinned. "He would say I've been wasting too much time fooling around with Ms. Right Now to find Mr. Right."

Sara turned and gently punched Hunter on the arm.

Chapter Seventeen

It turned out to be another restless night. Shortly after Hunter got home, the skies opened up, and for a long time she lay alone in her bed, watching lightning cut jagged streaks against the black sky through the skylight above the bed. She finally tumbled into sleep to the sound of the rain and the waves crashing on the shore.

Almost immediately, the dream returned.

It was always the same. No matter how fast she ran, Brenner still caught her. No matter how hard she tried to hold out, he still forced her to play his game. And no matter how well she played the game, her father still died.

As the night waned, she remained trapped in the past. Heart pounding, her breathing fast and irregular, her skin glistening with sweat, she struggled to break free until at last her own scream jolted her awake with a violent start. She opened her eyes to the crimson numbers on the clock beside her bed, watched them coalesce into the numerals four-three-nine. She groaned.

Terrific, she thought, conceding there would be no more sleep. She struggled to untangle herself from the sheets that had twisted around her and got out of bed, deciding a run in the predawn air would be preferable to spending more time lying in bed with ghosts.

She had always loved running early in the morning and tried to get in a run no matter where she found herself. But there was no comparison between running through congested city streets and the early morning solitude the beach offered. It was in the quiet of the early morning that she did her best thinking, and running, or any other kind of physical activity, always seemed to help her sort her thoughts—something she was particularly eager to do.

After a quick wash, she dressed in a pair of running shorts and a cutoff sweatshirt. She grabbed a baseball cap and slipped it on, adjusting it so her hair poked out the back in a loose tail.

A light rain was still falling as she stepped out the front door into the ethereal light of the misty dawn. The cool air brushed the bare skin of her abdomen, and she took a moment to breathe deeply as she stretched. She vaguely acknowledged when Conner and Adrienne got out of the black SUV parked near the front entrance to the house without saying a word, joining her in completing a series of stretches. They then set off, breaking into a light run along the cobblestone drive.

Beyond the gate, they jogged briefly along the road before turning onto a narrow path that meandered down toward the water. At the end of the footpath, they hit the sand running. Hunter chose to go in the direction of the Golden Gate Bridge, and running at a steady pace, their long strides began eating up the distance. The moist air was heavy with the smell of salt, pine, and cypress, and for the next hour, the only sounds that surrounded them were their running shoes hitting the wet sand and the colorful pebbles dancing in the waves along the shore.

As she ran, as if of their own volition, Hunter's thoughts kept returning to the previous evening. *And Sara.*

She had spent the better part of the evening enthralled by Sara. Imagining how her lips felt when she kissed, how her skin tasted. Wanting nothing more than to lose herself in her. But when Sara had raised the question of safety, it had been as effective as a cold shower on her libido.

In the end, she saw Sara safely home to Kate's house and left her with only a chaste kiss on the palm of her hand. For now, at least, that would have to be enough.

Hunter sighed as she remembered the look on Sara's face when she had dropped her off at the door. A look of confusion and disbelief—Sara undoubtedly wondering if she had misread the signals Hunter had been sending her all evening.

You certainly didn't, Hunter thought wryly and knew she would have to make amends at the earliest opportunity.

When the three women returned to the house just after six, Hunter wordlessly continued up the stairs until she reached the third-level master suite, leaving it to Conner and Adrienne to sort out between themselves who would shower first and who would make the coffee. She quickly stripped her rain- and sweat-soaked running gear as she walked into the bath. Then setting the water temperature, she slid into the shower. A moment later, she was enjoying the hot water cascading over her body. Briefly, she ducked her head, then slicked her hair back and just let the heat envelop her.

By the time she returned to the kitchen, the scent of fresh coffee was beginning to permeate the air. Standing in the doorway, she stared as she saw Conner by the fridge, her hair still damp from her shower. She was pulling together breakfast possibilities, and as Hunter watched, eggs and aged cheddar quickly joined the bread and half a stick of butter already on the counter.

"I take it you won the coin toss."

Startled, Conner looked up, then smiled sheepishly and nodded. "What can I say? Adrienne just seems to make better coffee than I do. And you really need to restock. You're out of milk. Can you handle the toast?"

"Possibly." Hunter reached for the bread and popped two slices into the toaster. "When do you suppose Adrienne will figure out you're using a two-headed coin?"

Conner grinned but didn't respond.

Hunter watched as Conner cracked the eggs into a bowl, added salt and pepper, then whisked them before pouring the mix into a hot skillet. When she turned down the heat and began to stir the eggs, Hunter drew closer. "I have to admit, I'm in awe of anyone who can fix a meal and have everything ready at the same time. But that doesn't look too difficult."

"It's not—difficult, that is. Is it something you're interested in learning?"

"Maybe. Why not?" For an instant, she pictured herself sharing a breakfast of scrambled eggs, bagels, and coffee, along with the Sunday paper, while spread out lazily in bed. Natural, normal, almost domestic—the image startled her back to reality. "Just because I've never done it doesn't mean I can't learn."

Conner refrained from commenting. Instead, she handed the wooden spoon she was using to Hunter. "Just keep stirring them," she instructed, "gently. Now let's add the cheese."

By the time Adrienne returned from her shower, Conner was buttering toast while Hunter piled scrambled eggs onto three plates and carried them to the table where juice and coffee had already been poured.

"Which one of you cooked?" Adrienne asked, her tone clearly suspicious as she stared at the plate in front of her.

Hunter raised a single eyebrow in a challenging gesture. "Is there a problem?"

Adrienne said a quick no and reached for a piece of toast before she changed the subject. "Anything on the agenda today?"

"I just need to pick up my new car this morning," Hunter responded calmly before adding, "and then I thought I'd go in to the office and meet with the whole team, so we can discuss who authorized these damned changes to my personal security. After that, I thought I'd lay out what will be considered acceptable on a go-forward basis."

She could see Adrienne swallow thickly and glanced at Conner, who was suddenly focused rather intently on her breakfast and did not look up. Obviously choosing discretion over valor, Adrienne ducked her head and followed suit. But Hunter could hardly blame her. After all, since it was likely either Matt or Peter arranged for all the security measures that were causing her displeasure, it was only fair they should be the ones to face her wrath.

Watching Adrienne and Conner, Hunter hastily swallowed a mouthful of coffee so she wouldn't lose it laughing.

❖

By early afternoon, Hunter was in possession of her new car, the rain had stopped, and her team was in a conference room, poring over reports. Connecting the dots on names in the hospital database of everyone who worked at the hospital ten years earlier and matched the profile in terms of age and gender. *Welcome to the information age.*

The reports they were generating were extensive and would eventually cover everything from employment histories and financial activities to relationships and travel patterns. Given a bit more time, they could probably determine what each of the subjects had for breakfast, Hunter thought dryly. More to the point, she wondered how many of the people on the list had traveled to New York in March.

Sitting at her desk, she twirled her pen absently in her hand while she scanned the latest contracts Tessa had drafted, giving them one last read over before scrawling her signature at the bottom of each page. Satisfied, she threw both her arms over her head in a stretch and was just about to wade into the next stack of printouts when Quito appeared at her doorway.

He smiled tentatively. "This came for you a little while ago," he said and waved the large manila envelope in his hands. "The courier was adamant it be delivered to you immediately, but I didn't recognize the sender. I hope you don't mind, but I had security scan it."

"Right thing to do. Thanks," Hunter replied easily, taking a sip of coffee. "Just leave it on the desk, and I'll take a look at it in a minute. I'm finished reviewing these contracts. Can you get them back to Tessa?"

She stared at the envelope Quito placed on the corner of her desk while waiting for him to leave. Once the heavy door clicked shut behind him, she took a deep steadying breath and picked up the envelope, uncertain why such a simple act was causing her trepidation. Chagrined, she ripped it open and spilled its contents on the desk.

And found she was staring at a photograph of herself. Holding hands and laughing with Sara as they left Club Vertigo just last night.

The blood drained from her face, and Hunter felt anger laced with fear welling up within her. Her nostrils flared, and her grip on her coffee mug increased until her knuckles stood out in vivid relief against the black mug.

Alongside the photograph was a note, handwritten and addressed to her.

> *Hunter,*
> *Enjoy the doctor while you can. Just remember…*
> *When the time comes, you are mine.*

Her eyes closed momentarily and she took another sip of coffee. Letting out a shaky breath, she made her way to the window, then about-faced and hurled her mug at the wall.

"Son of a bitch." Turning away from the coffee-stained wall, Hunter stormed out of her office past the conference room where her startled team watched her, questions in their eyes. "I'll be in the gym if anyone's looking for me."

❖

It was late afternoon when Sara exited the cab and approached the entrance to the Roswell building. She struggled to relax, anxious and uncertain because the previous evening had ended on what could only be described as a confusing note. The problem was compounded because Sara wasn't sure where the night had gone off the rails.

Although they had not spoken about it directly during the drive back to Kate's house, Sara knew she hadn't imagined the electrically charged atmosphere. There had been one moment in particular. A moment when her eyes had locked with Hunter's and the energy around them seemed to burn even brighter and hotter. As Sara had sat transfixed by Hunter's gaze, her heart rate had increased and her vision had narrowed until all she could see was this woman she barely knew yet felt she had known for a lifetime.

Unconsciously she had leaned forward, an inch at a time, then pulled back awkwardly, stopping at the last second as she realized she was about to kiss Hunter. The moment passed without either of them openly acknowledging it. But Sara had fully expected Hunter to follow her inside when they'd arrived at Kate's.

Instead, Hunter had walked her to the door, lifted Sara's right hand, brought it to her lips, and lightly kissed her open palm. She'd whispered good night, and without so much as another word or a backward glance, she'd moved down the walkway, her long strides taking her swiftly back to a waiting limousine.

What the hell did it all mean?

Sara hoped she was about to find out. Her throat was dry and her stomach was churning, but in spite of her nerves, she finger-combed her breeze-tousled hair, held her chin up, and entered the building.

As she reached security, she pulled out her ID and handed it to one of the uniformed guards, along with her weapon. He glanced at the ID before returning it—and her gun—and then passed her a small envelope.

"What's this?" Sara asked, not recognizing the bold handwriting that addressed the envelope to her.

"Ms. Roswell left it for you, Dr. Wilder," the guard responded. "The executive offices and operations center are on the top floor. The elevator's straight ahead, stairs are on your right." He then tapped his forehead in a brief salute and resumed checking visitors.

Moving to the side, Sara opened the envelope and found a small silver-and-black pin bearing the Roswell Group logo. The pin was accompanied by a brief note.

Thought this might help you keep my wolves at bay...H.

Sara looked down at the pin and recognized it as similar to the one Quito had been wearing in London. *Well, at least she's been thinking about you.* Smiling softly as she attached the pin to her collar, Sara easily cleared security and continued to think about the events of the previous evening.

Her recollections weren't coherent. Just a kaleidoscope of images of Hunter. The way she moved when she danced. Her incredible face. Her heart-melting smile. And her amazing eyes. Idly, Sara wondered what it would be like to see those eyes burn with passion, and she sighed.

Jesus, get a grip.

Any way she looked at it, she was asking for trouble. *Hunter did you a favor last night*, she told herself, *by stopping things from escalating any further and walking away.* Because getting involved with Hunter Roswell, on a personal level, had trouble written all over it.

If she was making a list, the fact that Hunter was a person of interest in a high-profile case should be near the very top of reasons not to get involved. The rules—both written and unwritten—were there for a reason. She was also Senator Patrick Roswell's only grandchild and the heir to the de León family empire. That made her bona fide royalty.

What could come of it?

If she wanted what was best for Hunter, she should keep their involvement to a business relationship. No strings, nothing personal.

But there was no denying she had one hell of a face. A dangerous face. A woman who allowed that face to draw her in would get exactly what she deserved…and probably enjoy every minute of it. Because she hadn't imagined the chemistry. Hunter could make her body sing and caused tiny sparks of sexual heat to sizzle along her nerve endings without even trying. And there was something deeper, something on a level Sara couldn't remember experiencing before. Something was telling her this gorgeous, enigmatic woman should be a part of her life.

Like a moth drawn to a flame, she was damned well going to see where this could lead. And at the same time, she was going to do her damnedest to protect Hunter from whoever wanted to play games with her. Simple. Nothing to it.

When she reached Hunter's office, she was surprised to find David there, conferring with Matt, Conner, and Adrienne by Hunter's desk. Just beyond where they were gathered, Quito was quietly picking up the remnants of a coffee mug, the pieces scattered on the floor in front of what looked like a huge coffee-colored Rorschach test gracing the far wall. Hunter was nowhere to be seen.

"What's happened?" she asked as she entered the room.

David shot her a tight-lipped look while Matt beckoned her over to the desk. Without saying a word, he placed the photograph and handwritten note he had been holding on the desk for Sara to see.

"What the hell is this?" As Sara glanced at the photograph, her breath caught in her throat. She looked back at Matt and David.

"I think this qualifies as direct contact, don't you?" Matt replied. "It was delivered by courier a little over two hours ago. The courier's behavior was a bit erratic, and Quito didn't recognize the sender's name, so he had security scan the envelope. It came up clean for chemicals and foreign substances and—what a surprise— no fingerprints, not even the courier's."

"Son of a bitch."

"The sender's address turns out to be a parking lot. And while the courier company is legit," Matt added, "they have no record of a delivery being made to this address today."

"Son of a bitch," Sara repeated, and then froze. "Do you think it was him? Do you suppose he tried to deliver the envelope himself?"

"That's a distinct possibility," Matt responded tightly. "I've already asked to have all of today's security discs pulled for both the parking lot and the lobby downstairs. If he attempted the actual delivery, we'll not only have him on the discs, we should be able to identify his vehicle tags as well."

"Exactly," David said softly. "Sara, can I talk to you in private?"

Distracted, Sara glanced at him. "Yeah, sure. In a minute." Turning to Matt, she asked, "Where's Hunter?"

"She went down to the gym," he responded.

"Then what the hell are we doing here?" Sara asked, her voice touched with incredulity and concern. "If the courier turns out to be her stalker, then he's escalating at an unanticipated rate. Hunter shouldn't be wandering anywhere by herself."

"The building is secure, but I agree with you she shouldn't be by herself." Matt shrugged and indicated the doorway. "Let's go."

After asking Adrienne and Conner to pick up the discs from the security office, Matt waited for Sara to precede him. But as Sara moved toward the door, David reached out and loosely grabbed her arm to stop her. "Sara?"

Exasperated, Sara shook his hand from her arm. Turning to face him, she snapped, "What is it, David?"

"I really need to talk to you before we go any further."

Out of the corner of her eye, Sara saw Matt leave the office and close the door, giving them some privacy. She took a deep breath and slowly let it out, trying to calm herself before turning to face David.

"What's the problem?" she asked.

David moved closer. He indicated the photograph on the desk with his index finger. "What's going on?"

"With what? That photograph? I'd say it means the UNSUB is following Hunter rather closely. Wouldn't you?"

"I can see that," David said, frustration creeping into his voice. "But let me tell you what else I can see. I can see trouble. You want to know why? Because I see a picture of you holding hands with someone who had been deemed a person of interest in a series of homicides. Christ, Sara. What the hell were you thinking?"

Sara was momentarily stunned. She looked at David in disbelief. "Excuse me?"

"I said—"

"I heard what you said, David," Sara shot back. "I just can't believe you said it. I'm also trying to figure out what concern it is of yours."

"Rule number three," he responded. "Never get involved with someone connected to a case."

She stared at him in silence, gathering her thoughts. "I'm making my own rules now, especially when they pertain to my personal life. And even if I wasn't, Hunter changes all the rules."

"Damn it, Sara. Don't you know this kind of thing can—"

"What, David?" Sara challenged, meeting his rising temper with her own. "Out me? I've been out since I was sixteen. Damage my career? Get me fired? The FBI can't fire me since I don't work for them anymore. And I haven't for almost eight months. It would seem you're the only one that's having a problem accepting that."

David sagged as if he had been punched, and his shoulders slumped. "You're right," he said. "I just thought—"

"You thought getting me to work this case with you would maybe get the juices flowing again. Maybe make me want to come back to work for the bureau," Sara finished softly. She looked her former partner in the eye, a gentle smile making its way to her lips. "I still have every intention of helping you with this case, David. But in my own way. Not as an agent. And I'm not coming back to work for the bureau. Not now and not when this case is over. I'm sorry."

"And the photograph…you and Hunter? You seem to have gotten close rather quickly. Is there something going on between the two of you?"

"Ah hell. I don't know." Her voice trailed off and she sighed. "All I can tell you is although I haven't known her for very long, she makes me feel things I didn't even know I was capable of feeling." She looked up at him and cringed slightly, aware that on some level, David also had feelings for Hunter. "I can imagine what this sounds like to you. But it's the truth. As for where this is going, I have no idea."

"Well," David said, "if the way Hunter's looking at you in that photograph is anything to go by, I'd say something is definitely going on." He paused for just a second. "Strictly speaking, you've never been one to follow rules. But just be careful, Sara. Hunter Roswell's—"

"Hunter's what, David?"

Lowering his eyes, David shrugged awkwardly. "She's got a reputation, and I just don't want to see you get hurt, that's all."

"Yeah, well, I guess only time will tell," Sara replied. "In the meantime, I think we have our work cut out for us, don't you? We need to head down to the gym and talk to Hunter. See how she's doing and make sure she's okay. And then we need to check the security discs and see what we have there. Maybe we caught a break."

David agreed thoughtfully. "He wanted to deliver the envelope directly to Hunter and he got foiled. That had to make him angry. Maybe angry enough he'll make a mistake we can use to find him."

"Yeah, maybe." Sara paused then asked softly, "Are we okay?"

David responded by draping a beefy arm around Sara's shoulders and squeezing. "Yeah, we're good." He opened the door and together they joined Matt who was waiting patiently by the stairway.

"Everything okay?" he asked, eyeing Sara and David as they approached.

Receiving twin nods, the three of them simultaneously hit the stairs.

CHAPTER EIGHTEEN

A s they approached the gym, the pounding rhythm of the music emanating from the sound system threatened to deafen anyone who dared come too close. Undaunted, Sara, David, and Matt stopped at the doorway and peered into the large area.

Not surprisingly, given the wall of sound, there were only two people working out—Peter, backing up and on the defensive, and Hunter, attacking aggressively. Judging from the saturation of their clothing and hair, they had been at it for quite some time. Hunter's skin was slick, and her ponytail scattered droplets of sweat with every movement.

"According to Peter, she's been working out like this since she went to London," Matt commented as he observed Hunter with a critical eye.

"What do you mean?" Sara asked.

"All out. Complete and total focus," he responded. "It's like she gets in a zone. Almost like a trance. At this point, Peter's the only one willing to spar with her."

Hunter seemed oblivious of her audience. She continued attacking with a near-absolute ferocity and tunnel-vision focus. As Sara watched, Hunter erupted in a series of explosive jabs and a sweeping high kick, her movements matching the hard-driving music pouring from the speakers. An instant later, she spun 360 degrees while airborne, dark hair flying wildly about her face as she delivered a kick that lifted Peter off his feet before dropping him hard, while Hunter landed with the grace of a cat.

For an endless moment, she stood with her sparring-gloved hands hanging loosely at her sides as she struggled for breath. Then she turned, and her eyes narrowed slightly as she caught sight of the trio standing by the gym entrance.

She inhaled and exhaled for several breaths, her eyes hot and brooding, her shoulders stiff. Tugging her gloves off and tucking them under one arm, she walked to the sound system and turned the music off. The sudden silence in the room seemed almost as deafening as the music had been.

When she turned back to face them, her face was devoid of expression. "Is there something someone wants?"

Her question hung suspended in the silent air between them until Matt finally responded. "We thought you might want to join us for a little show and tell. But if you're busy—"

"Planning on reviewing the security discs without me?" Hunter's voice was cool and calm, reflecting no trace of amusement. But Sara could see her eyes were laughing.

"Wouldn't dream of it," Matt replied.

"Damn, she's good," Sara murmured.

From across the room, Hunter's eyes met hers and Sara felt it. Instantly. A spark ignited deep within her and spread like a fire, burning away any thought of resistance she might have had. She didn't bother trying to hide her reaction from Hunter.

"I'll need a bit of time to get cleaned up before we review the discs. Say in an hour in conference room two?" Hunter's eyes remained locked on Sara's, and for a brief instant, a smile touched her face. "I believe I need a cold shower first."

❖

It was almost exactly an hour later when everyone gathered in the large top-floor conference room. Sara settled back into a chair at the long table and watched Quito set up the series of monitors and a large video screen while Conner cued the security discs.

Hunter was dressed in a cotton shirt and baggy jeans that hung low on her lean hips. Her hair was wet from the shower and falling freely around her face. As she leaned against the doorframe, she could hear the others talking tersely around her as if she wasn't there, and she knew if she closed her eyes, she could almost pretend she wasn't. But reality beckoned.

Matt caught her eye. "Back among the living?"

Hunter laughed softly and moved into the room. She chose a seat at the head of the table between Sara and Tessa. The tension in the room eased considerably, and she let the conversations drift as she watched the monitor in front of her come to life. Conner set up a split screen to cover both the exterior and interior views. "Hey, Q, what time did you get the call from security?"

"Twelve twenty-two."

"I'll start the disc at twelve hundred." Conner glanced at Hunter, received a nod of agreement. She swiftly input her selection then leaned back to watch her monitor as the images appeared. Beside her, Adrienne leaned forward in total concentration.

The exterior scanners enabled them to watch a steady stream of vehicles—cars, SUVs, vans—pull in and out. The vehicles picked up or dropped off passengers, and any arrivals were then captured by the interior scanners as they approached security. There seemed to be a lot of traffic.

"Smart boy, picking the lunch hour," Peter commented. "Lots of people coming and going. Maybe he thought that would help him slip through security."

Sara shook her head. "I don't think so," she said thoughtfully. "He may be escalating but he's not a fool. He'd have done his homework and had a good idea of the security systems that are in place. In fact, I'd hazard a guess this was not his first visit."

"How far back do you think we're talking?" Matt asked.

"We could be looking at anytime since you moved the Roswell Group into this location." Sara glanced at Hunter and saw her nod her head. An instant later, she saw her stiffen.

"Stop. Freeze that frame."

All conversation ceased and everyone directed their attention to the white courier van with green markings currently frozen on the screen. Almost immediately, Conner split the screen further, narrowing the focus and increasing magnification until the license plate became clearly visible.

David said, "Gotcha, you bastard."

At the same time, Hunter gave a sharp laugh.

"What is it?" Sara asked as she turned toward Hunter.

An uneasy silence fell in the room as faces turned to look at Hunter. "Don't bother to run the plates," she said easily.

"Why the hell not?" David asked.

"Because they're mine," she drawled easily. "The son of a bitch must have lifted the plates from the Maserati before he blew it up in the San Quentin parking lot. His idea of a joke, I guess."

"Cocky bastard. I'm not sure I like his sense of humor," Conner said as she tapped some keys and sent the frozen image of the van to the printer.

"Let's see what he does," Hunter said to Conner, who tapped another key. Hunter was watching intently, her eyes never leaving the screen, taking in every detail. The van on the screen resumed moving until it pulled into a designated short-term parking spot near the front entrance. A minute later, the driver's door opened and a man stepped out.

Sara felt immediate disappointment when she saw the brim of the baseball cap he wore pulled low, and his face further obscured by wraparound sunglasses. At best, they were left with an image of a pale face, a thin mouth, and short, light brown hair. He appeared to be of average height and weight and was dressed in dark green work pants and a pale green short-sleeved shirt with the courier company logo prominently displayed on the left pocket.

Hunter left her seat and moved swiftly over to where Conner was seated. Conner slid the keyboard toward her and in a heartbeat Hunter began to quickly tap a series of keystrokes while muttering softly to herself.

"What are you doing?" Sara wanted to know.

"Creating a sample biometric image." The answer came simultaneously from both Conner and Hunter.

"Hearing it in stereo doesn't help some of us," David chimed in. "Can we get that in English?"

"Most of the time, when I try to explain to someone what it is I do, they get this glassy look in their eyes," Hunter joked, never taking her eyes off the screen while her fingers continued to fly over the keyboard. "Are you sure you want to know?"

"Try us," Sara challenged. "But keep it simple."

"I'm not sure I can do simple, but I'll try," Hunter laughed. "Okay, I'm converting his image into something called a biometric template. Once we have that, we'll be able to do two things. First we'll take the partial image from the security video and construct an entire face from it using 3-D face-recognition technology. We will then be able to compare the output to previously stored templates and see if we can come up with a possible match that can be used to identify him."

David dragged his hand through his hair. "Assuming I understood half of what you just said, exactly what do you mean by previously stored templates?" He looked like he didn't really want to know the answer.

"The database containing staff photo IDs from San Francisco General," Hunter replied, grinning unrepentantly when David winced. "It'll be a bigger challenge because we're missing some key features, particularly his eyes. It just means it'll take longer, but it can still be done. We'll run what we have using a biometric face-recognition algorithm which calculates a match score. A high match score indicates a likelihood the corresponding images are from the same individual."

David sat up straighter. "I still don't fully understand, but I think you're telling me that just possibly he got cocky and screwed up." He whistled. "Son of a bitch."

"Let's hope so," Hunter replied softly, her eyes still glued to the face frozen on her monitor. "I'll let you know."

Hunter slipped back into her seat while Conner resumed running the security discs. Sara could see their target retrieve a large envelope from the van and enter the building, at which time the interior scanners immediately picked him up. He paused as he entered, and then looked up to his left and smiled directly into one of the cameras. Just before he turned away, his lips moved and he appeared to say something.

"Damn," she whispered. "He knows—"

"Mm-hmm," Hunter replied. "Just maybe he didn't screw up."

They continued to watch as their target reached the security desk. They could see his lips move as he spoke to one of the guards. Conner glanced at Hunter.

"I can give you audio if you'd like," she said.

Hunter nodded. "Do it. But back it up to where he first looked into the camera. See if you can pick up what he said."

Although Hunter had spoken with a practiced nonchalance, Sara watched as stormy emotions flashed in her eyes and noted the unmistakable tension visible in her neck and shoulders. Reaching under the table, she placed her hand on Hunter's thigh and squeezed it reassuringly.

It was a small gesture and at first there was no discernable response. But then she felt the warmth of a hand as it covered her own, which she kept pressed firmly against Hunter's thigh. Hunter turned to look at her and gave her an appreciative glance. An instant later the audio came on.

"You are mine, Hunter."

Almost immediately, Sara felt Hunter freeze. Turning, she saw her close her eyes. Watched as a fast-beating pulse danced at the base of her throat, and a sheen of perspiration filmed her skin. Saw her take a deep breath and fight to steady herself.

"Shit…" Hunter's voice died.

It more than what he's saying, Sara realized as she watched something resembling panic flash across Hunter's face. *It's his voice. She recognized his voice.*

"Are you all right?" Sara asked.

Sara's question allowed Hunter to focus on something other than the voice coming through the speakers.

You are mine.

She stared at Sara for long seconds, the muscles in her jaw clenching and unclenching in a rhythmic dance as she tried to maintain her composure. She wanted to move. Needed to do something. Anything to escape what she was feeling.

Finding it hard to breathe, Hunter closed her eyes and took a shaky breath. When she opened her eyes, she pushed her chair away from the table, stumbling slightly as she got up and moved to the window. She stood there for endless moments, just staring. Looking out but seeing nothing, she fought to keep herself from feeling too much, remembering too much.

You are mine.

As Hunter struggled to hold it together, Sara stood up and moved behind her. "Take long, slow breaths. Nice and easy," she instructed quietly. She placed her hands on Hunter's shoulders, her thumbs resting against the back of her neck, and gently kneaded the tense muscles under her fingers until she could feel them start to loosen.

Not caring that the others might be watching, Hunter sank into the touch with a sense of relief.

"Better?"

"Hmm."

"You need to take a break."

Hunter nodded as she turned her head and returned Sara's gaze. "I think you're right," she said. "Will you come home with me? I think…I think I'd like to talk to you about New York."

There was no hesitation, no question. "Of course."

As Sara waited for Hunter to speak with Matt and gather her things, she locked eyes with Tessa who gave her what looked like a quick nod of approval. Feeling pleased, Sara distracted herself by wondering what kind of car Hunter had bought to replace the Maserati.

CHAPTER NINETEEN

"This is one hell of a car," Sara sighed, reverently running a finger along the side of the sleek Lamborghini. "Somehow I don't think it qualifies as anyone's idea of inconspicuous, but it's a really, really nice car."

"I like it," Hunter replied, but her voice held an edge of unanticipated anger, and a frown creased her forehead as she held the door open for Sara.

Hunter's tone sent a chill creeping across Sara's skin, and her concern increased as she glanced over. Something had obviously happened during the twenty minutes between the end of their meeting and the time Hunter reappeared by the elevator. It was also readily apparent to Sara that whatever transpired had triggered the anger that had been on simmer all afternoon, so it now bubbled dangerously close to the surface.

"Do you still want to do this?"

"Yes." Hunter slowly let out a breath of air and didn't say anything else.

Once she was ensconced in the butter-soft leather seats, Sara leaned back and tried to relax. She watched as Hunter dropped into the driver's seat beside her, and seconds later, the powerful engine roared to life. A blip on the throttle yielded instantaneous acceleration, and the security guard manning the booth had to scramble to raise the gate. Sara saw him give a thumbs-up and heard him laugh with delight over the roar of the engine. Hunter gave him a cheeky salute in return before turning out of the parking lot and onto the busy street. A black SUV followed at a discreet distance.

"Brat," Sara said, admiring the smooth way Hunter handled the powerful car, downshifting and merging into traffic with a combination of ease and a requisite amount of aggression.

As she drove, Hunter glanced over periodically, her eyes intense and serious. Tilting her chin, Sara met Hunter's gaze the next time she looked over and felt something almost tangible pass between them.

Well, at least that answers one question, Sara decided, noting the look on Hunter's face and the corresponding heat that immediately radiated through her body in response. The seemingly mutual interest and attraction she had felt the previous evening was definitely alive and well, regardless of how the night had ended.

Turning her face, she looked out the passenger window and found herself staring at a reflection of the Lamborghini as they drove past a gleaming storefront. The reflection raised another question that needed to be answered. Sara frowned and contemplated broaching what would undoubtedly be a contentious subject. With all the security concerns circling in her head, the question begged to be asked. Even so, she silently waited for what she hoped was an appropriate length of time before venturing into turbulent waters.

"Has it occurred to you driving this car is a bit like having a matador wave a red cape in front of an already angry bull?"

Hunter felt the surprising slash of hurt and struggled to hide it behind a blank mask. The car was an argument she'd already endured twice. Once with Matt and again with Peter. And while she appreciated their concern, she was tired of defending her choices and felt frustration bubble to the surface. Shifting gears, she responded with an immediate, hard burst of acceleration, the roar of the engine coinciding with the surge of resentment rising from her core.

It took less than thirty seconds for the anger that flared to burn out. And once Hunter's anger was spent, she was left with only a curiously numb feeling as she slowed the car down. "If you have a point, make it."

"I thought I just did," Sara responded gently. "I think this is an amazing car, and I'd do just about anything for a chance to drive it. But the truth is it attracts too much attention. It is also far too easy to spot and will give your stalker an unnecessary advantage."

Hunter remained silent, focusing on traffic while maintaining a white-knuckled grip on the steering wheel. Her concentration broke when Sara reached out, her fingertips touching Hunter's arm. "You might want to consider—"

"I got the car because it was what I wanted," Hunter interrupted. She didn't want to argue, didn't have the energy to defend herself. But she didn't have a choice. "If this stalker has been watching me for the past ten years, he'll know I have a reputation for getting what I want. And since everybody knows I have a weakness for fast cars, I can't see how the damned car can be that much of an issue. In fact, I think the car is a *good* choice, since it's a match for what he'll expect from me. It will also give him the impression he's not getting to me."

She had a point, Sara conceded. She considered what she knew about Hunter's public persona—part genius, part rich playgirl—compared to the sometimes sweetly uncertain woman she thought she was getting to know. Studying Hunter's profile, the smooth line of her jaw, the subtle shift of muscles as she concentrated on the road, she found herself wondering what it was like to try to live up to an image that wasn't necessarily real.

After a moment, she folded her arms across her chest and stared out the window. But she could still feel Hunter's withdrawal, and part of her feared she would simply pull the car to the side of the road and tell her to get out. But instead, Hunter continued to stare straight ahead as she maneuvered through heavy traffic, the car negotiating the hills with ease.

Leaning back, Sara watched the city stream by. The late afternoon sun felt warm on her face, and music played softly on the stereo. When a telltale rumble in her stomach reminded her the last meal she ate felt like days ago, she looked at her watch. Glancing at Hunter, she made a swift decision.

"Have you eaten?" she asked.

The question appeared to startle Hunter out of her thoughts. "Pardon?"

"Food, Hunter. Sustenance. Have you eaten today?"

"I'm not sure, but I don't think so. I haven't really thought much about food lately." Hunter eased the car past slower-moving traffic. "Why? Are you hungry?"

"I'm a little hungry." Sara's stomach grumbled once again and she laughed. "Okay, actually, I'm starving. Do you want to stop and get something to eat first? Or do you want to wait until we get to your place? We could order takeout. Maybe we can talk about what happened in New York over a meal."

"Takeout sounds like a good idea." Hunter grinned unexpectedly. "Especially if we want you to live through the experience of eating at my place."

"You really don't cook?"

"Not much, no. Although, if you promise not to tell anyone, I've been experimenting a bit. How do you feel about Thai?" She reached for her phone as Sara nodded and punched in numbers from memory. "Is there anything in particular you like? Or do you trust me to order?"

"Implicitly." Sara was pleased to see Hunter starting to relax.

Hunter placed their order, a ghost of a smile hovering on her lips as she made her choices and arranged for the meal to be delivered. After their dinner had been taken care of, a comfortable silence settled between them. A short time later, Hunter turned onto an oceanfront cul-de-sac and hit the remote that operated a set of classic wrought-iron gates. The gates opened soundlessly, granting them access to a long cobblestone driveway that led up to the house.

Hunter bypassed the attached four-car garage and pulled up near the front door. The trailing SUV remained at the gate. As Sara stepped out of the car, the first thing she noticed was the quiet. There were no city noises here, no sounds of people or traffic. Instead there was only the sound of the surf and the rustle of a light breeze as it stirred the nearby trees.

❖

Sara had not given a lot of thought to where Hunter might live. At a guess, she might have pictured a high-tech condo or a trendy downtown loft. Instead, what she found was romantic architecture at its best and another glimpse into who Hunter Roswell really was. The entrance to Hunter's home featured a two-story foyer turret with a spiral staircase. Beyond the entrance hall, Sara could see a large sunken living room with walnut floors, beamed ceilings, and vast unobstructed ocean views from almost every vantage point.

"Wow," Sara said.

"I know," Hunter smiled wryly, looking around at the mostly empty rooms. "I've not gotten around to unpacking and decorating."

"That's not what I was going to say. I was simply going to say it's beautiful."

"Oh…thanks. I bought it not long before I went to London. There are still a lot of rooms that are only partially furnished and a lot of boxes that still need to be unpacked."

They stood overlooking the living room, where the late afternoon sunlight was reflecting on the gleaming surface of the baby grand piano, making Sara smile. "You play?

"Yeah. Next to running, playing is probably my favorite way to relax." Walking across the room, she ran her fingers across the keys, letting the notes resonate in the room. "Want to eat out by the pool?"

"Sure, it's a nice evening for it." Sara followed Hunter into the kitchen. "And…oh my God. This kitchen was taken straight out of my dreams." She turned in a circle, an expression of awe on her face as she took in the chef's kitchen with its limestone floors, granite counters, professional appliances, and built-in espresso machine. "It's a real shame you don't cook much."

Hunter glanced over, giving her a droll look. "At the moment, I don't cook anything most people would recognize or want to eat." She shrugged as she opened a cabinet. "I take it you do?"

"You play the piano, I cook." Sara grinned. "It's one of the things I do to relax."

"Well, Kate's always warning me about my poor eating habits. Anytime you're in the mood to relax and maybe take pity on me, you're more than welcome to come over and use my kitchen,"

Hunter offered. "If you can grab some plates and napkins out of there"—she indicated with a nod of her head—"I've got the rest."

Again, Sara thought she caught a flash of something in Hunter's eyes. She couldn't identify it, and in another instant it was gone, almost as if she had imagined it. She thought about pressing the issue, but decided to let it go. Instead, she opened the cupboards, picked up the items Hunter had asked for, and followed her outside.

"This is absolutely beautiful." Sara let a sigh escape as she stood on a multi-level patio surrounding a large swimming pool and Jacuzzi. It was unbelievably peaceful, the air blending the tang of salt and cypress with the intoxicating scent of sweet wisteria and other magical blooms.

She set the plates and napkins down on a table near the edge of the pool. She then finished opening the bottle of merlot Hunter had brought out, letting it breathe while Hunter responded to the intercom announcing the arrival of their meal. When she returned a few minutes later, the packages she carried added the tantalizing aromas of chicken, shrimp, jasmine rice, and spices to the evening air.

Hunter laid the food out and poured Sara a glass of wine, then one for herself. After casting a quick glance at the table making sure nothing was missing, she sat down, propped her bare feet on a spare chair, and picked up what looked like a complex TV remote. As she touched a series of buttons, the lights in the bottom of the swimming pool came on and Enigma drifted from unseen speakers.

"Food looks good, don't you think?" she asked softly.

Sara readily agreed as she plucked a fat shrimp with her chopsticks. She popped it into her mouth and gave an audible moan as she savored the delicate blend of spices. "Oh God, this is really good."

Hunter nodded and sent Sara a self-deprecating grin. "I make it a point to know where all the really good takeout can be found."

Sara ate a few more bites while watching Hunter's silent profile, and then bowed to the inevitable. "Tell me about New York. I know this was about six months ago. How long were you there?" she prompted gently.

Hunter's animated face became instantly still, and the sparkle in her eyes disappeared. The change was dramatic, and Sara regretted she'd been the cause of it.

"Hey. You okay?" she asked, when Hunter didn't speak.

Hunter didn't even try to lie. "No."

Instinct had Sara not touching her. "If you'd rather not do this—if you can't talk to me—you'll have to talk to someone. You know that. Look what it's costing you."

Hunter drew a deep breath to steady herself. *But where the hell do I start?* Stalling for time, she picked up a spring roll and dipped it into the sweet red chili sauce. Then, with a sigh, she said, "I really do want to explain myself to you. Explain what happened. It's just I'm not sure where or how to begin."

After a long stretch of silence, Sara reached out and gently turned Hunter's face toward her. "It's all right, Hunter. I'm not going anywhere. Take your time."

Hunter dropped the spring roll onto her plate untouched and drank her wine instead, barely tasting it. "New York was supposed to be a quick turnaround," she said softly. "I flew in that morning, and I was only supposed to be there a few hours. One meeting, in and out."

"Who were you meeting?"

"The client was Braddock Worldwide. They were looking to do a major upgrade on their security systems. We had already carried out intrusions at three of their locations and determined they were extremely vulnerable. We proposed a complete redesign and had been talking for a while, ironing out all the details. This was meant to be the final meeting to seal the deal. Just their CEO Max Braddock and me."

"Isn't that a bit unusual?"

"For someone else, maybe, but not for Max. Rumor has it that's how he made his fortune. One deal at a time and always personally involved at the end." Hunter turned her wineglass in her hands and looked a bit lost in thought.

"You like Braddock."

"More than that…I respect him." After a few seconds, she looked up, her expression pensive. "I never sit at the table without knowing who I'm going to be facing."

"And Peter McNeil gave you a file on Braddock at least an inch thick prior to your meeting," Sara said with a grin.

Hunter might have laughed if she hadn't been so tied up in knots. "Actually, Peter provided me with his usual thorough background check long before the meeting in New York," she said. "When Max dismissed his negotiation team and took over personally, then asked me to fly out and meet with him, it was right on schedule. I expected it."

Sara looked quizzically at her as if she could sense her sudden discomfort, hear the uncertainty in her voice. As if she knew intuitively Hunter's discomfort had nothing to do with Max Braddock or the negotiations they had conducted in New York. But instead of delving deeper, Sarah merely smiled. "Try the shrimp. It's really good." She topped up their wine glasses before gently nudging the conversation forward. "What happened next?"

Hunter struggled to recall the blurred memories she had of that fateful day. "As I said, I flew out in the morning, and I remember arranging for the limo to pick me up and take me back to La Guardia at six forty-five. But things went really well, and we were able to finalize the deal early, finishing everything just before five."

She paused and met Sara's eyes as she reconsidered the options she had faced and the decisions she had made that afternoon. "I suppose—no, the smart thing would have been to call and have the limo pick me up early. Or simply grab a cab. But we'd been working nonstop on this deal for so long, and the thought of having almost two hours to myself was too damned appealing to pass up."

Sara listened quietly to what was being said—both the spoken words and the unspoken ones—and tried to anticipate the events as they had occurred, trying to stay ahead of wherever Hunter was leading her. So much hurt there, she realized. So much pain. She wondered where it had its roots. "Where did you go?"

"That's the funny thing. I didn't actually go anywhere. Max and I had chosen to meet at a small boutique hotel on Park Avenue.

More informal, neutral territory. The hotel had a fairly nice little bar, and I just went in for a drink."

"And some quiet anonymity?"

Hunter's eyes widened slightly, and she gave Sara a startled glance. "Yeah, something like that," she confessed. "It was quiet, not too many people, but I remember this guy came over and sat down beside me. Kept insisting he wanted to buy me a drink and didn't want to take no for an answer."

"What did you do?" Sara asked quietly.

"I blew him off, finished my drink, and left shortly thereafter." She paused, moistened her lips, and when she looked up, her eyes seemed dark and haunted. "That's just about the last clear memory I have of that day."

"What did he look like?" *Did he have a pale face? Did he have a thin mouth and light brown hair? Did he look anything like the man on the security video?*

Hunter shook her head, her frustration evident. "That's just it," she said. "I don't remember. I mean, he could have been anyone. Nothing about him really stood out, and I wasn't paying much attention because I wasn't interested in whatever thrill he was selling. I just wanted him to go away and leave me alone."

Sara regarded Hunter silently. "What do you remember next?"

"Waking up in an alley near the East River about twelve hours later," Hunter said. The flatness of her delivery hid most of her pain behind a cool façade. "It was dark, and I was cold and dizzy and nauseous. I hurt all over and I kept passing out. I have no idea how long it was before I could remain conscious for more than a minute or two at a time."

"Sweet Jesus." Sara leaned forward. She noted Hunter was beginning to breathe more rapidly and resisted the urge to touch her. "What did you do?"

"When I was finally able to manage a coherent thought, I called Matt and let him know where I was," Hunter replied. "I told him what I could—which wasn't a lot. By the time I finished, my right eye had swollen nearly closed and my left eye wasn't far behind. I also seemed to be bleeding from a cut on my ribcage. I got the hell out of there while I still could and managed to get myself to an ER."

"Christ, Hunter. How badly were you hurt?"

Hunter smiled weakly for just an instant. "I looked like I went ten rounds with a Golden Gloves champ and lost every round. Fortunately, I really looked much worse than it was. Aside from the black eyes, a split lip, and an assortment of contusions, the worst injuries were a couple of cuts, bruised ribs, and a bruised kidney."

"If you say so," Sara responded. She waited a few seconds and then prodded gently. "But that's not all, is it?"

Hunter shook her head, reached for her wine, and drank it down in one long swallow. Her voice broke slightly on her next words.

"There were abrasions…ligature marks, actually…on my wrists. And the staff in the emergency department expressed surprise I was able to make it in under my own steam. According to one of the doctors, I was a chemical stew."

Sara studied Hunter's face and raised her eyebrows. "What exactly does that mean?"

"The toxicology screen came back positive for Ecstasy, benzodiazepine, and Rohypnol."

"And you didn't—"

"Not knowingly."

"Do you know if the doctor did a rape kit?" Sara asked evenly.

Hunter nodded. "Some of the blood on me wasn't mine, so unless there was a third person there, I can tell you he's A positive. But so is thirty-five percent of the US population."

She stopped and glanced at Sara before continuing. Her next words were stark and devoid of emotion. "There was also a fair amount of bruising, but according to the doc, there was no evidence of any recent sexual activity."

Sara's chest tightened as she heard the clinical response to her question, and she took a grateful breath. As selfish as it seemed, she didn't want to hear any more right now. She reached out tentatively toward Hunter before stopping herself from touching her. She wasn't sure the physical contact would be welcomed, and she was already treading on dangerous ground.

"There are a couple of other things you need to know about that night." Hunter's words continued to be delivered in a detached monotone. "He may not have left a lot of trace evidence, but he did leave me a note. I found it tucked in the front pocket of my jeans."

Sara gazed into stormy blue eyes and asked the question although she already knew what the answer would be. "What did the note say?"

"It said 'You are mine,' of course. Did you have any doubt?" Hunter stared down at her hands. "I should have told you before now. I mean that I'd had previous contact with your serial killer."

"Mm-hmm," Sara said. "You said there were a couple of things I needed to know. I'm going to assume the other is you recognized his voice this afternoon when we were viewing the security disc. Am I correct?"

"'You are mine.'" Hunter repeated the phrase like a mantra. Her words were whispered and toneless, but the flash of anger in the blue eyes was unmistakable. "He must have said that to me during those missing hours. It's the one thing I remember clearly. The damned phrase was still echoing in my head when I first regained consciousness in that alley." With suddenly trembling hands, Hunter reached for the wine bottle and emptied the remains into her glass. "How did you know?"

"Your reaction to the sound of his voice on the security disc this afternoon left little room for doubt."

Hunter gently swirled the wine in her glass. She watched as the glow from the swimming pool was reflected in the translucent liquid and swiftly downed the contents of the glass. Placing the empty glass on the table, she stood up abruptly and went into the house. Once in the kitchen, she stopped, feeling her knees go weak, and leaned against a wall for support until the sensation passed.

Her confidence had deserted her—that edge that helped her keep one step ahead—and she'd never felt more lost. She stood there for a long, hard moment while she shored up her defenses and battled an inexplicable and uncharacteristic need to weep.

Sara looked up when Hunter returned a short time later with a freshly opened bottle of wine in her hand. "What is it?" she asked in a soft voice.

"Sorry. I guess I had a bit of a flashback." Their eyes met, and Hunter let herself absorb the empathy she found mirrored there. "It also suddenly occurred to me I've no idea what he intended to have happen in New York. And for some reason, it's important." Her gaze was unwavering as she looked at Sara. "Do you think he meant for everything to begin and end there?"

"What exactly do you want to know?"

Hunter drew in a ragged breath and stared over Sara's shoulder, not really seeing anything. "Do you think he meant to play out the game to its logical conclusion?" She tried to keep herself together long enough to get out the next few words. "Was I meant to die in New York?"

When Hunter sat down, Sara took the wine bottle from her hands and refilled both their glasses. "I'm not sure what answer you're looking for, Hunter. I can only tell you I doubt he intended to kill you. What's important—what you need to focus on—is even if that was his intent, he didn't succeed."

Hunter nodded her head absently, her eyes fixed on the horizon. "No, he didn't succeed," she repeated. "My problem is I've no idea what happened that night. No idea where he took me. I don't know if he let me get away because that was his plan all along or whether I got away from him on my own. All I know for sure is five women have died since that night."

"You couldn't have stopped that from happening," Sara said softly. "For what it's worth, I believe he saw New York simply as an opportunity to escalate."

Hunter folded her arms across her chest, her eyes narrowing as she turned toward Sara. "What do you mean?"

"He's a stalker," Sara replied. "He's been following you for some time, playing a game and enjoying it. He knows you have a security team that's seldom far away. When he followed you to New York and saw you alone in the bar, it was an opportunity too good to pass up, and he decided to approach you."

"And it angered him when I blew him off."

"Probably," Sara replied carefully. "He slipped you something—most likely the Rohypnol—and simply waited. Roofies can have no color, smell, or taste, so there would have been nothing to alert you."

"And when I left the bar a short while later, he just followed me out?"

"You would have been dizzy. Disoriented. Having difficulty with motor function, difficulty speaking," Sara continued. "He may have had a car nearby, but considering you were in Manhattan, it's more likely he hailed a cab. He would have easily explained the condition you were in by saying you'd had too much to drink. He would have played the attentive lover."

Hunter nodded and tiredly rubbed her eyes. "I just can't remember any of it." She tried to ease the pounding headache that was beginning to make its presence felt and was making it difficult for her to think. "Or maybe I just don't want to remember any of it. I'm not really sure."

"It's okay, Hunter," Sara offered gently.

Hunter let out a shuddering breath. The fatigue was bone deep, leaving her too tired to argue. As if from a distance, she watched Sara capture one of her hands, squeezing it gently as she smiled, and knew she was trying to let some of the emotion bleed away.

"We've covered a lot of territory tonight. We'll talk again later if you're okay with that. In fact, why don't we put it away until tomorrow and simply enjoy the rest of the evening? Just two friends having dinner."

Feeling emotionally drained, Hunter readily agreed as relief settled over her and the last vestiges of tension melted away. She picked up her wine glass and slumped back in her chair crossing long, jean-clad legs. "I can do that," she said.

They sat in silence for a couple of minutes, and Hunter knew the next move was hers. She licked her lips and closed her eyes. "*Lord of the Rings*," she said softly.

Sara paused in the act of snaring another shrimp. "I'm sorry, what did you say?"

"*Lord of the Rings*." Hunter gave her a small crooked grin and shrugged sheepishly. "My favorite movie. What's yours?"

They looked at each other a moment longer before Sara started to laugh, as if she had clued in Hunter was attempting to make small talk.

"All right, it's a start." She looked at Hunter and grinned, her smile widening when it was instantly mirrored. "*Shawshank Redemption*. Favorite musical?"

"Movie or live theater?"

So it went for the next hour. They continued to exchange bits of personal information, maintaining a steady stream of easy conversation while they ate. Sara laughed easily and shared stories of her early days at Quantico. Hunter found herself relaxing and enjoying the easy camaraderie that unfolded.

Once they finished eating, they cleared the table, placed the leftovers in the fridge, and washed the few dishes. Returning to the patio, they sat in the gathering darkness as the wind whispered through the trees and the rays of the sun setting low painted an infinite horizon in shades of red and gold. Soon after, darkness descended completely, and it wasn't long before the glow from the swimming pool was the only source of light as they sat under a black, starless sky.

Eventually, Sara glanced at her watch. Beside her, Hunter had her head back and her eyes closed and as much as she didn't want to disturb her, Sara knew she should make arrangements to leave. "It's getting kind of late," she began.

Hunter gazed, heavy-lidded, at Sara. Her voice was soft and low, and she let the words slide out lazily. "Why don't you stay the night?"

"Hunter..." Sara whispered uncertainly.

Caught in the crystalline blue of Hunter's eyes, Sara remained silent while seconds ticked by. She wanted to ask Hunter what she was thinking, but some instinct told her now wasn't the time. She inhaled deeply, absorbing the scent of Hunter's perfume and something else that was distinctly her. And even though she knew Hunter's offer was meant to be strictly platonic, Sara still felt desire stirring deep within her.

"Sara?" Hunter gave her a lopsided grin. "Darlin', I've had too much wine to drive you back to Kate's tonight."

"I know."

"Which means I'll have to call the limo. But it's late, and there's no real reason why you shouldn't stay here. Logically, it just makes better sense to have you spend the night."

"I could just call a cab."

"You could," Hunter agreed. "But why bother? It's not as if we'll be tripping over each other in the dark."

"No, but—"

"Sara," Hunter said. "There are three guest rooms on the second floor plus a fully self-contained guest suite on the lower level. And while I may not have a lot of furniture, the guest rooms all have beds, and you can take your pick. I'm sure you'll find one of them to your liking. So please stay."

The dimly reflected light of the pool cast shifting shadows across Hunter's face, and Sara thought she had never looked more beautiful. Or more vulnerable. She could think of a handful of reasons why she should leave. But none of them could override the one reason she was choosing to stay.

Because Hunter wanted her to stay.

Chapter Twenty

S ara chose the second-floor guest room at the end of the hall. Spacious and bright with whitewashed walls and hardwood floors, it overlooked the patio and swimming pool, and offered an expansive view of the Pacific, currently cloaked by darkness and fog. There was a light breeze coming through the open window, and as she stood in front of it, she enjoyed the feel of the salt-tinged air against her face and the soothing sound of the waves.

Minutes later, Hunter came up behind her. She carried an oversized T-shirt and a blue silk robe. "I wasn't sure what your preference might be so I brought you something to sleep in. Is everything else in here okay for you?"

"Yes. Thanks."

"Towels are on the top shelf of that cabinet," Hunter explained, indicating the adjoining private bath. "You'll find toothbrushes and toothpaste in the drawer. Shampoo and body wash in the shower. Feel free to use whatever you need. Sleep well, Sara."

"Thank you. You get some sleep, too, and I'll see you in the morning," Sara responded. When she turned, she was surprised to find Hunter only inches away. Their eyes locked as Hunter moved closer, gently brushing a few stray strands of hair away from Sara's face with her fingertips.

"Sara."

She said it softly, her lips hovering only an inch away, and there was a slight tremor in her voice. Leaning closer still, she placed a gentle kiss on Sara's lips—the sweetest and most fleeting of touches—before she stepped back. A moment later, Hunter slipped quietly from the room.

Her lips had been softer, warmer, and more gentle than Sara had imagined. She whimpered at the loss of contact as images of Hunter's lips on hers flashed repeatedly through her mind. *Hunter.* She closed her eyes as the name echoed maddeningly.

A few minutes later, she padded into the bathroom and started the water running. *A shower is what you need. A cold shower.* The shower proved to be refreshing, and Sara found herself grinning as she pulled on the cotton T-shirt with Marvin the Martian on it, then sprawled out onto the bed, pleasantly tired if not necessarily sleepy.

Sometime later, she couldn't say what exactly awoke her from the deep sleep she had been enjoying. Feeling vaguely unsettled, Sara reached for her watch and saw it was just after three in the morning. She sat up, wincing at the twinge in her neck as she took in the room around her, listening for the sound she thought she'd heard. But only the silence greeted her, and after a couple of minutes, she settled back down onto the pillow and closed her eyes.

The sound of the waves had almost lulled her back to sleep when her eyes flew open once again. This time she heard it more clearly. The distinct sound of something or someone moving on the patio below.

Moving as quickly and quietly as possible, she reached for her bag on the night table and withdrew her weapon. She slipped the safety off as she inched toward the window and peered down.

At first, she could see nothing. Silently steeling herself, she waited, holding her position against the wall. Her patience was rewarded when she saw a silhouette move away from the shadow of the house. An instant later, the dark figure became clearer and morphed into Hunter. She was in the act of pulling the T-shirt she wore over her head as she moved. Sara watched as Hunter tossed it onto one of the deck chairs surrounding the pool, leaving her wearing a dark-colored thong. And nothing else.

"Oh Jesus," Sara said, licking suddenly dry lips as her ability to think flew right out the window. *The woman is obviously trying to kill me.*

She blinked and swallowed. Hard. She took a quick breath and tried to get control of her suddenly racing heart. Staring for what seemed like hours, she felt like a voyeur, but her eyes refused to obey her command to look away. Instead, she prayed Hunter would do her a favor and move back into the shadows.

She groaned softly as Hunter walked to the edge of the bottom-lit pool, unable to take her eyes away from the long, lithe body and the firm, muscular derrière. Watching her awakened something deep. Desire. Hunger. The need to touch her. Taste her. Claim her. She had never met another woman who possessed so strong an elemental sexual pull. It was sharp, almost painful, and Sara realized with a start that no other woman had ever caused her pain.

Oh, Sara, be careful, she told herself. *Be very careful.*

Finally, she released a small sigh of relief as Hunter dove cleanly into the water. She disappeared from view as she swam more than half the length of the pool underwater before surfacing and slipping into a strong crawl.

For the next several minutes, Sara watched Hunter as she swam laps. Then, without giving her own motivation too much thought, she put the gun away, grabbed a towel from the bathroom, and headed down to the patio.

As she stepped outside into the night air, she glanced indecisively toward the deck chairs before choosing instead to drop down at the edge of the pool, her legs dangling in the warm water. Sitting quietly, she watched Hunter continue to drive herself, maintaining a consistent pace as she swam lap after lap. Until finally, she began to slow down. Until finally, she pulled herself out of the pool and stood up, swaying slightly as she slicked her hair back from her face.

Sara stood up as well and stared as the water trickled slowly from Hunter's hair and ran down the angular planes of her face to her neck. Unable to look away, entranced, she followed the rivulets as they ran across Hunter's chest and down her smoothly muscled body.

She had a truly marvelous body. A swimmer's or maybe a runner's. It didn't really matter. All that mattered was it was long and lean and athletic with small breasts, narrow hips, and just enough softness covering her muscles. *Gorgeous.*

As she stepped closer, Sara could feel Hunter's breath, warm against the coolness of her skin. And once again, she felt the sharp tug of desire that seemed to constantly hover just beneath the surface whenever Hunter was near.

"Having trouble sleeping?" she asked softly.

Hunter regarded her and smiled uncertainly in response. "Something like that." She licked her lips and seemed unconcerned about her state of undress, oblivious to how attractive she was and totally unaware of the effect she was having on Sara. "Sorry, I didn't mean to wake you."

Sara stepped toward Hunter and wrapped the bath towel around her shoulders.

"For God's sake, Hunter, you're about to fall down," she said, feeling the skin beneath her fingers trembling faintly in the cool night air. "When's the last time you actually slept through the night?"

Hunter shrugged and smiled tiredly. "I'm not sure. What year is this?"

"Smart-ass." Sara bumped her forehead against Hunter's. "Come on. You need a hot shower. Then I'm tucking you into bed."

"That sounds promising." Hunter purred and quirked a half grin.

"Be good." Sara reached for Hunter's hand, precluding any further discussion, and led her back inside, stopping long enough for Hunter to reset the alarm before heading up the stairs. Still, she wondered idly what Hunter would think if she tried to join her in the shower. The thought caused her to briefly stumble, and she forced herself to concentrate on maintaining her footing before she did something stupid.

An hour later, with the lights in the master suite turned down low, Sara watched Hunter as she slept facedown on the bed beside her, and listened to her rhythmic breathing. Having totally exhausted herself, Hunter had not moved since she had dropped onto the bed, pulling Sara down with her after mumbling something about not wanting to be alone.

Sara indulged herself, transfixed by the relaxed features. Her eyes took in every contour and angle, every line, as she was drawn closer to the vortex that was Hunter Roswell. She seemed to have finally found some peace in a dreamless sleep. Her long dark lashes fanned her cheeks and a cloud of damp, tousled hair fell around her face. Gone for the moment were the haunted expressions of hurt and loss, anger and defiance. Instead, she simply looked young.

And so damn beautiful it made Sara ache.

Aware of the undeniable connection she had felt from the very beginning, Sara gave free rein to her thoughts, to her imagination. A smile crossed her face as she wondered what it would be like to make love with Hunter. To lie in this giant bed under the midnight canopy of the skylight, skin pressed against skin, limbs tangled, and unleash all the heat and passion Hunter seemed to keep barely contained.

The urge to touch increased until it became too strong to ignore. Surrendering to the pull, Sara reached out and gently laid her hand on Hunter's bare back, stroking, feeling the soft smooth skin covering the lean muscle. She could feel the flex of muscle beneath her fingers, and her breath caught in her throat. Feeling her pulse speed up, she caught her lip between her teeth and then sighed and wondered just what the hell she was doing.

Enough! Get it together, Wilder.

In her sleep, Hunter murmured incoherently. Reaching out blindly, she grasped Sara's hand and brushed a light kiss on it without waking. Sara felt her heart stutter in automatic response, felt quickening in the blood, and tried to concentrate on anything other than their interlaced fingers as they lay against the deep blue sheets. But her body betrayed her and forced her to admit the truth, if only to herself.

This attraction to Hunter had moved into previously uncharted territory. She had been sexually attracted to women on numerous occasions in the past. Had at times acted on the attraction. But this was different. This was much more than just a physical pull, a sexual attraction. In fact, she was certain she had not felt quite like this before about anyone.

But underlying that admission was the reality of their present situation. That she was here with Hunter at all was only because she had a job to do, to help her identify her stalker. To protect her. To keep her alive. Were it not for those circumstances, she doubted she would have ever gained entrance into Hunter's world, Hunter's life. And the fact that the attraction was quite possibly reciprocated did not change that reality.

Sara's eyes flickered across the shadowed planes of Hunter's face, and she swallowed as she felt the heavy surge of need and want and desire course through her. These were dangerous waters, and she was left feeling vulnerable, wondering what she was supposed to do now. Because still outstanding was the pressing question of finding out who wanted to hurt Hunter. Until that riddle was solved, everything else simply had to wait.

Didn't it?

With the questions tumbling endlessly in her head, Sara closed her eyes. And with the sound of Hunter's soft breathing murmuring to her, she let sleep claim her.

❖

When Sara opened her eyes, she found herself sprawled on the huge bed with the morning sun streaming in through the windows while the skylight overhead revealed a cloudless blue sky. A quick glance at the clock on the bedside table let her know it was already after eight. A further glance confirmed what she already suspected. She was alone in the bed.

The feeling of loss and disappointment was almost palpable. But inhaling deeply, she found Hunter's scent, so faint it was barely detectable, still drifted around her. It was like inhaling midnight. Cool with a hauntingly dark undercurrent. She closed her eyes, sighing contentedly.

You're hopeless.

"If you're wondering where Hunter is, she and Tessa went for a run on the beach about half an hour ago."

Sara's eyes flew open at the sound of the voice. She blinked at the sight of Kate's all-too-familiar body leaning against the doorframe, arms folded across her chest, a faint grin on her face. Just as quickly, Sara shut her eyes.

This is not happening. Oh God, kill me now.

After waiting what seemed like an appropriate length of time, she peeked through half-closed eyes, but the image in the doorway had not changed. "This isn't what it looks like," she said, a hot blush creeping up her neck and suffusing her face.

"Oh? And what do you suppose it looks like?" Kate asked.

Sara groaned. "I know it looks like Hunter and I slept together... but this really isn't...it's not what you think."

"So you keep telling me." Kate's grin was fast and amused, and she looked as if she was fighting hard not to laugh. "I think I walked in here and found you sleeping in Hunter's bed." She raised her brows. "But you tell me it's not what it looks like, and I'm supposed to believe you. No problem."

"Kate—"

Kate's laughter succeeded in cutting Sara off. "Come on, Sara. It's not as if I would think there's anything wrong with it if you are sleeping with Hunter."

Sara winced and Kate regarded her intently.

"On the contrary. I think it makes you a goddess among mortals, because the Hunter Roswell I've known for the past five years doesn't spend the entire night with a woman. Any woman. And she certainly doesn't bring them home to her own bed."

"Really?"

"Really," Kate confirmed. "Yet you have managed to accomplish both feats in short order. I'm impressed. Hell, I'm jealous. Why don't you tell me what's going on, Sara?"

"It's complicated."

"C'mon then, why don't you make it uncomplicated for me."

Sara sighed and ran her hands through her sleep-tousled hair. A moment later, her account of the previous evening came out in a softly worded tumble. "Hunter and I had dinner here last evening. We talked, ate takeout, and drank too much wine. When it got late, it seemed best…we decided it would be best if I spent the night. In one of the second-floor guest rooms."

A faint smile edged its way back onto Kate's lips. "And the house is so big you got lost on your way to this second-floor guest room?"

"No, smart-ass." Sara closed her eyes and pinched the bridge of her nose. Just thinking about it was enough to make her taste the hunger, feel the desire.

"Talk to me, Sara. What's going on?"

There was something quietly tenacious in the way Kate was looking at her, and Sara immediately understood she wouldn't have a moment's peace until Kate's curiosity had been satisfied. Bowing her head to the inevitable, she conceded.

"It's really quite simple. Hunter got up in the middle of the night. Nightmares, if I had to guess. I woke up when I heard her go outside. It looked like she was trying to exhaust herself by swimming laps, and I followed her out to make sure she was okay. When she went back to bed, she…she didn't want to be alone. Having me beside her seemed to calm her down. And I guess I fell asleep."

She stopped abruptly, ending the uncharacteristically long speech.

"That was very sweet of you," Kate teased. But her eyes gentled as she moved over to sit next to Sara on the bed. "I'm sure having you there helped Hunter get some much-needed sleep."

"It seemed to. I mean I guess it did. Of course, my feelings weren't entirely altruistic," Sara whispered softly after a long moment had passed. "Because more than anything, I really just wanted to grab her and make love to her until she forgot all about her nightmares. Until all she could do was scream out my name."

Kate's eyes widened with surprise, her gaze fixed on Sara's face. Reaching out across the bed, she took Sara's hand and squeezed. "Amen to that, sister," she sighed reverently. She paused as she peered more closely at Sara. "Oh my God," she said. "Does Hunter know?"

"Know what?"

"Does she know you're falling for her?"

"Am I?" Sara smiled sadly and stared up at the endless expanse of deep blue visible through the skylight. She'd never been good at denial. "No," she said, unable to pretend otherwise. "Hunter has no idea and it's just as well. Because nothing can come of it...nothing will come of it."

"Bullshit."

Kate might have argued the point, but Sara stopped her with a look. "Do I have to point out that I met her through the bureau? And believe me, the FBI has very clear rules about any involvement with someone they consider a person of interest."

"You no longer work for the FBI which means their rules don't apply. And she's Tessa's closest friend, just as you are mine. You would have met her eventually in a social context. Try again."

Sara tried to ignore the swell of emotions. Looking up at Kate, she attempted a different tack. "Have you ever just looked at her?" she asked softly. "I mean *really* looked at her?"

"Looked at Hunter?" Kate sighed. "Of course I have. Let's not forget I spent most of the first week after I met her trying to get her into my bed."

"Then you understand," Sara said. "There's something about her, but it's like she's not even aware of it. I think that's part of the attraction. She's so damned beautiful I find myself just staring at her. There are times I look at her and I forget to breathe. Damn, I'm a total mess."

Kate frowned. "What do you want to do?"

"I don't know. I don't seem to have a frame of reference for dealing with what she makes me feel." Looking down, Sara silently studied her hands. "We both know she could have anyone."

"Yeah, she could have anyone. But you also know she's not involved with anyone else."

"I guessed that was the case," Sara said. "But I also know between trying to identify whoever is stalking her and dealing with unresolved issues regarding everything that happened to her ten years ago, Hunter's already stretched pretty thin emotionally. This situation is forcing her to deal with all the ghosts she's been carrying for years, and I'm not sure she can handle one more thing right now."

"Even if it's a good thing?"

"Even then."

"What are you going to do?"

Sara took a long breath and let it out slowly before she looked up at Kate and smiled fleetingly. "I'm going to do what I set out to do in the first place. I'm going to help Hunter get through this and make sure she comes out whole on the other side. Anything else will just have to wait."

She hoped she sounded more confident than she felt. Running her hands through her hair again, she could feel them tremble. She bit her lip and looked away, suddenly afraid of what her face might reveal, especially to someone who knew her as well as Kate did.

Perhaps sensing Hunter wasn't the only one at her emotional limit, Kate backed off. "I've an idea," she suggested. "Why don't you have a shower in that religious experience Hunter calls a bathroom while I go downstairs and start the coffee?"

Sara gave a quick nod. "I don't suppose you happened to bring me a change of clothes?"

"No, but Hunter said you could borrow anything of hers you wanted to wear. I'll see what I can find that'll fit and leave it for you on the bed. When you're ready, you can come down and help me make breakfast before Tessa and Hunter get back. I was thinking we'd eat out by the pool. What do you think?"

"Sounds good," Sara said absently, grateful for the shift in focus. Throwing the covers back, she forced herself out of bed and padded toward the bathroom.

It took her three tries before she could figure out how to set the controls that worked the shower. But in the end, it was more than worth the extra effort. She slid the door open and eased herself into the enormous shower stall, sighing as the hot water and steam from the multiple shower heads enveloped her in a heated embrace.

She lingered in the shower, emerging finally after nearly thirty minutes, and slipped on the borrowed cargo shorts and navy polo shirt she found on the bed. After making her way downstairs, she picked up the plates and cutlery Kate had left on the counter and took them out to the patio.

She had just finished setting the table when she heard Tessa and Hunter returning from their run. She could hear Hunter laughing, a sound that immediately sent gentle shivers down her spine. As Hunter and Tessa came into view, she frowned when she saw Tessa was limping, but both women were smiling and nothing else seemed to be amiss.

Hunter caught and held Sara's attention. She looked gloriously healthy and radiantly beautiful. Especially now, with her hair damp and windblown, and her face flushed. Her racer-back tank top clung to her sweat-dampened skin, which made Sara take a longer second look and sent her pulse rate soaring.

As her eyes flicked along the length of Hunter's body, she became aware of the acute physical reaction she was having. With a soft groan, she forced herself to look away. *Talk about primal urges, Sara,* a little voice in the back of her mind chided. *I'm worse than a teenaged boy.* But she couldn't get rid of the delightful images that flooded her mind and weakened her knees.

"Hey," she called out, her voice sounding huskier that usual. She took a shaky breath and cleared her throat. "How was the run?"

A devilish grin pulled at the corners of Hunter's mouth. "Great, but we had to cut it short on account of Tessa's age and current physical condition."

She drew closer until Sara could feel the warmth of her overheated body. Giving in to an almost desperate need to see her eyes, Sara impulsively reached out and slid the sunglasses down Hunter's nose. Sara could see the questions evident in her eyes but was relieved the shadows in their depths had lessened considerably. She also couldn't miss the unguarded look of arousal.

Sara inhaled sharply and her world tilted on its axis.

"I'm only three years older than you," Tessa groused. "I'll have you know that makes me younger than both Kate and Sara."

"Really?" Hunter assessed Sara speculatively. "You don't look older than Tessa, and she's about to turn the big three-oh. Is it possible?"

"More than possible," Sara responded dryly. "I'm thirty-three...almost thirty-four."

"Damn, I could be in trouble here," Hunter said.

"Why?" Sara and Tessa asked simultaneously.

Hunter flashed a grin. "Because I think older women are *so* sexy."

Sara couldn't help but laugh, finding Hunter's grin infectious. "That may be, but right now Kate has breakfast just about ready and," she paused, "you both need to shower."

"You've got to love that kind of honesty in a woman," Tessa joked, sliding her arm around Hunter's waist. "Let's go have that shower. Wanna share?"

Sara watched Hunter drape an arm around Tessa's shoulder and laugh softly as they walked toward the house.

❖

As the late afternoon sun waned, the music drifted from the speakers through the patio. Counting Crows were singing goodnight to L.A., which told Hunter that Conner had chosen the latest selection. The level of noise and laughter coming from the barbeque pit increased in direct proportion to the amount of smoke that was billowing, thankfully away from the swimming pool.

As they gestured toward the volume of smoke rising into the clear blue sky, Matt, Kate, and Conner were arguing good naturedly about grilling techniques. Nearby, Peter was enticing Sara and Adrienne into trying the latest drink he had mixed at the makeshift bar. Hunter caught Sara gazing in her direction, a lopsided grin on her face. Hunter smiled back just as Sara answered her cell phone.

Stretched out by the pool, Hunter looked away and listened as the sounds of voices, teasing, and laughter blended. It made her smile. It also enabled her to ignore her quietly churning laptop, where an endless parade of faces flickered across the screen. Not that she needed to be watching it closely. She had an audible alarm that would signal her when one of her search engines located something she needed to see.

Come on, I know you're there. I can feel it. Let me see you.

It was ironic, she decided, that although she was doing everything in her power to speed up the identification process, illogically she found herself dreading the moment they would finally put a face to the man stalking her. A dread which was making itself known in the clamminess of her palms and the churning of her stomach. The touch of someone's hand on her shoulder interrupted her thoughts, and she looked up with a start.

"Hey, it's just me," Tessa said. "You look beat. Why don't you give yourself a break? How about a swim before the steaks are up?"

"Maybe in a minute," Hunter responded, distracted by the activity on the other side of the pool. Her gaze lingered on Sara, who had finished her telephone call and was now wandering slowly over to the barbeque pit.

Tessa laughed softly. "Or maybe you want to go and check on how the steaks are coming along before Matt and Kate manage to burn everything in sight including the salad."

Before she could respond, the laptop issued a faint sound. Nothing obvious. Just a small ping, really. A quick glance toward Tessa confirmed she had not heard it. Not over the music and voices and laughter. But then Tessa would not have been listening for it. Nor would she have recognized the importance of that seemingly insignificant sound.

A single musical note that indicated a high-probability match had been found.

With as much nonchalance as she could manage, Hunter reached out and angled the laptop until she could get a clear view of the screen. She got her first clear look at an ordinary-looking man with light brown hair, brown eyes, thin lips, and a pale complexion.

A singularly unremarkable looking man who had already killed five women.

A monster whose name was Dr. Eric Hamilton Collier.

Waves of nausea gripped her as she tried to absorb the details on the screen. The hospital records indicated ten years earlier, Eric Collier had been a surgical resident at San Francisco General. He had subsequently accepted a staff position, where he had remained until early March, when he had asked for and received an extended leave of absence.

You are mine.

Hunter could feel her body start to tremble, and she broke out in a cold sweat. Her mind reeled as a montage of images assaulted her. Images of a quiet bar in Manhattan.

Come on, beautiful. What's your problem? I just want to buy you a drink.

A new surge of nausea attacked her as darker, distorted images surfaced.

Hey babe, I understand you like games. Let's you and me play a game.

And then Brenner's mocking tone joined Collier's and filled her head until she couldn't distinguish one from the other.

What's it worth to you, Hunter?

She shuddered violently and covered her face with both hands, barely holding back the scream that she longed to release.

"Hunter?"

She registered the expression of concern on Tessa's face and opened her mouth to respond, but no sound moved past her throat. She tried taking one calming breath, then another, as she shut the laptop and pushed it away from her chair. As if the act would keep Eric Collier locked inside. An instant later, she jumped up and bolted into the house.

The kitchen was empty and quiet, and she pressed her forehead against the cool tiled wall. Her legs turned to water, and she slid down to the floor, her body trembling. She drew her knees up to her chin, wrapped both arms around her legs, and then pressed her head to her knees. Closing her eyes, she willed the room to stop spinning.

What's it worth to you, Hunter?

She didn't know how much time had passed when she felt someone rubbing her shoulder and gently stroking her hair, while a soothing voice said, "It's all right, Hunter."

Sara shifted position slightly, moving closer. Pulling Hunter into her arms, where she could feel her trembling. "I'm here. I've got you. I won't let go."

CHAPTER TWENTY-ONE

The night sky was cloudless, the air cooling slowly after the heat of the day. In the darkness, Hunter leaned casually against the Lamborghini and listened to a dog bark in the distance while she stared at the small house on the quiet, dead-end street.

A sign of the declining neighborhood, many of the single-family homes sat quiet and forlorn, with For Sale signs posted on overgrown front yards. And like the other houses on the street, Eric Collier's home was in obvious need of repairs and a fresh coat of paint. In fact, from the outside, there was very little to distinguish the house from its neighbors, whose tenants had scurried, melting away into the darkness at the first sign of police presence.

Collier's house appeared to be empty but for a faint flickering light visible through the front window. A bare bulb blinking on and off like a strobe light. It only served to confirm what Hunter's instincts had been telling her. That Eric Collier would not be found within the walls of the small house. At least not tonight.

From her vantage point, she could see what appeared to be numerous dark shadows, the members of the FBI, SFPD, and SWAT teams. Indeed, it seemed as if a veritable law enforcement alphabet soup was getting into position and converging on the house while she watched.

She knew that both David and Sara would be found somewhere among those shadows. Just as she knew that neither would be pleased to discover she was here. But then, neither had given her much choice.

"No way in hell are you going to be there when we take Collier down. That's final."

Had it been David who said that? Or Sara? Hunter was no longer sure. But then again, did it really matter? David's comments had certainly been the harsher of the two, but in the end, both had been equally adamant. Hunter would not be allowed anywhere near the address the DMV had on record for Eric Collier. David had actually taken it one step further, going so far as to threaten to place her into protective custody unless she agreed to stay away.

Hunter had not agreed. She had simply walked away, because it was an argument she had no interest in pursuing. Instead she resorted to a tactic she would normally eschew. She used the Roswell name—and all of its connections—to open doors. Fifteen minutes and two telephone calls and she had not necessarily what she wanted, but certainly what she needed if she hoped to put an end to the nightmare that was plaguing her. A front-row center seat at a well-orchestrated raid. But a raid that would yield…what?

She had no expectation that Eric Collier would be found in the house. But somewhere inside, there was something he wanted her to see. Or there would be a message of some kind. Of that she had no doubt. Otherwise Collier wouldn't have made it that easy for her to identify him and confirm Lindsay's suspicions. This was something he had allowed to happen when he had smiled into the security camera. Her eyes scanned the ongoing police activity while her fingers tapped restlessly against her leg.

"They're in position. We should be in any minute now. Then we'll know what we're dealing with," the low voice by her ear said softly.

Hunter turned her head slightly to her right and nodded. At forty-three, Special Agent in Charge Erin McBride was still as lean and fit as she had been the first time Hunter had met her. She had been part of the inner sanctum, working closely with Michael Roswell in those early days in her career. Over time, Hunter knew she had parlayed that connection and her experience dealing with domestic terrorism into overseeing operations in the San Francisco field office.

But she had never forgotten the career boost her former mentor had made possible. So when his daughter called looking for a favor, Erin had been more than happy to oblige—something Hunter understood and had counted on.

"I guess I can wait a little longer," Hunter stated quietly. "It's just that patience has never been my strong suit." She gave Erin a wry smile. "Of course, I don't know why I'm being this impatient since I really don't expect him to be there."

"You think this is some kind of setup, don't you?"

"I do, but not in the traditional sense. And before you ask, I really have no idea what Collier has planned. It's just that he's come too far to have it all end like this."

"What do you mean?"

Hunter shrugged. "He believes he's the superior intelligence here."

Erin leaned back, crossed her arms across her chest, and studied Hunter as a sardonic smile touched her lips. "Matched up against a woman with an IQ of what…over one eighty?" She shook her head in apparent disbelief. "How is that even possible?"

Her comment elicited Hunter's first genuine laugh of the night. "It's a scary proposition, isn't it?" Hunter watched Erin shudder slightly at the thought. "But Collier's medical school records put his intelligence somewhere in the top five percent relative to the general population, and while it may not match mine, his confidence isn't entirely without substance."

When there was no response, Hunter glanced at Erin and realized she was staring at Hunter's profile reflected in the Lamborghini's window. Lifting her chin, she frowned at the pale image of her own face in the glass and saw the ghost of her father looking back. When their eyes met in the glass, she saw Erin's brow lift in acknowledgment.

"You look so much like Michael," Erin mused out loud, her expression serious as she continued to study Hunter. "Same eyes. Same mouth. It feels almost a little eerie standing here with you. It also makes me wonder how deep the similarity runs."

"Working so closely with him, you would have known aspects of my father I never knew, so I can't really answer that."

"True, but I'd be willing to wager that you've much more in common than just a beautiful face." Erin's gaze briefly changed. "I still miss him, you know."

Hunter sighed softly before she replied. "So do I."

Lost in thought, she leaned back against the car and let the silence of the empty street wash over her until she heard Erin clear her throat.

"You accessed Collier's medical school records?" Erin asked, an edge creeping into her voice. "Please tell me the FBI won't find your fingerprints inside a classified system. That's a federal rap."

Hunter rolled her eyes, letting Erin know exactly what she thought of that possibility. "I don't leave tracks in computers." Her tone was dry but held a slight note of teasing.

"I hope to God you're right," Erin said fervently. "I know that, by reputation, you're considered the top in your field and your technical skills are supposed to be second to none, but still—"

"My technical skills *are* second to none."

Erin grinned. "That may be, but still, I would hate to have Michael Roswell's only child and, God help me, Patrick Roswell's only grandchild arrested. Please. Not on my watch."

"You're worrying needlessly," Hunter said reassuringly. "But I do believe that's become a large part of Collier's motivation. The challenge to prove he's superior. Invincible. Smarter than the police, the FBI. Smarter than me. And so far, there's been nothing to suggest otherwise."

"Because he's managed to commit five murders and, at least this far, has gotten away with it?"

"There's that." Hunter turned slightly so she could keep an eye on the house. "More so because he's still calling all the shots. We're all here because it's what he wants."

"So why would he help you confirm his identity? Doesn't it significantly increase our chances of finding and stopping him before he completes his agenda?"

"I'm not the expert on serial killers and their motivation. That's for the profilers and psychiatrists. But obviously it was important enough for him to take a calculated risk." Silence fell as she paused, tilting her head to look at Erin once again. "My guess is there's something in the house he wants me to see. Something that furthers his agenda."

Erin didn't respond immediately, her expression telling Hunter she was listening to a play-by-play. After a minute, she nodded and said, "The house is clear. You were right. No one was home."

❖

Hunter was already moving before Erin had the words out, her long strides eating up the distance to the small house. Just as quickly, two of the shadows materialized and were now flanking her.

Peter McNeil and Conner Reese immediately moved in lockstep with her. Both were sporting take-no-prisoners expressions on their faces. Both made it unambiguously clear that they were taking no chances where Hunter's safety was concerned, in spite of the overwhelming police presence.

The two agents at the door immediately moved to stop Hunter as she approached the house. A challenging eyebrow rose in response as they impeded her forward progress. But before the situation could escalate, Erin waved the agents aside as she walked past Hunter into the house. Both agents' eyes briefly registered their surprise at seeing SAC McBride walking up the front steps. But their surprise was immediately masked, and it was obvious neither was inclined to face her rather formidable wrath with what could only be a career-limiting move.

Hunter moved past the agents and stood in a small foyer. She could hear the sound of footsteps on the porch and knew that Peter and Conner were right behind her. Still, for a moment she hesitated and consciously slipped on the cool Roswell façade that she knew would make her appear composed even if she was anything but. Once she was ready, she moved beyond the foyer and stepped into the living room.

Hunter had no expectation of what she might find in Collier's house. Which was just as well, because the scene that confronted her left her dazed.

Her image covered every inch of available wall space.

There were photographs of all sizes along with pictures cut out of magazine and newspaper articles chronicling every stage of her life, both personal and professional, over the past ten years. A ski trip to Colorado. Dancing in the streets of New Orleans during Mardi Gras. Leaving a client meeting in Washington, another in Seattle. Even a private moment placing a flower on her father's grave had been captured.

Eric Collier had spent an inordinate amount of time dwelling in the shadows and the fringes of her life. Even as she struggled with that thought, another hit Hunter even harder. *All of this without my noticing. Without anyone on my team noticing. How the hell did that happen?*

Hands buried in her pockets, she turned in a small circle, her mind absorbing and cataloging the endless array of photographs. Nearby, several agents stopped what they were doing and watched her as she processed the scene. She was acutely aware of their scrutiny. But it had been a part of her life for as long as she could remember, and she had learned how to block it out. A well-learned lesson that served her a heartbeat later.

"What the hell are you doing here? Are you trying to replicate what happened with Brenner?"

Looking up, Hunter saw David approaching, with Sara following three steps behind, hurrying to catch up. David's face was a study in fury, and Hunter instinctively took a step back, wanting to avoid an open and very public confrontation that would hurt him— at least professionally—much more than it could ever hurt her.

But neither was she prepared to be run off the scene before she could have it begin to make sense. "You don't want to be busting my balls over this," she warned softly in a deathly quiet voice.

Before David could respond, however, another voice joined the fray.

"Is there a problem, Special Agent Granger?" The voice was low and menacing.

Sara watched David freeze, his anger temporarily forgotten as his boss made an unexpected appearance behind Hunter. She heard him swear under his breath as he glanced from Erin McBride back to Hunter and realized he'd been outmaneuvered. But when he opened his mouth to respond, she moved closer, stopping him with a soft touch on his shoulder.

She could feel the tension and the dark embarrassment vibrating from him as he tried to shrug her hand off impatiently. When she resisted, he turned abruptly toward her and caught her quick head shake. For the longest time, he appeared torn by indecision. But when Sara shook her head again, he gritted his teeth and bit back the words.

"There's no problem," he said and walked away.

"Smart move," Erin said, her eyes following David out of the room. When he was no longer visible, she looked at Sara, her eyes speculative. "He's a good agent. I'm told he was an even better agent with you as his partner. I don't suppose—"

Sara quickly shook her head. "Sorry, not interested," she replied, her attention singularly focused, her eyes following Hunter who was examining the photographs on the wall.

Erin nodded her head once and gave Sara an appreciative smile. "I guess I'm not surprised," she said and moved toward Hunter. She stopped an instant later when the small room began to fill with music.

It came at them from every possible direction—the floor, the walls, the ceiling. And with each second that passed, it increased in volume and intensity until the floorboards vibrated and the windows rattled. It continued to build until the electronic beat permeated every inch of the room and the hypnotic sound made it impossible to think.

"What the fuck?" an agent said.

"Somebody shut that damn music off," Erin ordered, shouting to be heard over the increasing level of sound.

"I can't figure out where the hell it's coming from," one of the agents yelled back, then looked around in sheepish confusion as the volume decreased on its own.

It took a second or two before Sara realized where she had heard this Enigma album recently. *At Hunter's house.* It had been playing in the background while they had dinner by the pool. She spun and moved toward Hunter, looking at her with increasing concern. "You were playing this the other night."

Erin approached them, her eyes moving quickly from Sara to Hunter. "Is there any particular significance to the song he's selected?"

Hunter released a humorless laugh. "I guess that depends on your point of view. The title is 'I love you...I'll kill you.'" She shrugged her shoulders. "What do you think?"

The three women stood shoulder to shoulder in the middle of the room without saying a word, staring at photographs covering ten years of history while the haunting music continued to repeat its dire refrain. Could Collier's message really be that simple? Pondering the possibilities, Sara watched Hunter unclip her phone from her belt and stare at it as it vibrated in her hand.

Hunter didn't recognize the number displayed by the caller ID, but she had no doubt who would be on the other end. *No doubt at all.* Moving past the FBI agents and SFPD investigators combing through the contents of the house, she stepped outside into the relative quiet of the front porch and brought the phone to her ear. "Roswell."

"Hello, Hunter. I thought it was time we spoke. Did you like my surprise?" The voice was male, soft, and slightly breathless. *He's excited.*

Hunter signaled to Peter and mouthed that she needed to have the call traced. She watched Peter reach for his own phone as she focused on keeping her voice steady. "What surprise would that be, Dr. Collier? Or may I call you Eric?"

While she waited for a response, she turned and saw Sara freeze near the front door in response to the name she had just uttered. Their eyes met and Hunter gave a brief nod before turning her attention back to the phone call.

A soft laugh reached her over the line. "There's never been a need for formality between us, Hunter. Please. You must call me Eric."

"Okay, Eric it is." Hunter closed her eyes, blocking out the activity around her while concentrating on what Collier was saying. She wanted to draw him out and fervently hoped any subtle nuance, any impressions she picked up would help uncover his whereabouts before another woman paid for his obsession. "You asked what I thought of your surprise. Are you talking about the photographs? Or your choice of music?"

Collier's voice sounded hollow as it echoed on the line. "Both, of course. I thought the photographs were a good representation of the many memories we've shared over the years. As for the music, we were listening to it the other night, and I happen to know it's a personal favorite of yours. Does it please you?"

He's totally delusional. Hunter bit back her instinctive reaction and forced herself to give what she hoped was an appropriate response. "Yes, you know it does."

"I'm glad." He paused. "But the best is yet to come. I have an even bigger surprise planned."

"Oh?" Hunter stiffened while fighting to keep her voice calm. "Are you talking about your plans for October and the feast of Hunter's Moon?"

"You really are a clever girl." Collier laughed once again but when he spoke, his tone was edged with arrogance. "But I'm talking about something much sooner than that. More immediate, I daresay. Tell me, Hunter. Do you like fireworks?"

Fireworks? "I suppose. I've never really thought about it. Why?"

"Because that's the surprise." A giggle this time, tinged with madness. "In about five minutes, I've got a special fireworks display planned for you. But you might want to move away from where you're standing. I wouldn't want you to get burned again like you did in the parking lot when your car went up in flames."

Jesus. He was going to blow up the house. Hunter caught Conner's attention and pointed to a notebook currently in the hands of a nearby agent. Without a word Conner reached out and snatched the notebook. Passing it quickly to Hunter over the agent's protest, she watched her scribble across the page.

Bomb in house. Get everyone out.

Conner didn't blink or question the message. She responded immediately, grabbing the notebook and thrusting it into Sara's hands. She then ran back into the house to find Erin. At the same time, Sara read the note. Sparing just enough time to glance toward Hunter, she quickly followed Conner into the house to help warn the others and get them to safety.

Over the phone, Hunter could hear Collier laughing. "Tell the doctor she doesn't need to rush. We wouldn't want her to get hurt, and believe me, there's more than enough time to get everyone out."

He's close by, she realized. *He's watching.* Numbed by the realization, she felt Peter grab her arm and allowed him to propel her away from the house. She arched both brows in unspoken question. *Have you been able to trace the call?* Peter shook his head.

When they stopped a safe distance away, she closed her eyes, anxiously waiting for Sara and the others to exit the house. Collier, in the meantime, continued to laugh.

Hunter tilted her head down and her hair formed a protective curtain around her face. "Why?"

Collier's laughter ended abruptly. "'Yet each man kills the thing he loves,'" he quoted dreamily.

"Oscar Wilde," Hunter said, "'The Ballad of Reading Gaol.'"

"Ah, Hunter, you continue to please me beyond my wildest expectations," Collier responded. "And just like the song says, Hunter, I'll love you forever. It won't be long, now, I promise."

The click of the call being terminated coincided with the blast as the house exploded and the flames lit up the night sky.

Sara's last glimpse of Hunter had been sometime during the chaotic moments following the explosion that leveled Eric Collier's house. Hunter had been standing by her car blanketed by four members of her OPS team as she spoke with Erin McBride. Sara found out later she had been verifying that everyone got out safely before the bomb went off.

A moment later, she'd seen Hunter slip into the Lamborghini and quickly disappear into the night. Two black SUVs followed closely behind.

Sara realized now that she'd made a mistake. At the time, she'd thought it best to wait until morning before connecting with Hunter. But that, as it turned out, was not the best decision she might have made.

In the morning, there was no answer to the call she placed to Hunter's home. Instead she was forced to listen to the telephone ring until the automated voice mail message kicked in announcing no one was available to take her call. *Just in case you haven't already figured it out.*

She ended up leaving an awkward message before moving on to the next contact number Hunter had given her. All the results were the same. No answer.

Finally, after several additional abortive attempts to make contact, she turned in frustration to the immediate job at hand. Aware that David and the task force were working on tracking Collier through a labyrinth of electronic records, she focused her attention on learning more about him and building a deeper psychological profile.

Over the course of several days following the explosion, she developed a clearer understanding of Collier as interviews with former teachers, classmates, and colleagues provided much-needed insights. They all painted a picture of a brilliant but often moody loner who had been searching for someone he could consider his intellectual equal. His soul mate. And he believed he had found his match in a seventeen-year-old patient named Hunter Roswell.

It quickly became apparent that Collier had been unable to keep his obsession hidden from the people around him. Or perhaps it was his arrogance that left him unconcerned about what other people thought. According to one former classmate—a fellow surgical resident by the name of Cassandra Doyle—ten years earlier, Collier had been captivated by the young celebrity patient from the moment he first heard about her. The stories circulating throughout the hospital about what had happened to her fascinated him. But as his obsession grew, he also became the target of some rather cruel and unsympathetic comments, particularly from the other residents.

"He was always a little creepy, but he got totally hung up on the Roswell girl," Cassandra said. "Constantly checking on her status, reading everything the newspapers had to say about her. Always hanging around just trying to catch a glimpse of her. It was sad, really."

Most other colleagues were far less kind.

"It was pathetic the way he lusted after that girl," one of the nurses exclaimed. "Like she didn't already have enough to deal with, and let's face it, she was so out of his league. And her family was never going to let someone like him get anywhere near her anyway. But he didn't seem to get that."

A medical supervisor put it succinctly.

"He was a bright and competent doctor. But he was also arrogant, condescending, and totally self-absorbed, which didn't exactly endear him to other staff."

Therein lay the challenge. The more details that came to light about Collier, the more it became apparent that he had no friends, which left no one who might be helping him hide. But it also left no one who could help identify where he might have gone to ground.

There was no family. An only child, nothing was known about his father, while his mother, a successful cardiologist in Los Angeles, had died only weeks before his first encounter with Hunter. His mother's sudden death raised suspicions and David checked it out thoroughly. But all reports confirmed that Collier had been quite close to his mother and had been devastated when she died in a traffic accident.

Far more likely, Sara thought, was that the death of his mother was pivotal to Collier's subsequent obsession with Hunter as he sought to fill the void in his life. It was also consistent with psychological studies which indicated that a large proportion of stalkers had experienced significant life-events preceding the onset of their stalking behaviors.

As his obsession grew and Hunter became his sole focus, it would not have taken a lot of effort on Collier's part to access her medical files. The knowledge he obtained—his confirmation of her intelligence, in particular—would have fueled his belief that he had found his one true love. What did become clear was that over time Collier embellished stories about his relationship with her to such an extent that several hospital staff actually believed that Collier's significant other was a rich and beautiful young woman named Hunter and had even seen photographs.

Collier's work computer also proved to be a treasure trove, filled as it was with articles from numerous sources chronicling the life and times of Hunter Roswell. Those files were the turning point, signaling the true beginning of Collier's obsessive behavior. Although his erotomania began with love and hope, it had disintegrated into resentment and anger with each story that surfaced alluding to Hunter's various relationships, as reality failed to match his dreams. As resentment built, the knowledge Collier had obtained began to feed his darker fantasies. Intimate knowledge that came from the audiotapes of Hunter's sessions with Lindsay Carson, found in his locker.

Listening to the audio tapes proved a much greater challenge than Sara had anticipated. Knowing Hunter—caring deeply about Hunter—had eroded a great deal of her objectivity, and Sara found it hard to listen to her give a monotone rendition of events.

But it had to be done. She needed to listen to the tapes and understand, as much as possible, what had happened to Hunter ten years earlier. Because it was while listening to those recordings that Collier's obsession with Hunter had evolved and he had begun to formulate his plan of action.

Of course, the recordings were also Sara's area of expertise: studying the victim, developing an understanding of how the lives of a victim and an unknown subject had intersected, then using that knowledge to anticipate what the UNSUB was likely to do next.

In this case, Hunter's encounter with Brenner had set her on the path that converged with Collier's. And her story—or some aspect of telling her story—had triggered his obsession with re-enacting what he had heard.

One particularly difficult moment for Sara came when Hunter's voice broke while relating an especially brutal experience. Lindsay had responded by telling her it was okay to cry. But after a brief silence, Hunter told the doctor not to get her hopes up, and she then continued to give up the details of what had happened to her at the hands of Kyle Brenner and his boys.

But as hard as listening to the tapes proved to be, there had also been one unanticipated benefit. After listening to the tapes, Sara found herself in a better position to understand the nightmares that continued to haunt Hunter. Nightmares born in the dark imaginings of a survivalist named Kyle Brenner that were now feeding the fertile mind of Eric Collier.

CHAPTER TWENTY-TWO

Nearly a week after the demolition of Collier's house, Sara walked into the Roswell building. She was uncertain what kind of reception she would receive, but she was determined to find some answers.

Collier was still nowhere to be found. It was as if he had simply vanished. The bank accounts and credit cards identified by the task force as his remained untouched while stakeouts at several properties they had located, listed under his mother's name, had yielded no results. It was as if he had simply ceased to exist.

More disturbing to Sara on a personal level, there had been no word from Hunter. The lack of contact or even information regarding her whereabouts had left Sara feeling stymied and discouraged. Erin McBride had also proven singularly unhelpful.

"Hunter Roswell is just fine where she is. What the task force needs to do is focus on looking for and finding Eric Collier before the next full moon. Any assistance you can provide in that regard will undoubtedly prove invaluable."

Sara had tried to do just that, but after five days she gave up all pretense of being able to concentrate. Instead, she found herself standing outside Tessa's office. She blew out a frustrated breath, then mustered her courage and pushed the door open.

"Where is she?"

Tessa looked up from the stack of documents she was methodically working her way through to see Sara standing in her doorway. "Do I assume we're talking about Hunter?"

"Of course we're talking about Hunter," Sara replied, her voice flat. "It's been almost a week since I last saw her. Collier, in the meantime, has disappeared into thin air. No one knows where the hell he is. All I know for sure is he's still out there somewhere making plans to kill Hunter, and somehow I'm supposed to help protect her. But I can't do that if I don't even know where she is."

"She's in New York."

Sara groaned. "What's she doing in New York? Jesus, Tessa, that's where she was when Collier grabbed her the first time. What the hell was she thinking?"

"She was no happier about it than you are, believe me. But it couldn't be helped. She had a series of meetings that she couldn't get out of, and if there's one thing Hunter understands, it's that stockholders and boards of directors wait for no one. Especially when it involves the Roswell and de León family businesses," Tessa explained calmly. "If it makes you feel any better, she's got her entire team with her, and they're all on high alert. Plus her mother and Nigel are there with their security people, and let's not forget her grandfather Patrick and all of his security people. All things considered, she's in good hands."

Pushing her chair back, Tessa swiveled her long legs away from the desk and stood up. Stretching her lean body gracefully, she walked over to the coffee service that sat on a nearby credenza. "You look like you could use a cup of coffee. How do you take it?" she asked as she filled two cups.

The change of subject surprised Sara, and she blinked in confusion.

A faint smile slashed across Tessa's face. "It's not that difficult a question, Sara. How do you like your coffee? Black? Cream and sugar?"

Sara blinked again. "Just cream, thanks."

Tessa added some cream to one coffee before passing Sara the cup. "Anyway, not to worry. She'll be back in the fold tonight."

"Hunter will be back tonight?" Sara was having difficulty keeping up. "How do you know?"

"Well, perhaps because I spoke with her just over an hour ago. She said they were just arriving at La Guardia, and she was hopeful they would eventually be cleared for takeoff," Tessa said and laughed. "The other reason I know she'll be back tonight is because she knows I'll kill her if she's not here for my thirtieth birthday. I understand you'll be accompanying Kate to the club tonight."

"The party at Vertigo?" Sara said and took a grateful sip of coffee. "I'd forgotten all about that. I'm sorry. Happy birthday."

"Thanks." Tessa paused but made no move to follow Sara as she walked to the window and stood staring out at the bay. "I'm not sure if you're aware I've known Hunter forever. Been mad about her for just as long."

The stiffening of her shoulders was the only sign Sara gave she was listening. She continued to look out the window and wondered where the conversation was leading.

"I'm not certain exactly what's going on between you and Hunter, but you need to know I only want the very best for her. Be warned if you hurt her in any way, I'll find a way to make you pay."

Every emotion Sara had been feeling was displaced by an instant surge of anger, and she turned abruptly to face Tessa. "Are you asking me my intentions, Tessa, or warning me off?"

"It looks like I've pissed you off. That's good. Makes me think there's more to this for you than merely solving a high-profile case and getting back into the FBI's good graces." Tessa grinned wickedly then continued speaking softly. "I just want to make sure you understand it's not just Peter and the wolves with guns protecting Hunter."

"I understand that," Sara said. "And you need to know hurting Hunter is the last thing I would ever want to do."

Releasing a soft sigh, Tessa leaned back and rested her hip against the desk. "It's funny, don't you think, that most people look at Hunter and see a woman who seems to have it all," she said. "But what they don't see is underneath the brilliant and beautiful exterior is a seventeen-year-old kid who is still trying to deal with what happened to her ten years ago."

"Don't you think I know that?"

"Maybe you do at that. You seem to know her very well for having known her just a short time." Tessa paused and gave Sara a gentle smile. "For as long as I can remember, I've been after Hunter to get on with her life. To leave the past in the past. At first she claimed she needed to focus on finishing her education, as if another degree would make any difference. Then it was building the business that prevented her from having a relationship with someone that lasted more than one night."

Sara opened her mouth, but closed it again when she could find no words. Then she closed her eyes as well as she waited for Tessa to finish. She tried to maintain a calm expression on her face, even though she felt anything but steady. Still, she was totally unprepared for Tessa's next statement.

"I assume David Granger gave you a file on Hunter." Sara gave her a slight nod of assent. "Good. I'm going to strongly suggest you read it."

"Why?"

"Because it's so very easy to fall in love with Hunter." Tessa's voice was soft and reflective. "I mean why not? She's rich, she's gorgeous, she's caring and smart as hell, and when she isn't being stalked by a serial killer, she has a wicked sense of humor and is actually a lot of fun. But you need to know—you need to understand—what you're getting into before you let things go any further."

"It doesn't matter what's in that file," Sara said bluntly. "It won't change what I think or how I feel."

Tessa's pause lasted several heartbeats, and when their eyes met, all Sara could see was compassion. "It's not you I'm worried about."

"Then what is it?"

"You need to anticipate how Hunter is likely to react. Don't give her a chance to get scared and push you away. Don't let her get away with any excuses."

Sara silently regarded Tessa. "Can I ask you a personal question?"

"Yes, we were lovers, but that was a long time ago. You've nothing to worry about where Hunter and I are concerned. Neither does Kate."

Sweet Jesus. "I already figured that part out," Sara stated unequivocally. "What I can't understand is why you're not still with her. How could you give her up?"

"Ah." Tessa looked momentarily uncertain, and then she smiled. "The truth is we were just kids. Christ, I was nineteen and Hunter was sixteen. We both knew what we had wasn't destined to become some kind of long-term commitment. And then what we thought became irrelevant when her father pulled her back stateside and Brenner happened."

Sara winced, then took a deep breath. "What about afterward?"

Tessa sighed, as if briefly caught in the haunting echoes of the past. "Hunter didn't immediately come back to England when she first got out of the hospital," she said wryly. "She took off, wandering through Europe and Asia, and partied with actors, musicians, models, athletes, you name it. I've no idea when she ate or slept. Mostly, I think she just lost herself in a haze of sex, drugs, and alcohol."

"Did you ever think to go after her? Even just as a friend?"

"Of course I thought of it, but truthfully, she would never stay long enough in any one place. By the time I would find out where she was, she had already moved on. I also couldn't hope to match her resources. So I stayed in England, figuring she would turn up eventually. And when she finally did, she was involved with someone."

"Dominique Kozlov."

"Mm-hmm," Tessa nodded. "Maybe you know more than I thought. Once she was back, Hunter focused on completing her doctorate, and we resumed our friendship as if nothing had happened. It stayed that way until just before I was due to leave England. Hunter knew I was planning to attend Stanford, and at one time, we had talked about getting a house together. But I thought she had forgotten those plans. Color me surprised when she told me she was coming with me."

"And you never considered—"

"We actually talked about it. But in some ways, we're too much alike, and we concluded while we would never last as lovers, we're unbeatable as friends."

Tessa reached for Sara's hand and gave her a lopsided grin. "And as her friend, if I can make one last suggestion—wear something sexy tonight. It'll drive Hunter crazy. And after five days of being smothered by security, getting lectures from her mother, and dodging her grandfather Patrick, she'll be more than ready for some kind of distraction. Plus you just never know where that might lead."

❖

The lower level of Vertigo was standing room only as many of the city's young, wealthy, and influential rubbed shoulders. At nine p.m., the opening band primed everyone, pounding out a lively beat. And then, for the next two hours, Darcy Cole took over the stage and turned up the heat. She drew the crowd to her and held them in the palm of her hand as she rocked the house.

Comfortably seated at Tessa's table, Sara reached for her drink and enjoyed the show. The crowd ebbed and flowed on the dance floor, undulating to the primal rhythm. She could feel her own innate response to the lure of the music—her body unconsciously swaying and her fingers tapping counterpoint to the hard-driving beat. There was only one thing missing from what would otherwise be a perfect night out.

Hunter.

The evening had begun with Tessa sending a limousine to pick up Kate and Sara and deliver them to the club in style. It was only when they arrived that Tessa let them know the Roswell jet would be landing in San Francisco later than originally scheduled.

There had been the anticipated, interminable delays at La Guardia. But as Tessa explained, "The delays kept them on the ground longer than expected, and shortly after takeoff, they ran into a major storm front."

Although Tessa shrugged the matter off, Sara knew how much she had counted on sharing this particular night with Hunter. She could see the disappointment reflected in Tessa's eyes, and on some level, Sara knew just how she felt.

With a mental shrug, Sara pushed her disappointment aside. She made a conscious decision to enjoy the evening and ensure the guest of honor had a good time rather than focusing on things that were entirely beyond her control. When Tessa crooked her finger and indicated the dance floor where Kate had already joined her, Sara followed willingly into the throng until just before midnight when her heart stopped beating. Or at least it felt that way.

The party was in full swing. Darcy Cole was entertaining the crowd, telling amusing anecdotes about the birthday girl to segue from song to song. And then suddenly Hunter was there on the stage beside her, looking like every fantasy Sara ever had.

She was stunning in black and white, a combination of leather and silk with black boots that added at least three inches to her already formidable height. With her dark hair loose and casually tousled, she looked long, lean, and wildly attractive as she stepped up to the front of the stage. Clutched in her left hand was a bottle of Krug's Clos du Mesnil 1995, while a long strap shimmered in the lights as it dangled from her wrist.

After receiving a long, lingering kiss from the singer, Hunter waited for the din to settle before unleashing a megawatt smile. "Made it just in the nick of time," she said, to the raucous approval of the crowd.

She then looked directly at Tessa. "Many years ago, Tessa gave me an incredible gift on one of her birthdays," she said. The deep, rich timbre of her voice was hypnotically seductive while her hands worked at uncorking the bottle of champagne. "At the time, I thought it was a little crazy that the birthday girl was doing the giving, but who was I to turn down such an amazing gift? In return, Tessa asked that, if it was at all possible, I should return the gift in some manner on her thirtieth birthday."

Hunter paused as she jumped down from the stage with fluid grace and walked toward Tessa. As she got closer, Sara realized that what was dangling from her wrist was a leash. Hunter handed Tessa the leash when she drew near. "Tessa, my love. I adore you. Happy thirtieth birthday," she said.

Her timing was perfect.

Just as she finished speaking, the cork popped. While she poured the champagne into the four waiting flutes on the table, members of the staff quickly circulated throughout the room with trays filled to overflowing with champagne for everyone. A minute later, Hunter picked up a flute and raised it. "Thank you all for being here to share this evening. Won't you please join me in wishing an amazing woman, an incredible lawyer, and the best friend I'll ever have a very happy birthday."

Eyes shining with unshed tears, Tessa picked up a glass and raised it toward Hunter before bringing it to her own lips. When she was done, she pulled on the leash. The action immediately drew Hunter's head closer to Tessa's until their lips met.

"You know I'll always love you," Tessa said softly, then took the leash and placed it firmly in Sara's hand.

Sara stared at the leash and tried to comprehend what had just happened. Instinctively, she knew the birthday girl had just given her a gift. An instant later, she felt Tessa squeeze her hand and heard her murmur, "Remember what I told you—and in the future, when you speak of me, speak well."

Sara looked up into Hunter's intense blue eyes. *A leash?* Perhaps she didn't want to know. Instead, she held out her hand. Hunter took it without hesitation as she slipped into the seat beside her.

"Hi." Hunter smiled.

They could have been completely alone as the crowd receded and everything faded into insignificance, except for the blue of Hunter's eyes and the warmth of her hand.

"Hi," Sara replied softly.

❖

The sky had begun to lighten by the time they left the club and got into the waiting limousine. Succumbing to exhaustion, Hunter sank into the seat. Stretching out long legs, she leaned her head back and closed her eyes. An instant later, she released a heartfelt sigh as the air conditioning began to cool her overheated body.

Sara slid in beside her and for the longest time quietly watched the shifting patterns created by the intermittent lights of passing cars and glowing signs as they illuminated the planes of Hunter's face. The signs of fatigue were more evident than usual. Had she managed to get any sleep in New York? Somehow, Sara doubted it.

But that had not stopped her from fully participating in Tessa's birthday celebration, including a memorable moment when Hunter and Tessa had joined Darcy on stage and the trio performed a raucous and bluesy rendition of Melissa Etheridge's "Yes I Am," much to the delight of the crowd. By then, Sara had discovered that Tessa and Hunter had met Darcy while the singer had been working the club circuit, and the three women had been friends ever since.

As she continued to study the woman stretched out beside her, Sara paused and lingered over Hunter's slightly parted lips and idly wondered what she was thinking to have brought out that lazy, sensuous smile. Momentarily lost in thought, Sara blinked, looked at Hunter once again, and then froze as her gaze was captured by Hunter's own.

"Sorry, you were quiet for so long I thought you had fallen asleep," she observed. "Penny for your thoughts?"

"Is that all you can spare?" Hunter responded teasingly, silk whispering as she shifted. "In this economy, I would have thought—"

Rolling her eyes, Sara laughed good-naturedly and nudged her with an elbow. "Bite me, Roswell."

Hunter bared her teeth and decided she liked the way Sara laughed. Even in the dim half-light, she could still see the sparkle in Sara's eyes, but they seemed to hold something serious in their depths. Something that drew her, tempted her, and as Hunter felt her heart begin to race, she found herself aching to touch Sara.

Even though she knew she shouldn't, Hunter reached out and rested her fingertips on the back of Sara's neck. She instantly felt the quiver of reaction that rippled across Sara's skin. Unable to resist, she drew her closer, inhaled the enticing scent of her perfume, felt the softness and heat of her skin. Bending down slowly, she brushed her lips on Sara's neck. *Just a taste.* Deluding herself into believing that would be enough.

"Hunter…" Sara shivered, took a deep breath, and let it out slowly. She drew the moment out as she leaned forward and brought her lips close to Hunter's ear. "I want you. Come with me to Kate's… be with me tonight," she whispered, her breath warm on Hunter's skin before she rested her forehead against Hunter's.

Hunter hesitated. She let out a shaky breath, and then shook her head and said, "I'm sorry. I can't."

Something in her tone caught Sara's attention and she sat up straight. She frowned but kept her voice deliberately light. "I believe that's twice now you've turned me down. A girl might start getting a complex if you're not careful."

Hunter pulled her closer, pressing her lips in a fleeting kiss against Sara's temple. Lifting her hand, she palmed Sara's cheek, then tilted her head just enough for their eyes to meet.

"If I haven't made myself clear, then let me quickly correct that oversight. You're a beautiful, desirable woman, Sara Wilder." She leaned forward and kissed her. A long, slow, sensuous kiss that whispered promises and left Sara breathless. "Believe me when I tell you there is nothing, and I mean nothing, I would rather do right now than take you home and make love with you."

Breathing had never seemed as difficult. "I hear a 'but' in there," Sara said as she reached for Hunter's hand.

"You're right," Hunter said, glancing at their intertwined fingers. "Sara, I'm not exactly sure what's going on between us. But I do know everything else in my life right now is—"

"Crazy?"

Hunter's smile reappeared, and this time it seemed genuine, as was the laugh that accompanied it. "Crazy, yes, and unfortunately, more than a little dangerous. And if I let myself follow through with this—with what I really want to do—I will be pulling you deeper into the abyss that is the current state of my life."

Sara tilted her head. "And that would somehow be bad for you?"

"No. It would be very good for me." Hunter's kiss this time was scorching. Hard and demanding, it left Sara groaning and dazed and with no doubt about how good it could be. "But I don't think it's fair to you."

"I see." *Why does that sound like a kiss-off?* Sara began to disengage and pull away. It wouldn't take a genius to see she was hurt.

"Sara—"

Sara stopped her. "No, damn it, just answer me this first," she said. "Are you always so goddamned noble?"

Hunter was rapidly reaching the point of no return. The taste of Sara's mouth still lingered on her lips, and she wondered if she was being a complete fool. "No. Usually when I see something I want, I just take it."

"Tell me you don't want this," Sara protested hoarsely. "Why are you afraid, Hunter?"

Afraid? Oh, yeah.

"Because you matter." Hunter reached over and tipped Sara's chin up to face her. "In spite of my reputation, I'm really not very good at this, and I don't want to hurt you."

Sara's hands moved up to Hunter's shoulders. "You'd hurt me more by not giving whatever this is a chance to see where it goes," she said softly.

"Maybe," Hunter conceded.

"What do you suggest we do now?"

Hunter's eyes closed and she leaned into Sara's touch. "I think because of everything else that's going on, whatever happens between us, we need to take it slowly."

"Are you sure that's what you want?"

"Yes." She had never been less sure of anything in her life.

"I can do slow." Sara paused. "It's only fair to warn you I don't have a lot of patience. But for you, I'm willing to try. Which means for now, we'll take it slow and see where it goes."

"Fair enough."

CHAPTER TWENTY-THREE

When Hunter stepped inside the small club and did a quick scan, the dull, aching pain brewing behind her eyes served as a reminder that she should not be anywhere without her wolves tonight. Although she was alone, this time she hadn't disabled the GPS units on her car, cell phone, and security pin, knowing Conner could track her electronically and relay her whereabouts as needed.

Still, the smart thing would be to simply go home and get some sleep. *Preferably the deep and dreamless variety*, the pragmatist in her head added wryly.

But she knew there was no point in going home, because sleep would not be forthcoming. Not tonight.

Instead, much as she had always done, she attempted to find something that would help her forget the chaos around her, at least temporarily. Tonight, that meant a spontaneous change of plans and venue, and a small, noisy club where the lights were low, the music was loud, and the dance floor was crowded.

The drink the bartender set down in front of her burned her throat. She winced at the taste and shuddered as she put the glass down. Leaning back and propping her elbows on the bar, she surveyed the crowd, her eyes flicking over the scene in front of her without really seeing it. She could feel the blaring music pumping through her veins as she watched the sea of people on the dance floor. Could feel the heat of their bodies against her skin.

Several times, she was approached by strangers who pressed close against her in the crowded space and asked her to dance. But she smiled and shrugged them off. She hadn't come looking for company. She just didn't want to be alone.

But what does it mean? the pragmatist asked.

That she didn't want to be alone was, in itself, a revelation. Especially considering she had seldom been alone during the two weeks since her return from New York.

She let her mind slowly drift, hazy thoughts that began and ended with Sara. During the past two weeks, Sara had become integral to her life in ways she could never have anticipated. And much to Hunter's surprise, she found herself enjoying it.

In the mornings, they fell into an easy pattern of Sara joining her for a run on the beach with Conner and Adrienne. Afterward, they would gather for breakfast, which Sara insisted she eat. Sara teased her incessantly about her newfound appetite. *I told you there was more to a nutritious breakfast than coffee,* Sara said one morning, as a mountain of fresh fruit and French toast disappeared. *I guess having me around is not so bad after all.*

Once breakfast was over and the kitchen tidied, Sara would accompany her to the office. There, between the meetings, the design work, and the endless negotiations, she would find Sara working tirelessly with both the task force and Hunter's OPS team. They had turned a conference room into a war room as they tried to piece together the puzzle that was Eric Collier. They were determined to find where he was hiding. Determined to anticipate when and how he would make his next move.

Sometime during those two weeks, Sara had even managed to convince Hunter of the benefits of using the limousine to travel to and from work. The time was primarily spent reviewing any progress the task force was making toward finding Collier. But it was also during those moments, alone in the back of the limousine, that they enjoyed some of their best personal conversations.

Sara shared stories of growing up the middle child of three, with an older sister who was a school teacher like their mother and a younger brother who had followed their father into medicine. In return, Hunter offered up tidbits on what it was like to be Patrick Roswell's only grandchild and the sole heir to both the Roswell and de León family dynasties.

Hunter felt the minute shifts in her life. And as her friendship with Sara grew, at times she found herself struggling to rein in the growing feelings that had her, on more than one occasion, contending with the desire to drive over to Kate's in the middle of the night and crawl into bed beside Sara. For two weeks, she had wanted nothing more than to bury her face in Sara's hair and breathe in her essence. For two weeks, she had simply wanted Sara.

The thought shook her to her core.

When a petite blonde cruised her, Sara's face came sharply into focus in Hunter's mind. The image lasted only a second or two, but it distracted her long enough for the woman to feel encouraged and draw nearer. Closing her eyes for just a moment longer, Hunter forgot where she was and concentrated on the image her mind had conjured. Until she felt lips whispering a suggestion close to her ear.

The image shattered like shards of glass.

Leaning her head back slightly, she considered surrendering to the casual seduction. It had been too long, and maybe, if only for a little while, she could banish thoughts of Sara from her mind until she could see things more clearly. Torn by her own indecision, she opened her eyes again and caught a glimpse of someone standing just a few feet away. Very obviously watching.

Her heart jolted. The mood was broken. And then a ghost of a smile touched her face as the shadow morphed into a familiar face.

Tessa studied Hunter and sighed. "What the hell are you doing, Hunter?"

Hunter's smile faded. She sat up straighter and gently pushed the blonde away. "Sorry, baby," she said. "Perhaps another time."

The woman looked like she wanted to argue the point. But one glance in Tessa's direction quickly convinced her it wasn't an argument she wanted to engage in. As she disappeared onto the crowded dance floor, Tessa leaned against the bar and picked up Hunter's discarded drink.

Taking a dubious sniff, she touched the glass to her lips, tasted the contents, and grimaced. "Shit, what's in this?"

"Scotch."

"Who made it, Exxon?" Tessa shook her head in disbelief then looked at Hunter.

Hunter took the glass out of Tessa's hand and drained it before sliding it back toward the bartender and asking for a couple of Coronas. When the bottles arrived, she nudged one toward Tessa. Tipping her bottle back, she let the chilled beer run down her throat before asking, "You want to tell me what you're doing here?"

"I would think it's rather obvious I've been looking for you," Tessa said. "In fact, I've been looking for you for the last two hours. There's a full moon tonight, in case it escaped your notice."

"Don't you think I know that?" Hunter studied Tessa as frustration seeped into her voice. "Don't you think I'm fully aware that somewhere out there, a woman is going about her business, doing whatever it is she normally does on a night like this, because she has no idea her life is about to end?"

"Hunter, you're not—"

"Not what? Are you going to tell me I'm not responsible?" Hunter retorted angrily. *So much for control.* "How can I be anything but responsible? Damn it, Tessa, some woman is going to die tonight for two simple reasons. Because she happens to look like me, and because I failed to find Eric Collier."

"Do I need to remind you the FBI and the SFPD have also been unable to find Collier?" Tessa spoke in a calm, moderate voice.

"That just spreads the blame. It doesn't alter the fact that he's still out there, free to kill someone."

"Is that why you're sitting here alone in this place? Want to tell me what's going on?"

"Nothing…not really…I've just got things on my mind."

"You always have things on your mind, but you don't usually end up drinking in a bar by yourself," Tessa said softly. She waited for Hunter to respond, but when she failed to say anything else, she asked, "Where's Matt? Or Peter and your security team?"

Hunter chose to remain silent in spite of the angry heat she could feel emanating from Tessa. She knew Tessa had always been protective of her. Just as she understood Tessa wouldn't let matters rest until she had whatever answers she was looking for. But she was too tired to have this conversation. Too much had happened. Too many defenses had begun to shift and crumble.

"Actually, you don't need to answer," Tessa finally snapped. "I'm quite aware you slipped away from your security team. What the hell were you thinking? Jesus, Hunter. Like Brenner didn't do enough damage to you, so you thought you'd give Collier a shot?"

"I'm not a seventeen-year-old kid this time."

"So what, Hunter? Do you think your black belts are going to defend you when you've got a gun pressed against your head?"

The question reverberated as a kaleidoscope of ghostly images flashed in her head. "Why are you doing this, Tessa?"

"Because you're my friend and I'm concerned about you. You should know that about me by now." Tessa's voice became soft and cajoling as she continued to watch Hunter. "So…do you mind if I sit?"

"Sit if you want, but I'd rather be left alone if it's all the same." Her hands were icy cold and trembling slightly. Swearing just under her breath, she clenched her hands tightly and battled control back into place.

"Thanks, I think I'll sit for a while," Tessa said as she eased onto the barstool beside Hunter. "Tell me, how long have we been friends?"

Hunter arched an eyebrow in question. "Is this where I get the lecture on everything I'm doing wrong with my life?"

Tessa grinned. "No, this is where you get to sit back and tell me what's troubling you."

"Are you my shrink now as well as my lawyer?"

"If that's what it takes." Tessa laid her hand on Hunter's arm, only to have it shrugged off. "Damn it, Hunter, you really need to go home. When was the last time you slept? Or ate? You look like hell. What's going on with you?"

Biting the corner of her lip, Hunter just shook her head. "There's nothing going on."

"Then tell me why you didn't show tonight at Antoine's to have dinner with Kate and Sara and me like you were supposed to. Why did I have to get Conner to use the GPS on your security pin to—" Tessa cut herself off. "And don't even think about giving Conner a hard time for tracking you down for me. She knew we were worried."

Hunter remained silent, but Tessa showed a willingness to wait her out, and after a prolonged silence, she sighed. "I've no intention of giving Conner a hard time. And my reasons for not showing up for dinner are not all that complicated," she said softly. "I don't think you have a full appreciation of the logistical nightmare it would create at Antoine's to have a diner show up with an entourage that includes eight armed bodyguards."

Tessa tried to keep a straight face and failed miserably. "When did your wolf pack increase in size to eight?"

"This morning." Hunter gave a mirthless chuckle. "I guess I wasn't supposed to notice. But obviously Matt and Peter haven't fully bought in to my theory that Collier will wait until the full moon in October before coming after me."

"Then they should have talked to me. Or better yet, Sara, since she's the behavioral expert, and she happens to agree with your assessment," Tessa replied. She moved closer, resting a comforting hand on Hunter's shoulder. "Sara doesn't believe Collier can change his agenda any more that he can stop himself from breathing. She thinks he's driven by his obsession, and the timing is part of the symbolism he needs for his fantasy."

Hunter nodded her head slightly. "I know. We've talked about it."

"Of course, it doesn't matter what Sara or you or I believe. What's important here is what Collier believes," Tessa continued. "And after tonight, none of it is going to matter because you will be his entire focus, which means he'll be close by."

"Yes, but at least that should make things a little easier."

"What makes you say that?"

"Up until now, Collier has selected his victims at random. It's made it impossible to stop him because no one has had any idea who was going to be targeted. Just that they were going to look a lot like me."

"Kind of like me?" Tessa rolled her eyes and sighed when Hunter nodded. "Is that why I've had a couple of your wolves following me around all day?"

Hunter's lips twitched. "Unlike all the other victims, you don't have blue eyes. But I ran the probabilities and talked to Sara." Sara had concurred that the odds of Collier going after Tessa weren't high. But Hunter was still concerned. "You weren't supposed to notice them."

"After being around you all these years, how can you say that?"

"And I should have told you what I was doing." Hunter's grin widened briefly. "I'm sorry. But after tonight, there won't be any question who Collier will be targeting next, and that will make it easier. I mean, it's better to know the target than to guess. Measures can be put in place."

"Yes, you'd think so, wouldn't you," Tessa said calmly, her eyes thoughtful. "But it's still going to be difficult to defend against Collier because you're not going to know how he's going to come at you. The lone gunman. Is that what's bothering you?"

"That's part of it."

"Hunter." Tessa reached for her hand again and clasped it tightly. "If having a serial killer stalking you isn't the problem, then what the hell is it? Damn it, talk to me."

In an already fragile state of mind, the simple gesture—the touch of Tessa's hand—proved to be Hunter's undoing.

"It's—" She stopped and made a frustrated sound in the back of her throat.

"Complicated, I know. But I'm not going anywhere, love. I'm right here, and you need to talk to someone, so you might as well talk to me."

There was no point in arguing or resisting the support Tessa was offering. "Fair enough." But what Hunter left unsaid was by now there would be at least a dozen security personnel keeping watch outside. Which meant, at least for tonight, Collier wasn't getting anywhere near either of them. Hunter reached for her beer and swallowed another mouthful, buying time while she sorted her thoughts.

"I've been thinking a lot about Brenner."

Tessa waited, clearly uncertain where the conversation was going. Hunter could see it in her eyes. With amazing clarity, Hunter suddenly remembered the dark and rainy afternoon when she had finally told her about Brenner. Tessa had been horrified, and that was only knowing as much as Hunter had been able to tell her.

"Brenner may have started out seeking revenge against my father for the death of his son," she began softly, "but he didn't just want to kill him. It was really all about control. He wanted to be able to control my father. Hurt him—deeply. So he went looking for his Achilles' heel…and found me."

"You were just a kid—"

"Everyone keeps telling me that," Hunter snapped. "I was seventeen. Old enough that I should have known better. Certainly smart enough. I should have trusted my father enough to know there had to be a damned good reason for what he was doing."

She stopped for just a second. "All that damned intelligence. You'd think I would have used it to figure things out. But no, I had to have a fit of teenage rebellion, and instead, I used my brain to slip the security detail. Just to prove I could. And gave Brenner the tool he could use against my father. And if that wasn't enough—if I hadn't already fucked things up enough—I gave Brenner the ability to control me, to force me to play his game."

"Hunter"—Tessa hesitated—"you were trying to survive."

"I know that. Believe me, I've thought about it often enough. I know that initially I was driven by the basic need to survive. Maslow's hierarchy. Basic things like getting something to eat, something to drink, stopping the pain." Hunter paused and steadied her breathing the best she could. "But that stopped working when I realized he had no intention of letting me go. I truly believed he was going to kill me. So why let him win, you know?"

"But you continued to play Brenner's game," Tessa prompted.

The gentle tone had Hunter nodding. "That's the point. I had to, don't you see? Because I handed Brenner something much more powerful than my own survival. Something he was able to use to bend me to his will. It was a brilliant move on his part. My mistake. I didn't give him enough credit."

"What do you mean?"

"I let him see how much my father meant to me. In turn, he was able to use my love for my father to control me, to force me to override my own survival instincts. To continue to play his damned game."

Hunter's eyes fixed on Tessa. She watched Tessa work through what she had just told her and knew the moment the pieces suddenly fit together.

When Tessa spoke, the words emerged slowly, deliberately. "You're afraid of what will happen if Collier tries to do the same, aren't you? You're afraid he'll try to manipulate you by somehow using how you feel about the people who are important in your life. How you feel about your mother, or me—or Sara."

Hunter remained quiet, absorbing the words. Leaning back against the bar, she let her head fall back and sighed. Then she straightened, squared her shoulders, and nodded. "I really care about her," she said softly.

Tessa remained still for a moment. "Let me make sure I understand what you're telling me," she said. "Are we talking about Sara? Did I just hear you say you care about her?"

Hunter nodded mutely.

Tessa tried to stop her smile with little success. "Well, that's good…no, that's excellent. You must know you've had me worried for some time. I thought you were going to shut yourself off from humanity for the rest of your life."

"What the hell's that supposed to mean?"

"You know damn well what I mean, Hunter Roswell," Tessa retorted. "For nearly ten years, other than Dominique, can you honestly tell me you've had a single relationship? Jesus, can you even tell me who you've slept with more than once?"

Frowning, Hunter held her ground. "I don't have a problem admitting I've had my fair share of lovers. And I'm well aware I don't do relationships worth a damn."

"Of course not. Shit, you can barely count your encounters as one-night stands, because you would've had to spend the night with someone to be able to do that."

"You don't know what the hell you're talking about."

"Don't I?" Tessa sighed and shook her head. "Hunter, the truth is you can barely count Dominique."

That stopped her. "Why not?" she asked mildly.

Tessa's expression softened. "Because, my beautiful friend, while I don't deny you might have been crazy about each other, neither of you had any expectation of forever. Never mind that both of you knew she'd never leave—oh God, what the hell was her husband's name?"

"Dimitri."

"Right. You both knew she'd never leave Dimitri." Tessa paused and met Hunter's eyes. "But it's different with Sara."

"How do you know that?"

"Because in all the years I've known you, I've never once seen you look at a woman the way you look at Sara. And if she didn't mean something to you—if you weren't experiencing real feelings for her—you would have already slept with her and moved on."

Hunter concentrated on finishing her beer. "You might be right," she said a minute later. "I mean, it certainly looks that way. But I don't want to think about it right now."

"Good. Don't think about it. You think about things too much." The words were softly spoken. "Don't let your fear stop you from loving, Hunter. Because it's love—or the possibility of it—that's going to get you through the next few weeks."

Hunter remained silent, thinking about what Tessa had said. But before she could respond, her phone began to vibrate. And while she didn't recognize the number on the call display, she anticipated she was about to hear choice words from one of the other women who had been expecting her at Antoine's.

As she brought the phone to her ear, she noticed Tessa smirking at her. "Roswell."

"Hello Hunter. I have another surprise for you."

Hunter's smiled vanished and her grip on the phone tightened. She listened without speaking and suddenly felt very cold. It was as if all the heat had been drained from the room, from her body.

When the call ended, she sat for endless seconds, still holding the phone against her ear as she tried to force her heart rate to slow down. At last, she put the phone down and looked at Tessa. "That was Collier," she said, her voice strained. "He wanted to let me know where he left the body of his latest victim."

❖

The scene was chillingly familiar as Sara and David pulled up to the curb. There were several black-and-whites and unmarked police vehicles parked haphazardly in front of a three-story walk-up, and yellow crime-scene tape was strung across the lawn.

It was a neighborhood that boasted spectacular views of the bridges and islands in the bay and attracted young professionals. A neighborhood that was unused to the kind of violence that had visited it earlier that evening.

David exited the car first. Sara watched him approach two uniformed police officers. As they engaged in conversation, she took a minute to gather herself.

The disappointment she'd felt earlier in the evening when Hunter failed to show for dinner had given way to concern as the evening slowly progressed. Hunter had left a brief voice mail, apologizing and assuring Sara she was fine. But Hunter should have been with them. Safe. Instead she'd been alone somewhere, leaving herself an unprotected target in the event they had misread Eric Collier's intentions.

When Tessa located Hunter through Conner Reese, Sara had immediately wanted to go to her, but Tessa had convinced her to wait with Kate, that she was the better choice to chase Hunter down. But in spite of a wonderful meal and Kate's attempts to cheer her,

Sara's unease had gnawed at her, and when her cell phone began to vibrate, she grabbed it, hoping the caller was Hunter. But those hopes were dashed when David's number flashed on the call display.

In that instant, her emotions had swung like a pendulum. She'd known she was about to hear that Collier had struck again. But for a brief, all-too-terrifying moment, she feared the worst had happened. That they had been wrong and Hunter had been the target after all.

Knowing that wasn't the case had done nothing to ease her discomfort. For in spite of their best efforts, another young woman had been killed. And the clock was now ticking down with Hunter squarely in the killer's sights.

The passenger door suddenly opened and, startled, Sara looked up at David's quizzical expression. "Everything okay? You coming?"

Sara shuddered slightly and quickly exited the vehicle. She followed David across the walkway and up to the second-floor apartment. And although there was no longer any need to hurry, they both took the stairs two steps at a time.

A young officer was stationed in front of the door and stepped aside to allow them entrance.

"Were you the first on the scene?" Sara asked.

"No ma'am. He's inside."

The first thing Sara noticed as she stepped into the apartment was the metallic smell of blood. It hung thick and heavy in the small room. Rick Wilson, the lead SFPD investigator, was just inside, talking to the medical examiner. To their right, a crime scene tech was photographing the latest message.

Hunter, you are mine.

Just beyond them lay the victim, the pool of blood around her head still wet and glistening under the glare of the overhead lights. As she looked, Sara realized just how fresh the crime scene actually was. And as the scene played out in her head, it became too easy for her to picture it. *Hunter's body lying on the floor. Hunter's lifeblood spreading out around her head. Hunter's eyes staring sightlessly.*

"Sara?" David's voice sounded distant, and as she turned toward him, he shot her a quick look of concern. "C'mon, Sara. You need to breathe."

Sara could feel David's arm around her waist, providing support as she drew in several long breaths through her mouth. And though she didn't get sick, she knew the members of the task force working the scene were watching her, obviously surprised someone with her background and experience would react as she just had.

Like a rookie, she thought with disgust.

But she knew her reaction had nothing to do with the body or the blood that covered the murder scene. What shook her more than anything was how easy it would have been for that body to be Hunter's.

"Hey," Wilson said as he approached. He looked curiously at Sara but refrained from making any comment. "We've got a Caucasian female, five foot nine, approximately one hundred and thirty-five pounds. Victim's name is Kristin Colby, twenty-nine years of age. The ME puts the estimated time of death at less than two hours ago."

"Christ, she hasn't been dead that long," David said. "How the hell did you guys get here so quickly?"

Wilson shrugged and indicated they should follow him. They stepped out of the apartment and followed him down the stairs. "We got a call telling us we would find victim number six here."

"What the fuck?" David's eyes narrowed. "Are you telling us that son of a bitch Collier called you?"

"Not directly." Wilson shook his head and pointed to the street where his partner was talking to someone. "It's more like the call came from his intended next victim."

Sara let out a hiss of shock as she recognized the two tall figures speaking intently with Inspector Sanchez. "What's Hunter doing here?"

Wilson shrugged tiredly. "According to Ms. Roswell, Collier contacted her earlier this evening. Among other things, he told her where we could find his latest victim. She immediately called it in, and as luck would have it, Sanchez caught the call. As soon as he realized who was on the line, he asked Roswell to meet us here."

"You're not bringing her in to make a statement?" David asked.

"Not a chance, buddy." Wilson rubbed his chin. "In case your keen powers of observation missed it, that's Roswell's lawyer standing beside her. Of course, we also didn't count on her showing up with a cadre of bodyguards in tow, but considering what's upstairs, I can't say as I blame her."

"Among what other things?" Sara asked suddenly. When Wilson appeared confused, she tried again. "You said that among other things Collier told her where you could find his latest victim. What else did he say to her?"

Wilson hesitated, and Sara's anxiety level ratcheted up another notch. Wilson finally spoke. "I don't have all the details. Sanchez was getting them. But my understanding is Collier told her he was looking forward to getting together with her real soon. That when the time came, she would come to him, and he wouldn't let anything stand in her way. Not the FBI. Not her personal security team. Nothing."

"Damn it." Sara tried to make eye contact with Hunter. But it was too late. Hunter had already turned and was walking away with Tessa, flanked on all sides by the wall of security Matt had put in place earlier in the day. Just in case.

Moments later, the headlights on the Lamborghini and four black SUVs lit up the darkness before the vehicles pulled away from the crime scene.

Chapter Twenty-four

The fog had rolled in and hung heavy and low as Sara exited the cab in front of the wrought-iron gates. David had offered to drive her, but Sara had refused, wanting—no, needing—some time alone. It hadn't occurred to her until now, as she watched the cab pull away, that Hunter might not be alone. Tessa could still be with her. Or any number of bodyguards.

But by then it was too late.

Turning her collar up against the cool dampness in the air, she waited for Rachel and Scott to let her in. Scott made a point of deliberately looking at his watch just before he opened the gate, his eyes questioning what she was doing there in the middle of the night.

Two other men she didn't recognize stood in the shadows and checked her out thoroughly but said nothing, even as the sensors picked up the weapon she was carrying. Sara shrugged and moved past them without a word, then made her way up the cobblestone drive under watchful eyes.

As she walked by the Lamborghini, she continued to feel the faint whisper of doubt tickling the back of her mind. It bothered her that Hunter had left the crime scene without exchanging a word with her. It bothered her more that Hunter had chosen to face this night alone. She hesitated briefly before knocking on the door. It was now nearly one in the morning, and more than anything, she felt uneasy about Hunter's possible frame of mind.

When the door opened, she got her answer as she noted the glass of mahogany-colored liquid in Hunter's hand.

Hunter stood stiffly in the doorway without saying a word, blocking the way inside. It was obvious she hadn't been prepared to find Sara standing there, and for an instant, surprise touched her features. Watching her, Sara feared Hunter would simply close the door again, refusing to let her in. But after an interminable pause, she moved aside wordlessly and Sara stepped around her.

Once inside, Sara took the time to study Hunter's appearance critically. Fresh from a shower, she looked tense and pale, standing barefoot in worn, fitted blue jeans with shredded knees and a ribbed white tank top. Shadowed blue eyes met her stare.

Sara took the drink from Hunter's hand and brought it to her own lips, grimacing at the taste. "Scotch? Jesus, Hunter, wouldn't it be quicker if I just got a baseball bat and hit you over the head with it?"

"What the hell is everyone's concern with what I'm drinking tonight?" Hunter said darkly. Her face was devoid of expression, and there was a weariness in her voice Sara didn't like.

Taking the glass back, Hunter emptied it in one long swallow. She sighed softly and walked back to the counter for the bottle. "I'm sorry. It's one o'clock in the morning and I'm running on empty. Something's got to give."

Sara silently agreed as she removed both the bottle and glass from Hunter's hands and placed them on the table. "Maybe, but you don't need that."

Hunter looked at her, her gaze focused and intense. "And what would you propose I need instead?"

Sara responded instinctively and without thought. She leaned in and brushed her lips over Hunter's.

Hunter remained perfectly still. "What are you doing, Sara?" she asked, a mix of uncertainty and hunger flickering across her face.

I have no idea, Sara answered silently. *I have absolutely no idea.* She placed her hands against Hunter's shoulders, and then let them slide down her arms, reveling in the feel of the soft, warm skin and the solid muscle that lay just beneath.

Her breath caught in her throat as she watched Hunter's eyes darken and glide hungrily over her face. Her vision narrowed until it encompassed nothing more than Hunter's mouth. She ran her fingers through Hunter's damp hair as she had wanted to do for far too long, and in a move she had rehearsed in her mind a thousand times before, she pulled Hunter's head down and kissed her again. Long and slow and deep.

"Sara." Hunter murmured her name, mouth against mouth, her voice rough and filled with need. "What are you doing, Sara?"

Hunter wasn't sure if Sara answered her. The only thing she was aware of in the seconds that followed was the way her lips suddenly brushed against Sara's—or was it Sara's against hers? She didn't know which and didn't really care, because it no longer seemed to matter.

Even so, she tried one last time to rein things in. She leaned her forehead against Sara's, closing her eyes. "I thought we agreed to take things slow."

"Actually, you wanted to take it slow…which we did…until now." Sara brushed her lips against the hollow of Hunter's throat. "I believe I also warned you I didn't have a lot of patience. Now we're changing the pace. I'm changing the pace."

"We can't," Hunter said, tasting regret. "Sara, I still don't know what's happening with my life. Another woman died tonight. Everything is spinning out of control, and I don't want you to become collateral damage." Her breath hitched. "And getting close to me right now is a surefire way for you to get hurt."

"Then you should have thought of that earlier," Sara whispered, closing the fractional distance between them to lightly brush Hunter's lips with her own. "Before you made me want you. And I do…want you."

Hunter swallowed. "It's dangerous—"

"You think too much," Sara interrupted. "Don't think so much. For once, just feel. Just let me…" She brushed her lips against Hunter's yet again.

Let me touch you. Let me love you. Let me hold you while you sleep, even if it's only for one night. She used her hands to caress and soothe while her mouth continued to slowly seduce. *But oh God, please don't let it be only for one night.*

In the back of her mind—just a fleeting thought—she allowed herself to wonder exactly how bad it might be if she only got this one opportunity to be with Hunter. And then Sara decided if she was going to go over the line, if she was only going to have this one chance, then she wanted to remember everything about this moment. She was going to memorize Hunter's scent, the feel of her skin, the taste of her lips, the heat of her mouth.

Lowering her hands from Hunter's back to her narrow hips, she pulled her against her body and kissed her again. This time, though, her lips lingered, and this time, she was certain she felt Hunter begin to respond.

"I love the taste of you." She looked up again into Hunter's eyes. They were dark and wild with need and desire, and Sara felt a quickening in her blood.

It was then she realized she had been wrong.

Totally wrong.

The heat in Hunter wasn't going to be cooled with soft strokes and gentle touches. Acting instinctively, she thrust her hands in Hunter's hair. "Touch me," she demanded and crushed her mouth against Hunter's.

In that instant, she felt Hunter's tightly held control snap.

Sara found herself spun around and pushed backward until she was pinned against the wall, her hands digging for any kind of handhold as her knees grew weak. She felt long fingers wrap themselves around the back of her head as hungry lips covered her mouth and Hunter fed upon her.

Sara's breath quickly grew ragged, and she uttered a soft moan as she gave herself up to the onslaught. She felt Hunter's hands on her, impatiently pulling her shirt open, her lips following the trail of increasingly exposed flesh. She felt Hunter slip her hands under her open shirt. Touching her. Tasting her. Devouring her.

And she responded with abandon. Losing herself in a haze of soft lips, warm hands, and a hot, ravenous mouth. She cried out as her body began to writhe under Hunter's intoxicating assault.

Hunter's mouth, hot and hungry, closed over her breast, teeth grazing hypersensitive skin. Sara inhaled sharply and arched her back under the searching hands and seeking mouth, urging Hunter on. Her blood boiled as her zipper was tugged down and her pants were pushed to the floor. Long fingers stroked up the inside of her thigh, nails making muscles twitch, leaving contrails of fire across her skin.

"Hunter—"

Hunter was lost, her senses on overload. Her whole world had condensed to a single point of focus—Sara. The texture and taste of Sara's mouth, Sara's skin. How Sara fit against her. Denial had never been her forte, and she had denied herself for far too long.

She groaned, dizzy with the feel and scent of Sara's arousal and the need to touch her. Taste her. Absorb her. Sara was so hot. Hot and wet and smooth and tight, hips pumping as Hunter's fingers slid into her. She could feel the exquisite silky softness against her fingers as she drove her toward that first peak. She wanted to... *needed* to feel her come.

"Let go—"

"For you—"

She could feel Sara start to shatter, but instead of letting her crest and begin to slide gently back down, she drove her ruthlessly back up again and kept her there. Pushed her to her limits. Even as Sara shuddered, Hunter drove deeper inside of her, pushing them both to the brink of madness. And finally, with her mouth possessing and consuming Sara, she sent her crashing over the top in a shudder of sensation so powerful Sara's breath tore out in a wrenching sob.

Whatever Sara might have imagined making love with Hunter would be like, it was nothing resembling this. She had never expected anything to feel like this. Hunter was a combination of passionate and tender and seemed to give her entire focus to pleasuring her partner. Nothing else intruded, nothing else mattered. The result infused Sara with a deep and wild hunger that robbed her of breath and left her aching. She was shaking, unprepared for the rush of emotions that came with each touch, and her hands clutched feebly at Hunter as she poured—heart, body, and soul—into Hunter's hand.

"You're so beautiful," Hunter breathed into her ear.

Her low, sultry voice was almost enough to send Sara over the edge again. Reaching for Hunter, all Sara could think of was *more*.

"Tell me what you want."

"You—in every conceivable way."

Hunter awoke before first light, surprised to discover she had slept for two solid hours. She had only a vague recollection of having dropped into oblivion like a stone, and it took almost a full minute before her mind was clear enough for her to remember how she and Sara had stumbled up to her bed, leaving a trail of clothes in their wake.

She had a much clearer recollection of feeling emotionally and physically spent and wrapping herself around Sara. The thought brought a wry smile to her face as she noted the tangle of their arms and legs.

She had to admit it was unusual for her to awaken with someone beside her, and she was faintly surprised to discover that it didn't bother her. She would have expected it to feel awkward, perhaps uncomfortable. But instead, it simply felt right.

She could also still detect the lingering scent of their lovemaking. It surrounded her, filled her, and as she inhaled deeply, she grew aroused again. Shifting slightly, she let her mind drift while she began to softly stroke the expanse of smooth, pale skin visible above the twisted sheets.

Aware that reality was lurking just around the corner, she closed her mind to the impending daylight and concentrated on Sara, sleeping quietly beside her. She listened to the sound of her slow and even breathing. Felt the steady rhythm of her heartbeat. And felt her own blood stir, desire blossoming as a burning, aching need deep within her.

She savored the need and slowly pressed her lips against the delicate skin on Sara's shoulder, bestowing a light kiss. A second kiss soon followed, and then a third. Hunter risked a tentative taste of salt-laced skin with her tongue, before moving up to trail more kisses along Sara's collarbone. Every touch, every taste just made her want more.

When Sara stirred, Hunter paused, watching her float between the realms of sleep and sensual haze. After a moment, she resumed slowly making her way up Sara's neck. Teasing an earlobe with the tip of her tongue, nipping a pulse point with her teeth. Easing Sara onto her side, she settled her thigh between Sara's. Hard muscle against soft, wet heat. Threading her fingers through Sara's hair, she captured Sara's bottom lip between her teeth, tracing it with her tongue before sucking gently.

Sara's lips parted for her, slow and easy and arousing, and the kiss deepened. Their tongues danced as hunger met need. But even as her body ached and her heart began to pound, Hunter kept the rhythm loose.

They continued to kiss, exploring each other's mouths while Hunter caressed Sara with a touch as light as a feather. Sara whimpered as fingertips lovingly traced the swell of her breast, and she brought her leg up, hooking it on Hunter's hip and rocking insistently.

Smiling, Hunter reached down and slid her hand between them. She found Sara hot and wet and ready, and entered her with ease. She kept her movements slow and languid until there was nothing but a flood of sensation and the sound of her name carried on a whispered breath. She felt Sara press into her, clenching around her fingers as she began to peak. She felt her soar, tremble, breathe her name again, as her body shuddered convulsively. Almost simultaneously, her own breath caught, and her body hummed with arousal as Sara's moan mixed with hers.

Bringing her mouth to Sara's once again, her body went taut with pleasure, and she finally let herself go. And when the pounding in her ears lessened, and her heart rate and breathing returned to normal, Hunter framed Sara's face with both hands, palms lightly cupping her jaw, before whispering, "Good morning."

"Mmm," Sara murmured, stretching like a cat. "I could become addicted to how you say good morning." She reached up and brushed Hunter's hair out of her eyes, tucking long wayward locks behind one ear. She let out a breath, drew another in as she stared at her in wonder. "Not that I'm complaining, but what are you doing up this early?"

Hunter smiled and moved her hand in a tantalizing caress along Sara's side until she stroked the curve of her breast and teased a taut nipple. "I've got a video conference call scheduled with New York in about an hour."

Sara captured the wandering hand and gave it a quick squeeze. "Then I guess I should let you go." She inched closer, inhaled the lingering undertones of her haunting scent, and nuzzled the vulnerable curve of her throat. "But then again—"

Sliding sensuously against her body, she felt the slight tremor beneath Hunter's skin, and as she gazed at her, all she could see was how beautiful Hunter was. All she could think was she looked wild and utterly perfect.

Using her teeth, she nipped at Hunter's full bottom lip and found she wanted her again with an intensity she'd never felt before—one that almost frightened her. She blinked and tried to make sense of it all. But as Hunter brought her hand up to brush the hair from her face, Sara realized the why no longer mattered.

"God, you have the most amazing effect on me," she said. "I'm afraid I've become insatiable."

"Is that a fact?"

"Mm-hmm. Do you have the faintest idea how much I want you? Enough that it's starting to hurt."

Hunter's smile deepened. "That can't be good."

"I guess that depends. If I do even half of the very interesting things I'd like to do with you, we won't be getting out of this bed anytime soon. Certainly not in time for you to have your conference call. But I can guarantee one thing—it will be very good."

As Hunter laughed, Sara took the ends of Hunter's hair, wrapped a length of it around her hand, and pulled. And as she drew Hunter toward her, she said, "Give me your mouth, Roswell. I don't believe I got nearly enough of it before."

She brushed Hunter's mouth once, twice, and then claimed her, devouring her until she felt Hunter yield, and a deep shuddering sigh shook her body. Her response ignited a hunger Sara had not known she possessed. Hot and greedy. And as the taste and scent of Hunter exploded inside her, she knew she had to have more.

She couldn't get enough of her mouth, her throat, her breasts. With a twist, she rolled them both over until she was on top. "Don't move," she whispered, scraping her teeth across Hunter's chest before capturing a pebbled nipple. She felt Hunter arch beneath her in response, and as she pressed her abdomen against her, she felt the slick, welcoming heat.

"Sara—" Hunter took a shuddering breath and leaned into her, aching for contact. The touch of Sara's mouth left her trembling and filled her with a dark, edgy need. Try as she might, she couldn't remember the last time she had relinquished control to another woman. She'd always held a part of herself back. But it suddenly didn't seem to matter, and she realized the more she opened herself up to Sara, the more she wanted to.

She moaned deep in her throat as Sara began a slow, torturous exploration and made her way down her body, tormenting her with lips and tongue and teeth. Creating a trail of fire that burned across her skin. Licking and biting with just enough pressure to drive her mindless. Responding to an increase in pressure, Hunter parted her legs farther, leaving herself open and vulnerable. And then she felt Sara claim her with her mouth.

Hunter was stunned by the wildly primitive urges in her blood. She anchored her hands in Sara's hair, threw her head back, and cried out. And then she splintered. There weren't words. Her body pulsed and contracted, and she lost all sense of time and place. All she could feel was Sara holding her while she came apart. All that mattered was the moment. The rest would take care of itself.

❖

As Hunter's breathing steadied and the pounding in her chest took on a more recognizable rhythm, she realized she was sprawled across Sara's chest, her arm and leg locked possessively over her. Glancing at the clock, she saw that she needed to get up, although she had no desire to move.

"Are you okay?" Sara said against her hair

Oh yeah, she was more than okay. Raising her head, she saw Sara staring back at her with uneasy eyes. "I'm good," she said. Heat bloomed in her face and a grin twitched at the corners of her mouth. "You gave me exactly what I needed."

Almost immediately, she felt Sara's body relax and saw her close her eyes with a sleepy, contented sigh. "That's good."

"Mm-hmm. Why don't you get a bit more sleep," Hunter whispered. She gently smoothed Sara's hair, tucking the short, curling strands behind her ears. Lulling her with her touch, her presence. "I'll wake you when I'm done, and you can decide what you'd like to do today. I'll be happy to provide some suggestions if you can't think of anything."

She heard Sara moan softly and resumed her gentle stroking until Sara's breathing deepened and sleep claimed her once again. Hunter watched her sleep a minute longer, placed a featherlight kiss on her forehead, and then eased her way out of bed.

Video conference call? Right. She paused, ran a hand through her hair, and grabbed a T-shirt from the dresser.

Sara awoke gradually. The first thing she became aware of was the warmth of the sun now streaming though the skylight. Stirring, she stretched an arm lazily toward the vacant side of the bed before remembering that Hunter was no longer there. *Conference call? Yeah, that was it.* Rolling onto her back, she inhaled deeply and smiled contentedly. The breeze through the open windows carried the fresh scent of salt, cypress…and coffee.

Turning her head, she grinned with anticipation as she saw the large mug on the bedside table. She sat up, pushed her bangs out of her eyes, and reached for the mug. *Yes.* Freshly brewed coffee with a dash of cream, just the way she liked it.

Thank you, Hunter.

As she sipped the steaming beverage, she heard the distinctive sound of running water coming from the shower. She also picked up the spicy scent of the soap Hunter favored, and her smile widened. Still holding the coffee, she slid out of bed and silently made her way to the adjoining bath.

The soft, gentle flickering of the candles in the room reflected a golden glow on the naked woman leaning against the wall, arms crossed. As she watched Sara approach, her eyes darkened with seductive intent.

Sara's mouth went dry, and she felt an instant surge of heat. Unable to look away, her gaze roamed hungrily over Hunter's body. "So," she asked as she put her coffee down, "do you mind sharing a shower?"

Hunter smiled and held out a hand without saying a word. She drew Sara into the warm mist and let the pulsing water spill over both of them. Pulling her closer, she traced the edge of Sara's jaw with her tongue before bringing her mouth down on the soft lips beneath hers.

A groan escaped her as she felt Sara begin to respond, and she smiled to herself when she heard Sara's breath catch and then become labored. She briefly deepened the kiss before dropping slowly to her knees, her lips gently tracing a deliberate pattern down Sara's body as she descended.

Sara opened her eyes halfway and mumbled something unintelligible.

"I can't seem to get enough of you," Hunter said and touched her mouth to Sara again, letting the intimate kiss deepen slowly. Silkily. "Do you mind?"

"No, I don't mind," Sara answered breathlessly. "Sweet Jesus, Hunter. Do you have any idea how you affect me...Oh...my... God..."

The rest of her words were lost to the steam and the sound of the running water as Hunter continued her languorous explorations. Sara drifted in a place of pure heat and sensation, and she lost herself in Hunter's mouth. She wanted to prolong the moment, hold out as long as possible, but knew almost immediately that wasn't going to happen. She moaned as she got closer, started to shudder as her orgasm tore through her. Waves of pleasure strangled in her throat. A sob exploded from her lips, and she arched her back, calling out Hunter's name as her limbs gave out.

She would have collapsed but for the strong arms holding her up. Hunter stayed where she was, on her knees, Sara's hands entangled in her hair. As her breathing returned to normal, Sara looked down at the beautiful face pressed against her abdomen. Hunter seemed lost in thought, her expression distant.

"Are you okay?"

Hunter nodded and pressed her lips against Sara's skin. When she looked up, her eyes met Sara's with an intense gaze. "My life… it's still crazy."

As if hearing what Hunter left unspoken, Sara framed Hunter's face in her hands. "What are you afraid will happen?"

"I don't know," Hunter replied. "The only thing I know for sure is I don't want to regret this. Not with you."

"I don't want that either." Still holding Hunter's face, Sara bent down and kissed her forehead. "We'll just have to make damned sure neither of us has any cause for regret."

Hunter grinned wryly as she got to her feet. "And how do you propose we do that?"

Sara smiled. "I don't know," she said, as she put her hands around Hunter's neck and brought her mouth closer. "But this is a good place to start. The rest we'll figure out together with time."

CHAPTER TWENTY-FIVE

The late afternoon sun felt wonderful on her face, and with the temperature in the midseventies, Hunter knew her decision to go for a run was the right thing to do. After working through most of the night on a new simulation program, she had been left inexplicably restless and edgy all day. She should have gone home to bed, she thought ruefully, as she rubbed her burning eyes.

But part of her felt the need to somehow touch her old self and the life she might have had if—what? If Brenner hadn't gone looking for revenge? If she hadn't been brought back from England? If she hadn't slipped the security detail? If her father hadn't died?

She knew the skein of events and circumstances that shaped her past was tangled and there were no simple answers. That was why she chose the Presidio for her run, undoubtedly the most scenic former army post in the country. Now part of the national park system, she had picked it in part because it boasted the Golden Gate Bridge as a backdrop. But mostly because the air was thick and redolent with the past.

She felt a hint of guilt at having turned down a number of offers for company. She knew the OPS team was trying hard to give her breathing room. Once October's full moon drew nearer, she knew they would leave her with no choice but to accept their constant presence in every aspect of her life. But until that time, they would concede there were times when her need to be alone outweighed all other considerations.

As she locked her car, she made a mental note to make it up to them.

After a few minutes spent stretching, she started off at an easy pace to give her muscles a chance to warm up before she pushed them. She pounded steadily along, letting the rhythm soothe her jangled nerves and tired mind. And thought of the green eyes and beautiful smile of the woman who lately had occupied nearly all of her waking thoughts.

One recent telephone conversation came to mind.

"What are you doing?"

"Trying to determine the best way to break into the Palace Casino's vault."

There was a moment of silence. "And you would be saying that while an as-yet-undetermined number of FBI agents and SFPD officers are just down the hall from you...why? Do I need to ask Tessa to start arranging bail?"

Hunter laughed. "The chief of security operations at the Palace heard we redid the systems at the Royal Palm and asked us to test their security. He seems to think it can't be breached. Fancies himself a security expert. Told me he designed it himself."

"And?"

Hunter stared once again at the schematics on her computer screen. "And having checked it out, I could crack it in my sleep," she responded dryly. "Which is why I thought I might do something a little more creative."

Sara's amusement came through over the phone line. "He annoyed you."

"You're dangerous," Hunter said. "Or I'm starting to become predictable. Should I be worried?"

"Never."

"Right. So what are you up to?"

"Well," Sara said, "I was just sitting here thinking how much I'd like to walk down the hall to your office and have my way with you on your desk."

Hunter was speechless. For just an instant, she looked around at her desk, cluttered with stacks of blueprints and program code. "Give me thirty minutes," she said and then paused. "No, wait. What the hell am I thinking?"

"Hunter…Jesus, I—I can't believe I actually said that. Do you suppose you could pretend I didn't?"

"Uh-uh," she replied. "After all, this is my company."

"I know. I'm—"

"That means I can delegate some of this stuff that needs to be cleared off my desk so I can turn my attention to…other pursuits. Give me fifteen minutes instead." A deliberate pause. "And Sara?"

"Um, yes?"

"Don't be late," Hunter said in a low drawl. "If you're not here in fifteen minutes, I'm starting without you."

She could hear Sara struggle to breathe as she hung up the phone.

The memory made Hunter's heart skip a beat, and she felt an intense rush of adrenaline that had nothing to do with running. It also brought a smile to her face as she maintained her pace for twenty minutes, and then kicked it up a gear for the next twenty. Salt-laced air filled her lungs as her breathing increased to match her exertion.

For the final twenty minutes, she picked up the pace again, enjoying the endorphin high a hard run always gave her. Finally, concentrating on her breathing, she slowed down to a jog, letting the sea breeze blow her damp hair back off her forehead. She turned away from the water and onto the inland path that led back toward her car.

As the path bent to the right, Hunter caught a glimpse of movement—a group of runners coming in her direction. There was nothing remarkable or unusual about them, but Hunter felt a twinge of unease as they drew near. She slowed her pace, an uncertain smile playing on her lips, her senses on alert.

As the lead runner passed her, she thought she caught a glimpse of something dark in his hand. *A gun.* There was no time to react. In the next instant, she felt a searing flash of pain as she was lifted off her feet. Her body stiffened and she lost all motor control.

No, not a gun. A Taser, she realized. Not that it mattered. Her body relaxed and folded as soon as her attacker stopped the stun.

Completely cognizant of what was happening, but helpless to do anything about it, Hunter felt a hard kick as it caught her in the ribs, sending her into a short rolling slide. A follow-up blow to the solar plexus knocked the wind out of her and left her gasping. Through the ringing in her ears, she heard a laugh as she fought to regain her breath. But she could do nothing to stop yet another blow as it caught her high on the right shoulder, and her arm went numb.

Time slowed. She felt hands grabbing her arms, pulling her helplessly to her feet and holding her upright. As muscle control slowly returned, she began to struggle and lashed out with the only weapon left to her—her legs—connecting violently with one of her assailants, eliciting a grunt of pain as she grappled for some kind of advantage. But there were too many of them and it was much too late. She was unable to break free, and an arm came around her neck in a chokehold while a series of blows battered her ribs.

For a long time, the world stilled. And then when she was no longer held, Hunter felt her knees start to buckle. She looked up at blurred, unfamiliar faces and tried to focus. But something exploded against the side of her head just before she hit the ground. Her last clear memory was the scent of the past and the sound of the waves lapping gently against the shoreline, and then her world went black.

Just before six o'clock, Sara poked her head into Hunter's office and was surprised to find it empty. She checked her watch and confirmed the time, then decided that Quito would probably be the best one to tell her where Hunter could be found. Turning, she ran directly into Matt's broad chest.

"Hey," he smiled. "I was just coming to see if the resident genius wanted to grab some dinner. I'm glad you're here. Maybe you can help me convince her coffee isn't the only food group."

Sara laughed. "Actually, Hunter and I had agreed to meet up for dinner around this time, but she's not in her office. I was just going to check with Quito to see if he knows where she is."

"She went for a run," Quito said when they found him.

"What time was that?" Matt asked.

"Maybe two o'clock," Quito replied. "Sorry, Matt. She dropped some papers on my desk as she was heading out and asked me to run some revised numbers for her on the new hotel contract. Then she told me not to work too late and she'd see me tomorrow—like maybe she wasn't planning on coming back to the office. I guess I hoped she was going to go home and get some sleep after her run. Is everything okay?"

"Everything's fine. Don't worry about it," Matt reassured him. "I'll just ask Peter to locate her."

"She went to the Presidio for a run," Peter responded promptly when asked a few minutes later. "Conner and I both offered to go with her, but she begged off and it was obvious she needed some alone time to clear her head. Especially after working on that SIM program all night—bloody piece of genius that it is. Have you seen it?"

"Is she still there? At the Presidio?" Sara asked.

"No." Peter glanced at Matt and Sara quizzically. "I kept an eye on her car, and it started moving about half an hour ago. Actually, if you head down to the parking lot, you'll find she's pulling up to the front of the building as we speak. Is there a problem?"

"No problem," Matt said. "Just as I suspected. Nothing to worry about. Let's go catch Hunter before she comes back in and take her out to dinner. How do you feel about Japanese? Do you like sushi?"

❖

Awash in a world of pain, Hunter maneuvered the Lamborghini carefully through the security gate, intent only on reaching the building. *So damn close,* she thought, as she breathed through her mouth and fought past the pain that punctured her senses. Just a little bit farther.

As she neared the overhang at the front entrance, the pain inside her head intensified, and unable to concentrate any longer, she allowed the car to coast to a stop. Once it was no longer moving, she reached for the ignition, turning the key as she slumped forward against the steering wheel.

It was the pain that brought her around. Radiating in waves. Her ribs burned, her shoulder throbbed, and oh God, everything hurt. She could taste the blood, feel the warmth and wetness of it as it trickled into one eye and down her face. She tried to focus, but she suddenly couldn't concentrate on anything other than breathing and on not making a sound. On not screaming.

Another long moment passed, and Hunter forced herself to pay attention, knowing that losing consciousness again was not an option. She knew she had to hold it together but wasn't sure anymore how...or why. With her remaining strength rapidly depleting, time became slow and hazy.

"Hunter?"

Matt's voice. Security must have called him—probably after the Lamborghini bumped against the building and she didn't get out of the car. The fact that she could reason reassured her somewhat. But then Hunter felt another jolt of raw pain, and she stopped trying to think.

She opened the car door, pushed her legs out, and managed to climb out of the vehicle. She stood off balance as her vision swam and her legs began to buckle beneath her. Nausea swept through her, and she reached out, grabbing the car door and trying desperately not to fall.

Sara started moving toward Hunter, whispering, "Jesus, Hunter," half prayer, half expletive. It didn't take a medical degree to know that Hunter was hurt. The only question was how badly. There was a gash over one eye which was bleeding freely. Blood was smeared across her cheek, joining the dark purple bruising that covered her jaw and throat. Another bruise was forming under her other eye, and she stood unsteadily, swaying, eyes blinking and unfocused.

Sara took another step closer and could hear Hunter's breathing—shallow, harsh, labored. She noted the blood that stained

Hunter's hands, the scraped knuckles, the bruises on her arms. Whatever had happened, she had not gone down quickly or easily.

Hunter blinked again, shivered, and tried to remember where she was and why she was there. She had been trying to get somewhere, but she was so tired and her body felt so heavy.

"Hunter?" Sara said softly.

"Hey, Sara." Hunter's normally smoky voice sounded hoarse and confused. "When did you get here?"

Hunter swayed and dropped to her knees. Sara moved quickly to her side and wrapped both arms firmly around Hunter and eased her to the ground. Sara's stomach clenched, and she swallowed convulsively as she rested the palm of her hand against Hunter's face. She could see that her features were taut with pain, and her breathing was uneven and erratic, but Sara could tell she was trying to push past it.

Pulling herself together, Sara began to whisper reassurances. "Easy. I've got you, Hunter. You're going to be okay."

Hunter's only response was a low groan that bubbled up from deep inside as she gritted her teeth.

Unable to keep her hands still and needing the contact, Sara reached down and brushed Hunter's hair out of her face, examining the cut and the bruises more closely. Hunter responded with a faint smile and reached for her hand, linking their fingers together. Behind her, Sara could hear Matt barking instructions on his cell phone, and she became conscious of others arriving to help.

"Hunter, I need you to concentrate for just a minute," she said, watching as Hunter's eyes drifted shut. "Come on, love, stay with me. Can you do that for me?"

Hunter opened her eyes again, but she seemed to struggle to focus, and her movements were growing increasingly slow. Sara could see the signs. Whatever adrenaline had gotten Hunter this far had dissipated, and she was going into shock.

"She needs a hospital," she said to Matt as he crouched down beside her. "At a bare minimum, she's going to need a CT scan, and I'm not sure, but this cut over her eye might need stitches."

Matt nodded. "That's what I figured. Conner's on her way with one of the SUVs and she's a trained EMT. You stay with her," he added, "because Hunter's going to be pissed when she finds herself in a hospital."

"Wouldn't have it any other way. Did you hear that, Hunter?" Sara asked. "Just hang in there, love. We'll get you fixed in no time at all."

Hunter could hear Sara's voice, found her touch comforting. She felt herself drifting. The world was spinning, fading. But it was okay because Sara was there, and Sara would look after her.

"Ah, shit," she managed, before the world receded.

❖

She'll be all right.

It all blurred, as the words kept repeating in her head, a silent mantra. Sara felt close to panic as images of Hunter, bloodied and beaten, continuously invaded her mind.

She'll be all right.

Seated in the waiting room, she clenched her hands as they began to shake. Her relief upon seeing Kate on duty when they had brought Hunter into the emergency department had long since vanished. Now she was desperately waiting for word—any word—on Hunter's condition.

She closed her eyes, fighting against the tightness in her chest, the fear in her heart, and realized with startling clarity the depth of the feelings she had for Hunter.

Hunter completed her. She was the missing piece of the puzzle, and for the first time in her life, Sara knew she had fallen in love.

She's got to be all right.

"Sara?" The voice was pure Texas and could only be Conner's. "How are you holding up?"

"I'd be a lot better if they'd let me back there where I can see her," she replied, turning back from staring distractedly out the window. "Is that coffee I smell?"

There was an awkward silence, and she felt Conner's eyes quickly assess her. Apparently satisfied with what she saw, Conner released a grin and winked. "Not just coffee. I managed to score Starbucks instead of the usual hospital brew."

"You're a goddess," Sara grinned back weakly. She accepted the tall white coffee cup with the familiar green logo, took a sip, and sighed. And then she leaned back and closed her eyes while she continued to wait.

Almost two hours passed before Kate walked back through the swinging doors and into the waiting room. By then, it seemed as if everyone in the room was there hoping for some word about Hunter. Tessa had arrived just behind Matt and Peter and had dropped into a chair beside Sara without saying a word. In the interim, David and a number of task force members had also arrived.

As Kate approached, Sara stood up quickly. The sudden movement, coupled with the emotional overload and the lack of food, made her sway slightly on her feet. Conner and Tessa immediately jumped up beside her, each grabbing an arm to hold her steady.

"Easy," Tessa said. "One of you in the hospital is more than enough to handle right now."

Sara nodded. She was actually surprised her legs were able to hold her upright. But she was prepared to crawl, if necessary, to reach Kate. She focused on her face, searching her eyes anxiously. "How is she?"

The reassuring response came quickly. "She's going to be fine."

Sara's shoulders slumped in relief. "Are you sure? Can you tell me more without a subpoena?"

"She gave me permission to share details with you and her security team. Her vitals are strong. That's not to say she won't be hurting when she wakes up. She was pretty disoriented and we had to sedate her. She had a partial dislocation of her right shoulder, which we were able to reduce."

"Were there any other injuries we should be aware of?"

Kate gave a slight nod. "She's got badly bruised ribs, but luckily, there were no fractures. She's also got a nasty bump on her head, a sprained wrist, and an assortment of contusions and lacerations, mostly to her face and torso. Given her medical history, we had some concerns about the bruising on her right cheekbone, but thankfully, there was no fracture this time."

"Why does that sound—" Sara froze.

"It sounds a lot like Hunter's original injuries from ten years ago," Matt interjected.

"That's probably because there's a close match," Lindsay offered as she walked into the waiting room and confirmed the thoughts running through Sara's head. "In fact, I'd say deliberately so. I've been reviewing Hunter's file since I was told she had been brought in, and I believe this was an attempt to replicate her original injuries."

"If we're looking at the full moon as Collier's target date, then the timing would be right," Sara added. "Brenner held Hunter for three weeks, and she got most of her original injuries shortly after she was kidnapped."

"I don't get it." Matt spat out furiously. "She's got two damned black belts. Christ, she can take Peter down, and that's no easy feat, so tell me how the hell Collier did this to her. Was she drugged like in New York?"

Kate shook her head. "She got taken down with a Taser. There are twin burn marks high on her chest."

"Son of a bitch."

"It also didn't help that she was badly outnumbered," Kate added softly. "From what Hunter was able to tell me before we sedated her, there were five of them. She indicated they were all white males in their mid- to late-twenties, for all the good that will do you in trying to identify them."

"Five of them," Matt snapped as he turned to look from David to Sara. "He's replicating everything. When Brenner and his boys originally did their number on Hunter, there were five of them. How did we not see this coming? Someone tell me, how the hell did we miss this?"

Sara ran her hands through her hair and shook her head. "I don't know," she said bleakly. "I think in part because until now, everything indicated Collier was only practicing his end game. Brenner's game. It just never occurred to me—"

"It didn't occur to any of us, including Hunter." Tessa wrapped a supportive arm firmly around Sara. "And Hunter's the last person who will be looking to assign blame."

Lindsay nodded. "Tessa's right. What's important here is that, at least physically, Hunter's going to be okay," she said. "But we'll need to keep an eye on how this affects her psychologically, which is probably the reason *he* did this. He likely wants to cause dissention on the team. At the same time, he wants Hunter rattled and off her game. Vulnerable. He's smart enough to realize it's the only chance he's got to beat her."

"It also means we can't afford to make a mistake like underestimating Collier again," Matt added. "Hunter may be smarter than him, but this little bastard has managed to stay at least two steps ahead of us."

And that was the crux of the matter, Sara thought. Collier was smart. He not only continued to elude capture, he was now trying to goad Hunter into reacting emotionally. He would have listened to the tapes of Lindsay's sessions with Hunter countless times and would use his intimate knowledge of her past to try to manipulate her.

He obviously wanted Hunter alone and at odds with her team. He wanted her to provide him with the same kind of opportunity she had given Brenner ten years earlier—a chance for him to grab her. Then he wanted her to play Brenner's game with him.

And if they weren't careful, he just might succeed.

David scratched the stubble on his chin. "Doc, I know you said she got Tasered, but is there any chance she did some damage to whoever did this to her? Enough that they might be in need of some kind of emergency medical attention themselves?"

"It's possible," Kate said. "But from the bruises on Hunter's arms and neck, I'd say two or three of them had a pretty good hold on her."

"Maybe," Matt said. "But her knuckles were bruised, and maybe she got a couple of shots in before they grabbed her. She had a lot of blood on her when we brought her in, including some on her hands and on her running shoes. Maybe it wasn't all hers. Maybe we should start checking out the local emergency departments, starting with this one."

David nodded. "I'll call it in."

"The question now is did anything else happen during the three weeks immediately before Michael Roswell was killed that we should know?" Sara asked as she turned back to Lindsay. "Because that's what Collier is using to create his plans, and we can't afford any more miscues."

"I'll go over the tapes again, but I don't believe there's anything else in them that will prove helpful." Lindsay paused thoughtfully. "But you need to consider the natural reaction to what just happened will be to place Hunter in the equivalent of protective custody, which is, of course, what her father unsuccessfully tried to do when Brenner started making threats."

Matt stiffened visibly. "What are you trying to say?"

"She's saying our natural instinct to smother Hunter in a protective blanket is more likely to drive her crazy and make her bolt, which will give Collier the access he'll need to get to her," Sara said. "It's how Brenner was able to grab her, and Collier knows that."

Matt scowled. "Then what the hell are we supposed to do?" he asked, and whether or not it was a rhetorical question, it seemed no one had an immediate answer.

"I want to see her," Sara said softly, looking at Kate.

CHAPTER TWENTY-SIX

Pain washed over her in waves, pulling her from a comfortable oblivion. *That's good*, Hunter thought groggily. *If you can feel pain, it means you're still alive.*

Breathing, she quickly discovered, was painful, but not unbearably so. Testing her hypothesis, she took a deeper breath. *Okay, that hurts.* She bit her bottom lip to keep from moaning, but apart from a strangled little sound at the back of her throat, she was able to hold herself rigid and fight the pain as she tried to remember what had happened. But everything remained unclear, and before she could determine where she was or why, the drugs in her system took her back under.

The next time she opened her eyes, there was a woman she didn't recognize standing next to her. She blinked several times and concentrated on bringing her surroundings into sharper focus. She finally realized the woman was wearing medical scrubs and was checking the IV in her arm, adjusting the flow. She lay perfectly still and listened to the steady, low beep of the heart monitor. She smelled the distinct scent of antiseptics.

This is not good.

She licked dry, swollen lips and tried to speak. She worked her mouth open, but despite her best effort, no sound came out. The movement, however, seemed to catch the nurse's attention.

"Ah, you're awake. That's good. How are you feeling, honey? Do you know where you are?"

Hunter blinked. The world appeared to be moving in slow motion as she considered the question. She closed her eyes for a few seconds—or maybe it was longer—as she tried to formulate an answer. When she opened them again, the room was dark and she was alone. But there was no doubt in her mind this time. She knew exactly where she was. She was in a hospital. She could feel the panic start to rise and tried to concentrate on what she knew she had to do.

I've got to get out of here.

Her first attempt to sit up was definitely not a success. She tried to push herself up and didn't even make it to a sitting position. The room swam, her head whirled, and she was hit by an almost instant wave of nausea. It didn't help that her movements were restricted by the shoulder immobilizer she was wearing. *Separated shoulder*, the pragmatist said. Felled by dizziness, she was forced to lay her head back down.

Okay, you can do this.

She focused on keeping her breathing even and on controlling the fear that threatened to overwhelm her. After a few minutes, she tried again, and this time her effort met with substantially more success as she managed to get her body upright. Gritting her teeth and working through the pain, she swung her legs over the side of the bed. In the process, she dislodged the lead for the heart monitor and set off the alarm.

"Ms. Roswell?" A nurse came through the door, hurried over to the bed, and silenced the alarm. "What do you think you're doing? Ms. Roswell, you need to get back in that bed. The doctor said...I wouldn't recommend—"

"I need to get out of here." Hunter barely managed to get the words out. Her throat was raw and dry and the words did not come easily. Ignoring the nurse, she slid out of the bed slowly and felt the vertigo hit hard and fast as her feet touched the cold floor. She managed to grab onto the nurse to stop herself from falling.

"Ms. Roswell—"

Hunter tried again. "You don't understand," she said hoarsely. "I really need to get out of here. I cannot spend the night in this hospital. Please believe me. I'm not trying to give you a hard time." She drew in a deep breath and grimaced. "Look, just give me whatever papers I need to sign so I can leave AMA. But I need them now."

"I can't do that, Ms. Roswell. Now, whether you leave against medical advice or not, I really need you to get back into bed while I go and find Dr. Montgomery."

Hunter sighed. Her head was pounding and the pain in her side was becoming more intense. "Fine, you do what you have to do. But tell Kate not to bother coming to see me unless she's bringing the papers I need to sign so I can get out of here."

"Ms. Roswell—"

From the doorway, Sara cleared her throat. "Nurse," she glanced at her name tag, "um, Lorraine, why don't you give me a few minutes to speak with Hunter? In the meantime, maybe you can find Dr. Montgomery."

The nurse nodded and quickly left the room without a backward glance. Sara turned her attention back to Hunter, who looked as if a slight breeze would topple her and had yet to acknowledge her presence in the room other than with a quick initial glance.

"Hi," Sara said softly, smiling at Hunter. "How are you doing?"

"Still breathing, sort of," Hunter said, turning to face Sara and grimacing. "But I'd be doing a lot better if I could just get out of here. You think you can help?"

Sara tilted her head to one side and studied Hunter. Her right arm was held firmly in place by a shoulder immobilizer while her left was tenuously tethered to an IV. Her eyes were glassy and dazed, her face ashen, the only hint of color the angry purple bruises that covered most of the right side of her face. The bruising then spread downward across her neck before disappearing under the faded blue hospital gown she wore.

"Actually, you look like you're about to fall flat on your face. How about I help you back into that bed for a minute while we talk about it?" Sara suggested gently.

Hunter stared at Sara as she allowed herself to be maneuvered back into bed.

"Would you like some water?" Sara held a glass of water with a bendable straw up to Hunter's lips and waited until she had managed a few sips.

"Thanks," Hunter said, mumbling something as her eyes closed.

Sara set the glass on the side table. "Sorry, what did you say?"

Hunter tried again. "When did you get here?"

"I've been here since we brought you in, about eight hours ago. Matt, Tessa, most of your OPS team, and, I swear, over half the task force are just down the hall."

Hunter frowned. "Eight hours?"

"Mm-hmm. I've been in and out of your room since they moved you up here, but you've been pretty much out of it, so I'm not surprised you didn't notice. How bad is the pain?"

Hunter stared up into Sara's eyes. "My head hurts," she said darkly. "And it hurts just to breathe. I think I banged up my ribs."

Sara couldn't help herself and chuckled. "Yes, you certainly did. You also dislocated your shoulder," she added helpfully.

"That would explain the damned immobilizer." Hunter raised an eyebrow. "I think they've given me so much medication I can barely think straight."

"The bump on the head probably isn't helping you there." Sara grinned. "That's the main reason they want to keep you here for observation. It's just to be on the safe side. I'll even stay with you, if it makes you feel any better." She grabbed Hunter's good hand in hers and squeezed it gently, conscious of the scraped knuckles and the intravenous tube.

Hunter shook her head and her eyebrows furrowed as the movement intensified the throbbing in her head. "I—it's not that I don't appreciate the offer, because I do. I really do. But it won't help. I just can't stay here." She swallowed hard, her breathing becoming more shallow and rapid.

I can't breathe oh God please help me there's not enough air...

"Hey, what is it? Hunter?" Sara asked, her voice tinged with alarm.

"Sara," Hunter whispered with her last ounce of strength. "Please…I—I can't…breathe…in here."

Sara gazed at Hunter as understanding dawned. The monitors registered no physical reason for the shortness of breath. *Panic attack. Ah hell. We've brought her back to a place that is tied to so many of her nightmares.*

"Okay, Hunter," Sara said reassuringly, keeping her voice soothing. She leaned over and brushed Hunter's disheveled hair back, then kissed her forehead. "It's going to be okay. As soon as Kate shows up, I'm going to get you out of here. I promise. I'll have you home in no time."

❖

The trip home from the hospital in the early morning took them through the nearly deserted streets without incident. Sara concentrated on driving but was constantly aware of the black SUVs that had her flanked on all sides. Protecting Hunter, who was stretched out in the passenger seat, dozing quietly from the effects of whatever medication Kate had administered.

Sara wasn't sure what it was Kate had given her, but it had worked with amazing speed, and for that she was grateful. It had been difficult watching Hunter swaying unsteadily, each movement obviously sending waves of pain radiating through her body while they'd waited for the orderly to bring a wheelchair. And before they left the hospital, Kate placed a small bottle of pills in Sara's hand, along with instructions to give Hunter two as soon as they got her home and into bed.

Hunter awoke as they pulled into the driveway, groggy and disoriented, then leaned on Sara as she guided her slowly up the stairs.

"I don't know what I would have done if I'd been forced to stay in the hospital." With her words slurring from the medications coursing through her system, Hunter wrapped her arm around Sara's shoulders, gave her a lopsided grin, and kissed her. "Thank you for understanding and being there for me," she whispered against Sara's lips.

Sara felt herself fall that last little bit, realizing she was truly, madly, and absolutely in love. "Any time, Hunter."

Sara swallowed hard as her heart raced in her chest. She could feel her emotions starting to spill over, and she needed to keep them in check. Now, more than ever, Hunter would need her to be calm and rational.

"How about a bath before I tuck you into bed? It'll make you feel better and probably help you relax enough so you can sleep." *It will also remove any trace of the attack that might be lingering.*

"You just want me naked." Hunter's tone was surprisingly light, almost playful.

"Anytime I can." Cautiously maneuvering Hunter and leaving her leaning against the wall, Sara began to prepare the bath. "How's the pain?"

"I'm not really feeling anything."

"I'm not surprised. You're so wasted," she said with a smile, filling the huge tub. Once it was ready, she helped Hunter remove the immobilizer and her clothes before easing her into the warm water.

"Oh God." The words slipped unintentionally from Sara's lips as she got her first look at the lurid bruises that covered most of Hunter's torso. Was it only hours since she had touched every inch of that skin with her lips? She felt a flash of fury when she saw bruises that looked like finger marks on her upper arms and the twin puncture marks where the Taser had hit her before bringing her down.

"It must look really bad if you're praying," Hunter said and then gave Sara a hopeful look. "Are you getting in here with me?"

"Not this time, love."

"No fun..." Hunter tried to pout, ignoring the protest from her split lip for an instant, before she gave up and closed her eyes. She sank slowly beneath the water, allowing her mind to float in a drug-induced haze that had no discernible pattern. When at last she brought her head back up above the water, she released a deep sigh bordering on a moan as her battered body absorbed the heat. Within minutes, the tension around her mouth and eyes began to ease.

Sitting on the edge of the tub, Sara carefully washed and rinsed Hunter's hair. She then began using a sponge to gently remove any lingering traces of sand and blood from her bruised and battered body. And when the water began to cool, she helped Hunter out of the tub and dried her with a thick white bath towel before helping her get into bed.

Her final act was to bring Hunter a glass of water and two pills. Hunter raised a questioning eyebrow, and Sara shrugged in response. "I've no idea what they are, honey, but Kate said to give you two and put you to bed. Please don't fight me on this. Kate's going to drop by later today to check on you. In the meantime, you need to try to get some rest."

Sara watched Hunter swallow the pills without further protest and waited until her eyelids grew heavy and closed. "I'll be right here when you wake up," she promised softly.

Hunter seemed to fight her sluggish mind in an attempt to respond before surrendering, as her fingers intertwined with Sara's grew lax. Sara remained perched on the edge of the king-sized bed for a few minutes longer, simply watching her, needing to reassure herself that Hunter was indeed all right before she went downstairs. When she heard her breathing deepen and knew for certain Hunter was asleep, she quietly left the room.

She found Matt, Peter, Conner, and Adrienne sitting at the kitchen table reviewing plans to upgrade Hunter's security, while Tessa tried to get the espresso machine to work.

"How is she?"

"She took a couple of the pills Kate sent home with her, and now she's sleeping."

"She took the pills willingly?"

Disregarding the shocked comments, Sara listened in but didn't participate as the ongoing discussion resumed. Instead, she helped Tessa finish making coffee, then kept herself busy for the next hour, making breakfast for everyone and tidying the kitchen. When she was done, she prepared a small tray with some toast and fruit juice in case Hunter was hungry when she awoke, then added a glass filled with ice chips as an afterthought.

"You should get some sleep," Tessa said. "That's what I'm planning to do, in case anyone's looking for me."

"Sounds like a plan," Sara responded tiredly. She and Tessa parted company on the second-floor landing. As she continued to the third level, she could feel Tessa's eyes following her.

She found Hunter much as she had left her. She lay sprawled on her back, and Sara could see the pain that marked her face even in sleep. Setting the tray on the bedside table, she showered quickly and changed into a clean T-shirt. She then sat on the edge of the bed, content to watch Hunter sleep.

A few minutes later, a small moan escaped Hunter's lips, and she stirred restlessly in her sleep. Sara stroked the soft dark hair, trailing an index finger across the badly bruised cheek before bending and brushing her lips briefly on her forehead. She could feel the heat radiating from the bruises on Hunter's body and slipped her hand under the sheet, tenderly caressing the smooth skin until she could feel Hunter's breathing begin to relax.

"Sara?" Hunter said. Her eyes were glazed, her voice thick with pain and exhaustion.

"I'm right here," Sara replied. "How are you feeling? Are you hungry?"

"Not really, no. My stomach's not feeling particularly friendly. Maybe some water?"

"Well, open up," Sara instructed, feeding Hunter some of the ice chips when she obediently complied.

Hunter sighed as the ice eased her throat. "Thanks. What are you doing still awake?"

"Watching you," Sara admitted. "You're beautiful."

"Oh." Hunter's breath caught and her lips parted slightly in a hazy smile. "Why haven't you come to bed? Is something wrong?"

"I—" Sara stopped, uncertain how to explain the insecurities that were suddenly plaguing her. Especially in light of all the people in the house. This was definitely not the time for a discussion about exactly what was going on between them. They had to have that conversation, and Sara hoped it would happen soon. But not today.

"Sara?"

Sara looked down and sighed. "You've a house full of people. I guess I didn't want to assume anything, so I thought maybe I should go down to one of the guestrooms."

Hunter wondered whether she'd heard the fleeting note of insecurity in Sara's voice or not. She groaned faintly and struggled to focus. "We probably need to talk—" She tried to move and sucked in a sharp breath, hissing at the stinging pain the motion caused. "Damn."

"Hunter, don't move," Sara said quickly. "For God's sake, you'll only end up hurting yourself more."

"Now you tell me." Hunter dropped her head back onto the pillow and closed her eyes. "Sara, in the last ten years, I haven't— I've only ever been with one person for any length of time. So I'm really not very good at this. If it bothers you having anyone downstairs know we're involved, that's one thing. But if I'm the one causing whatever discomfort you're feeling…if I've not been clear, or you're finding it difficult to read me, then for now, can you accept that I need and want you close to me and just come to bed?"

Sara brought her fingers to Hunter's lips, stopping any further discussion. "Yes, I can do that." She slipped under the silky sheets and lay on her side. "Is this better?"

"It helps," Hunter said.

"Go back to sleep, Hunter. I'll be right here when you wake up." Sara gently stroked Hunter until her own exhaustion took over and her eyes closed.

Chapter Twenty-seven

Sara leaned her elbows on the table, her frown deepening as she watched Hunter.

Since the assault at the Presidio several days earlier, Hunter had become increasingly frustrated with her physical limitations. She continued to fight blinding headaches, and her slowly healing body left her incapable of working out or going for an early morning run. Unable to relax, her moods had deteriorated and she had grown progressively more withdrawn.

Today had been the worst.

All day long, Sara had felt the heat of Hunter's frustration radiating like waves. Her expression was dark and stormy, and it was only a matter of time before something triggered her simmering temper. That something, it seemed, turned out to be Matt, when he walked in with Peter and said, "We need to talk."

Hunter leaned against the counter and sighed. "Why is it nothing good ever follows that sentence?"

"I'm sorry, but this can't be helped," Matt replied. "Peter and I have been talking, and we think until this thing with Collier gets resolved, you need to postpone or cancel any trips or meetings you've got planned. If there's anything that can't be rescheduled or canceled, just let me know, and I'll go with the team in your place. But until this mess is over, you need to consider yourself grounded."

Hunter's smile faded and she stared at Matt without making a sound. When she finally spoke, her response was succinct. "That's not going to happen."

Matt turned to Sara, plainly seeking her input and support, but she silently shook her head. This was not her battle, and although she understood Matt and Peter's motivation, she didn't agree with their approach. Their intervention was the very thing Lindsay had warned against. In their own way, they were replicating what Michael Roswell had done ten years earlier when he brought Hunter home without explanation—they were taking matters into their own hands and not giving her any say. And they were risking Hunter reacting in exactly the same manner. Slipping away from the protection her wolves provided and giving Collier an opportunity to get to her.

Still, Matt would not be swayed. "Look, Hunter, be reasonable. The smartest thing you can do right now is stay here—out of sight."

"We can put extra security in place and add a couple of sharpshooters on the roof until it's all over," Peter added. "I know some guys who are available, and I promise, you won't even know they're there."

Hunter spun around to face Peter, redirecting the heat of her anger toward him. "Don't even think of it."

Sara frowned and thought Matt should have recognized the combative tone in her voice. But perhaps his frustration with the lack of progress in finding Collier had him craving a fight as much as Hunter was.

"Don't think of it?" Matt repeated. "Christ, Hunter, does Collier really have to kill you? Is that what you want? Answer me, damn it. Is this how you finally rectify Brenner's mistake when he let you survive instead of your father?"

A stunned, drawn-out silence hung in the room between them.

Hunter stood white-faced and furious.

"Fuck me," Peter muttered.

"Damn, Hunter. I'm so sorry, I shouldn't have said that," Matt said. "I know that's not what you want, but can't you see that it's you Collier wants? That all the others have just been practice? Why are you giving him a chance to get to you?"

But Hunter was clearly not ready to forget his remark about Brenner and would have no part of his apology. "Back off, Matt," she warned softly.

"No, damn it—I have every right, as your friend and business partner—"

"Do you think that grants you the right to dictate how I live my life? You've got to be kidding. Do you really want to test how quickly I can have Tessa dissolve our partnership?"

"You can't—"

"Do you have any idea how much I detest those particular words?" Hunter's voice, low and winter cold, seemed to echo in the room. "Of course I can. Watch me."

"Damn it, Hunter."

The next few moments were like watching a train wreck. As if in slow motion, Sara watched Matt grasp Hunter's arm as she turned away from him. It was obvious that, in the heat of the moment, he forgot just how bruised she was. Matt froze as he watched Hunter's face turn ashen. But in spite of the pain he had to have caused her, she didn't utter a sound.

Instead, she met his eyes. "Remove your hand," she said quietly. "Now, or I'll remove it for you."

He complied immediately. "Ah hell, Hunter, I'm sorry. I didn't mean to do that. You've got to believe me."

The pain was still starkly evident in her eyes as she turned away from him, pausing for only an instant. "Do us both a favor, Matt. Be gone by the time I get back," she said and walked out the door.

They all waited for her to slam it shut. Somehow it seemed worse when the door closed quietly, as Hunter demonstrated she was still in control.

Peter remained frozen, staring at the closed door while Matt made a move to follow her. Sara quickly intervened.

"Don't, Matt. Give her some space right now," she suggested gently. "She didn't mean what she said. You'll see once she's had a chance to calm down."

He shook his head. "Doesn't she get it? Doesn't she realize how much danger she's in?"

"Of course she knows. You just pushed her at the worst possible time," Sara said. "We all need to remember that she's got a lot to deal with right now. It's not just having Eric Collier lurking in the shadows waiting for the next full moon. She's still in a lot of physical pain, and the anniversary of her father's death is fast approaching. Think how that must be affecting her emotionally."

"I know she's got a lot going on. But damn it, Sara, I just want to make sure she's safe, and she's not making it easy," Matt said. "Collier has managed to kill six women. *Six*. And no one—not the FBI or the SFPD—has been able to stop him."

"Now it's Hunter he's got targeted," Peter added quietly. "And for all our collective know-how, the only thing we can come up with to protect her is to go into lockdown mode and wait him out."

"Believe me, I understand," Sara replied. "But you need to try to look at it from Hunter's perspective. That means if there's a decision affecting her that needs to be made, you need to involve her in making it."

"It's not going to be easy." Matt looked at Sara. "Because in the meantime, she's going to be Hunter Roswell—hurting like crazy and not letting anybody in."

Matt might have been wrong in his approach, Sara decided, but he was right in his assessment. She glanced at her watch and decided enough time had passed. It was time for Hunter to let her in—whether she wanted to or not.

Hunter spent the better part of an hour walking on the beach. The October winds were chilly, but she found comfort in the solitude, and as always, the rhythm of the waves soothed her overloaded nerves. She was grateful Matt hadn't followed her out of the house, but thought perhaps the wisdom of that decision had come at Sara's urging. Only Sara could have watched what happened with Matt and immediately understood any further conversation would have had disastrous consequences on a relationship that was too important to both of them. The reprieve she'd been granted enabled her to calm down and regain some perspective.

Aware that her wolves were flanking her, she walked close to the water's edge until the pain in her head became too intense and her knees threatened to buckle. Dropping onto the cool sand, she rested her arms on raised knees and watched a trio of pelicans circle and dive into the surf to feed.

The birds, in combination with a throbbing ache in her temple, kept her distracted until Sara was almost at her side. Sensing her approach at the last instant, Hunter's head came up and she looked around. Their eyes met with an almost tangible intensity, then Hunter's shoulders slumped and she sighed. "Sorry I'm being such a bitch."

"Were you?" Sara asked blithely. "I hadn't noticed."

Hunter lowered her sunglasses and regarded Sara. "Liar." A rueful smile made a brief appearance before it faltered and disappeared as she looked away.

At that moment, Sara wanted nothing so badly as to reach across the distance Hunter had created between them. But she wasn't certain how or where to begin. Torn by indecision, she simply dropped onto the sand beside her, their thighs touching. She was pleased that at least Hunter didn't pull away. But for the first time, the silence between them was decidedly uncomfortable.

Waiting what she hoped was an appropriate length of time, Sara made the first attempt to break the silence. And though the question had to be asked, she hoped she wasn't risking another flash of anger. "Do you want to talk about what happened?"

"No." Hunter retreated into a deafening silence. She continued staring at the waves before finally tilting her head toward Sara. "Can I ask you a personal question?"

Sara sat up straight. *Why does she feel like she needs to ask permission? What could she possibly want to know?* "Of course," she answered evenly. "You should know by now you can ask me anything."

"Why is that, do you suppose?" Hunter asked. "But more to the point, why hasn't some woman come along and claimed you?"

It was the last question Sara expected, and she gave a small laugh. "I'm not sure…what I mean is, I'm…" She glanced at Hunter who was regarding her with gentle amusement. "I guess I'm not really sure how to answer that."

"Try."

"Okay." She stretched the word out, then looked out at the water and sighed. "When I was younger…I guess I never really thought about committed relationships. I was totally focused on achieving certain goals…to the exclusion of everything else. And while I knew where my interests lay, women were just—"

"Distractions? For fun? Stress relief?"

"You're making it sound worse than it was." Sara felt a heated blush. "After I got recruited by the FBI, I became totally caught up in the work I was doing. I also didn't think any woman would put up with the hours and the uncertainty, so relationships took a backseat and I just focused on being the very best. At least, that's the way I felt until the Pelham case."

She stopped and shrugged. "In hindsight, I think I never met anyone who captured my attention. I never met anyone who made me want to stay and try to build some kind of future."

"Not even Kate?"

"Good God, no," Sara laughed. "Even if she wasn't more consumed by her career than I was, Kate and I have always been amazing friends. Neither of us has ever wanted to risk that."

"And now?"

Sara looked at Hunter. "Since I quit the bureau, I've had a lot of time to think about what I really want in my life. And while I haven't figured out where I'm going professionally, I admit that I now find the idea of having someone in my life appealing."

She watched Hunter nod to herself and stretch her legs out on the sand, content to sit in silence and watch the ocean. When she remained silent for more than a few minutes, Sara leaned into her.

"Your turn," she said.

"My turn?" Hunter echoed with a whisper of uncertainty. "I don't know. I've never—I think I come with too much baggage. Who the hell wants that?"

Sara shook her head. "Uh-uh, Roswell. I'm not buying that. You're gorgeous and sexy as hell. Try again."

"You think I'm sexy?" The words were teasing.

"You're damned right I do," Sara said as her ears grew hot. "Now, no more evasions. Try answering the question."

Hunter's smile faded and a frown appeared before she turned away to look at the swirling water and stared into the past. "I think it's part of Kyle Brenner's legacy."

Her voice was calm and even, but Sara caught the uncertainty more clearly this time. "What do you mean?"

"He taught me to fear."

"I have a hard time believing you're afraid of anything."

"I don't know about that," Hunter said. "You scare the hell out of me, you know that, don't you?"

The comment surprised Sara, but the vulnerability clearly evident in Hunter's face stopped her from pursuing clarification. "What did Brenner make you afraid of?"

"I think he made me afraid of needing anyone too much, of caring too much, in case they get taken away from me," Hunter admitted after a moment, her voice growing soft and distant. "I think that's why I've never let anyone get close. Why I've never stayed long enough with anyone to find out if there might be anything else there."

"Because of what happened with your father."

"Mm-hmm." Hunter regarded Sara intently. "Pretty fucked up, wouldn't you say?"

"Not so much, no. Understandable." It certainly explained the many walls Hunter had built to isolate herself. The irony, Sara knew, was Hunter didn't see how many cracks already existed in those walls. Didn't see how many people she had already let get close and were now an integral part of her life. People like Tessa and Matt. Quito and his family. Lindsay Carson. Even her wolves.

Sara got up onto her knees and framed Hunter's face with her hands, using her thumbs to stroke soothingly. Leaning closer, she kissed her. "I want you to listen to me. And I mean really listen. It happened, Hunter. You can't change that fact, no matter how much you may want to. Nor can you go back and change the outcome."

She placed another kiss near Hunter's temple and felt her tremble, then wince. Holding Hunter closer to her, she said, "You're chilled and it's obvious you're in pain. Let's get you back to the house where you can get warm. I'll make you some hot cocoa, and you can take something to ease that headache."

Hunter nodded, willingly following Sara's lead back to the house and settling on the couch. Sara even managed to tuck a blanket around her and start a fire before making her way to the kitchen.

By the time Sara returned, the fire was crackling and snapping in the hearth, its light bathing the room in swirling shadows, and the air was filled with the rich scent of wood smoke and chocolate. She handed Hunter a steaming mug. "There's more on the stove if you want some," she said. "Just let me know."

Hunter looked up. "Thanks. Aren't you going to sit?"

"Sure…lift," she said, watching as Hunter obediently lifted her legs. Sara slid under them and took a seat next to her. "Here, before I forget," she added and gave her two tablets.

"Thanks." Hunter dutifully swallowed the pills.

Watching the fire, Sara's eyes strayed to a framed image on the mantle—a photograph of a much younger Hunter with her parents. It was a candid shot taken at a happier time, all three faces windburned and grinning as they sat in the stern of a sailboat. Sara could see the strong resemblance between Hunter and her beautiful mother in the slashing cheekbones, but the vibrant blue eyes and sensual mouth were unquestionably a mirror of her father's.

"It was taken on St. Barts the summer I was fifteen," Hunter said. "I've been thinking about him a lot."

"Not surprising, given the date and what's happening in your life." Sara captured Hunter's hand and felt her fingers curl around her own. "I'm here for you to talk to, whenever you want."

Hunter nodded. "I know." Her voice grew soft, her eyes unfocused. "He was the first person who looked at me and really saw me. Not just the prodigy, the whiz kid, but the person inside. The person I thought only I could see."

"That's the person I see," Sara said quietly.

CHAPTER TWENTY-EIGHT

The blazing fire had been reduced to smoldering embers, and the warmth in the room had long since dissipated. Still, Sara didn't want to move, content to watch Hunter as she lay dozing, her head now nestled in the sanctuary provided by Sara's lap.

So beautiful, she thought, dizzy from the scent of her, mixed with the faintest touch of wood smoke from the dying fire. She could still see the bruises in the faint light. *And I'm crazy about her.* Hunter's hair felt like silk running through her fingers. Her fingertips moved to Hunter's cheek, stroking gently. An instant later, she inhaled sharply as Hunter captured her fingers and kissed them.

"I thought you were asleep."

"I was." Hunter smiled as she reached up and gently drew Sara closer until their lips met, brushing the sweetest of kisses on her mouth. "But then I woke up with this insatiable need to kiss you."

Sara grinned. "I noticed." She bent her head and kissed Hunter once again, tasting her lips and teasing gently with her tongue, watching her eyes instantly grow dark with arousal. She was so damned responsive. Sometimes, all it took was a look. A touch. And each touch became so much more than a physical act. "Any other needs I should know about?"

Although it was said with a trace of teasing, Hunter's smile faded and was replaced with a faint frown. Sara saw the change in her expression but couldn't interpret it. "Hey, what's going on?"

"Actually"—Hunter met Sara's appraising look and struggled to sit up—"I just remembered there was something I needed to ask you. I can't believe I forgot."

"Then ask me."

"Right," Hunter said. "It's just my mother and Grandfather Patrick have arranged a memorial service, the day after tomorrow, to commemorate the tenth anniversary of my father's death."

"I know."

It had been all over the news for the past several days. One network had put together a film retrospective of Michael Roswell's life and career which included stark photographs from the fateful day. Sara had difficulty erasing one particular frame from her mind—a shot of Michael Roswell as he lay dying in his daughter's arms. Hunter's face was shadowed by a curtain of dark hair, but there was no mistaking who it was.

Foolishly, Sara wondered if Hunter had seen it. *Of course she has*, she decided. It would explain her increasingly haunted expression. "I would imagine you'll want to attend."

"I was unable to attend my father's funeral," Hunter said. "I will not miss his memorial service."

As Sara absorbed the words, all she could think was how much pain she could hear in Hunter's statement. Taking Hunter's hands, she stroked them gently with her thumbs, wishing she could find a way to exorcise the past and help her truly embrace the present. "What can I do to help you?"

"I was hoping you would come with me."

Sara frowned. "Of course I'll be there. You don't even need to ask." In her mind, she quickly flashed back to an earlier conversation with Peter and Conner as they reviewed plans to increase security at the cemetery. In addition, the task force would have a discreet presence, and Patrick Roswell would also have security. Would that be enough? *Surely Collier wouldn't try anything under the glare of the media spotlight?* "I know Collier is still a threat, but I don't think—"

Hunter sighed. "Sara, I'm not asking you to be there to protect me. I don't mean for you to sit in the shadows with the task force or my wolves." She hesitated. "I mean I'd like you to come with me. Be with me."

"Well, of course, if that's what you really want." Sara tilted her head and thought about what that meant for just an instant. Comprehension dawned. "Oh."

"Yeah, *oh*." Hunter grinned weakly. "We're just talking a short graveside service. Private. That means my mother, Nigel, and my grandfather Patrick will be in attendance. Of course, that means the addition of politicians, reporters, and media types. The service will be followed by a family dinner, but I can guarantee that will be a strictly private affair. Just family. Will any of it present a problem for you?"

Sara shook her head, uncertain what to say as endless possibilities danced in her head. "Are you sure—"

"I'm sure." Hunter's grin widened. "I promise it won't be as bad as anything you are probably imagining."

Her mother, Nigel, and Patrick Roswell. Oh God. Sara cast a sideways glance and swallowed, almost unable to speak. "Should I be afraid?"

A dark eyebrow arched. "I guess that depends on how easily you scare."

❖

The day dawned cool and gray. But even the comfort of Sara's presence hadn't stopped the nightmares. Tired and light-headed, with shadows beneath her eyes underscoring her lack of sleep, Hunter remained quiet and introspective—almost withdrawn—all morning. Now, as they waited for the limousine, she could feel Sara watching her, could sense her concern.

"Are you okay?" Sara asked.

Hunter rested her forehead against the window. "Just a headache."

"Can I get you something for it?"

Hunter turned and stared at her for several seconds and then reached out and wrapped her fingers around Sara's wrist, pulling her closer. The faintest of smiles ghosted over her face. "I've got something for it right here," she murmured and forgot about everything except the gently smiling woman in her arms.

All too soon, she heard the sound of someone clearing their throat. Turning her head slightly, she saw Conner standing by the door.

"Sorry to disturb you, but the limo's here."

Nodding, Hunter looked at Sara and gave her a wry grin. "I guess it's showtime."

Less than an hour later, they stood at the graveside, Hunter between her mother and Sara, a single long-stemmed white rose in one hand. She could feel the gentle breeze blowing across the quiet hillside as it whispered through the trees, stirring memories and ghosts.

Crossing her arms in front of her and bowing her head, she stared silently at the large gray stone. The name Roswell stood out in deeply engraved letters across the center, and she found herself repeatedly tracing her father's name with her eyes. Michael Hunter Roswell. Beloved husband and father.

Somewhere to her right, Patrick Roswell was speaking. Quiet, heartfelt words, eloquently used to describe a man who loved his family. His wife. His child.

She closed her eyes as wisps of memories came back to her.

What's it worth to you, Hunter...

The incessant voice in her head caused her to stiffen, continuing until she was certain it would drive her to the brink of madness. Just as the October sun broke through the low gray clouds, Hunter reached out blindly and grasped Sara's hand, drawing her near, unconsciously rubbing a thumb over her hand as she tried to stay connected. She continued to stare at the cold gray stone without seeing it, as the past reached out and consumed her.

Hold your fire...Hold your fire...We're losing him...

Lost in the past, she watched her grandfather Patrick's mouth move but couldn't hear his words. In her mind, all she could see was a montage of violent images. All she could hear was Kyle Brenner whispering in her ear.

Don't you want to know why, Hunter? Don't you want to know why I never killed you? Why I killed your father instead?

"Hunter?" Sara's voice was a low murmur. "Are you all right?"

The concern in the quiet voice broke through, and Hunter started abruptly. She recognized she was being given the time to get her bearings, to gather her thoughts, and she was grateful for that. She felt dizzy and swallowed hard.

Releasing Sara's hand, she took a deep breath and straightened her shoulders. Rolling the rose between her fingers, she hoped her mother couldn't see how badly her hands were shaking. She stepped forward and placed the rose on the grave with infinite tenderness. Her eyes closed and she drew in another deep breath.

"I still miss you, Dad," she whispered softly. *I'm so sorry—it should have been me.*

The family dinner that followed the memorial service was held in the penthouse suite of the Citadel—the newest addition to the de León family chain of hotels. As they entered, Sara deliberately lagged behind and found herself standing with Nigel. She wanted to give Hunter time to speak with her mother, an opportunity that had not been available prior to the service. Nigel seemed to be affording Marlena a similar opportunity.

Both women bore evidence of their shared grief. Not on open display, but it was visible nonetheless. And while Sara could not claim to know Hunter's mother—after all, they had yet to be introduced—the resemblance between mother and daughter was striking and enabled Sara to see things more clearly.

Michael Roswell must have been an incredible man, to have two such amazing women all but brought to their knees by their grief, even after all these years.

"Michael was a force to be reckoned with in everything he did or touched." Nigel regarded her calmly when Sara turned toward him. "From the day he met her until the day he died, he was totally and passionately in love with Marlena. And he was convinced the sun rose and set in his little girl, and then she hung the moon."

Sara watched Hunter turn and smile at something her mother was saying. The smile made Sara catch her breath. It was the kind of smile that spoke of unconditional love and made everything worthwhile.

"Is Hunter very much like him?"

"Amazingly so." Nigel's own smile widened, and the affection in his voice was unmistakable. "Don't misunderstand me. There's a lot of Marlena in Hunter as well, especially when it comes to business. But the daredevil risk taker is all Michael. And he seemed to know it from the moment that child was born. Had the girl flying planes before she was ten, and the two of them loved nothing better than to go hang gliding and skydiving. And if they weren't up in the clouds, then they were on the water, or under it."

"How did Marlena handle that?"

"With amazing grace," Nigel responded wryly. "More times than not, Michael and Hunter's choices terrified her, but to her credit, she never held them back."

"Not that I could have stopped them, even if I had wanted to."

The deep, husky voice behind her was enough like Hunter's to startle Sara, except Marlena's voice still retained some traces of her Spanish heritage in the soft accent. Sara turned and came face-to-face with the dark-eyed, strikingly beautiful woman who happened to be her lover's mother. "Oh, I'm sorry," she began and held out her hand. "We've not yet been introduced. I'm—"

"Sara Wilder. Yes, I know." Marlena smiled graciously as she accepted the outstretched hand. "Michael loved all things physical. He used physical activity as a way to relieve stress."

"Hunter's much the same," Sara said, aware that in spite of a welcoming smile, Marlena was openly assessing her.

But then what had she expected?

Being here with Hunter was a coming out of sorts, a kind of public acknowledgment of their evolving relationship. *You're here as her daughter's lover*, she thought wryly. But while Marlena de León Roswell had a reputation for being a formidable woman, Sara had told Hunter she could handle this, and she wasn't about to let her down now. Feeling both anticipation and dread, she expelled a breath and met Marlena's gaze head-on.

"It's good to know some things don't change." Marlena's expression was tempered with humor. "As a child, Hunter seemed to have no fear—of anything. And she and Michael loved to conspire. Michael's role was to choose their activity, while Hunter was expected to provide me with detailed explanations of thermal updrafts and drag coefficients. I believe those explanations were meant to somehow reassure me."

Sara laughed. "And did they reassure you?"

"Well, it's hard to argue with the laws of physics, especially when they're being explained to you by a ten-year-old genius," Marlena responded dryly. She took a sip of her wine while she continued to regard Sara. "Will you tell me something, Dr. Wilder?"

The quiet question rattled her. To calm her nerves, Sara tried to focus on Hunter who was standing across the room from her against the far wall. But that didn't help. At that moment, Hunter appeared unhappy and seemed intent on finishing the drink in her hand as she stood listening to something her grandfather was saying.

She turned back to face Marlena and smiled. "Please, it's Sara. What would you like to know, Mrs. Roswell?"

"You must call me Marlena. And I need to know how Hunter is really doing. I would also like a solid reason why I shouldn't take my daughter to my family home in Spain where she can be kept safe. At least until the next full moon is a memory and the authorities have captured this madman who seems intent on harming her."

As Sara contemplated her answer, she wondered who was keeping Hunter's mother informed. "Your first question is easier to answer. Hunter is healing physically from what happened at the Presidio. She is also finally trying to come to terms with what happened to her ten years ago. Unfortunately, that means facing a lot of things she had previously managed to suppress, and as you can tell, she's not eating or sleeping much. But on the positive side, she is starting to talk more openly, and that can only help her. As for your second question, I'm afraid you won't like my answer very much."

"Oh? Why is that?"

"If you force Hunter into hiding, Collier will most likely continue his killing spree. The deaths of more women will destroy Hunter as surely as anything Collier can do to her."

Marlena's expression revealed a momentary trace of surprise. "You seem to understand my daughter quite well," she said softly. "Why do you suppose that is?"

"I'm a psychologist, so you might say understanding Hunter is my job." Sara paused. "And your daughter means a great deal to me. But then, you already know that."

"You're right." This time, there was no change in the calm expression on Marlena's face. "Please understand that unlike Patrick, I try not to interfere in the choices my daughter makes. I simply want Hunter to be happy. But I make it a point to know what is happening in her life, and I make no apologies for utilizing whatever resources may be available to me. I am also most certainly going to take notice when a former FBI agent is all but living with Hunter."

Sara sent her a cool stare. "Did Special Agent in Charge McBride have a particular problem with that?"

"Touché," Marlena admitted with a sharp laugh. "And no, actually, Erin was both reassuring and quite complimentary, and I felt infinitely better knowing Hunter's safety was in the capable hands of someone who cares about her."

"You can count on that."

"That's all I ask." Marlena nodded approvingly. "Now that we have put our cards on the table, so to speak, perhaps you can tell me what I'm supposed to do to help keep her safe. I lost Michael to one madman. I doubt I would survive if I were to lose Hunter to another."

"Then I'd say you have nothing to fear, Mother, because you're not going to lose me," Hunter said softly as she approached.

Sara watched Hunter stop behind her mother and slip an arm around her, holding her tight. Marlena seemed to revel in the embrace before turning and resting her fingers on the faint bruise still evident on her daughter's cheek.

"What about you, querida? Are you afraid?" she asked.

Hunter didn't answer right away, obviously giving the question serious consideration. "I don't think so," she said in due course. "At least, not about Collier."

Marlena looked from Hunter's face to Sara's and then back again before she slipped her arm around Hunter's waist, drawing her closer. "You look tired and you've lost more weight since I saw you in New York. Are you still having trouble sleeping?"

Watching Hunter hesitate and seeing the exhaustion clearly etched on her face, Sara wanted to answer for her. She wanted to say *Yes, damn it, she's having trouble sleeping and it's getting worse. Most nights she wakes up screaming and then can't seem to get back to sleep. All I can do is hold her and try to reassure her that it's only a dream.* Instead she remained silent as Hunter met her mother's gaze and gave her a rueful grin.

"I'm fine," she protested wearily. "Don't fuss."

"It's a mother's prerogative to fuss, *hija*," Marlena replied with a faint smile. "And I know you too well. Just promise me you won't take any unnecessary chances, Hunter. I love you and I need you to promise me you'll try to stay safe."

It was quickly obvious to Sara that Marlena didn't expect a reply, as she reacted with unguarded surprise when Hunter said, "I promise."

Sara was equally surprised when Hunter reached for her and threaded an arm around her waist. "Thank you for being here with me," she said quietly, her voice low and subdued.

Feeling the faint tremors running through Hunter's body, Sara grasped her arm, as much to offer comfort as for the physical support she could provide. "There's nowhere else I would want to be."

Hunter gave her a lopsided grin, and her hand tightened reflexively around Sara's waist. Tilting her head, she looked at her mother, a thoughtful expression on her face. "I was also thinking it might be nice to open the beach house for Thanksgiving this year. What do you think?"

Marlena regarded her daughter and graced her with a radiant smile. "I think that's a wonderful idea, my love," she responded. "Something we can all look forward to. Isn't that right, Sara?"

CHAPTER TWENTY-NINE

The nearly full moon hung low over the Golden Gate Bridge, caressing the mist-covered city with the tenderness of a lover. The night air held the faintest hint of a chill, and standing beneath a canopy of distant stars, Hunter shivered as she inhaled the sweet scent of night-blooming jasmine and tried to sort her jumbled and confused thoughts.

All day long, voices had drifted out of the past and twined themselves around her psyche. But here, in the solitude of her home, the breeze was blowing gently and the sound of the waves lulled her as she gazed into the endless darkness. Here she could pretend she didn't remember, if only for a little while.

Somewhere in that darkness, she knew that at least eight of her wolves had been strategically positioned around her neighborhood. Just as she knew that somewhere inside, Sara was on the phone with David, reviewing whatever plans the task force had put in place to cover the next twenty-four hours.

Just thinking of Sara seemed to be enough to still the restlessness inside her. Even as she braced herself to face Eric Collier. The thought both pleased and terrified her. But there would be time enough to understand what it all meant after Collier had been dealt with—at least she hoped so.

That, in itself, was something of a revelation. For the first time in years, she was looking forward to the future.

Notwithstanding the guilt she had carried for having been the one to make it out alive ten years earlier—survivor's guilt, Lindsay had called it—she wanted to live beyond the next twenty-four hours. Then she wanted to take her time and explore the endless possibilities that Sara represented in her life. But first, she had to get through the next twenty-four hours and come out the other side with mind, body, and soul intact.

She had no doubt that the day would bring a face-to-face confrontation with Eric Collier. Until now, he had planned all his moves too carefully to leave this final act to chance. There was no way Collier would allow her wolves, the FBI, and the SFPD to distract him from his goal. For whatever reason, he was determined to play out Brenner's game, and she had no doubt they would be playing before tonight's full moon set.

She scowled into the distance. All she needed to do was find a way to live through the experience a second time.

Don't you want to know why, Hunter? Why I never killed you?

No. I never wanted to know for sure.

"Are you all right?"

She hadn't heard Sara approach. It wasn't until she heard the softly spoken question and felt herself being turned around that she realized she was no longer alone on the terrace. Hunter blinked and brought Sara's face into focus. "Mm-hmm, I'm fine. Why do you ask?"

"You were talking to yourself when I came out here." Sara watched Hunter's eyebrows furrow, saw the confusion in her eyes. "You said you never wanted to know. What don't you want to know?"

"Oh, sorry. Bad habit," Hunter said. "I was thinking about Brenner. Remembering something he said to me when I went to see him in prison. He wanted to know…he asked me if I knew why he didn't kill me when he had the chance."

Sara opened her mouth to say something, but nothing came out.

Hunter's voice was a near whisper. "He said—" She stopped, and a heartbeat later shrugged her shoulders before continuing. "It really doesn't matter what he said. I don't know why I keep thinking about it. How crazy is that?"

Not so crazy. Sara caught the slight waver in Hunter's voice, the hint of bewilderment and pain tearing at her. "Is there anything I can do? Do you want to talk about it?" Without waiting for a reply, she pulled Hunter into her arms, simply intending to hold her. But feeling Hunter's body pressed against hers seemed to routinely short-circuit something in her brain, driving every other rational thought from her mind, and as always, it awakened the hunger that lurked inside.

She opened her eyes and found herself less than an inch away from Hunter's mouth. She ran a finger over her full lower lip, staring at it intently. And then Hunter leaned in and that hot, sweet mouth was kissing her with a fierceness and possessiveness that surprised them both.

When the kiss ended, they stared at each other. Always intense, there was something in Hunter's gaze that was different this time, but Sara couldn't read it. "Hunter? What is it?"

Hunter's hands moved in a tantalizing caress. "I want you." Her breathing grew ragged as she reached for Sara's hand and led her inside.

Sara watched her as she lit candles in every corner of the bedroom while, in the background, a saxophone played, low and sexy. With her body illuminated by the glow of the dancing flames and flickering shadows, Hunter moved toward her, approaching with feline grace. She didn't stop when she reached Sara. Instead, she backed Sara up against the bed, pushing her onto her back before stretching out on top of her.

Hunter hovered over Sara, eyes dark, taking in every inch of her. It was almost as if she was trying to memorize the moment. Almost as if she was afraid it might never come again.

Then slowly, she extended a trembling hand to trace the line of Sara's jaw with a gentleness that bordered on reverence. Just as slowly, tenderly, she began to kiss, taste, and touch her, and Sara was lost in the heat of Hunter's hands, the softness of her skin, the warmth of her mouth.

"Look at me, love. Open your eyes and look at me. I need to know you're here with me," Hunter said as she slowed her movements.

"Always." Sara's breathing hitched, almost stopped, and all thought vanished.

❖

Sara awoke from a deep sleep, feeling vaguely disoriented by the total darkness that surrounded her. It took a minute before she realized that the candles had long since burned out, their ethereal scent wafting only in memory. She wasn't sure what time it was. All she knew for certain was it was closer to sunrise than when she had tumbled into bed with Hunter.

She reached out for her now, imagined she could still feel the heat radiating from Hunter's body, still feel the beat of her heart. But instead, she found the bed empty, the sheets cool to the touch.

She sat up slowly, listening to the relative silence of the house. There was only the ever-present sound of the surf, a distant whisper as the waves broke and washed up against the shore.

For a few minutes longer, she sat without moving. Listening. Wishing somehow for this day to be over. Wishing she could simply concentrate on Hunter and how she felt about her and what it all meant instead of being afraid. Afraid that Collier would find a way to get past all the security measures that had been put into place. Afraid that he would get to Hunter. Terrified that he would kill her.

Pushing the dark thoughts aside, she swung her legs to the floor and got out of bed, raking her hair with her fingers. She grabbed a cotton shirt that was hanging on a doorknob and threw it on. The shirt held faint traces of Hunter's perfume, and Sara felt comforted by the familiar scent as she made her way out to the terrace, instinctively knowing that was where she would find Hunter.

She was leaning against the railing, dressed in baggy black cotton pants and a matching haphazardly buttoned shirt. The air was rain scented, and the soft breeze played with her hair as she stared into the darkness and listened to the waves. Sara approached and wrapped her arms around Hunter's waist from behind, trailing light kisses across her shoulders and back.

"I had hoped you'd sleep longer. Did you manage to get any sleep at all?"

"Some…enough." Unable to stop the faint trembling in her hands, Hunter ran shaky fingers through her hair, pushing it back from her face as she turned toward Sara. "How come you're up? Did I wake you?"

"No," Sara responded with a small smile. "I got lonely."

Hunter smiled back. "It was difficult to leave you alone in that bed." She chose her next words carefully. "But I don't want to spend any part of the next twenty-four hours sleeping..." Her voice faded, and she left the thought unsaid. *Just in case I don't survive my encounter with Collier.*

"Hunter—"

"Sara," Hunter interrupted her. "Would you do me a favor?"

"You know I'll give it my best shot."

"Let's not talk about Collier. Let's not talk about him at all."

"Hunter—"

"Please," she whispered. "I don't know what's going to happen. I do know I don't want to waste time talking about or thinking about Eric Collier. I won't give him that much power."

Sara rubbed Hunter's back soothingly while fighting to suppress the emotions that surged through her. She needed to focus on why she was here. To help Hunter, to protect her. And to stop Eric Collier. That was all that counted now. Sentimentality had no place in the equation.

But it was no longer that simple.

Sara sighed softly as she cupped Hunter's face in her hands. She kissed her brow, her eyelids, her nose, her cheeks. She kissed her mouth, a slow, gentle kiss that held all the emotions she was feeling. It was the kiss of a woman in love.

"I'm not going to let anything happen to you," she whispered. "You know that, don't you? I don't care what I have to do."

"Then I don't have anything to worry about, do I?" Hunter turned, lifting her hands to gently hold Sara as she looked into her eyes. "Let's not forget I promised to take you to Paris when this is over, and I always keep my promises." She smiled slightly and lowered her head to press soft kisses along Sara's collarbone.

"Mmm." Sara shivered and let her head fall against Hunter's shoulder. "If you actually take me to Paris, people are going to think I'm just with you for your money."

"You mean you're not?"

"No, I'm actually with you for the mind-blowing sex."

"That's what they all say."

Sara involuntarily stiffened and silently cursed herself when Hunter drew back and looked at her more closely. "Hey, I was just kidding. What's going on?"

Sara gave a shaky laugh. "It's nothing." But she couldn't help feeling a twinge of unreasonable and unfounded jealousy. It also didn't help that she suddenly felt as if Hunter could see right through her and knew everything she was thinking.

She tried to smile back, but under the intensity of Hunter's gaze, her smile faltered. *Can Hunter see what I'm feeling? How would she react if she knew the depths of my feelings?* She pulled away and stared at the floor. This was neither the time nor the place to have this conversation.

Hunter frowned. "Sara, talk to me. What is it? Please, tell me what's wrong."

"Nothing's wrong."

"Don't give me that. Please, just tell me."

Sara blew out a deep breath. "I need to tell you something. It's nothing bad. At least I don't think so. I just believe…I think maybe you should know I'm crazy in love with you."

The words came out in a rush. Once they were said, she found her breathing steadied and the tightness in her chest eased. She hadn't realized how much she wanted to say those particular words until that very moment.

She forced her eyes back to Hunter's face and saw only a stunned expression. *Oh shit. Too much. Too soon.* The warmth in Hunter's eyes had vanished, replaced by an unfathomable stare.

"What did you say?"

She could pretend she hadn't said anything. The odds were better than even that Hunter would let her off the hook. But that really wasn't what she wanted. Sara sighed, knowing there was no going back.

"I said I'm completely, utterly, totally, and helplessly in love with you." She met Hunter's gaze directly. "I've wanted you from the first time I saw you in London. I didn't plan it. In fact, I never expected to feel like that. But there you were. You were magnificent, you know. Arrogant one instant, vulnerable the next. Since that time, I haven't been able to think of anything except you."

She wasn't sure what she was expecting. Some kind of response. Anything from unbridled joy to anger. But instead, Hunter said nothing.

"Sara"—Hunter drew in a sharp breath and stared at Sara for what seemed like forever. Finally, she shrugged helplessly—"I don't know what I'm supposed to say. How I'm supposed to respond. I'm sorry. I—I don't think I can say anything right now. Please. Don't ask me to say anything right now."

Sara felt as if she was in emotional free fall, her head spinning and her throat constricting as she swallowed an overwhelming sense of heartbreaking disappointment. She knew for certain she didn't regret telling Hunter how she felt. She was equally certain she didn't want Hunter to feel pressured into responding. But as she watched the struggle evident on Hunter's face, she realized she especially didn't want to hear that Hunter didn't feel the same way. Because if Hunter walked away from her, Sara knew she'd survive, but she knew she wouldn't want to.

Jesus, she's beautiful. Why does she have to be so goddamned beautiful?

"I didn't tell you because I wanted you to respond." Sara turned away for just a moment, not wanting to see the sadness and remorse on Hunter's face. But it didn't help. The image was burned into memory.

"Sara, please." Hunter rested her hands loosely on Sara's waist and drew her closer. "How about I make another promise? How about I promise we'll finish this conversation after the full moon has set? Can we please do that?"

In the silence that followed, Sara heard the almost-seductive whisper of the wind coming in off the water, imploring her to do as Hunter asked. Doing what she asked, giving her more time—just twenty-four more hours, really—had to be less painful than forcing the issue when Hunter wasn't ready.

For several seconds, Sara tried to think of something clever to say. But in the end, she kept it simple. She took a deep breath and nodded her head. "Yeah, we can do that."

"Thank you." Hunter smiled. It was a nice smile, even though it failed to reach her eyes and was all too brief.

And she was still more beautiful than any other woman Sara had ever known.

Brushing her lips lightly against Hunter's, Sara maneuvered her onto the nearest chaise lounge and then settled herself in the space between Hunter's parted legs before reaching for Hunter's arms and threading them around her waist. "When was the last time you stayed up to watch the sunrise?"

"Should I remind you we're on the wrong coast for a sunrise over the ocean? Never mind that it's going to rain." Hunter's low, sexy voice tickled Sara's ear.

Sara growled playfully. "Then we'll watch daybreak instead."

Hunter's long arms tightened around her waist. Leaning forward, she rested her chin on Sara's shoulder. "Sounds like a wonderful plan," she said, and together they watched as the darkness gave way to the pale light of the new day.

Hunter walked into the bedroom wet from the shower she'd just taken, a towel casually wrapped around her hips, another draped around her neck. Sara was speaking on her cell phone, and although Hunter could hear her talking, only part of the conversation registered.

"I can be ready in five minutes…"

Hunter raised an eyebrow in question and searched Sara's eyes as she waited for the call to end.

"The task force got an unexpected hit," Sara explained a couple of minutes later. She reached for a pair of jeans and pulled them on. "Collier used a credit card to check into a small motel near Monterey. David's offered me the chance to be there when they take him down. I agreed to meet him."

"I heard," Hunter said. "You can borrow an SUV from one of my wolves, if you'd like."

Sara took a step closer to Hunter. "I didn't plan on leaving your side today. But if there's a chance we can bring this to a close…" She moved her fingers briefly to Hunter's face and stroked her cheek before dropping her hands awkwardly and jamming them into the pockets of her jeans.

Hunter moved away, suddenly needing to put more space between them. "I understand." And she did. She didn't have to like it, but she understood.

"While I'm gone," Sara's voice softened, "you should try to get some rest. It's going to be a very long night."

What's it worth to you, Hunter?

Hunter made an effort to silence the voice in her head, then reached over and brushed her knuckles against Sara's cheek. "You just focus on keeping your head down and staying out of the line of friendly fire. Don't worry about me. I'll be fine."

Hunter deliberately kept her face expressionless. But even though she attempted to keep her tone casual, there was something in her voice that stopped Sara. "I promise this won't turn out anything like what happened to your father," Sara whispered. "But then, you really don't believe we'll find Collier, do you?"

"No." Hunter shook her head. "This isn't how today is going to play out. Collier's planned everything for too long to make a mistake of this magnitude and blow it now. Not when he's this close to getting what he wants."

"You mean finding a way to get to you and forcing you to play Brenner's game with him, don't you?"

They stared at each other silently. "Yes."

Sara squeezed Hunter's hand gently as she studied her. Part of her wanted to call David back and tell him she couldn't leave Hunter. Not now. Not like this. But she was torn by conflicting obligations. Conflicting needs. "Promise me you won't take any chances while I'm gone. Promise me you won't leave the house until I get back."

Hunter shrugged and gave a rueful smile.

❖

It was only later that Sara remembered Hunter had not given her any kind of answer. By then she knew Hunter had been right. Eric Collier was not at the roadside motel. If indeed Collier had ever been there, he had gone to ground long before the noise from the flashbangs finished echoing in the small room.

What she didn't understand was why Collier had sent them on this particular wild goose chase. What purpose could it possibly serve? It had not reduced in any way the security surrounding Hunter, nor had it brought him any closer to her, and at this stage, that should be his only motivation.

Then why did he do it?

Feeling a sense of unease she couldn't shake, she took the stairs to the parking lot two at a time. She wanted nothing more than to get back to Hunter and see this day out. Nothing else mattered.

As she rounded the landing, she heard someone call out to her. But as she turned, a blast of pain shot through her body and knocked her off her feet. She stumbled helplessly down the last few steps, striking her head as she fell and landing in a crumpled heap at the bottom of the stairs. Dazed and unable to speak or move, she felt hands turn her over onto her back and looked up in horror at what was now a familiar face.

Still holding the Taser in his hand, Eric Collier smiled. "I can't believe it was this easy, my dear."

Oh God, Hunter. I'm so sorry.

She tried to scream but it was too late, as darkness overcame her.

❖

The darkening sky and gathering storm clouds did nothing to alleviate the ever-increasing anxiety Hunter had been feeling all day as she alternated between pacing restlessly and staring out the window. The tightness in her chest did not change. Neither did the sense of foreboding that had plagued her since Sara left—one she instinctively knew would remain with her until Sara returned.

Hunter shivered and wrapped her arms around herself as she looked toward the ocean. Her head was hurting again and she absently rubbed it. On some level, she was aware of what was going on around her—Tessa was rummaging in the kitchen cupboards, looking for anything that resembled food, while Conner and Adrienne killed time playing cards at the table. All perfectly ordinary.

"I gave up trying to find anything and ordered pizza and salad," Tessa said a while later. "Can I ask how often you shop for food?"

"Whenever I have no other choice. Why?"

"Consider yourself there."

Hunter stared at Tessa for an instant and then started to laugh. Why bother keeping food on hand when she would have to deal with it? The telephone rang, interrupting her musing. Hunter reached for it as she watched Tessa flirt with the teenaged pizza-delivery boy, making him stutter and blush.

You are so bad, Hunter mouthed.

A minute later, the tantalizing aroma of spicy pizza filled the air while Erin McBride confirmed what Hunter already knew. Eric Collier had not been in the motel room and was still at large, free to continue whatever plans he had made for tonight's full moon.

"We're going to find him," Erin assured her, but Hunter was not really listening. Her mind had already moved on to other matters. The good news was it meant Sara should be on her way back.

Three pairs of eyes were watching her intently as she hung up the phone. "Erin wanted to let me know there was no one in the motel room. If he was ever there, Collier was gone by the time the FBI got there." She closed her eyes, feeling suddenly as mentally weary as she was physically tired. She opened her eyes again when she felt a hand on her shoulder.

Tessa was standing very close, her expression one of concern. "It's going to be a long night. You need to eat something."

To please Tessa, Hunter walked over to the table, picked up a slice of pizza and nibbled on it, but couldn't have said what was on it. Turning, she watched Tessa pour two cups of coffee before passing one to her.

Putting the barely touched pizza down, she found herself once again in front of the window. She stood there for several minutes, silently drinking her coffee. The rain had started to fall, streaking across the windows and obscuring her view. She thought of Sara, wished she would hurry back. *I'm crazy in love with you.*

Yeah, they needed to talk.

"Hunter? Are you all right?" Tessa asked.

"No." Hunter shook her head. "No, I'm not." She took a deep breath and turned to face Tessa. "But if I somehow manage to survive the day, I think I will be."

❖

The stack of poker chips in front of Hunter had grown steadily for the past hour. This in spite of the total lack of attention she was giving the card game, much to the dismay of the others.

"All these years and I still can't figure out how you do it," Tessa said as she threw her cards on the table. "Are you dealing from the bottom? Is that it?"

Her rant was short-lived, stopped by Hunter's phone as it suddenly began to vibrate and dance on the table.

Hunter reached for the phone, checked the display, and smiled. "Hey, where are you? The pizza's almost all gone."

"Dr. Wilder will be sorry to hear that," a soft male voice responded. "But I'm afraid I must extend her regrets. She's not going to be able to join you."

The world around Hunter ceased to move, all the colors were leeched, and the people in the room with her faded, then disappeared. Hunter swallowed her anger and fear and forced her voice to remain calm as she switched the phone to speaker. "If you've hurt her—"

"I believe I have something of value to you," Collier said, "so I don't think you're in any position to make threats."

"What do you want?"

Collier's sharp laugh was clearly audible. "You know what I want. It's what I've always wanted. Just you and me. Face-to-face."

"Tell me where and when." Her mouth went dry and she was barely able to speak. She forced herself to breathe slowly and tried again. "But I want to speak with Sara first."

"Your parents' beach house." He paused. "In two hours."

Hunter's despair gave way to fury, and her voice shook with barely controlled rage. "I want to speak with Sara."

There was a longer pause followed by the sound of muted conversation, and then Hunter's world tilted momentarily on its axis. "Hunter?" In spite of the strain evident in Sara's voice, nothing had ever sounded as sweet.

"Are you all right? Has he hurt you?"

"I'm okay. Please don't—" There was a muffled sound and then Collier's voice came back on the phone.

"As you can see, she's safe for the moment," he said. "But I can guarantee if you're not here within the next two hours, Dr. Wilder's situation will take an unfortunate turn for the worse. Maybe she can take a turn playing the game with me. In fact, that might prove entertaining. What do you think?"

"You don't need to do that," Hunter said tersely. "I'll be there."

"Dr. Wilder's counting on it." Collier laughed. "You've got two hours, Hunter, and I expect you to come alone. I don't need to tell you if I see any of your security people or the FBI, you won't like the results."

The instant he terminated the phone call, Hunter felt as if her fragile link with Sara had been severed, and she fought to keep her knees from buckling. She took several deep breaths in rapid succession, and then slowly turned around.

"I'm going to ask that we not waste what little time we've got arguing," she said to the three women watching her intently.

"You're going to meet him," Conner stated.

"He has Sara." The thought made Hunter's blood run cold. "Six women have already died instead of me. Sara wouldn't be in jeopardy now except for me, and I will do everything in my power to ensure that she does not become Collier's seventh victim. I don't care what it takes."

"Hunter?" Tessa said softly. "Surely there's something else—"

"We're out of options. Given the weather conditions, it's going to take every minute of the time he's given me to get to the beach house. My only hope is I can get him to let Sara go once he's got what he wants, which would be me." She felt Tessa tighten her grip on her arm. "But whether or not I'm successful, I'm counting on the three of you to work with Matt and Peter and get both Sara and me out of there alive."

"That's your plan?"

"My only plan is to distract Collier long enough to try to get Sara safely away from him. Beyond that," Hunter arched an eyebrow and shrugged, "is why I've got a whole team of security experts and lawyers."

Tessa groaned.

"You can count on us," Conner replied.

"What about Matt and Peter?" Tessa asked. "Do you want to talk to them first or do you want me to do it?"

"You call off the wolves at the front gate and stall the FBI long enough to give me a head start. I'll call Matt once I'm on the road." There was so much more she wanted to say, but she was out of time. "I'd best be on my way."

She grabbed her jacket and headed for the door. She made it half way across the room before Tessa grabbed her and pulled her into a furious embrace, burying her face in Hunter's hair and holding on.

"Damn you, Roswell. I almost lost you once. I love you, and I don't know what I'll do if I lose you for real this time."

"You won't lose me."

"You've got that right." Tessa's voice tightened a little. "So you're not going to take any unnecessary chances with that psychopath. You're going to stall for time, keep your head down, and let your wolves do their thing. Don't do anything crazy. Do you hear me?"

Hunter gave her a faint smile, brushed a kiss against Tessa's cheek, and then pulled away and turned toward the door.

CHAPTER THIRTY

Hunter had no clear awareness of driving to her parents' beach house, just an innate and all-consuming need to reach her destination. As she drove along the Pacific Coast Highway, the urban sprawl of the Bay Area gradually gave way to the open road. She downshifted and pressed harder on the accelerator, the car dancing skittishly as it followed the ribbon of wet asphalt.

The rain clouds hovered low over the coastline like a soft gray shroud and made visibility a challenge. In the rearview mirror, the faint lights of the city lit the gloom like fireflies in late summer, while up ahead in the darkness and shadows, the highway wound its way along the coast as it paralleled steep ocean cliffs and curved past beaches and inland mountains.

The wipers kept up a steady, monotonous rhythm and the heater pumped out blasts of hot air, reminding her that she wasn't dressed for this weather. Her leather jacket was adequate, at best, for the coolness of the fogbound coast and would offer only limited protection against the rain that had been steadily falling over the past few hours.

But then she had not been thinking when she had left the house. She had simply been reacting to the fear she felt deep inside. Fear caused by the knowledge that Collier had Sara.

One more task, she thought. Gritting her teeth, she reached for her phone and turned it on. Within seconds, it started vibrating, indicating an endless barrage of recent messages. Grimacing, she ignored the voice mail and speed-dialed Matt's number.

"What the hell are you doing?" he asked immediately, concern and frustration warring in his voice. "The teams assigned to the outside perimeter of your house reported you left in your car but said they had been ordered to stand down. Conner would only say I needed to speak to you, and I've been trying to reach you, but your damned phone was turned off."

She remained silent a moment, then spoke quietly. "I'm sorry. Do you remember my parents' beach house?" She paused as she battled to get the next words out. "Collier's there and he's got Sara. He's given me two hours to get there or he'll kill her."

"Ah Christ."

She heard muffled sounds as Matt spoke to someone. In the background, she could hear Peter respond. A moment later, Matt came back on the line.

"Hunter, listen to me. Once you get to the beach house, I need you to wait by the gate. Don't do anything until the team gets there."

"I can't do that." She glanced at her watch and swore. "Matt, I couldn't stop what happened ten years ago. By taking off, I put my father's life in jeopardy, and then, no matter what I did, I couldn't save him. I've had to live with that every day since."

"Damn it, Hunter. *You* didn't put your father in jeopardy. The truth is it was his job—his connection to Brenner—that put *you* in jeopardy. As for saving him, of course you couldn't save him. Jesus, you were just a kid."

"Everyone keeps reminding me of that like it makes a difference. Well, I'm not a kid this time. And it's because of me that Collier has Sara."

"Wait for me," he pleaded. "That's all I'm asking. Just give me time to put a team in place."

It was a full minute before she found her voice. "Go ahead and get the team in place, but whatever you do, stay out of sight until you have a clear shot. I'm not willing to do anything that's going to put Sara in more danger than she already is. Collier wants to meet with me alone, and that's just what I'm going to give him."

There was a prolonged silence on the line, and when Matt spoke again, his voice was softer. "What do you think you're going to do on your own? Have you thought this through?"

"It doesn't matter." Hunter's breathing hitched. "Don't you see? I'm the one he wants. All of this—six women killed, Sara in danger—it's all been because that twisted psychopath wanted to play mind games with me." She took another ragged breath and fought for control. "I may not have started this, but I'm going to finish it. I'm going to give him what he wants, only hopefully, it'll be on my terms."

"All I'm asking is that you wait for me."

She heard Matt's breathing change, along with the cadence of his voice, and knew he was running. She could visualize him, running down the stairs as he headed for the parking lot.

"I've run out of time. I've got to go. I'm sorry," she said, eyes straight ahead on the road. She heard Matt's final words echoing as she turned the phone off and tossed it on the console. *He'll kill you if he gets the chance.* That was certainly a possibility, she conceded, but not one she was prepared to give a lot of thought.

She pressed ahead, accelerating along the winding road. She knew she was driving much too fast for the current road conditions— the fog, the rain, and the slick pavement—but she was counting on her reflexes and the responsiveness of her car to keep her out of trouble. Warning signs flashed past, and there was the once-familiar bridge spanning a deep, somber gorge. The road surface was opalescent from the standing water, and she was forced to ease off the accelerator, battle for control. Then she was through.

As she drew near, she was assailed by echoes from the past. *The road forks. Follow the right fork until you can't go any farther.* She kept right, following the coastline. The turn for the long drive approached rapidly on her right. She spotted the gates to the house through the trees as the pines gave way to a clearing, and she brought the car to a sliding stop.

The house was not visible from her vantage point, but Hunter could picture it clearly in her mind. Like the nearby town, it had always reminded her of a movie set and looked so perfect that, at times, she expected to walk through the front door and find only empty space. A façade constructed of make-believe. But the house was real, nestled amid the trees, and offered stunning views of the valley and the endless expanse of turbulent ocean.

She got out of the car and slipped quietly into the waiting night.

Shivering, she raised her collar against the dampness and cold, but the rain still managed to seep down inside her jacket, chilling her. As she approached the gate, she was surprised to find the security system activated. Still, it took only a few seconds for her to disable it. She swung the gate open and steered her car through, leaving it nestled under the pines just inside the gate. Then she jammed her hands into her pockets and turned toward the house.

On either side of the long, winding drive, the trees loomed like ghostly sentinels in the swirling mist. Hunter knew the trees and rain would mask the sounds of her arrival, just as the rhythmic pounding of the surf muted the sound of her footsteps. Not that it mattered. Collier would have known she had arrived from the moment she deactivated the alarm. Even so, she approached the dark house cautiously. Fog snaked around her feet, broke apart at her long strides.

Collier chose the stage for his final act well.

It was a community of large homes, with tennis courts, swimming pools, and small private beaches. She knew the closest neighbor was a mile up the beach. The next neighbor another mile farther still. The landscape was rugged with redwood and pine groves, low cliffs, jagged rocks. It offered privacy and solitude.

She stopped as she reached the front door, assailed by questions and doubts. She knew Eric Collier was waiting just beyond the door. Waiting to destroy her in the childhood home that previously held nothing but the ghosts of happier times. She shook her head to dispel all thought and focused on the task at hand. She attempted the door handle, heard it click, granting her entrance.

Welcome home.

As she stepped into the house, Hunter could hear the beams creaking overhead, blending with the pounding of the surf. Closing the front door, she took a deep breath and moved around the central staircase, instinctively going to a doorway on her right—the library.

She struggled with the elusive wisps of memory as past and present continued to converge and collide.

The eyes of the child she once was saw the room as enormous. Bookcases filled with endless wonder towering over her head. There were three large windows covering most of the west wall, and the glow from the fire in the hearth was reflected on the mist-coated glass. She could hear the hiss and crackle of the flames, feel their warmth on her face. She could smell the smoke as it gently rose above the dancing flames, then dissipated.

Pressing her nose against the cold glass of the window, she saw the trees looming just beyond the house, their branches bare. The trees gave way to a ribbon of sea grass and jagged rocks, and finally to a stretch of sand pounded smooth by the relentless waves.

It was here in this house that she had felt happiest as a child, and the library had been her favorite room. Her safe place, secure in her father's lap while they read. It seemed ironic that her life had come full circle. That circumstance had brought her back to face her demons here in this house. In this room.

She opened the door to the library and stepped inside.

The light in the room came predominantly from the fire burning in the hearth, but was aided by the Tiffany lamp sitting on a side table. Hunter could see Sara. She was seated in a large wood-and-leather high-backed chair, her hands and legs restrained by wide leather straps. As she drew nearer, she could see that Sara's jaw was bruised and her eyes appeared glassy. But Hunter couldn't tell whether that was due to the reflection of the flames or if Collier had drugged her.

You're a dead man, Collier, she thought. If for no other reason than the bruises he had put on Sara's face.

Sara turned her head as she stepped into the light, her eyes filled with shock and dismay upon seeing Hunter standing there. "Oh God, what are you doing here? You shouldn't have come."

Her words were slurred, confirming that Collier had drugged her. Hunter shrugged apologetically. "How could I not come?"

Turning her gaze slightly, for the first time she could just make out Eric Collier standing in the shadows to Sara's left. She had difficulty discerning his features in the near darkness. But there was no mistaking the glint of the gun in his hand.

"Thank you for joining us," he said.

"It's not as if you left me any choice." The words snapped out, the anger just behind them as Hunter kept her eyes on the gun. "I did as you asked. Now it's your turn, Eric. Let Sara go. She doesn't matter to you. It's me you want and I'm here. Let Sara go, and you and I can talk about this."

Collier responded by stepping forward into the light. Hunter saw the gun pointed toward her.

"Do it," Hunter challenged softly. "Go ahead. End it now."

A flicker of doubt flashed across Collier's face as he realized she was serious.

"Hunter, please." Sara's voice was strained.

Collier laughed. "I'm afraid Dr. Wilder's right. After all this time, I can't have you end things just yet. Not like this."

Hunter fought to control the chaotic state of her emotions. "What is it you want?" she asked tiredly. "You have to know it's just a matter of time before we're surrounded by Roswell security and law enforcement agents. This is not going to work out the way you planned, so why don't we just end this now while we still can."

"But you've no idea what I have planned." He cocked his head as he approached and assessed her. "I'm afraid I have to check you for weapons."

Hunter removed her leather jacket. Holding it up in one hand, she raised her arms and turned in a circle, allowing Collier to see she was unarmed. As she turned back around to face him, Collier took a step forward and ran his free hand down her sides and back, confirming for himself that she had not concealed a weapon beneath the loose cotton shirt. His smile as he stepped back seemed pleased.

Hunter started to speak when the backhand caught her. The powerful strike rocked her head back and dropped her to one knee. She clenched her jaw and tried to breathe slowly through the pain but refused to cry out, intent on robbing Collier of the satisfaction.

Collier grunted but did not move, as if mesmerized for an instant by the blood Hunter could feel trickling from her mouth.

He wants you unsettled—uncertain. Lindsay had helped her understand that during the three weeks Brenner had held her, he had wanted her psychologically off balance. Keeping her that way had been an essential element to breaking down her resistance, and Collier had obviously learned that key lesson while listening to Lindsay's tapes. The problem was Collier didn't have the luxury of time Brenner had enjoyed.

Collier walked back and sat at the table beside Sara. He then indicated the seat across from him. "Please come and join us, Hunter. I need you to sit down and place your hands flat on the table."

Sara watched Hunter's indecision and silently willed her to do what Collier asked, if only to buy some time. She breathed a sigh of relief when Hunter got back to her feet, approached the table, and did as he asked.

"Good. Now we can begin." Aiming the gun he held in his right hand at Sara, with his left hand Collier removed a second revolver that had been tucked in his waistband. "Tell me, Hunter. How well do you remember your time with Kyle Brenner?"

"It's not something I'm likely to forget." There was a slight tremor in her voice. "What in particular interests you?"

"Games. I'm particularly interested in the games." He flipped the swing-out chamber open and closed with a flick of the wrist. It was a move done for show, but he had made his point, demonstrating the revolver held only one round before spinning the cylinder and placing the gun on the table. "And this is one of my favorite toys. It's a Smith & Wesson Model 60, which I'm told is one of the preferred concealed-carry weapons for law enforcement officers. It has a five-round cylinder in which I've chambered a single thirty-eight special round."

Although she had expected it, Sara inhaled sharply. She was very familiar with the weapon, having carried one as a back-up at one time in her career. Even as she pulled against the straps that bound her to the chair, she knew it would prove to be the gun used to kill six women. But as she stared at it, she remembered listening to Lindsay's earliest sessions with Hunter, could still hear Hunter describing her ordeal at the hands of her captors, and knew the cost of her own rescue was already too high.

"Hunter?" The blood trailing from Hunter's bruised mouth had reached the open collar of her white shirt, but she seemed oblivious to it.

Hunter didn't respond, but for just an instant, Sara saw her mask drop. Saw both grief and rage burning in her remarkable face. But just as quickly, Hunter's expression became dark and frighteningly vacant.

Sara turned to Collier with the faint hope of distracting him. Buying time for Hunter's wolves and the task force who surely had to be nearby. "You don't want to do this."

"Sara, please," Hunter cautioned wearily. "Stay out of this."

"I would listen to her if I were you, because you're wrong. I've dreamed about doing this, and as far as I'm concerned, you've already served your purpose. I believe the term is Judas goat, is it not?"

Sara shook her head slowly, trying to clear away the dizziness. Denying his words even as she understood them and knew them to be true.

Collier leaned back and laughed. "Of course, at this point, it would be far simpler if I just killed you."

"No." Hunter started to rise from the table but stopped cold as Collier turned and touched his gun to Sara's temple. Sara flinched and froze, unable to do anything other than wait for the scene to be played out.

"Sit down. Hands flat on the table."

Hunter stared at Collier. She would have given anything at that moment for a chance to go one-on-one with him. Anything except Sara's life. But realistically, she knew she could never make it across the table before he pulled the trigger. Breathing hard, she reined in her rage and focused on shutting it down. Taking a deep breath, she sat.

Collier resumed speaking as if there had been no interruption. "As I was saying, it would be simpler if I killed her now. However, it is apparent you have feelings for her, so it serves my purpose to keep her alive. I seem to recall you telling Lindsay Carson about the deals you made with Kyle Brenner." He indicated the revolver on the table. "With that in mind, I'm prepared to offer you a deal. Just to get us started."

Hunter stiffened, but her face remained impassive. "I'm listening."

"I want one pull of the trigger and in return, I let Sara live." He slid the revolver handle-first across the table toward Hunter. He placed the gun between her hands, but kept his own hand over it. "One pull of the trigger. A one-in-five chance. Is she worth the risk to you, Hunter? I seem to recall you thought your father was worth the gamble. Of course, daddy's girl wasn't able to save her father, was she? Do you suppose she can save her girlfriend?"

One pull of the trigger. The words echoed and rattled in Hunter's mind as the voice morphed from Collier's to Brenner's and then back again.

"What happens if I'm unlucky on the first try?" she asked, her voice tired and empty.

"I would be…disappointed," Collier replied. "But you have my word. I'll let Sara live."

Sara felt her heart thunder as she watched Hunter's hand move in what seemed like slow motion toward the revolver. "Hunter, please stop. You don't have to do this. There's got to be another way. Please."

Hunter heard Sara only as a broken sound coming from a great distance. Her eyes remained fastened on Collier as she reached for the gun. She felt as if she slipped through time, lost between past and present, until she could no longer distinguish between the two. She only knew that neither offered a safe place.

What's it worth to you, Hunter?

"I think you've overlooked something, Eric." She breathed deeply, once and then again. "I have nothing to lose. Because we both know I was dead the moment I walked in here."

What's it worth to you, Hunter?

She glanced at Sara.

Everything.

Lifting the gun almost nonchalantly, in one motion she placed it against her temple and pulled the trigger.

The hollow click of the empty chamber echoed in the stillness of the room. Collier exhaled loudly and indicated with the gun in his hand, watching as Hunter placed the revolver back on the table.

Sara gasped and struggled against the straps that held her bound to the chair, only to stop at the ragged sound of Hunter's voice.

"You got what you wanted, Eric. Now let Sara go."

Collier shook his head with obvious delight. "That wasn't the deal. No. Our deal was that I would not kill her." He stopped and seemed to savor the moment. "However, if you are prepared to raise the stakes, you know what it will take. One pull of the trigger. You give me another pull of the trigger without spinning the cylinder, and I will let her go."

"Is that what it will take?"

Collier nodded. "Of course, the odds have changed. One-in-four. Is she still worth the risk? What's she worth to you, Hunter? I mean, isn't that the question? What are you prepared to sacrifice? Is she worth your life?"

Hunter struggled to steady herself as her eyes met Sara's. *Yes.*

"Oh God, Hunter. No, don't," Sara shouted as soon as she realized Hunter's intent, but her words had no effect. Instead, she watched with horror as Hunter picked up the revolver, placed the barrel against her temple, and pulled the trigger in one quick, fluid motion.

The sound of the hammer striking the firing pin devastated Sara. She wanted to scream, but more than anything, she wanted to take Hunter away from Collier and all of his madness. She didn't believe things could get any worse until she looked across the table and saw Hunter was still holding the gun against her temple in a visibly trembling hand.

"Hunter?"

It was as if she hadn't uttered a sound. Hunter remained frozen, the gun resting against her temple. Her face was pale and drawn, and she was staring blankly, no longer aware of her surroundings.

As Sara looked into Hunter's eyes, it was as if she could glimpse the shattered pieces of her soul.

"Hunter? Please look at me."

The seconds dragged out interminably, but still Hunter didn't respond. The only sounds in the room were the crackle of the fire and the distant breaking of the waves.

Hunter's silence unnerved Sara. Just when she thought she couldn't take much more, Hunter shuddered. Slowly, she lowered the revolver and blinked several times, looking around with only stunned confusion in her eyes.

"Damn you." Sara's wrists burned as she continued to strain against the straps. Still groggy from the drugs in her system, she glared at Collier and her frustration mounted. "Can't you see what you're doing to her? Why don't you stop this?"

For the first time since he had taken Sara down in the parking garage, Collier seemed uncertain. She could see it in the sudden hesitation of his movements and the tentative set of his mouth. As though he had spent years dreaming of this moment and Hunter's response had somehow surprised him. Left him confused about what to do next.

"I didn't want it to come to this. The first time I saw her, she was so bright. So beautiful. I knew I had to have her, and for so long, things were really good between us."

Sara stared at him as he came and stood over her. There was something almost reasonable in his voice, and she realized he believed what he was saying. He had slipped totally into his delusion.

"But then it somehow fell apart. I followed her and tried to make things right, but instead, she ignored me. Wouldn't even have a drink with me. All I wanted her to do was talk to me."

"You mean in New York?"

"Yes, of course. I didn't mean to hurt her, but she made me so angry when she wouldn't stay with me. She had to be punished although it hurt me to do so." He stopped and looked at Sara as if seeing her for the first time. "Then she took off to England, and when she finally came home, you got in the way. And really, do you think you're what she needs? Well, you're not. She is mine."

"Fine." Hunter's hollow voice surprised Sara and shifted Collier's focus.

Collier stared at Hunter. "What did you say?"

Hunter stared back at him for a few seconds. "I said fine—you win." Her voice was soft and low. "We both know what you want. Just you and me. But only if you let Sara go first."

"You're saying you'll come back to me?"

"Only if you let Sara go."

"You are mine." He whispered it almost as if to himself as he approached Sara and began to undo the straps that held her.

"Sara," Hunter said, never taking her eyes off Collier. "You'll find my car by the gate. The keys are in it. Take it and get as far away from here as possible."

Sara shook her head. "No. I'm not leaving without you. Don't ask that of me."

"Commendable loyalty, Hunter," Collier observed. "But I don't think she understands."

"No?" There was a faint edge of rancor in Sara's voice. "Then help me understand."

Collier looked briefly at Hunter. "Hunter and I have been destined to come together like this since the first time we crossed paths that night in the emergency department," Collier said, undoing the last of the straps. "This is her destiny and mine. I need you to leave."

As Collier stepped back, Sara rubbed her wrists where drops of blood seeped from the abrasions. She tried to stand, but the room spun and she dropped back onto the chair. She silently cursed.

"Move," he said with growing impatience. He waved his gun in her face. "This is your only chance to leave. She doesn't want me to hurt you, but I will if I have to, so walk away while you still can."

"Go to hell," Sara said quietly. "You're crazy if you actually think I'm leaving Hunter with you."

"Damn you. Don't you understand?" Collier grabbed Sara, pulling her roughly to her feet, and then pushing her toward the door. "She's mine. This is her destiny and mine."

Hunter had been watching through half-closed eyes. When Collier turned his back to her, she pushed through the detritus of the past that had immobilized her and got to her feet. He must have heard her, heard the sound that reverberated in her throat when he laid rough hands on Sara. Just as he turned back to face her, she launched herself at him.

❖

Sara knew the three weeks of inactivity since the Presidio attack had left Hunter ill-prepared to take Collier on. Her timing was off. He deflected her initial attack far too easily, and her follow-through was weak and ineffectual.

Collier countered, fighting back like the madman he was with strength, cunning, and timing, as he lashed out twice before ramming a knee into Hunter's abdomen, dropping her to the floor. Bouncing lightly on the balls of his feet, he watched as she pushed herself upright, limping and off balance.

"You didn't count on this, did you?" He gave a soft laugh. "I've spent years training, Hunter. Just for this moment. I wanted us to be equals."

He quickly lunged with a series of punches that Hunter barely managed to block. An instant later, he broke through her defenses with a blow that connected and sent her stumbling awkwardly, gritting her teeth against the pain.

She tried to shake off the rust, fought with everything she had. But before she could regain her balance, Collier landed another combination of rapid-fire punches and capped his assault with a powerful shot to her jaw. The impact sent her spinning into the table, and pain exploded in her head. Her vision blurred as she crashed to the floor.

"You shouldn't have left me." Sweat trickled down his face.

Dazed, Hunter managed to roll over onto her hands and knees, but Collier followed with a driving kick, lifting her from the floor with the force. He laughed and talked to himself as Hunter tried to catch her breath, and then kicked her again. She doubled over in agony, coughing and unable to draw a full breath. Barely able to see, she managed to roll away from him, bracing herself with her hands as he lunged at her.

With Collier's attention focused entirely on Hunter, Sara dropped to the floor, scrambling but unable to locate either of the weapons that had fallen. She teetered, desperate to help Hunter somehow. But she was debilitated as much by the drug-induced dizziness as by the fear that she would prove to be a distraction to Hunter rather than assistance. She couldn't take the chance.

Shuddering with pain, Hunter struggled to get to her feet. She was out of time and she knew it. She hoped she had something left in reserve to stop Collier, but as she wiped the blood out of her eyes with one hand, she had no confidence in the outcome.

As if he could sense victory, Collier waved for her to come closer. Hunter swayed and tried to respond. She absorbed another blow, her right arm hanging limply at her side. She was defenseless. She staggered and realized she had nothing left. She could not see Sara and hoped she had found her way to Matt and Peter. Resigned, she waited for Collier to finish her.

As he moved toward her, Hunter pushed herself and sent one final kick with what strength she had left. She felt her foot connect with his head just before she collapsed. Through blurred vision, she saw Collier stumble backward as he fell, his head striking the floor with an audible crack. She waited for him to get back up, then pushed slowly to her knees. When he failed to move, she reached cautiously with her left hand and picked up the revolver that lay discarded on the floor. Standing unsteadily, she tilted her head to one side and stared at him.

Collier remained where he had fallen, his eyes closed. Hunter licked her lips. Her heart pounded fiercely as she tightened her grip and leveled the gun. She fought to bring Collier into focus.

Sara reached out, touched Hunter's shoulder. "Hunter, listen to me. You don't want to do this. This isn't who you are. Please. Give me the gun."

Hunter turned vacant eyes toward Sara. For one terrifying moment, Sara watched as Hunter turned back toward Collier and steadied her aim.

One bullet. A one-in-three chance, Sara thought. It was almost as if she could hear the thoughts in Hunter's mind and realized she was turning Collier's game—Brenner's game—against him. Sara vaguely wondered if Collier was feeling particularly lucky. "Hunter, don't. Please."

Hunter took a shallow breath, her knuckles white as she strained to hold the gun steady. A moment later she slowly eased her finger from the trigger and lowered the revolver. Turning her head, she stared tiredly as a familiar face came into focus. "Sara?"

"I'm right here." Sara could feel tears welling in her eyes as she took the gun from Hunter's hand. "It's over, love. I've got you."

Sara reached for her, wrapped her arms around Hunter and held her.

Hunter swayed and leaned more heavily into Sara. She started to respond just as a sound drew her attention. Collier had staggered to his feet. His expression was wild, and she found herself staring down the barrel of the gun in his hand.

"Hunter!"—he screamed as he pulled the trigger—"I'll love you forever."

Sara fired simultaneously.

Hunter never heard the volley of weapon fire. She had started to turn, but got no further as the bullet slammed into her. She stared at Sara without comprehension. A look of total surprise registered on her face as the punch of the bullet's impact stole her breath away. She stumbled, her legs buckling beneath her, and then all strength left her and she collapsed. She struggled to breathe, dimly aware of Sara calling her name.

Sara rushed first to Collier, kicking his gun away and ensuring he was truly down. Sara then looked at Hunter in disbelief. "Hunter! No...no...no..."

Time slowed.

Even as Sara's mind denied what she had just witnessed, her body moved into action, her hands desperately trying to stanch the hot blood that flowed freely from Hunter's chest. Familiar faces appeared and converged around her—members of the FBI, SFPD,

Matt, Hunter's wolves—as a scream gathered strength somewhere deep inside her, only to be choked back.

As she tried to hold on, Hunter watched Sara's frantic attempts to stem the tide of blood with something almost bordering on amusement. "It's not going to stop," she whispered, sounding surprised. There was no fear. Only a vague sense of regret.

Sara cradled Hunter's face with gentle hands red with blood. "Hunter, it's going to be okay. You've got to stay with me, sweetheart. Stay with me. We're going to get you out of here, do you hear me? Look at me, Hunter. It's going to be okay. You're going to be okay." *It will not end like this. Please. It cannot end like this.* "I need some help here," she yelled.

"Sara—" Hunter coughed, her breathing weaker, shallow. The only thing that was clear was Sara. Sara touching her. She turned her head and looked up into Sara's worried face. She absorbed the comfort of Sara's touch, finding strength in it.

Sara looked into Hunter's eyes, saw the glimmer of light slowly fading as her eyes closed. "No, stay with me," she said, watching as her eyes fluttered open again. "That's it. Stay awake. Stay with me. You're going to be just fine. Now stay with me."

"Sara, you need…to know…" The pain was white hot and unrelenting. It hurt so bad she could hardly breathe.

"Know what, baby?"

"Only—" Blood sprayed from Hunter's lips as she coughed weakly.

"Only what?" Sara repeated in confusion.

"Only ever fell in love…only once…you're the first…"

"Oh God." Sara felt her heart shatter into a thousand pieces. "Damn you, Hunter, don't you dare say something like that to me and then leave me. You will not die, do you hear me?" She tightened her grip, feeling the hot blood soaking her as she grabbed Hunter's hand, squeezing it as tight as she could. "You will not leave me. I won't let you."

Hunter was cold, shivering with shock. It was getting harder to breathe. Every breath hurt. She closed her eyes as her body sank into the cocooned comfort and security of Sara's arms. Her mind drifted, floating on a cloud, and she slipped into the welcoming darkness.

"Please...oh God...stay with me...hold on to me." Sara begged. Heedless of the blood, she wrapped her arms around Hunter and pulled her closer, rocking her gently. She looked around frantically. "Where the hell are the EMTs?"

Time resumed.

Suddenly Tessa was there, kneeling beside Sara as paramedics converged on the two women. There was anguish on her face and in her voice. "Sara, let her go. Come on sweetie, let the paramedics do their job."

But Sara continued to cradle Hunter in her arms, even as Tessa tried to get her to relinquish her hold. Finally, Tessa and Matt urged her away, giving the paramedics room to work.

"Sara." Tessa held a struggling Sara close. "You're covered in blood. Is any of it yours? Are you hurt?"

Sara shook her head numbly, her eyes never leaving Hunter. A silent mantra—*she'll be all right she'll be all right*—echoed in her head.

CHAPTER THIRTY-ONE

What does it all mean?

It had only been a couple of hours, but already Sara could barely remember making the trip from the beach house to the hospital. All she could think of was her last clear image of Hunter—her face pale and lifeless while the EMTs worked furiously to keep her alive. All she could focus on was finding her way back to Hunter's side and never leaving it again.

The swift efforts of the response team gave Sara hope. And despite the rain and fog, the FBI was on hand with critical-care transport to the trauma center in San Francisco.

Once the gurney carrying Hunter had been wheeled away and loaded onto the medevac chopper, Sara numbly allowed Tessa to take control. The rain had stopped, but the night air was cool and damp, and as she began to shiver, Tessa settled a jacket over her blood-soaked clothes. Almost immediately, a familiar scent penetrated her senses, and for an instant she became convinced that Hunter was standing behind her, wrapping her arms around her.

But just as quickly, she realized the scent was coming from the soft leather jacket—Hunter's jacket. She clutched it to her chest, drawing in her scent and finding some desperately needed comfort. She tried to say something, but her mind wouldn't cooperate, and she felt her world fall out from under her.

"How are you holding up?" Tessa asked while looking her over.

"I'm okay," Sara said as Tessa took her by the hand, pulling her past FBI agents and police officers and Hunter's wolves, giving her no choice but to follow. Sara stumbled along behind her until they reached the Lamborghini. She looked at Tessa as fear and anger and confusion swirled in her head.

Jesus, she'd killed a man. She'd spent years in the FBI without ever having discharged her weapon other than in training drills, and tonight she'd taken someone's life. But what choice had there been? There was nothing she could have done differently. "I can't leave… I—I shot Collier. I'll have to give a statement—"

"Not right now. I spoke to David, and he'll catch up with you at the hospital."

There was clearly no point in staying or arguing. Or resisting Tessa's support as she tucked Sara into the passenger seat and buckled her in. She stared blankly for a moment and then watched as Tessa brought the powerful engine to life and headed out onto the highway toward San Francisco.

The trip was a blur of speed and passing headlights and fathomless darkness. By the time they raced into the hospital, all Sara wanted was to have one question answered. "Is she alive?" No one responded fast enough. "Is she *alive*?"

Silence descended until someone—one of the trauma unit nurses—told her Hunter had been rushed directly into surgery.

Waiting was the worst part. Sara had never been good at waiting. She leaned against the wall in a room filled with people and waited. She was so lost in herself she didn't sense Tessa approach until a paper cup filled with muddy-looking coffee was thrust in her hand.

"Sit," Tessa ordered kindly.

Sara realized her legs were shaking and sank to the floor.

Tessa sat down beside her, her arms crossed and her head bowed. The dark curtain of hair shielded her from curious eyes. But Sara could still see the pain etched in her pale face, and she wondered how many childhood prayers they were remembering between the two of them.

At least another hour passed before the hushed conversations in the room suddenly ceased. Sara felt the tension increase, and her mind screamed that it was much too soon to hear anything from the OR, while beside her Tessa murmured, "Oh shit."

Filled with a sense of foreboding, Sara looked up. But instead of Kate's familiar face, she recognized Hunter's grandfather. He stood framed in the open doorway, a tall, handsome man with a craggy face and a full head of silver hair, wearing a dark suit and cashmere overcoat. His movements were restrained and controlled as he surveyed the room. As soon as his eyes lit upon Sara, he made his way to her, people automatically moving out of his way like the parting of the Red Sea.

"What the hell are you doing here?" he demanded of Tessa, his voice a low, deep rumble. Without waiting for a response, he turned his attention and fury in Sara's direction. "And you—what the hell happened? I thought you were supposed to protect my granddaughter from that madman. Why is she in surgery fighting for her life?"

Sara slowly stood up, straightening her shoulders as she looked squarely at Patrick Roswell. This was a man with a history of conducting emotional hit-and-runs on Hunter. But he was Hunter's grandfather nonetheless. "I'm sorry, Senator. We did everything possible—"

"Well, it certainly wasn't good enough, was it? And as far as I'm concerned, you have no business being here. This room is intended for family, and that's my flesh and blood in the operating room."

Sara clenched her jaw and struggled to remember that the senator was overwrought. But he was talking about Hunter, who was strong and beautiful and fearless. Her Hunter. "The woman in the OR also happens to be the woman I love, Senator," she replied softly, trying not to give in to the anger rising inside of her. "And I have every intention of being here for her as long as she wants me to be."

The senator's face turned a deep shade of red. "I won't have it—"

Before he could continue, a soft voice interrupted. "Stop it, Patrick, and leave the girl alone, or I'll ask security to have you removed from the premises."

Marlena Roswell stepped closer, pressing between Sara and the senator, forcing him to step back. Sara saw Marlena's jaw tighten as her eyes fixed on the dark stains covering the front of Sara's shirt. "Are you injured, Sara? Have you been checked out?"

"It's not necessary," Sara responded quietly. "It's not my blood, it's—" *Oh God, it's Hunter's blood and this is her mother I'm talking to.*

She might as well have spoken the words out loud. Sara watched Marlena flinch and saw a flash of pain cross her face.

"That's my daughter's blood," Marlena said, more to herself than to Sara. "You were holding Hunter?"

Sara nodded.

Marlena stared at her chest a moment longer and then appeared to regroup. She nodded her head faintly and maintained her composure. "All right, I'll be back in a few minutes," she said as she wrapped her arm around the senator's waist. "Come along, Patrick. I'm sure we can find a more comfortable place for you to wait for some news."

Sara watched Marlena draw Patrick Roswell away, then shuddered involuntarily as the fight-or-flight surge of adrenaline dissipated. She remained silent for a moment longer, before finally turning toward Tessa. "You want to tell me what's up between you and the senator?"

Tessa shrugged and then flashed a weak grin. "He blames me for Hunter's sexual orientation. Seems to think I perverted her with my wicked ways while we were roommates at Oxford."

"You're kidding."

"What can I say? I mean, I might have been Hunter's first, but there was never any doubt which team she played for."

Sara felt an inexplicable urge to laugh as she sat back down.

Almost fifteen minutes passed before Marlena returned to the small waiting room. "I'm sorry about Patrick's behavior," she said. "He's always been controlling where Hunter's concerned, and since Michael died, she's the only one who's ever been able to stop him." She held out a pale blue scrub shirt. "I got this for you from one of the nurses. It occurred to me if Hunter sees you in your present condition, she's likely to get upset."

Sara swallowed, acknowledging the dried blood on her shirt, and accepted the clean top. "Thanks." *Actually, if Hunter sees me like this, she's more likely to kick my ass.*

The thought made the turbulent and tangled emotions she was feeling bubble close to the surface, and in her mind, Sara screamed out her heartache and rage. She needed Hunter in her life. The thought of not having her terrified her, and she vowed that when Hunter came through this, she'd make her understand what they could have together.

The pressure in her chest increased, and as she closed her hand around the soft cotton top, she felt Marlena briefly grasp her fingers, holding them tightly. Sara looked up into her beautiful face and saw the tears swim in her eyes, only to be hastily blinked away.

Rising quickly to her feet, Sara held herself together long enough to step out of the waiting room and into the nearest washroom. The enormity of the day's events came crashing down upon her. Her body shook, and she covered her face with her hands, overwhelmed by all the emotion she had kept under tight control since Hunter's shooting.

Several minutes passed before she realized she was no longer alone. She felt the presence of another person standing close, stroking her back, and through the haze of grief and embarrassment, she saw Marlena.

"I'm so sorry," Sara whispered and bit down hard on her lip to keep her voice from breaking. "It was my fault. I should have been paying better attention."

"Sara—"

"No, it's true. If I had been paying attention, Collier would never have gotten near Hunter. I promised to protect her, and instead, she nearly died in my arms. Because of me, she's in the OR right now, fighting for her life." Another tear spilled over and she wiped it away impatiently with the back of her hand. "I don't even know what I'm crying for. Or who."

Marlena didn't say anything. Instead, she put her arms around Sara, gathering her into a tender embrace. Sara stiffened, but after the initial shock, her defenses broke down and she felt herself drawn in. As she wept, she felt Marlena weep with her, and they forged a bond through their tears and their mutual love for Hunter.

"You've been holding that back for a while," Marlena said when Sara's tears were finally spent. "Let it all go, Sara. None of that matters anymore. What's important is Hunter is strong. She's a fighter, and you must have faith she will survive this."

"I know." Sara nodded weakly. "Thank you."

Wiping her own tears from her face, Marlena gave Sara a faintly amused smile. "There's no need to thank me, querida. Just listen to me. Wash your face and change your shirt, then come back to the room where Tessa is waiting. She shouldn't be alone." There was a slight tremor in her voice as she paused. "I had someone check with the operating room. They said it will be some time yet before we'll know anything, and I think it's important that we all wait together. At least we know she's still fighting."

Doing as she had been told, Sara washed her face and changed shirts. In the mirror, she watched Marlena will her own tears away. And knew it cost her. The knowledge nearly brought Sara to her knees and she couldn't do much more than follow Marlena back into the waiting room. Once there, she leaned tiredly against the wall, gripped Tessa's hand with her left and Marlena's with her right, as they waited together.

Finally, Kate stepped into the waiting room. Sara felt herself grow weak at the expression on Kate's face. She licked her lips and tried to move, tried to meet her partway. But instead, she remained frozen. Fearing the worst. Expecting the worst.

"How is she?" As Marlena voiced the question, everyone stopped talking, stopped moving, and stood waiting to hear the response.

"Still breathing." Kate tiredly pushed a sweat-soaked surgical cap from her head. "She's a fighter."

"How badly—"

"We managed to stop the bleeding and repair all the damage, but the blood loss was extensive and it was close. Very close."

She stopped and a smile surfaced past the exhaustion and strain visible on her face.

Sara closed her eyes and heard Tessa ask, "Is she going to make it?"

"She has a fighting chance, that's the best news I can give you right now," Kate replied evenly. "But she's still not out of the woods. The next forty-eight hours will be critical."

"But she's a fighter and she's going to pull through," Marlena responded reassuringly, giving Sara strength. "Now let's go see her. She needs to know we're here for her."

❖

Four days later, Sara was convinced the wait was too long.

Much too long. And Hunter looked so fragile. Her skin was pale beyond belief, almost translucent, and her eyes were deeply shadowed. There was an IV hooked up to her right hand, and there were lights flickering across the various machines that monitored her vital signs.

But the good news was that they had moved Hunter into a private room, and she was breathing on her own. That had to be considered progress.

Sara closed her eyes and briefly prayed to every deity she could think of. Bargaining, pleading, begging. She no longer cared what it took or what she had to offer. She just wanted Hunter back. Soon, damn it.

Kate had tried to explain. Sara knew the medical people had been monitoring Hunter for internal bleeding while allowing the damage to her lung to heal. But Sara hadn't been paying that much attention. All she knew was the chest tube was now gone and the doctors had finally withdrawn the sedation. They said Hunter would awaken when her body was ready for her to wake up, and all anyone could do was wait.

But this was taking far too long.

Of course, Sara wasn't going anywhere until Hunter was back—healthy and whole. She needed to see her open those amazing blue eyes. Needed to hear her laugh. Needed to feel her strong arms wrapped around her. She hadn't had nearly enough time with her, and there were still a million things they needed to explore.

Things like Paris...and things like being the first...and only.

Marlena and Nigel had been there earlier, and both of them were quite optimistic by the time they left. Sara also knew there was no one else scheduled to visit tonight. She wasn't sure how, but Marlena had somehow arranged for her to have this uninterrupted time with Hunter, and she would be forever grateful. Now Hunter just needed to cooperate and wake up.

She approached the bed, leaned down, and kissed her lightly on the lips, then glanced at the monitors over the bed. According to one nurse, her vital signs were good and getting better. She listened to Hunter's heartbeat, rhythmic and strong, and felt reassured. Pulling a chair closer to the bed, she reached for her hand and held it. "Hunter, I want you to squeeze my hand."

She watched the pale, beautiful face, looking for a sign. Marlena had mentioned that Hunter had drifted close to being conscious several times earlier in the day, but Sara desperately needed to see it for herself. She needed to know Hunter was going to pull through. "Come on, love, give me something," she said dispiritedly. "I'll take anything."

She kept talking, whispering words of love, rubbing the back of Hunter's hand. She leaned close to her ear. "It's all over, you know. There's no reason for you to stay away. Collier's gone. He can never hurt you again, but you have to fight." Still nothing.

"Come on, Roswell. Everyone says it's not in you to give up, so you need to wake up. We need to start a life together and I—" Her voice broke. "Damn it, I need you."

She felt the movement then. A quick brush of Hunter's thumb as it moved across the back of her hand. Her gaze snapped up to Hunter's face.

It was several minutes longer—although it felt like an eternity—before Hunter's eyelids fluttered open and she groaned softly. "Sara?"

Sara whispered her thanks to whatever deity had heard her and impatiently brushed the dampness from her cheeks. She caressed Hunter's face, pushed her hair back from her forehead, and leaned closer to the bed. "Hey you. I'm right here. How're you doing?"

Hunter tried to speak, but the words didn't seem to come easily. "I—" She started to cough and grimaced, the pain clearly showing on her face.

"Easy, love. Take your time. Don't rush it."

Hunter paused to take another few breaths before trying to speak once again. "Sorry…how long…?"

Sara lowered the side rail so she could move closer to Hunter. "How long have you been here? Almost four days."

Hunter remained silent for a minute or so, as she tried to process what Sara had said. "It's a blur…I can't seem to remember anything…after I got hit," she said hoarsely. "You okay?"

"Absolutely."

"How bad…?"

"The bullet fractured your left shoulder blade and you have a few broken ribs."

"A few?"

Sara grinned. "Okay, five. And a punctured lung, and you lost quite a bit of blood—which gave Kate a few tense moments in the OR. The good news is they gave you a few pints of fresh blood, patched you up, and you're expected to make a complete recovery."

Hunter stirred slightly and winced. "No wonder everything hurts."

"I know, love," Sara said soothingly. "But the doctors say you'll be up in no time."

"That's good."

A few minutes passed in silence as Hunter fought to stay awake, absorbing the wonder of being alive, while Sara sat on the edge of the bed beside her. She started when Hunter reached for her hand.

Sara leaned closer. "What is it, love? Do you want some water?"

Too tired to speak, Hunter shook her head.

"Do you need anything? Should I get the nurse?"

"No…I'm good…just wanted to hold your hand."

Sara hadn't thought she could love Hunter more than she already did. She'd been wrong. She had so many things she wanted to tell her, there were so many things they needed to talk about. But first things first.

"I'm so sorry," she said quietly.

Hunter sighed, her breath soft against Sara's face. "Nothing to be sorry for."

"How can you say that? I nearly got you killed." Sara touched a fading bruise on Hunter's cheek. "Can you forgive me?"

"Nothing to forgive."

"Hunter? I—" Sara's voice trembled and broke on the word as she stared at Hunter. Releasing a small choked sound, she leaned into Hunter, burying her face in the curve of her neck, and no more words were needed.

Wrapping her arms around her, heedless of the IV and the monitor leads, Hunter gathered Sara closer. The movement made pain rip through her chest, and her vision wavered. Swallowing an involuntary moan, she held her breath for a moment and steadied herself.

"Don't cry," Hunter whispered. "Please."

"It's just…I've missed you."

"I've been right here—at least I think so."

Sara laughed and pressed a kiss against her neck before she eased back slightly, studying Hunter's face. "What's wrong?"

"Sorry, I can't seem to stay awake."

"It's all right, love," she said. "Don't fight it. Go back to sleep."

"I know we need to talk." Hunter wanted to say more but found it increasingly difficult to keep her eyes open.

"We can talk when you wake up again. What's important right now is that you rest and get better. Everything else can wait. Okay?"

"Okay." Hunter swallowed as another wave of weariness broke over her. "Will you still be here…when I wake up?"

"I'll be here for as long as you want me to be."

"Promise?"

"Absolutely. Now try to get some rest."

Hunter closed her eyes. Sara's body felt warm and strong against hers, and she could smell the sweet scent of her shampoo. She bit her lip as the words threatened to spill over. And then she whispered, "I love you."

For an instant, there was no reaction. But then she felt Sara's heart racing as she pressed against her chest, and heard the unmistakable sound of joy in her voice as she replied. "Oh God, Hunter. I love you, too."

CHAPTER THIRTY-TWO

Three weeks after she was released from the hospital, Hunter stood by the window in her parents' beach house, listening to the sound of the ocean as the waves crashed to the shore. The shutters were open, allowing the breeze to circulate through her old bedroom under the eaves, filling the room with the sound and scent of the ocean. It felt wonderful.

Sara had been concerned that it was too soon for her to comfortably make the two-hour drive to the beach house. But it was Thanksgiving, and she had promised her mother both she and Sara would be there. So they had compromised, and Hunter arranged to use the company helicopter for the trip to Monterey.

"But you'll have a nap once we get there," Sara had said as she brought their bags out to the helicopter pad.

She was really very good at giving orders, Hunter thought with a grin, but she indulged her. In part because she still tired much too quickly. But mostly because it made Sara smile.

And she had to concede, she awoke from a two-hour nap feeling much more refreshed. After a quick shower, she pulled on fresh jeans and a black turtleneck, then headed downstairs to look for Sara. Near the bottom of the stairs, she could hear voices coming from the library. Nigel was relating a story and eliciting laughter. She paused on the verge of joining, choosing instead to stand in the doorway. Smiling as the story reached its inevitable and familiar conclusion.

Voices carried and faded. Delicious scents and muted laughter emanated from the kitchen, where she knew her mother was dealing with last-minute preparations for the Thanksgiving feast. But Hunter was conscious only of Sara, who came and stood at her side. Sara draped an arm around her waist in comforting solidarity, then slowly eased her into the room. In no time, she found herself seated on one of the large sofas between Sara and Tessa, and she was drawn into the lively conversation.

From time to time, Sara would look at her quizzically, but didn't press. *We need to talk. Isn't that ironic?* the pragmatist said, just as Sara wrapped a warm arm around her shoulders and pulled her closer.

Several hours later, her ribs aching from the near-constant teasing and laughter, Hunter took Sara by the hand, and they bid everybody goodnight. Once their bedroom door was closed, she held herself very still as Sara reached up, slid her arms around her neck, and kissed her.

"Your mother and Tessa want to help me shop for furniture for your house."

Hunter considered the ramifications of responding incorrectly to that statement. "Is that what you want to do?"

Sara leaned back and gave her a long, hard look, but stayed within the circle of her arms. "You may have more of your grandfather Patrick in you than I thought. Are you considering a future in politics?"

Hunter laughed softly. "How would you like me to answer that?"

Sara nibbled on her neck. "Just tell me the truth."

"That was the truth. Sara, I love you. So much it hurts. So much that, no matter what, I know I'll love you for the rest of my life. And I want you in my life. I don't care where or how we live—my place, a new place—all I care is that I have you with me."

"You have me…and I love your house…it just needs—"

"Furniture? Yeah, I know. And for the record, it's *our* house."

Sara grinned. "Yeah? Okay. Then maybe we can *both* go shopping with Marlena and Tessa."

"If that's what you want, we can do that. Or I can give them my credit cards and send them shopping, while you and I stay home and make love."

"I like how you think, Roswell." The next moment, all conversation ceased as Sara leaned in and kissed her.

Hunter loved the way Sara kissed her. Bold and sensual, she used her lips, her tongue, and her teeth to draw her in and ensnare her, robbing her of the ability to think and breathe. She groaned deep in her throat as pleasure washed over her, and she told herself she couldn't possibly come from just a kiss. Then she pulled Sara tighter against her and sighed contentedly. Sara felt so right in her arms, her body pressed against hers.

"I think it's my turn," Sara said.

"You're insatiable," Hunter laughed as Sara pulled the turtleneck over Hunter's head and tossed it to the floor behind her.

"I'm in love." Sara kneeled, licking a line down to the snap of Hunter's jeans. She unfastened the jeans and pushed them down, then took her with her mouth. Hunter whimpered, making a sound that was a cross between a moan and a purr, and threaded her fingers through Sara's hair. She needed something to hold on to as she felt her bones melt. When she could stand no longer, Hunter collapsed on the bed, pulling Sara on top of her. Wrapped in each other's arms, she surrendered completely to Sara.

"You're mine," Sara whispered against her skin.

Hunter smiled. *I certainly am.*

She was hers alone.

About the Author

Transplanted from Cuba to Canada as a child, AJ lived in numerous places before finally settling by the lake in Toronto. When not working as a consultant, she can be found indulging her passions for writing, reading, and photography. Willing to travel at a moment's notice, AJ loves exploring new places with her Nikon.

Books Available from Bold Strokes Books

Three Days by L.T. Marie. In a town like Vegas where anything can happen, Shawn and Dakota find that the stakes are love at all costs, and it's a gamble neither can afford to lose. (978-1-60282-569-7)

Swimming to Chicago by David-Matthew Barnes. As the lives of the adults around them unravel, high school students Alex and Robby form an unbreakable bond, vowing to do anything to stay together—even if it means leaving everything behind.(978-1-60282-572-7)

Hostage Moon by AJ Quinn. Hunter Roswell thought she had left her past behind, until a serial killer begins stalking her. Can FBI profiler Sara Wilder help her find her connection to the killer before he strikes on blood moon? (978-1-60282-568-0)

Erotica Exotica: Tales of Magic, Sex, and the Supernatural, edited by Richard Labonté. Today's top gay erotica authors offer sexual thrills and perverse arousal, spooky chills, and magical orgasms in these stories exploring arcane mystery, supernatural seduction, and sex that haunts in a manner both weird and wondrous. (978-1-60282-570-3)

Blue by Russ Gregory. Matt and Thatcher find themselves in the crosshairs of a psychotic killer stalking gay men in the streets of Austin, and only a 103-year-old nursing home resident holds the key to solving the murders—but can she give up her secrets in time to save them? (978-1-60282-571-0)

Balance of Forces: Toujours Ici by Ali Vali. Immortal Kendal Richoux's life began during the reign of Egypt's only female pharaoh, and history has taught her the dangers of getting too close to anyone who hasn't harnessed the power of time, but as she prepares for the most important battle of her long life, can she resist her attraction to Piper Marmande? (978-1-60282-567-3)

Contemporary Gay Romances by Felice Picano. This collection of short fiction from legendary novelist and memoirist Felice Picano are as different from any standard "romances" as you can get, but they will linger in the mind and memory. (978-1-60282-639-7)

Pirate's Fortune: Supreme Constellations Book Four by Gun Brooke. Set against the backdrop of war, captured mercenary Weiss Kyakh is persuaded to work undercover with bio-android Madisyn Pimm, which foils her plans to escape, but kindles unexpected love. (978-1-60282-563-5)

Sex and Skateboards by Ashley Bartlett. Sex and skateboards and surfing on the California coast. What more could anyone want? Alden McKenna thinks that's all she needs, until she meets Weston Duvall. (978-1-60282-562-8)

Waiting in the Wings by Melissa Brayden. Jenna has spent her whole life training for the stage, but the one thing she didn't prepare for was Adrienne. Is she ready to sacrifice what she's worked so hard for in exchange for a shot at something much deeper? (978-1-60282-561-1)

Wings: Subversive Gay Angel Erotica, edited by Todd Gregory. A collection of powerfully written tales of passion and desire centered on the aching beauty of angels. (978-1-60282-565-9)

Suite Nineteen by Mel Bossa. Psychic Ben Lebeau moves into Shilts Manor, where he meets seductive Lennox Van Kemp and his clan of Métis—guardians of a spiritual conspiracy dating back to Christ. But are Ben's psychic abilities strong enough to save him? (978-1-60282-564-2)

Speaking Out: LGBTQ Youth Stand Up, edited by Steve Berman. Inspiring stories written for and about LGBTQ teens of overcoming adversity (against intolerance and homophobia) and experiencing life after "coming out." (978-1-60282-566-6)

Forbidden Passions by MJ Williamz. Passion burns hotter when it's forbidden, and the fire between Katie Prentiss and Corrine Staples in antebellum Louisiana is raging out of control. (978-1-60282-641-0)

Harmony by Karis Walsh. When Brook Stanton meets a beautiful musician who threatens the security of her conventional, predetermined future, will she take a chance on finding the harmony only love creates? (978-1-60282-237-5)

Nightrise by Nell Stark and Trinity Tam. In the third book in the everafter series, when Valentine Darrow loses her soul, Alexa must cross continents to find a way to save her. (978-1-60282-238-2)

Men of the Mean Streets, edited by Greg Herren and J.M. Redmann. Dark tales of amorality and criminality by some of the top authors of gay mysteries. (978-1-60282-240-5)

Firestorm by Radclyffe. Firefighter paramedic Mallory "Ice" James isn't happy when the undisciplined Jac Russo joins her command, but lust isn't something either can control—and they soon discover ice burns as fiercely as flame. (978-1-60282-232-0)

The Best Defense by Carsen Taite. When socialite Aimee Howard hires former homicide detective Skye Keaton to find her missing niece, she vows not to mix business with pleasure, but she soon finds Skye hard to resist. (978-1-60282-233-7)

After the Fall by Robin Summers. When the plague destroys most of humanity, Taylor Stone thinks there's nothing left to live for, until she meets Kate, a woman who makes her realize love is still alive and makes her dream of a future she thought was no longer possible. (978-1-60282-234-4)

Accidents Never Happen by David-Matthew Barnes. From the moment Albert and Joey meet by chance beneath a train track on a street in Chicago, a domino effect is triggered, setting off a chain reaction of murder and tragedy. (978-1-60282-235-1)

In Plain View, edited by Shane Allison. Best-selling gay erotica authors create the stories of sex and desire modern readers crave. (978-1-60282-236-8)